Peach Passion
Publications

A Dangerous Love 8

A Love Like Ours

The Carter Family

JPeach

Contact Information

Email: j.peach0509@hotmail.com,

Instagram: authorjpeach

Facebook: Peach Johnson

Facebook Group: JPeach's Spot

Facebook Like Page: JPeach1088

Twitter: JPeach1088

Dedications

To my two amazing kids, DaJah & Da'Vion if it weren't for wanting to be better for you two, I wouldn't have had the drive or determination to continue this amazing writing journey I'm on!

Acknowledgment

To my readers that has stuck with me and given me unlimited support and encouragement, no amount of words can't even begin to describe how much I absolutely love and appreciation each and every one of you!

Thank y'all so much for sticking with me and loving these crazy characters of mine!

Chapter 1

Peaches

After eight hours of assisting in surgery, I was beyond tired and all I wanted to do was go home and go to bed. Once I made it to the locker room, I quickly changed out of my scrubs and into my black fitted capris, and red tank top. When I got dressed, I snatched my scrubs up off the floor and stuffed them into my bag, then slugged it over my shoulder.

The doors came opened and I looked up to see Mariah walking in. "Hey, Peaches, are you leaving?" She asked, staring at my changed clothes.

My eyes rolled at her. I did not like that damn girl—which she knew—so I couldn't understand why the hell she even spoke to me. Mariah was just too damn slutty to me. I still wasn't over the fact that she had flirted with Blaze over a year ago. Even when she found out he was happily married, that didn't stop the little hoe from trying to get with him. Blaze thought the shit was funny until I was about to break my foot off into her ass.

I loved my job and that was the only reason I hadn't beat the hell out of her ass *yet*. Without saying a word to Mariah, I stood up and closed my locker, then headed for the door. Purposely, I bumped into her and left out the room. As I made it to the elevator I dug in my purse and grabbed my cell phone. I called Blaze.

He answered after the first ring. "What's up?"

"Hello to you too." I responded as a smile came to my lips. Even after being with him for over thirteen years and married for seven. Blaze was still the same old Blaze given he had matured and grown a whole lot. Attitude wise, though nothing had changed.

"What's up, baby girl? You just getting off?" He laughed into the phone.

"Yeah, I am. Where you at?" I looked at the time to see it was just now one o'clock.

2

"I'm at the Lot. Why? You tryna meet up? Hm?" He hummed, and I knew that low tone of voice all too well.

"No, I'm not, nasty. I just got off and was calling my husband to see what he was doing is all." I got off the elevator and made my way out the hospital.

"Hm, yo husband? Shid, this ain't my wife because if it were, she would be tryna ride. You know she don't ever turn down a quick meet..." He trailed off and I could just picture that sexy smirk his lips were stretched into.

My lips pursed tight together as I tried to contain my laughter. Same ol' horny ass Blaze however, he wasn't lying though, I was always down for a quick meet just to get a quickie. Hell, with three kids who thought your room was theirs it was sometimes hard for us to be together sexually. We literally had to setup a meeting time just to have sex.

Even though, Blake was now sixteen he was still a momma's baby. When he had nothing else to do, he stayed in our room with us, which I knew he only did for my benefit. The same with the twins, at seven years old they barely slept in their rooms. They always ended up in our room with BJ at the bottom of our bed and Brianna in the middle of me and her daddy.

3

"Peaches, let me ask you this." He started saying.

I gripped my bottom lip to contain my smile because I knew it was going to be something stupid. "Okay, ask me what?"

"Peach, you been giving my shit away? Yo ass been acting real stank when it comes to fuckin' now. Man, don't make me have to come to that hospital and fuck some shit up—"

I couldn't hold it in, and I let out a scream filled laugh. "B, get off my damn phone. Wait, didn't we just have sex this morning in the shower?" I laughed at him.

Blaze let out a snort. "That's different. Shid, we had to be quick because of yo damn worrisome ass kids. I'm about to put all y'all asses out and go get me a blow up."

I came to a stop light and started laughing. "Ugh, I can't stand you. And you mean our kids. They just like yo ass! Bad and needy." I told him as I pulled into a Steak & Shake.

"Fuck you, Peaches. I'mma show yo ass needy and bad when I get home, bet that. I'm locking the kids outside and we gon' have the house to ourselves." I could tell from his tone of voice he was giving that sexy little smirk that I loved.

"Mmm, papa bear don't tease me." I moaned before laughing. "Bae, hold on a sec." I put the phone on mute, then placed my order. Once I finished, I took the phone off mute. "Okay, I'm back."

"What the hell you doing that I gotda be on hold? Who in the car with you? Peaches, don't get fuck'd up." Blaze threatened me.

Again, I laughed. "Bae, for real stop it. Hey, did you go to the twins' school?" Since the twins started second grade, I've been getting calls back to back from their teachers. I was starting to think she just didn't like my babies for some reason.

I pulled to the window and once again put the phone on mute as I paid for the food and got it.

"Yeah, I went up there this morning. Yo damn kid's, man. Brianna just talk too much but BJ little ass is the class clown. I walk in the room and his ass playing around. The teacher yelling for him to sit down and he done told the woman to shut up talking to him. Man, I yoked his little ass up so damn quick. I wanted to beat his ass." Blaze said.

I had to admit that no matter how long Blaze and I have been together it always amazed me to see how he transformed from an inconsiderate, mean, rude hood, into a mean, rude *but* mature, respectable husband and father, was simply phenomenal. And every day I fell even more in love with him because of that.

"You should have tore his little ass up. I keep telling him about playing around in class. He always telling me it's the boys or girls talking to him. And he told her to shut up." My head shook and a sigh left my mouth. BJ was something else. To me he was way worse than Blake at that age. All I could really do was put the blame on Blaze because they took all his genes. I was never that bad especially not in school. My mom and dad would have killed me.

"Oh, I'mma tag his ass when he gets home. Little bad ass." He mumbled into the line.

Our kids were beyond spoiled and got whatever they wanted. Even so, when they needed to be put in their place, Blaze was the one to get them straight and fast. My baby had no problem going up to the kid's school and embarrassing them. He was an all-around amazing father.

I pulled into the Lot and parked by the front door. I shut off my car, grabbed the food then got out. "Papa Bear, you know I love it when you go into father mold." I told him as I walked into the building. A receptionist went to speak but I quickly put my finger to my lips, shushing her.

"Why you wanna play, you know my dick just got hard when you said that. Wifey, come meet me. Matter fact, I can get off right now and meet you at the house."

"Baby, I'm not on my way home. I got some stuff I need to get so I can't meet you right now." I told him as I stopped in the hallway.

"And that shit can't wait until later? Man, where yo ass at for real?" I could hear the irritation in his voice.

I started to whisper into the line. "I'll tell you later I have to go. Love you, bye." As I hung up the phone, I heard him call my name. He was going to be pissed that I hung up on him. I waited outside the room door for a few seconds before I walked in. "Papa Bear." I greeted Blaze with a small smile. "Where you about to go?" I pointed to the keys he held in his hand.

"On my way to find yo ass." He sat his keys down as I laughed. I wouldn't doubt he would have GPS'd my ass real quick. "Why you playing? I was hoping I caught yo ass with somebody." He walked over to me with a mean mug on his face. He backed me into the office door. "Peach, you been giving my shit away." His lips pressed against mine.

I nodded as I kissed him back. "Only to my Papa Bear." I mumbled in between pecks.

"Is that right?" His hand slapped against my ass. My head nodded again. "Can I be yo Papa Bear right now? Yo nigga don't gotda know."

Laughing, I pushed him back. "You crazy. Here, I brought you something to eat."

Blaze grabbed the bag of food and tossed it on his desk before he turned back to me. "How was your day?" He took hold of my hand and led me to the couch that was in his office. He sat down and I got on top of him, straddling his hips.

"It was good. I can't really complain. I kinda wished my husband would've brought me some lunch but I'm not complaining. I know how busy he is." My arms wrapped around his neck and I kissed him again.

"That mothafucka slippin'. His ass better get his shit together before I take yo ass from him." He bit at my bottom lip as his hands slid to my booty.

"How can you take what's already yours?" I held up my hand while waving my ring finger. A thought came to me and I hit him. "B, why yo little girlfriend gon' speak to me today?" My eyes rolled playfully at him. His face furrowed up in confusion. "Don't look stupid, Mariah slutty ass."

Blaze barked out a laugh. "Man, Peach, that damn girl don't be thinking about my ass. She ain't even my type any ways. I got who I wanna be with. Hell, I married her crazy ass just to show that shit." He slapped my ass again before he pushed his hips up. "You gon' ride before my wife pop up here?"

My eyes rolled at him, but I ended up laughing no less. "I love you." I lowered my head to his and stuck my tongue out.

"Show me you love me." Blaze tongue came out and I pulled it into my mouth, sucking on it. He moaned as his hands slid under my top to my bra. He broke the kiss while he unhooked my straps. He then pulled off my shirt and bra, dropping them to the floor. Blaze cupped both of my breast into his palms then brought his mouth to them.

His tongue flicked over my right nipple then the left, pulling it into his mouth. He sucked on the small nub then moved his head back, letting it pop from his lips.

I pulled his head back and brought my lips to his. My head tilted as his tongue danced with mine. My hands went to his shirt and I pulled it off.

Blaze turned us over on the couch, he sat up on his knees and grabbed my pants. We both made quick work with taking off our jeans. My hips raised and I pulled off my pants and panties as Blaze pulled his down his hips. I sat up and took hold of his dick.

My hands stroked him as my tongue swirled around his rim, licking the precum from his leaky tip. I then pulled the mushroom shape head into my mouth and started sucking.

"Mmm, shit." Blaze grunted as he gripped my ponytail tight.

I took him deep into my mouth until my lips kissed his pelvis. Moaning around him, my head started to bob as I massaged his sack.

Blaze pulled my hair from the tie then ran his fingers through it. He got a good grip of my hair and his hips started to thrust as he fuck'd my mouth. "Mm, fuck, Peaches," he groaned.

I felt his muscles tighten and he pulled me away from his dick. "Baby, where are you going?" My tongue ran over the bottom of my top lip.

"I ain't tryna nut yet. Damn." He took off his shoes then pants fully.

I laid back on the couch and widened my legs. I brought my fingers to my mouth, sucking on them, getting them wet. I then brought my fingers to my throbbing pussy and began playing with my clit. My tongue swiped over my parted lips as I pushed two fingers inside me. "Papa Bear, you gon' eat my pussy?"

10

Blaze squeezed the head of his dick while he watched me. "Damn you sexy as fuck."

I brought my free hand to my clit and started playing with the swollen nub. My fingers continued to stroke my inner walls as my body started to twitch.

Blaze came and kneeled in front of me. He removed my hands and his mouth latched onto my pearl, and he started sucking. He pushed two fingers inside of me, then pressed down, hooking my pelvic.

My hand cupped the back of his neck and I began to grind against his mouth as my orgasm built higher. "Ooh, baby just like that! Ooh, shit." My toes curled and my lower body raised off the couch. "Ah, ah, ooh, baby I'm about to cum. Oh, my God, Blaze!" My nails bit into the back of his neck as I came hard. "Mmm, shit!" A moan left my mouth once Blaze pulled his fingers out of me.

He kissed my thigh then made his way up to my lips. His tongue slid into my mouth, twisting with mine.

My hands slid down to his ass and I pulled him to me. Blaze grabbed his man and slapped it against my clit before he brought it to my opening. "Wait, wait get up." I patted his arm.

He let out a groan. "Why?" He grabbed my arm when I got up. "Hold up, where you going?" He pulled me back into his lap and brought his mouth to mine.

"To get a condom out your drawer." I mumbled between our kissing. Blaze lifted me up and brought his dick to my opening. He pushed his tip inside of me. "Baby, wait, I haven't gotten my pills refilled yet."

He pushed deep inside me as his fingers dug into my ass.

My face fell into the back of the couch at the feel of him. "Mmm, Blaze." My teeth gripped the tip of his ear as my hips rocked back and forth on him. "Ooh, fuck, you feel so good." I panted while rocking faster on him.

Blaze slapped my ass, then gripped my cheeks tight, holding my pelvis to his. "Damn, Peach, fuck!" His hand came down on my ass again.

My pussy muscles squeezed around him as my hips moved faster. I could feel my orgasm at its peak.

Blaze fingers came to my clit and he began to toy with the swollen nub.

"Ooh, shit, baby. Oh, my God!" I moaned loudly as I came once again.

Blaze held me to him as his hips jerked upwards and he came inside of me. "Ah fuck, Peach. Damn, I love yo ass." His hand tangled into my hair and he pulled my face to his, bringing his lips to mine.

A small laugh left my mouth as I kissed him back. "I love you too. Waaaay too much." Panting, my hands went to his knees. I leaned back and just stared at him. My smile couldn't be contained. "Papa Bear, you know you sexy as fuck. Damn." I had to give it to my baby. He was still handsome as hell after all these years. I could never get enough of him.

Blaze eyes roamed over me before he cupped my breast. His mouth came to my right nipple, sucking it into his mouth. "And you beautiful as fuck." He mumbled against my breast.

Laughing, my hand ran over the back of his head as his tongue continued to play with my nipples. A light sigh left my mouth as I started to move my hips on him again. "Papa Bear, can you handle another round." I bit at his bottom lip and moaned. "You think you can make me cum again?"

"Peach, you better stop—" Blaze started to say but was cut off as his office door swung open.

"Dad—" Blake walked into the room and his eyes landed on us. "Damn! Y'all asses." His hands quickly went over his eyes and he turned around.

I swear we could never get any alone time because of our damn kids.

Chapter 2

Peaches

"**B**lake, I'm gon' beat yo ass!" Blaze snapped at him. He mugged our son as if he were ready to beat his ass. Groaning, I tossed Blaze is clothes off the floor so he could get dressed. I then quickly grabbed my top and put it on then my pants.

"Man, y'all shouldn't be doing that in here anyways. Y'all to damn old for that." Blake looked through his fingers to peek at us. Once he saw that we were dressed, his hand left his face and he walked fully into the room. He went to Blaze desk and sat on top of it. "What you got to eat?" He picked up the bag from Steak & Shake and looked inside of it.

"Boy, what the hell do you want?" Blaze pulled on his shirt and walked over to Blake. He slapped him on the back of his head, then snatched the bag of food from him. "Give me my shit. What I tell yo ass about just walking into my office. Yo ass don't know what the fuck I be in here doing." Blaze snapped at him as he went to his chair and sat down.

Blake rubbed the back of his head, then snatched the bag of food from his dad. "I did knock and heard you say come in." Blake retorted as he took the burger out the bag. He unwrapped it then took a big bite.

Blaze head tilted at Blake before he laughed. He pointed to me. "You heard yo momma say she's cumming, not come in with yo dumbass."

Blake stopped eating and gagged.

"Blaze, you're ignorant. Why would you tell him that? Shut up, I didn't even say that!" I laughed at them as I walked over to the desk where they were. "You better stop just walking into rooms. Yo ass to damn old to still be doing that." I rubbed the back of his head then kissed the side of it.

Blake's head quickly jerked away from me like I had burnt him. "Ma, don't kiss me. I know yo mouth ain't clean. Gon', Ma, that's nasty." He wiped the side of his head irritably.

Blaze broke out laughing. "That mothafucka sholl ain't, B. Yo moms' nasty as hell."

"Shut up, Blaze. Blake don't get yoself slapped." I pushed him away from me, then went over to Blaze and sat on his lap. "What are you doing here anyways? Don't you have basketball practice?" My arm wrapped around Blaze's neck and my fingers slowly started to caress the back of his head.

Blake shrugged as he finished off the burger. He threw the paper in the trash, then started on the fries. "I do. I don't have to go for another hour and a half, so I stopped up here to see if dad wanted to go get something to eat. Never mind now though, that Steak & Shake hit the spot. I don't even feel like going to practice no more." He rubbed his stomach as he stood up and stretched.

I looked at my oldest boy and just smiled. He stood, six, two, he was medium built and muscular like an athlete. His jet-black hair was smooth and thick with ocean waves. A thin beard lined his face neatly. He was a spitting image of his dad. He had his same beautiful light brown skin complexion, he inherited Blaze's gorgeous light brown eyes. Blake had grown to be a handsome young man.

Blake had grown up so much from that little badass kid he was. He still had a mouth on him, which I sometimes wanted to bust him in, but he was so smart and mature for his age. He was also focused on his schoolwork and looking to get a basketball scholarship. I couldn't have been prouder of my baby.

"I wish I had of known, I would've told you to pick up the twins from your nana's house." I grabbed Blaze's phone from the desk to look at the time.

"They cool, momma don't mind them over there for a couple of hours." Blaze took his phone from me and put it in his pocket.

My eyes squinted at him. "So, I can't use your phone now?"

"What?" Blaze asked, looking confused.

I waved him off then opened his drawer as I spoke to Blake. "Why you really stop by here and I know damn well it wasn't to take your daddy to get something to eat." I knew my son all too well. He wanted something and it wasn't to take Blaze out either.

Blake's head tilted to the side. "Man, you so dang on nosey, it don't make no sense. I came to talk to my pops, not you." Blake hopped off the desk when I looked up at him. He started laughing.

18

"Hehehe hell. You ain't ever too old to get your ass whooped." I fussed at him before I spotted the box of condoms in Blaze's desk drawer. My eyes squinted and my head tilted as I stared at the empty box of Durex condoms. "Babe, who's are these?" I pulled out the box and showed it to him.

I kept condoms in Blaze's office for whenever I popped up on him and we had sex to prevent me from becoming pregnant again. Those condoms however wasn't ours. I never brought Durex, we always used Magnums.

"Ours," he said simply.

Even if they were ours, why was the box empty? I bought the box of magnums a couple of weeks ago. Since then, I only did three pop ups on him and today we didn't even use a condom.

"You know damn well these ain't our fuckin' condoms. When have we ever used Durex and why the hell is the fuckin' box empty if they're ours?" I got off his lap and threw the box into his face.

Blaze face twisted up as he mugged me. "Peaches, you better sit yo ass down some fuckin' where. If yo dumb ass trying to imply I'm cheating, you better rethink that shit and get on somewhere with that bullshit." He laughed at me.

I didn't find anything funny at all. "Where the condoms come from then, Blaze? We never once used this brand. So, you had to have bought and used them?"

"Peaches, shut yo ass up with that dumb shit. If I wanted to cheat, I wouldn't have married yo ass in the first place. Why the fuck would I choose now after all these damn years to cheat? Man, now ain't the time or place to discuss this." He stated, looking over my shoulder at Blake. "We'll talk at home." His nonchalant tone and attitude pissed me off. "Peaches, if yo ass hit me Blake gon' see you get yo ass whoop, I promise."

I was so tempted to smack the shit out of him. I turned to Blake trying to sound and look as cool as possible. I was so pissed off and the fact that Blaze seemed so gotdamn uncaring about the condoms, wasn't helping me at all.

"Blake, can you go get the twins from your nana's house for me, please?"

"No, you gon' go get them—" Blaze tried to send me off.

"Are you being serious right now? Blaze, I'm trying so hard not to knock the shit out of you. Blake, get out, please." I was about to try and whoop Blaze ass. I was not about to deal with his cheating bullshit not now after all these damn years we've been together.

"Peaches, calm yo ass down, man. I ain't cheat on you. I'ight? Why would I lie to you about that? When have you ever known me to go to the damn store and buy condoms? Besides why the fuck would I buy an off brand and leave the shit in my damn desk? Especially when I know you nosey as fuck, and go through everything in this bitch? Sweetheart, you have to give me more credit than that. I ain't no dumb mothafucka, I wouldn't be careless to leave that shit around like that. In all the years you've known me when have I ever been careless, Peaches? Think about it now? So gon' get the idea I cheated out yo damn head." He explained.

When he explained it to me, it did sound reckless and that just wasn't Blaze, he was careful with everything he did.

"I'll let y'all finish talking. I'll pick up the twins and take them to practice with me." Blake said then hurried up and left out the room, closing the door behind him.

I turned to Blaze. "Okay, you're careful, so who used your condoms and replaced them with the wrong ones?" My arms folded over my chest and I glared at him.

Blaze laughed, then ran a hand over his mouth before he shrugged. "Shid if I know. And if I did, I ain't no snitch so I can't tell you."

"So, you would rather let me think you're cheating than to tell me where the condoms came from?" I looked at him confused. "What sense does that make, Blaze?"

He grabbed my arms and pulled me into his lap. "You not gon' think I cheated for the simple fact that I love the hell out of my wife. Can't no other chick out here make me look their way when I got you. Peaches, you know I don't even like condoms, that's why I never buy them mothafuckas. Somebody else used the condoms and replaced them with the wrong ones." His hands went under my shirt and he rubbed my lower back. "Peach, you really think I'll cheat on you?" He bit at my bottom lip.

My lips twisted to the side and I rolled my eyes wanting to be mad. However, I couldn't be, I knew Blaze and he never gave me any signs that he was unhappy with our marriage or with me sexually. Beside the condoms there was never anything that made me think he would cheat.

"No, but why would you rather have me think you are instead of telling me the truth? Blaze, that don't make any sense…" It wasn't until after those words left my mouth it dawned on me what Blaze had said. "Wait, who would you be snitching on that I would care about?" And like a light bulb turned on in my head, I hit Blaze in the chest.

"Why the fuck yo ass hit me for?" He laughed.

"Blake is taking your condoms. That's why he came here? And you're willingly giving them to him? Blaze, he is not old enough to be having sex! Oh, my God, I can't believe you." I fussed whereas Blaze laughed at me. "B, it's not funny. Who is he having sex with?"

That only made him laugh harder. "Peach, I don't know. Look he came to me last year and told me he wanted to poke his needles into some skins, so I took him to get some condoms. He's usually good with keeping them but when he runs out, he stops by here and get a couple." He shrugged like nothing was wrong with what he said.

My eyes were wide from learning the news. "A year? Blaze, he was only fifteen a year ago. And you let him have sex?" I just couldn't wrap my mind around my baby having sex. Blake wasn't supposed to want to have sex yet, school was supposed to be his main focus, not girls and sex. He didn't even tell me he liked someone.

"How the fuck you sound? I let him?" He stared at me as if I was crazy. "I didn't let him do a damn thing. He told me what was up, and I talked to him, then went out and got him some condoms. Peaches, not everybody is you. Mothafuckas not gonna wait until they're older to fuck. So calm yo ass down, you getting to worked up about it. At least we knew and he ain't out here fuckin' these little girls raw." Again, Blaze shrugged like it was cool.

"*We?* I didn't know shit. B, you did, you knew. Okay it's cool. Now when Brianna turns fifteen and come tell me she's ready to have sex, I'll just go out and buy her a box of condoms then." My lips pursed together as I made a point, and as I suspected Blaze glared at me hard.

"I wish the fuck you would do some bullshit like that. You and Bri-Bri gon' get y'all asses beat and that nigga gon' die. I promise that shit. Get the fuck off me." He pushed me off him. He was pissed off.

"My point exactly. I can't believe my baby is having sex. But why wouldn't he come and talk to me." I just felt like crying.

Blake having sex was a sure sign of him growing up and I just wasn't ready for that. Keeping secrets wasn't something Blake and I did. He had always been open with me. I couldn't understand why he would keep this away from me. My feelings were so hurt.

Blaze must have sensed my inner turmoil because he sighed and grabbed my arms then pulled me back into his lap. "Peach, baby don't cry over that man."

It wasn't until he said that I realized I was actually crying, but I just couldn't stop my tears. My baby was growing up and I wasn't ready for that. "Blaze, why wouldn't he come and talk to me about having sex. Blake is growing up to fast, next he's going to be talking about moving out, probably to another state and won't even tell me." I wiped my eyes and sniffled.

"Baby, I..." Blaze started laughing once again.

I hit him. "You are so damn insensitive. I swear to God."

Blaze wiped the tears from my eyes then shook his head. "Peach, that damn boy ain't moving nowhere anytime soon. That overgrown fucka still bring his ass in our room and jump in the bed with us. Baby, Blake ain't gon' stay yo little boy no matter how bad you want him to. You gotda let the idea of him always being yo baby go. That's a man, if he wanna go out there and poke his needle into some skins let him. Hell, when his ass turns eighteen, I'm putting him out anyway. He got another year to go and his ass is gone. I ain't about to take care of no grown ass man and yo ass ain't either. Maybe his needle will fall into some rich skin—"

I started laughing. "Would you stop saying that. I don't want his needle poking into anything. I can't believe he didn't tell me."

"Why so you could've talked him out of it only to have him sneaking around fuckin' and shit? If that would've happened yo ass would've been taking care of yo baby, babies and treating his ass for some type of STD. It's been a year after his talk with me and he ain't got no STD's no bad ass, snot nose ass babies running around either. So, stop all that damn crying, I'm on my daddy shit. Now say, *thank you papa bear* and give me a kiss." Blaze instructed, making me laugh.

One thing I will forever love about Blaze is that no matter what the sad situation for me is, he can always take my mind off it. I knew what he was doing, but I didn't call him on it. I needed a distraction.

My arms wrapped around his neck and I kissed him. "Thank you, papa bear, you're the best and I love you." I pressed my lips to his once more.

Blaze's arms tightened around me and he stood sitting me on his desk. He grabbed the hem of my shirt and pulled it off, then removed my pants. "You gon' give me another baby?"

For years Blaze been talking about having more kids. Although I wanted more, I just didn't want to push them out. Regardless of that, my head nodded, and I kissed him again. "Yeah, we can have another baby."

26

Even though I didn't want to go through those painful contractions, I would simply because I love my husband. During these past several years, Blaze been patient with me as I got into the career field I wanted to be in and for that, I would give my papa bear another baby.

I got up off his desk and undid his jeans. Once I pulled them down to his knees, I pushed him into his chair then squatted down in front of him.

I took hold of his man, spitting on it I started to stroke him up and down. My hands worked his shaft as my mouth sucked on his tip until he was fully erect. I cupped his sack, massaging his balls as I took him deep into the back of my throat.

"Ah fuck!" He grunted while grabbing a handful of my hair. I glanced up to see his head had fallen back and his lips were parted. His pleasurable grunts and moans turned me on something terrible.

Moaning around him, my head started to bob faster. I released him with a pop then sucked on his tip once before I moved down to his balls. I sucked his sack into my mouth and moaned while I gave his tip a slight squeeze.

"Gotdamn, Peaches." Blaze pulled me away from his dick. He picked me up and placed me on his desk. Grabbing his stiff man, he lined it up to my opening and pushed deep inside of me.

He then proceeded to make love to me on his desk.

***

"Can I taste it?" Blaze arms wrapped around my waist once I sat the lasagna on the counter. He kissed the side of my face, then my neck as his hands rubbed my hips.

My lips were stretched into a wide smile. "You know you can have anything you want."

"Don't tell me that. I'll take full advantage of you." He bit at my neck.

Laughing, I elbowed him. "Stop." I got a forkful of Lasagna and blew on it, to cool it off. I turned slightly, holding the fork out to him.

Blaze ate it then moan. "That shit hot." His mouth formed into an O as he tried to blow the food in his mouth. Once he swallowed it, he shook his head. "I couldn't even get a good taste, that shit was so hot."

Now I knew he was lying, but I didn't call him on it. Instead I got another forkful and blew on it. However, before I gave it to him that time, I touched it with my tongue to make sure it wasn't hot. "Taste it."

He ate it. "Damn, that taste better than the first bite," he leaned down and kissed me.

"You're so damn crazy." I let out a small laugh as I kissed him back. Blaze was suddenly pushed back away from me.

"Can I taste it, please?" Brianna asked, standing in between us.

"Why you hating, Bri-Bri?" Blaze laughed at her.

Brianna climbed on top of the counter. "I'm not hating." She pulled Blaze to her, then wrapped her arms around his neck and her legs at his waist, forcing Blaze to pick her up. He had no problem with doing so. "Mommy, can I taste it?" She then turned to Blaze and wiped his mouth off before she puckered up her big full size lips for him to kiss.

Blaze kissed her on the mouth, then laughed. He looked at me and shook his head. "Brianna, why you gon' wipe off yo mom's kiss? You a hater."

"She really is, ol' big head little girl." I muffed her head to the side making her laugh.

"I'm not a hater. You always kissing my daddy." She laughed before eating the food off the fork. "That's good. Can we eat now? I'm so hungry, I'm about to pass out." Brianna's head fell on Blaze shoulder and she sighed.

"You are so dramatic like yo damn momma it don't make no sense, crazy ass." Blaze laughed at her. He kissed her cheek, then put her down. "Go tell your brothers to come eat."

"Okay. Oh, Blake not here. Some girl called him, and he left—" Brianna started to tell but Blaze cut her off.

"Bria, shut up and go get BJ." Blaze waved her off.

"What girl?" I asked, looking at Blaze and he shrugged.

"Janae with the big butt." Bria once again replied. I looked at her shocked. "What? That's what Blake call her." She looked over at her dad then took off running out the kitchen.

I turned to face Blaze. "You better call Blake and tell him to get his ass home. And he got five minutes to get here otherwise I'm coming to find his black ass. Call him, Blaze. I'm not playing either."

Blaze shook his head at me and laughed. "Peaches, leave that man alone. He ain't did shit. He knows what time he got to be back home. I ain't about to call him. Brianna! BJ!" He yelled as he grabbed the plates and held them out to me.

"So, you're not going to call him?" I glared hard at him.

30

"No, now gon' make them plates. We hungry." He pointed to the food, urging me to do what he said.

I snatched the plates from him and started putting food on them. "Stupid ass gets on my nerves." I mumbled, handing him the plates as I fixed them, and he sat each one on the table.

I grabbed some cups and went to go put them on the table, but Blaze stopped me. "Lose that damn attitude. Didn't I tell you not to worry about him, Peaches? He's good, man, so calm yo ass down, i'ight?"

I smack my lips not wanting to listen to him. I knew I had to accept the fact my baby was growing up and he would be an adult in just a few more years. Even so, I wasn't ready for it to happen. The years had gone by so fast. It seemed like he was just that two-year-old little boy I had gotten yesterday. Now he was suddenly sixteen and having sex.

"Peaches, you hear me?" Blaze asked me. My lips popped once more, and I didn't answer him. Blaze grabbed my chin and tilted my head back. "So yo ass don't hear me talkin' to you?" He fussed at me.

"I ain't cool with that, B. I don't care what you say, but whatever." My eyes rolled at him.

That seemed to make him smile. "I still got that ass in check though. Now gimme a damn kissed before I slap yo ass." He pressed his lips to mine.

A stupid smile came to my lips. "You ain't even funny." That time I kissed him.

"Ahh!" I heard BJ scream before the sound of footsteps thumped hard down the hallway.

My face fell on Blaze chest and I groaned. "And you want more kids."

Blaze laughed as the kids ran in the kitchen with us. "What the hell is y'all doing?" Blaze asked them.

"That stupid little girl hit me in the head with a shoe. I'm about to knock her out." BJ fussed, trying to get to Brianna.

I grabbed my youngest son and held him back. "Bria, why would you hit him?" I didn't even have to ask if she had done it or not because I knew her all too well.

"I didn't mean to hit him hard. I told him to come eat and he was ignoring me, steady playing that stupid game." Bria explained.

"No, I wasn't, I told her I was coming, and she hit me with the shoe for no reason. I promise I'mma knock her ugly butt out." BJ threatened.

I swear my youngest had his father's attitude and temper. It was all bad with him.

"Where she hit you at?" I asked, rubbing his head.

"That damn shoe ain't hurt him. His ass ain't even crying. Stop babying him and Bria you hit him with another shoe, I'mma tag yo ass. You understand me?" Blaze fussed at the three of us.

Brianna's lip poked out and her shoulders sagged. "I understand. I'm sorry, BJ."

"It's okay." BJ told her. "But don't hit me no more, otherwise I'mma knock yo ugly butt out." He snapped at her.

Brianna popped her lips. "Shut up. You not gon' do nothing but cry to your momma. *Whine, whine*, momma, Bria hit me." She mocked him while making crying noises.

My hand covered my forehead as I tried not to laugh. Those were Blaze's gotdamn kids to the fullest. Those damn Carter's was nothing nice, they took all his genes and none of mine.

And here we were trying to have more of them.

Lord help us.

Chapter 3

Blake

My nails scratched over my head as I sat in my car outside of Janae's house. I was stressing like a mothafucka waiting for her ass to come out.

Janae was a girl I been messing around with for about a year, back when she transferred to my school. From the moment I laid eyes on Janae, I was immediately attracted to her. She was medium built with a beautiful almond skin complexion, pretty and natural long brown hair, with a pair of gorgeous light brown eyes. Shorty was simply beautiful. On top of that, she was cool and smart as hell. I was feeling the fuck out of her, honestly.

Janae fuck'd me up when she told me she was five weeks pregnant. I went to talk to my dad about it, but my momma was with him and I didn't plan on telling her ass shit about what was going on. I already knew she was going to flip the fuck out. Hell, she still thought I was a gotdamn virgin.

I wasn't ready for no kids right now. I had to much planned for my future to be thinking about a baby. Fuck'd up thing with that was, Janae wanted to keep it.

"Fuck!" I grabbed my phone and called her again.

"Hello?" She answered.

"Man, what the fuck are you doing? I'm outside, bring yo ass on." I hung up on her as I ran my hand over my head. A few seconds later I saw her front door open. She came outside with a throw-blanket wrapped around her shoulders.

She jogged to the car and got in. "You didn't have to call snapping. I was in the bathroom getting sick when you called the first time. I had to clean myself up. Damn, sorry." She fussed while folding her leg up under herself. She let out a heavy sigh, then laid her head back on the headrest.

"My fault, i'ight?" I reached over and ran my fingers through her hair.

Janae looked over at me and grabbed my hand, entwining it with hers. "It's okay, I know you're just as stressed as I am."

I hummed, nodding my head. "You told yo momma yet?"

"No, I wanted to talk to you and see where your heads at about this." She sighed. "I want to keep the baby, but this is a decision we both need to make." Janae let out a breath and pulled the blanket tighter to her.

When Janae found out earlier during the day that she was pregnant, her ass told me she wanted to keep it. That was basically the end of the conversation about it. I never told her what I thought or how I felt.

I licked my lips and was honest with her. "Nae, I ain't tryna have no kids right now. Neither one of us is ready for a baby, we both got big futures we trying to pursue and having a kid right now gon' either stop those plans or slow them down. And ain't no basketball scholarship gon' wait on me. On top of that, I'm not with having my folks taking care of my kid. If you have this baby now that's exactly what's gon' happen. My folks gonna pick up that responsibility and I don't want that. I would rather have my own first before bringing a shorty into this world. Nae, now just ain't our time, sweetheart." I was feeling Janae without a doubt, but a baby just didn't fit in my plans. I hope like hell she saw it my way and thought getting an abortion was the better option.

Janae had never met my folks and vice versa, and now her ass was pregnant. We didn't know if we were going to be together in a month or a year from now so why should we bring a baby into that unknown situation? We were just kickin' it and having fun.

Janae wiped her eyes. "Blake, I don't think we're ready, but I don't want to kill my baby either. This is so messed up. Like, I don't know how the future will play out between us. Rather we end up together or not I just don't feel right getting an abortion. No, this don't fit into our plans, but I can't do that." She cried.

"Baby, you ain't doing this by yoself. I'mma be with you every step of the way. I don't want you to get an abortion either," I felt a little bad that I was lying to her, but I had to say whatever was needed. "But we can't have this baby right now. Janae, I haven't even met yo folks and now you gon' introduce me as the dude that got you knocked up? Man, that shit ain't about to go right at all and my moms' gonna flip the fuck out. But whatever you decide to do I'm with you. If you get an abortion, I'll be right there with you." My thumb ran across her cheek, wiping her tears away.

"You're not mad that I'm pregnant?" She suddenly asked me.

My eyes squinted at her and I shook my head. "Why would I be mad at you? If anything, I'll be pissed at myself but I'm not mad at you. I mean shit happens, you getting pregnant wasn't intended. Shid, I wished this had of happened a couple of years from now when we're both financially stable. If that was the case abortion wouldn't even be mentioned." A small smile came to her lips. "I'm dead ass serious. But that ain't the case. I'm sixteen, Nae, you're seventeen and we can barely take care of ourselves."

"I know." Again, she let out a sigh. "Can you give me a few days to think about it. And if I decide to do this, you'll come with me?" She asked.

"Yeah, I'll be there with you. What kind of question is that?" I looked at her like she was crazy. Her lips twisted and she started chewing on the inside of her jaw, which she did whenever she was nervous. "Come here," I let my seat back then grabbed her hand.

"Nah, Blake—"

"Man, get yo ass over here." I gave her hand a slight tug.

She looked around us while biting into her lower lip. "What if my momma pulls up. She gon' kill you."

"I don't give a fuck. My windows tinted so she can't see shit." I gave her hand another tug and she climbed into my lap. "Now why you think I wouldn't be there with you?" I grabbed her chin then leaned up and kissed her.

Janae shrugged. "I mean, you're this," her fingers moved like quotation marks, "star everybody loves and I'm this, newbie nobody, who done got pregnant by the jock. So, I honestly thought you would think I tried to trap you or something, I don't know." Her eyes rolled into her head and again she shrugged. "My dad was apparently the same as you and he left my momma when she got pregnant with me because of his so-called career."

"Yo father's a bitch. That's why he ran. I'm not running. Hell, my momma wouldn't let me and if she even knew we were talkin' about abortions. She'll 'bout beat both of our asses, real shit. But I ain't going nowhere." After hearing that her father left her momma, I felt bad about trying to get her to have an abortion. But we couldn't take care of a kid at the moment.

She leaned into me, "I hope you don't," she mumbled as her lips played with mine.

"I'm not," I grabbed the nape of her neck and slid my tongue into her mouth, tangling it with hers. My hand slid under her skirt, I started playing with her clit through her panties. Janae's pussy quickly became wet and she started grinding harder against my fingers. "Hold up, get over there and take yo panties off." She did as I told her. While she was doing that, I undid my jeans, pulling my pants and boxer-brief's down my hip. I started up the car then grabbed my phone. I put an address into the GPS then hooked the phone on the dock.

"Blake, what are you doing?" Janae asked confused with furrowed brows.

"You're about to drive me. Come on." I grabbed her hand, but she pulled away.

"What? I'm lost." Her facial expression showed that she really was confused.

Laughing, I pulled her into my lap. I laid back and closed my legs. I had her back facing me, with her legs on each side of mine.

"Blake, what are you doing?"

"Raise up," I reached between her parted legs and guided my dick to her opening. I thrusted my hips forward, pushing my tip inside of her and immediately her pussy started to suck around my dick.

"Mmm, shit, Blake." She moaned.

I pressed down on the brakes, then put the car in drive before I started the GPS. "Take us there." My hands grabbed her hips and I started moving her up and down on my dick.

"What? I can't drive like this. Dude you're crazy as hell." She laughed, thinking I was joking.

But I was serious as hell. "You can. I wanna see how good you are at multitasking. I'mma work the paddles and you tell me either brake or gas while you're steering and riding my dick. If we die then shid, we'll be happy. Now gon' head."

"You're serious?" She turned her head around to look at me.

Smiling at her, I nodded. "As fuck, now go." I reached between her legs and started playing with her clit.

"Blake, I can't. Oh, my God," She moaned as her inner muscles squeezed around me.

I took my foot off the brake and the car started rolling as I pressed on the gas. I grabbed her hips and started lifting her up and down on my dick.

41

"Mmm, ooh, Blake, you're going to fast." She moaned so I slowed down her movement. "I mean you're driving too fast."

I eased my foot off the gas and started to move her faster with one hand while the other continued to play with her swollen clit.

"Oh, my God." She leaned forward causing the horn to beep. "Ooh shit."

Out of all the chicks I've messed with Janae was the only one I ever went raw in. Nae's shit was so tight, and it felt so gotdamn good. Her pussy fit me like a glove.

"Brake Blake!" She said loudly. Once I hit the brakes her hand went into her hair and she started bouncing. "Babe, I can't drive no more. Ooh, Blake, please." She moaned while bouncing faster.

The cars behind us started to blow but Janae didn't care, she was too busy fuckin' my dick.

"Nae, ah shit!" She was rocking her hips and working her pussy muscles, I was ready to nut. "Damn, Nae, fuck." I grabbed her hips and started to thrust up into her.

"We missed the light." She laughed out a moan but didn't stop.

My phone started ringing. "Damn!"

"It says Unc." She moaned out, not once stopping her movement.

"Answer it." I told her and I heard my Uncle King on the phone laughing. "Yeah?"

"Nigga, I know damn well yo ass ain't doing what the fuck I think you doing?" He asked, cracking up.

I tapped Janae to slow her down. "What the fuck is you talkin' 'bout, Unc?"

Janae pace picked back up. "Ooh, ooh, ooh," She panted loudly rocking faster.

"Lil B, man if you don't get yo ass off the fuckin' road with that bullshit." He continued to laugh. "I done missed this fuckin' light because of y'all ass. Nigga I'm tellin' yo damn momma."

I grabbed Nae's hips trying to slow her down, but she wasn't. "Ah, fuck. I'ight, Unc. Baby, hang up the phone."

"Babe, go." She panted.

I pressed on the gas paddle and we pulled away from the light. I wasn't worried about my Unc tellin' my momma shit. If anything, he was most definitely going to tell my dad, but again I wasn't worried about it.

"Baby, slow down, I have to turn."

I did as she said. I took my foot off the paddle. I leaned my upper body back into my seat as I planted my feet to the floor. I held her to me as I started to thrust my hips upwards, pounding into her harder.

"Oh, my God, ooh, mmm, I'm cumming. Blake, ooh God!" She cried out as she came.

"Ooh fuck," I grunted still holding onto her hips as I nutted inside of her.

Janae suddenly started laughing. "Oh, my God. I can't believe you just made me do that. Oh, my God, your uncle gonna tell your mom. And we missed our stop."

"You loved that shit. And don't worry about my uncle." I told her as I stopped the car. "Get over there and put yo panties back on." Janae climbed back over, grabbing her underwear.

I adjusted my seat, then turned the car around. Pulling in front of my house, I shut the car off.

"Where we at?" She asked, looking around the neighborhood.

"At my house, come on." I fixed myself back in my jeans then got out the car. This would be the first time she's ever been to my crib.

"Blake, I'm not dressed to go inside your house. I look like a bum and I have on house-shoes. Why would you bring me here?" She fussed, looking shocked. She pulled the sun visor down and started fixing her hair.

"Man, ain't nobody gon' be looking at yo ass like that. You always look like a damn bum, for real, so who you tryna impress?" I asked her and she rolled her eyes at me. "Get yo ass out the damn car before I drag you out."

She slammed the sun visor closed, then got out the car with an attitude. She then slammed my car door.

"I can always take yo stupid ass back home too. I don't give a fuck." Her damn attitude was gon' make me knock her ass out.

"Then take me home because I don't wanna meet yo folks dressed like this." She folded her arms over her chest with a pout.

I didn't expect her ass to say that. Laughing, I locked my car doors. "You better wrap yo ass up in that damn blanket you got." I put my arm over her shoulder and pulled her into my side.

"You ain't even funny. I can't believe you brought me over here like this." She said before smiling.

"Fuck you smiling about? Come on, I'll sneak you in through my window and I'll be there in a minute." Her smile quickly dropped. I broke out laughing. "I'm bullshittin' come on."

We went to the front door and I unlocked it. "Ma!" I yelled as we walked in. "Ma! Where you at?" I yelled again.

"Stop yelling." Janae whispered nervously. She held onto my arm, hiding slightly behind me.

"You just fuck'd me driving my car and you nervous to meet my folks? Yo ass twisted." I laughed at her.

"That's not funny and I look tacky." She hit me in my arm.

With my arm around her I pulled her into the living room. "Ma!"

"Rashad, if yo ass don't stop all that gotdamn...yelling." Her fussing faded as she saw Janae. "Why are you yelling? Make me slap you." She threatened.

Janae started laughing. "That's where you get that from." She whispered.

"Where he gets what from?" My momma asked her.

"Um, threatening to slap people." She mumbled before her lips twisted and she started biting on the inside of her jaw.

"Rashad?" My momma eyes slid to Janae. "Who's your friend?"

"Oh, Ma, this my friend Janae, Nae this my crazy momma." I introduced them.

"Hey, Mrs. Carter it's nice to finally meet you." She held her hand out for my momma to take.

"You too, sweetheart." My mom gave her a friendly smile. "Are you staying for dinner?" She asked her. "You can if you haven't eaten yet."

"Um," Janae looked back at me.

"What you looking at me for? She's talkin' to you. Do you wanna stay or you don't?" I asked her.

"Oh God." My momma grunted out. She touched her forehead, then grabbed Janae's arm. "Come on sweetie." She then looked at me with pursed lips. "You have to excuse my son. I promise I didn't raise him like that. It's in his DNA. He can't help it." She explained to her. Laughing, I followed behind them. "Blaze, this is Blake friend, Janae."

"Janae with the big butt?" Brianna blurted out.

"What?" Janae looked back at me.

"That's what Blake say. Janae with the big butt, Janae with the really big butt. He told Ace he couldn't look at you because you were his

47

girl." Brianna repeated parts of a conversation I had with my best friend.

"Brianna, shut up. What I tell you about repeating everything you hear?" My momma fussed at her.

"Her booty ain't really that big, though." BJ's head tilted to the side as he looked at Janae's ass.

"What the hell, dude. Ma, get yo kids. Tell them to shut up!" Had I known this was going to happen, I wouldn't have brought her over to the house.

Janae broke out laughing. "Oh, my God, y'all are to funny and so cute."

"Thank you." Brianna smiled at her.

"I ain't cute, I'm handsome." BJ rubbed his chin. "You wanna play video games with me?" He looked her up and his eyes squinted together. "Why you got on house-shoes? You don't have no real shoes?" BJ continued to question her.

Laughing, Janae nodded. "I do. But your brother didn't tell me we were coming here. I thought we were just going to sit in front of my house."

"Okay, you wanna come play games with me?" BJ asked again.

"Man, leave that gotdamn girl alone. BJ, finish yo food then go do yo damn homework." My dad snapped before he looked at me. "Why the hell do that girl got on a damn blanket?" He pointed at Janae but was looking at me.

"Why are you asking me?" I looked at her with the throw blanket wrapped around her shoulders. I didn't know why her ass came out the house like that. "Dad, she's kinda special." I shrugged.

My dad looked at her then shook his head. "Yup you a Carter. We like them dirty and ghetto."

Janae mouth dropped as did my momma's.

I broke out laughing.

Yeah tonight was going to be long and fun.

***

"Dinner was really good, Mrs. Carter." Janae said as she finished her food.

"Thank you and call me Peaches." My mom returned Janae's smile then stood up and grabbed my dad's plate. She put it in the sink, then came back to the table. As she walked past my dad, he smacked her on the butt then pulled her into his lap.

"Blaze, when I smack the shit out of you, yo ass gonna be mad." She snapped at him.

"I'm not gon' be mad. I'll just smack yo ass back." My dad quickly grabbed my mom's arms, laughing. "Gon' now, Peaches. Why that girl can't call you Mrs. Carter? That's yo name ain't it?" He picked with her.

Janae leaned into me and started laughing. "Why I have to be *that girl*, though?" She whispered to me.

"Shid, he doesn't know yo name. Yo ass lucky he ain't callin' you, *dirty girl*." I whisper to her. My dad was terrible with names either that or he simply didn't care to know them. I looked over to my parents to see them kiss. "Y'all, we going to my room." I stood up and grabbed Janae's hand.

My mom pulled away from my dad and looked at me. "Why you have to go in your room? I haven't seen you all day and I'm just meeting your friend." She stood up but my dad pulled her back down.

"Peaches, we need to go handle that thing and make sure the twins in the bed." My dad started whispering in her ear making her eyes roll.

A Love Like Ours: *The Carter Family*

I pulled Janae out the kitchen and took her to my room. Once inside I locked my door and flopped down on my bed.

"Your folks are crazy." She laid down beside me. "I like your momma. She's nice."

"Yeah they are and my moms real cool." I shrugged, kicking off my shoes. Janae got on top of me and let out a sigh. My hand ran over my head. "What's up?" She shrugged her shoulders as she started chewing on the inside of her jaw. I glared at her and she rolled her eyes at me. "Why the fuck you lying? What's up, Nae?"

"Blake, what are we? Like are we dating or just friends because I'm confused. I don't want to be telling folks we're together and you're saying we're not. Like tonight." She folded her arms over her chest with an attitude.

I was confused as hell because I didn't remember telling nobody she wasn't my girl tonight, or any other time for that matter. "What the hell are you talking about? Tonight when?"

She sighed and rolled her eyes. "When you introduced me to your momma as just your friend and not girlfriend. So, I need to know what we are to you."

Again, my hand ran over my head. "Why we need labels? Labels and shit really don't matter to me. If I'm fuckin' with you, then I am. And to

51

be honest, I'm not worried about you tellin' folks we're together. Shid, what we do ain't nobody's business anyway." I was feeling Janae, but I wasn't trying to be committed to anybody. Shid, I was sixteen, a young dude and being serious with a chick was the last thing on my mind.

"Blake, that didn't answer my question. Okay, fine, a label may not mean anything to you, but it does to me. I need to know what we are because I don't want to be holding onto you if that's not what you want. Like, if we're not together, cool. Just tell me so I can move on." Janae got off me and I knew she was mad because of the shit that was coming out of her mouth.

Sitting up, I rubbed my bottom lip as my head nodded. "Janae, don't threaten me with that bullshit. That's only going to piss me off, real shit." I felt the glare overtake my features as what she said hit me. "Who the fuck you gonna move on to? Huh?"

"Nobody... I'm just sayin'—"

I cut her off. "Yo ass ain't just saying shit. You obviously thought about moving on with some mothafuckin' body. So, who the fuck is it?" I asked her.

"It's no one, Blake. Damn. You don't know what you want us to be. So, why should I be claiming we're together when you don't even know. You saying labels don't matter but it does to me. I'm not about to just be sleeping with a nigga when we're not dating." She snapped, sounding dumb as hell to me.

What she said just didn't make no damn sense. "Bruh, yo ass several months too late to be saying this bullshit. Especially since we fuck'd a week after we met." I laughed at her. She was talking out her ass with that dumb shit.

"I only had sex with you because I thought we were together! I don't just open my legs for anybody—"

"You thought we were together a week after we met? If I didn't tell you that then you shouldn't have thought no shit like that. We've never talked about the shit, we just started hanging out." I shrugged.

Janae's head nodded. "Okay. We're not together, fine, cool." She rolled her eyes at me. I could see it in her eyes that her feelings were hurt. "Can you come take me home."

My hand rubbed over my head and I groaned. I wasn't trying to hurt her feelings, but I didn't see the point of us having a label. I didn't give a fuck what she told folks about us because I never paid it no mind. Even so, at the end of the day, I fuck'd with her.

"Nae…" I grabbed her hand, but she pulled away from me. "Man, gon' with that dumb shit. You pissed because I don't see a point in us being labeled? Sweetheart, you're missing the bigger picture, look where we're at." I motioned around my room. "You know how many chicks I done brought home to meet my folks?" Her lips twisted and she looked away from me. "None. Zero. You the only female that done been here. At the end of the day, Janae, you know you're my girl. So why the fuck do I even have to say that shit?"

"I thought we were together, but I didn't know, which is why I asked. Like I said, when you introduced me to your mom, I was simply your friend not your girl." She pointed out once again with an attitude.

I looked at her like she was stupid. "For a smart mothafucka yo ass dumb as hell. Man, I told yo ass what it is. You can take that shit how you wanna but I'm over this conversation." I grabbed the remote then laid back down. I turned on the TV and started flipping through the channels.

"You not gonna take me home?" She asked still standing in the middle of the room.

I looked down at her. "When I feel like droppin' yo ass off I will. If you can't wait, then you're free to walk." I could admit I was wrong

54

but fuck her. I don't see why the questions was suddenly coming now after all that damn time we spent together.

"Yo ass is so irritating. I swear." She flopped down on the bed with her arms folded over her chest.

I kicked her as I laughed. "But yo ass ain't gone nowhere either."

She hit my foot. "Stop. And I'm not gone because you won't drop me off." She snapped at me.

Laughing, I reached out and grabbed her ponytail, pulling her head back. Janae fell on the bed. "Yo ass don't wanna go home for real. You just want me to baby yo black ass."

Janae slapped my hand away from her. "No, I don't. I wanted to know if we were together and you done already told me we weren't. So, I actually do wanna go home." I grabbed her arms and she pulled away from me. "No, gone, Blake."

I sat up, grabbed her by the waist and pulled her to the top of the bed with me. "Why you wanna fight with me? Huh? You know yo ass ain't gonna leave me because I'm not gon' let you. So why we gotda do all this?" Committed or not Janae wasn't going anywhere, I wasn't going to let her. She was a cool ass chick that I liked hanging with. I wasn't ready to let her go, on top of that she was pregnant, so it wasn't no quitting for us just yet.

She rolled her eyes then turned away from me. "We don't have to go through anything. Blake, stop, I'm being serious right now and you wanna play." She snapped at me as I kissed her neck.

I turned her around to face me and her eyes rolled. My head leaned down, and I kissed her. Janae kissed me back then sighed. "Nae, tell me what's really wrong with you. And don't give me that bullshit about clarifying us being together because that's not it. Tell me what's up?"

Throughout the whole time we've been together, whether we were official never came up. All of a sudden, though she wanted to make it a big deal and whine about the shit. So, I knew it had to be something more to it.

Janae lifted her head up and kissed me again. "I'm sorry I'm being a bitch to you." She apologized then sat up. She turned around and faced me. "Blake, I just wish we were older, and I didn't have to even think about an abortion. I know what's best for us right now, but I don't like that I have to do this. I know you're say you'll be here for me, but once I get the abortion then what? Where does that leave us?" She asked me.

56

"Ain't shit gon' change between us, Nae. I done already told you that. You saying once you have the abortion then what? Look, you having the baby is not gonna make me stay with you if I don't want to. You understand? Same thing if you get an abortion, if I don't wanna be with you then I'm not going to be. That's it on us being together. As for you keeping the baby, I'm leaving that decision up to you. I told you how I felt about it but at the end of the day it's your choice. And if you keep it, then I'll take care of my responsibility regardless." I wished like hell her ass didn't get pregnant and I honestly did want her to have the abortion. But rather she did or didn't wasn't going to stop me from fuckin' with her.

"I know you don't have to be with me either way. But I feel like once I have this abortion it's going to be over between us and I don't want that. And I know keeping it isn't going to make you stay with me." She let out a sigh. "I don't know." She stressed.

"Nae, who's to say that tomorrow you probably won't want to fuck with me anymore?" I asked her straight up. Shid, we didn't know when we were going to get tired of each other.

"I'm to say because I'm not going to feel like that." She mumbled but I still heard her.

My brows raised because she sounded sure of herself. "What make you so sure?"

She let out a heavy breath and rolled her eyes. "Because…" Her words turned into low mumbles so I couldn't hear what she said.

"I don't understand that shit. Open that big ass mouth of yours and talk. Don't mumble shit."

"I said I'm not going to feel like that because…" She let out a groan. "Because Blake… I love you…" She looked down at her hands as she chewed on her lip.

"Janae." I called her name and she looked up at me.

Her hands covered her face. "Stop smiling like that. Ugh, you get on my nerves."

I couldn't stop myself from smiling. I thought it was cute that she tried to start a dumb ass fight all because she was in love. I didn't know if I loved her. But I liked her ass to the point I wasn't ready to stop fuckin' with her. "Janae." I grabbed her hand, but she pulled away.

"No, Blake, stop smiling at me like that." She whined.

"Stop that. I can smile." I pulled her to me then picked her up, sitting her on my lap. "You love me?"

She nodded her head. "Yeah, I do." Janae's hands covered her face once more.

"Don't get shy on me now." I pulled her hands from her face. "Nae, you got me, i'ight? Don't worry about me going anywhere… yet."

That made her laugh and she hit me. "You're not funny." Her arms went around my neck. "So, I got you?" She bit at my bottom lip.

"Mmhm, you got me for right now." I grabbed the hem of her shirt and pulled it off.

Janae pulled my shirt over my head, then stopped. "What about your folks?" She whispered as I undid her bra.

"They're not gonna hear shit. Hell, knowing my folks, they're probably in their room doing the same damn thing." I rolled her over then got up. I pulled her skirt and panties off, tossing them to the side. I then removed my pants and boxers. "Yo ass just gotda be quiet." I told her as I turned up the TV.

Laughing, she pulled me down on top of her. "I don't even be loud. Mmm." She moaned as I pushed inside of her. Janae's arms went around my waist and she lifted herself up, so that her tongue licked at my bottom lip before she sucked it into her mouth. "Blake, I love you." She moaned, kissing me.

I didn't know why but hearing her say that made my dick throb and I started pounding into her harder and faster.

It probably wasn't love I felt for Janae, but I knew I definitely had a heavy like for her. Then again, I honestly didn't know but whatever it was. I wasn't ready to let it go just yet.

***

Once we finished, I took Janae into my bathroom so we could take a shower.

"You think they heard us? They probably not gonna ever let me come back over here." She whispered to me.

I turned her around and started washing her up. "Man, they ain't hear shit. Believe me if my momma did, she would've kicked that damn door down. And dragged yo ass out by your hair." I half joked. My momma was kind of crazy and it was really no telling what she may have done. But I didn't need Janae thinking about that. Hell, that was the last thing on my mind. "So, stop worrying about my folks." I pushed her under the shower head and rinsed her off.

She spit water from her mouth. "Why you do that. Stupid self." She laughed.

My fingers ran through her wet hair. "But you love my stupid self, though." I walked her under the shower head again as I kissed her. I turned off the water and moved back.

"I do love yo little ugly ass." She kissed me then opened the shower door. I smacked her on the ass hard. She turned around so fast her hand swung hard and I ducked back. She didn't even hit me, and I felt that hit. "Yo ass play to damn much. That shit hurt! I'm wet you stupid, ugly ass fucka!" She snapped.

"Shut the fuck up with yo crybaby ass. That shit ain't even hurt that bad." I laughed as she mugged me hard. I grabbed the towel and wrapped it around her.

"How the hell you know? You ain't feel it." She was pissed off.

I took hold of her ass and squeezed it. "I'm sorry."

She bit into her lip and looked away from me before she started laughing. "Whatever." We went back into my room and she walked straight to my closet.

I dried myself off then grabbed a pair of black basketball shorts and pulled them on.

"Why come you never let anybody wear your jersey on game day?" She asked, holding up my basketball jersey.

61

"Why come? It's, how come." I corrected her and she laughed. "Why do I have to let somebody wear my jersey?" I pulled on a white beater then a pair of socks.

She shrugged. "It's just a question. But all the players let either their girls or somebody wear their jersey's. You never have, so I was just wondering why not." She took my Jordan shirt off the hanger and put it on.

"That's my favorite shirt. You bet not mess it up." I grabbed my jersey and hung it back up in my closet. "Every chick that asked to wear it. I don't fuck with." I put on my Nike slides, then grabbed my keys off the dresser. "You ready?"

"Yeah." She pulled on her skirt then grabbed her stuff. She went back into my closet and took my red and black Bulls hoodie.

"Why the fuck you takin' my shit?" I laughed at her.

She pulled it on. "Because I want to wear it. Dang." She laughed, kissing me. "Come on before my momma start calling."

"You gon' leave yo bra here?" I pointed to the bed. She snatched it up and put it in the hoodie pouch. "Man, lets go." I opened my room door to see Brianna running into her room. My brows raised and I followed behind her, opening the door.

Her eyes got wide and she dropped the pack of cookies on the floor. "Blake, please don't tell." She immediately begged.

"Yo ass supposed to be sleep. Take yo ass to bed!" I laughed at her.

She looked around me to Janae. "So, you his girlfriend? You want a cookie?" Bri asked her.

"Yeah I'll take a cookie." Janae walked to the bed and grabbed a cookie.

"Is you his girlfriend?" Brianna questioned again.

"Yeah, she is, now take yo ass to bed." I told her, then left out her room.

"She is just to cute." Janae linked her arm with mine.

I shrugged. "She straight."

She popped her lips. "Shut up!"

We walked in the living room to see my mom and dad laying on the couch watching TV. When my momma saw me, she sat up. "I didn't know your friend was still here. I thought you was sleep." She stated, looking between the two of us.

"We did fall asleep watching TV. I'm about to drop her off now though." She stared at me for a long while and I looked away from her. My nails lightly scratched at the back of my head.

"Man, go take that damn girl home." My dad shook his head at me before he started laughing.

I didn't need to be told twice as I pulled Janae out the house and to my car.

Once we got in, she started laughing. "You're a terrible liar! You just looked so guilty!"

My Mom was a gotdamn psychic or some shit. No matter how many times I tried to lie she always called me out on my bullshit. I could lie good as hell to anybody else except her ass. "I'm a good ass liar. I just don't like to lie to my momma." I shrugged as I pulled out the driveway and took her home.

Chapter 4

Blaze

"**I** was behind his ass for damn near two blocks. At first, I didn't know it was him until I saw the *Ballers* tag on the plate. I keep telling his ass those windows ain't that damn dark."

King sat in my office telling me about what Blake did yesterday. His head shook and he started laughing.

"I'm telling you that little mothafucka held up traffic fuckin'. I wanted to be mad as hell, but I couldn't. That nigga had shorty driving while he was fuckin' her. I call his ass to make sure I'm not trippin' and her ass moaning when he answered the phone. Man, I had to pull the fuck over just to laugh at that shit."

I'm glad King wasn't the type to run and tell Peaches ass anything because this would've killed her dramatic ass. I had to talk to my damn son, he was getting out of hand with these damn girls. One or two was cool but that nigga fell into some pussy and done lost his fuckin' mind.

"Here," King held out a blunt to me.

"That nigga starting to do some dumb ass shit. His ass come and tell me he was ready to start fuckin'. Cool, I got his ass some condoms. So that little cheap mothafucka don't like to use his own money to buy condoms. So, his ass pops up on me during his lunch break, asking for a condom. I tell his ass—*take what you need but replace my shit because yo momma pop up on my ass and we use them.* That little mothafucka uses up all the fuckin' condoms, then go and buy some fuckin' Durex. But check this, he used those and leave the fuckin' empty box. Peaches see that shit and flipped out. Crazy ass gon' accuse me of cheating. That nigga got him some wet and now he's losing his damn mind." I pulled on the blunt, inhaling.

"That's yo damn son." He laughed.

"Yeah, but he gets that stupid shit from Peaches dumb ass. I ain't claiming that bullshit."

Biological mother or not, Blake stupid behavior he gets straight from Peaches dumb ass.

King started laughing. "Don't blame that shit on her. That's his ass. You need to talk to him. That little nigga something else for real."

I nodded my agreement and grabbed my phone as it started ringing. The kids school number flashed on the screen. "I bet this BJ's black ass." I showed King the phone then answered it. "Hello?"

"Hey, Mr. Carter, I'm sorry to have to bother you, but Blaze was in a fight. Is it any way you can come up here and talk with the principal and myself?" Ms. Richardson, BJ's teacher asked.

"Yeah, I'm on my way." I ended the call and ran my hand over my head. "That little mothafucka right there, yo. Every fuckin' week I'm getting a call about his ass." I passed King the blunt then got up. "What the fuck did you want?" I asked him. We never got to the point of why he was in my office.

"Oh, shid I don't even remember. When I saw yo ass that shit with Blake popped in my head." He said following me outside. "Gon' take care of yo fatherly duties. We'll meet up later at the courts."

"Yeah, I'll be there." We shook up then jumped into our cars and went our separate ways.

***

"Blaze initiated the fight. I tried to defuse the situation and calm him down, but he was pushing me away from him. I let him go and he walked over to the other boy, threatening him. The boy stood up and asked Blaze to get out of his face and that's when Blaze just started hitting him. I did not hear the other student say anything to him—"

BJ cut her off his tone of voice was nothing but straight anger as he spoke. "He was talking about my momma, so I hit him. I told him to shut up talking about my momma and Ms. Richardson didn't say nothing. Just told me to sit down and be quiet. I did because I didn't want to get in trouble again. Then when we were in line Mikel kept walking on the back of my shoes on purpose. I told her again and she told me to be quiet. Then Mikel called momma the *B* word, so I beat him up. She ain't even telling the truth, man. Dad, I promise she's lying. You can ask anybody in the class, and they'll tell you." He explained defending himself.

"Is that what happened?" I asked her and Mr. Baily, the principal.

"Bits of it—" The teacher started to say.

My brows furrowed. "So, why am I here? If my son came to you and said something about the little boy messing with him more than once. It was yo place to step in and correct that kid. Not wait until my son done got picked at repeatedly and pissed off to react. When he said something to you the first time you should have acted right then. You gonna say BJ initiated the fight when he was defending himself. Do yo ass not know the damn difference between the two?" I looked at her like she was stupid.

I pointed to Ms. Richardson. "Had you stepped in the fight wouldn't have started. So why you tryna suspend him when he was defending himself because you didn't?" I was never one to hide how I felt, and I knew at times my expression gave my feelings away. I was pissed the fuck off that this bitch had me down there for nothing. "Did you know about the *bits* of his story before you called me down here?" I asked the principal, mugging him hard as hell.

"No, I did not. This is the first time I'm hearing about the little boy picking at Blaze. We do not tolerate bullying of any sort but given the fact that the altercation turned physical. Even if he didn't start it, there was a fight so both students will be suspended. And for his story not being told upfront I will look into that." He looked at BJ's teacher as he said that last bit.

I wiped my mouth and nodded. "This what I'mma tell y'all, I don't condone fighting, but I also don't tolerate bullying. If a kid picks at my son, he is to tell y'all and if you don't do nothing after that second time, he has every right to defend himself. My kid ain't no gotdamn toy to be played with. He got my permission to fight if nothing is done *after* that second complaint. And y'all ain't gon' be suspending him for defending himself. Especially not when the shit could have been avoided if her ass would have stepped in and done something. Now, I'mma take him home today but he'll be back tomorrow." I got up out my seat. I didn't need for them to tell me shit else because they were on some straight bullshit. I was trying not to flip out because I had BJ with me, so it was best I got my ass away from that damn school.

"Am I in trouble?" BJ asked as we walked to the car. I didn't respond to him right away, I just kept walking. "Dad, I promise I was trying to be good and wasn't gonna fight him, but then he made me mad." He continued to explain. "Ms. Richardson just don't like me. Ooh, I swear if I get a whooping because of her. Ooh." He gritted out mad. BJ got in the truck and slammed the door.

I believed he was telling the truth. I got in and started up the truck.

"Dad, am I?" He turned in his seat and looked at me.

"Man, put on yo damn seatbelt, and no you're not getting a whooping this time." I pulled away from the school. I glanced down at my youngest son. "Did you beat his ass?"

BJ looked at me and started laughing. "Yeah, I beat him up. If he didn't call momma a *B* word, I wouldn't have hit him." He shrugged as his body relaxed since he knew he wasn't getting a whooping. "Where we about to go?"

I looked at the time to see it was close to Peaches lunch break. "You wanna go pick up yo moms and take her out to eat?"

"Yeah. We should go to Friday's." He let the seat back then folded his arms behind his head. "Dad, you should let me be suspended. I need a break from school. It was only for two days."

I started laughing at him. "Man, shut yo ass up. This is yo damn break. I should drop yo ass off to your nana—"

"No! Please don't take me over there. Nana make us go to the laundromat and clean up around the shop. I just cleaned up my room, I'm tired of cleaning up." BJ grunted then sat up and grabbed the bottle of Sprite from the cup holder. "Can I have this?"

"That shit hot as hell and I'm telling your nana what yo ass said too." The kids stayed talking about my momma. I couldn't blame them even after all these years she was still the same. She was nosey as hell and talked to damn much.

BJ shrugged then opened the pop. I shook my head at him as we pulled into the hospital. "Come on." BJ hopped out the truck and waited for me to make it to his side.

We walked into the hospital and I sent Peaches a text letting her know I was in the lobby.

"Dad, can I go to the vending machine? I'm thirsty." He held his hand out for me to give him some money.

I reached into my pocket and pulled out my wallet. I held out the ten I had and showed it to him. "I don't have no change. So, you shit out of luck."

"Give it here, I'll ask somebody for change." He tried to grab it, but I pulled the money out of his reach. "Come on man, I'm thirsty. I'mma about to pass out." He fell back on the chair dramatically, like he had passed out.

I started laughing as did someone else. I looked back to see Mariah standing there. "We can't have you passing out now, can we?" She asked walking in front of us.

"No." BJ replied with a shake of his head. "Do you have change for a ten?" He asked her.

"BJ, you can wait for yo momma to get down here. Calm yo little ass down." He was gonna get our asses killed if Peaches caught us talking to that damn girl. She already thought Mariah liked my ass.

She smiled at me. "He's okay." She then looked at BJ and nodded. "I actually do have change. I was just looking for a solid ten." She looked at me and held her hand out.

"I gotda see yo money first." I told her.

Mariah sat beside me, then reached into her purse and grabbed her wallet. After going through it, she pulled out ten singles and held them out to me.

We swopped and I gave BJ the money. "Here, hurry up and get your drink before yo momma come down." BJ took the money and ran across the room to the machine.

"He is so handsome. He looks just like you." Mariah smiled looking at BJ.

"Thanks." My boys were spitting images of myself whereas Brianna looked just like Peaches ass.

"I haven't seen you up here in a while. What you been up too?" She tried to make conversation.

"Did you see my wife up there before you came down?" I glanced at her just in time to see her eyes roll. "What the fuck you doing that for?"

"It's a habit when she's mentioned. I don't know why but she doesn't like me." Mariah laughed. Her head tilted to the side and she licked her lips while looking me over.

I pointed to her face. "That's why she don't like yo ass now, because of that sex look you be giving me." Looking away from her, I glanced over to BJ who was getting something else out the vending machine.

Mariah let out a laugh as she hit my arm. "Sex look? I don't have one of those." Her hand rubbed over my forearm.

I pulled my arm away from her. "Sweetheart, I'm a happily married man. It ain't shit you can offer me that my wife can't amazingly do already, and I mean marvelously." I smiled at her as I thought about the things Peaches could do.

"How would you know what I can do when you haven't tried me?" She got up as BJ ran back over with an arm full of junk. "I'll see you around, Blaze." She waved at BJ then walked off.

I paid what she said no mind. I wasn't stupid enough to fuck around on Peaches and risk losing her ass again, wasn't no bitch worth it. I damn sure wasn't crazy enough to fuck with somebody she worked with. I loved and respected her way too much to do some dirty shit like that. "Dude, yo ass said a drink. We about to go eat in a minute." BJ had four bags of chips, a Sprite, and a Snicker.

"I was hungry. Now you don't have to take me to the store." He sat down beside me and opened a bag of chips.

I shook my head at him. Knowing BJ, he was most definitely going to ask me to take him to the store later. I grabbed his pop. "Give me some of this."

"Let me give you a waterfall." He grabbed the pop back and twisted the top off of it. "Hold yo head back." He pushed at my chin.

I pushed his hand away from me. "Man, give me that damn pop." I looked at BJ and started laughing. My youngest was bad as hell and spoiled like a mothafucka. Hell, all my kids were, even so, I love the hell out of all of them. Never in my young life did I ever think I'll be a damn father let alone somebody's husband.

These past thirteen years with Peaches had definitely changed me for the better. I just couldn't picture what my life would have been like without her or my kids. Hell, I would've been dead no doubt and to think I almost fuck'd up everything I have now.

"There go momma." BJ got up and ran to Peaches.

"How come you're not in school?" She hugged him.

"I got suspended for fighting." BJ shrugged it off like it was cool.

Peaches eyes widened. "What?" She grabbed his face and started looking him over. "You got into a fight? With who?"

"Peaches, calm down." I leaned down and kissed her.

She kissed me back as her arm went around my waist. "Why didn't you call me? Why was he fighting?"

I looked down at her while putting my arm over her shoulder. "Because I took care of it." I pushed her chin up and kissed her again.

"You still should've called me." She mumbled against my lips.

Peaches couldn't help but be the worrying type. Had I called her ass she would've came home from work and made it bigger than it was. "I was gon' tell you when you got home." I opened the passenger side door for her.

Peaches got in and fell straight back. "Oop!" She squeaked out loudly, before sitting up right in the seat. "BJ, why would you leave this damn seat back like that? Don't sit yo black butt back in this front seat. I don't know why you have to adjust the dang on thing." She fussed at him as she fixed the seat.

"Sorry momma. I forgot." BJ told her before he started laughing.

Chuckling, I closed the door then made my way to the driver's side. On the side of my door was a hot pink post-it. *Try me*, it read with a phone number. I got in the truck and handed the paper to Peaches. I didn't want no bullshit. I knew sneaky bitches like Mariah and all they brought with them was drama.

"What's this?" She asked with a confused look.

"It was just on my door. Yo girl Mariah left that shit." I let the TV in the back down and started playing Transformers for BJ.

"You saw her?" She questioned.

I nodded before I started telling her the conversation that was had between us while driving to the restaurant.

"I told you that damn girl liked you. I can't wait until I run into her ass at work—"

My hand waved, cutting her off. "I don't know why because yo ass ain't gon' say shit to her." I knew Peaches ass was crazy and she would definitely beat the fuck out of Mariah with no hesitation, hell she been itching to tag that girl for damn near a year. Even though, her ass had grown up didn't mean her hood side had left. She was still quick to pop off when needed.

"Oh, yes the hell I am. She know you're married and knows who your wife is and still she's asking you to try her ass out? I'mma drag her ass all through those halls. Ugh, I hate females like her." Peaches fussed.

"Man, you heard what I said. Yo ass ain't gon' do shit to that damn girl. I could see if I was giving her the attention she wanted, then cool. But I ain't trippin' off that bitch, man. And if you ain't planning on quitting yo job then what's the point? Baby, you know where I'm at. Can't no bitch come between us. So, chill out." I turned off the car and looked at her.

"Yeah, I hear you, but that still don't change anything. I don't even understand why you would sit there and have a conversation with her." Peaches' lips pursed together, and her eyes rolled hard.

"Shut the fuck up with all that. If I ain't sitting here telling you—*I wanna take that hoe for a test drive*—yo ass shouldn't even be mad. Laugh that shit off because you know she can't get me. This yo shit remember." I grabbed her hand and ran it down my chest.

Peaches lips twisted before her eyes rolled once again. "You're so stupid." A laugh slipped through her lips. "Yeah it's all mine." She leaned over the seat and kissed me.

My tongue came out and slid into her mouth as I grasped the back of her neck.

"Y'all do know I'm still in here, right?" BJ hand pressed against my forehead and he pushed my face back. "Can we go eat now. Or y'all just wanna stay in here and kiss?" He asked sitting on the middle console and putting his arm on the both of our shoulders.

He was just sitting there chillin' like everything was good. "Sit yo ass back. Yo ass know better."

"You better say please first." BJ said before jumping back in his seat.

Peaches hand covered her mouth as she laughed. "Don't look at me that is all you baby."

"BJ, you gon' make me whoop yo ass. Peaches, shut up. Let's go." I got out the truck then walked around to Peaches' side and opened her door. "Bring yo short ass on."

She grabbed my hand and got out. "Why you pick Friday's?" She asked.

"That was yo son. He wanted to come here." I shrugged I didn't really care where we went. As long as they ate.

"BJ, come here." She waved him back. "What you want from here?" She asked him.

"Cheese sticks, a burger and a blue slushy. Blake always bring me and Bri here when he picks us up from school." BJ told her as we went inside.

Once at the table we ordered our drinks and food, already knowing what we wanted.

"Blaze Jr. tell me how the fight at school started." Peaches stared at him with a serious expression. "And don't lie either."

BJ, blew out a breath. "I'm not gon' lie. So, Mikel…" He jumped into the story of what happened at school.

***

"Peach, I'm not playing with you don't say shit to that damn girl. You hear me?" I grabbed her chin and tilted her head back, making her look at me. "I'm serious, Peaches."

She popped her lips. "Okay, Blaze, I'm not gon' say anything but if she looks at me wrong and say something first. I'mma go off and whoop her ass." She said with a promise.

"I'ight, just don't get yo ass arrested. My kids can't have a felon for a momma." I went to kiss her, but she jerked her head back.

"Nigga, you a gotdamn felon. What are you talking about?" She pushed me away from her as she broke out laughing.

"Oh, damn, fuck you Peaches." I laughed, pushing her back as she made a grab for me.

"Baby, stop, I'm playing. I promise I'm not going to touch her. Only because you told me not to." Peaches stood on her tiptoes and kissed me.

"I'ight. You gonna have to pick the kids up from my momma's crib. When I get off, I'm meeting the boys at the court." My arms wrapped around her waist and I picked her up.

"Okay, I'll get them." She kissed me again and I put her down. Peaches started to walk away.

"I love you, Peaches." I called out to her.

She looked back at me and started smiling hard. "I love you too. Bye, husband!" She waved once more then walked into the hospital.

I turned to go back to my truck only to see Mariah standing there with three other chicks, looking my way, and smiling.

"Hey, Blaze." She waved.

I paid her ass no mind as I hopped in my truck. "You coming to work with me or you wanna get dropped off at Nana's house?" I asked BJ.

"Can I go to Pop's gym?" BJ climbed into the front seat and put on his seatbelt.

"Why you don't wanna come to work with me?" I looked down at him as I pulled away from Peaches' job.

"Because you gonna make me stand outside and hold that sign again. It's too hot outside for that." His head shook before he reached over and pressed play on the TV screen.

BJ ass was something else. Little dude was too damn grown for his own self. "Yo ass ain't in trouble so you don't have to hold the sign today." Whenever he got in trouble at school I would either take him to the lot or my car garage and make him hold a big ass advertising sign.

"I still wanna go with Pops." He shrugged then turned up the TV as he got into Transformers.

I grabbed my phone and called Marcus to see if it was cool to bring BJ to the gym.

***

"Come on, Unc, yo ass cheating. You can't be holding onto me." Blake pushed King off of him.

"Man, shut yo crybaby ass up and ball." King tossed Blake the ball.

"I ain't crying. I'm saying if yo old ass can't keep up get off the damn court." Blake snapped at him.

We fell out laughing at the two of them. King and Blake stayed into it when we played ball.

"Would the both of y'all shut the fuck up and ball. King, yo ass is grabbing that man. Yo ass holding the hell out of his shirt." Mac laughed while pushing King back.

"Nigga, fuck you. I ain't holding his ass. I can't help it if that nigga can't shake me." King leaned down, putting his hands on his knees.

"I can't shake yo ass because you keep holding me. Nigga grabbing on me like he my girl or some shit. *Don't wanna get left behind ass*, nigga." Blake clowned as he bounced the ball. "You got yo breath back or you still need a minute?" He asked King, even though he was panting just as hard.

"Nigga, keep talking shit and I'mma show yo ass just how we can get down. Yo little ass ain't never too old to get fuck'd up."

"Now you tryna beat me up, Unc?" Blake picked at him. "Come on, baby, it's just a game. Come whoop my ass on this court and it's all love."

We had been out there for damn near an hour hooping. Blake, Mac, and I were on teams against Bell, King and Sam. I was tired as hell and those two mothafuckas wanted to argue every other minute.

"If y'all don't come the fuck on. Blake take the damn ball out." I grabbed the bottom of my beater and wiped my face.

Blake took the ball out then tossed it to Mac. Immediately Bell was on him. Mac shook him then tossed the ball back to Blake.

"Come on, Unc, there you go with that holding shit." Blake faked left then went right, he threw me the ball.

I pulled back, away from Sam, then shot.

"Sam, what the fuck is you doing?" Bellow snapped at him. "Nigga, get on his ass. Hold onto that mothafucka if you got to. You better do what King's ass doing."

"Nigga, fuck you. I was on his ass." Sam retorted.

I walked off the court. I wasn't about to stand there and listen to their ass argue. We been doing this same shit for years and not a damn thing had changed. We all still balled hard and fought just the same. The only thing that changed was the bet, instead of putting up $200 we did $600, and that only got them rowdier to play.

I grabbed a bottle of water out the cooler and poured a little over my head. It was hot as shit out there and a cold shower was definitely needed.

"B, toss me one." Mac jogged over to me. He caught the bottle of water I threw to him. "Them niggas a damn fool. I don't know why the fuck King ass keep wanting to stick Blake ass." Mac laughed as he drunk some of his water.

"That mothafucka think his ass still young. I keep telling him he can't keep up. My nigga getting to damn old." I tossed the bottle back.

"Y'all come on!" Blake yelled over to us.

I pulled off my beater and wiped my face with it then sat it on the cooler. Mac and I then jogged back to the court. King took the ball out and the game started again.

We played for another hour until we reached one hundred.

"That was a good game." Sam said, sitting in the middle of the court panting.

"Yeah, y'all niggas worked hard out there. Now pay up." I rubbed my fingers together for Sam to give me the money.

"I'll be right back." Blake said then ran off the court. My eyes followed him as he jogged over to the chick he brought to the house.

"Here…" Sam slapped the money in my hand. "Y'all mothafuckas was out here cheating. Mac fouled Bell ass so many gotdamn times—"

"And that nigga shot every time y'all asses called that shit. Get the fuck outda here with that bullshit. Now yo ass gon' blame us for him missing half of those fuckin' shots too, huh? Man, kill that fuckin' noise. You mothafuckas suck simple as that. Nigga, King ass rode Blake throughout the entire fuckin' game. Man, shut the fuck up with that cheating shit." I pushed Sam away from me as I laughed.

"I wasn't holding that nigga. His ass just losing his touch, and that's why." King pointed to Blake and his girl, laughing. "That nigga got his nose so far into pussy, he can't focus on the game."

"Yo ass ignorant. Lil B was walking yo ass all over this fuckin' court, so don't talk shit nigga. Yo ass was holding on him, clinging to that nigga like a bitch, talkin' 'bout, *don't let me go*." I joked while shooting the ball.

"Yo ass got jokes. Fuck you." King laughed, throwing me the ball.

I shot again then walked over to the cooler, grabbed my shirt, and wiped my sweaty face before getting another bottle of water.

"Hey, Mr. Carter." Blake's little friend spoke with a wave.

"What's up." I looked down as I felt the top of the cooler hit my leg. "Yo, this some stalker type shit right here."

"No, not really because I didn't follow you up here. My sister actually lives up the street. I just brought my nephew up here to play basketball." Mariah pointed to a little boy who was shooting on one of the side courts by himself. She then looked over at Blake's girl and spoke to her. "But it is nice to see you around here." She smiled then let her eyes roam over me. "You look hot, want some?" She twisted the top off the bottle of water and started drinking it.

I tilted the bottle further back as she drunk the water, causing it to spill up her nose. "Yeah, drink that whole mothafucka because yo ass thirsty as hell."

Mariah spit out the water as she started choking. "Blaze! Why would you do that?" She wiped her mouth and looked at me surprised. Mariah's expression quickly changed as she started to laugh. She grabbed my beater and started patting her chest down.

My hand rubbed over my head. "Look, don't talk to me, i'ight? We ain't friendly or none of that shit. I know what type of bitch you are, sweetheart and I ain't interested, period, man. I told you, I'm a happily married man and ain't no hoe gon' come between that. So gon' 'bout yo business."

Mariah's hand stopped moving and she stared at me, shocked. "Who the hell you calling a bitch? And you don't know shit about me—"

"I'm calling you a bitch, with yo disrespectful ass. I know you a hoe. That's all I need to know about yo ass." I snapped at her. "Standing yo ass right here tryna flirt and shit. Bitch, I told you I'm married. Now get the fuck on somewhere. Go babysit." I pointed to her nephew who was still playing by himself.

"You know what? Fuck you, Blaze—" She started to fuss.

I cut her off. "Nah, sweetheart that's why yo ass mad now because I won't give yo ass this dick." I smiled and winked at her.

"Fuck you." She pushed me away from her then stomped off, pissed.

Blake barked out a loud laugh as he made it over to me. "Dad, I think you hurt her feelings."

"Man, I don't give a fuck about her damn feelings. Hoes like her would fuck up a whole ass family. Plus, that bitch works with yo momma, fuck her. I don't know what the fuck is wrong with these young dumb ass chicks. Bitches will do anything to fuck up yo life and it ain't even worth it." I learned that shit a long time ago.

Females were fuckin' crazy. Sam's little sister, Tishana taught me that. Those mothafuckas was no different from a nigga when he was pissed, hurt, and set on revenge. I could never forget the shit that happened over seven years ago.

"I thought she looked familiar. That's where I saw her at before, the hospital." His head shook before he chuckled. "She must don't know momma crazy as hell." Blake grabbed his shirt off the floor and dusted it off.

"Hell, she must not know." My hand ran over my head. That chick was crazy. I didn't know what the hell Mariah ass was on or what the fuck she was thinking to even come over and start talking to me like we were cool. I didn't have time to be dealing with no crazy ass bitch.

"Dad, you good?" Blake snapped his fingers in my face.

He pulled me out of my thoughts. "Yeah. You out?" I pointed to his clothes that he held.

"Yeah, I'm about to drop her off at the crib." His arm went around ol' girl's shoulder. She looked at me then moved closer to Blake.

"Her ass just got dropped off up here. Why the fuck whoever brought her here ain't take her ass home?" I asked him, but then redirected my question to his friend. "Why the fuck you ain't get dropped off at the crib?"

Her mouth opened then closed before she looked over at Blake. "Um—"

"Dad, come on man, you trippin'. I told her to get dropped off up here." Blake laughed and his hand came out. "I'll see you at the house later."

We shook up and gave each other a one armed hug. "I'ight. Oh, and you know I'm fuckin' you up about that empty box of condoms." I whispered then pulled him further

90

down the courts so his friend wouldn't overhear us.

"Damn. Dad, I'm sorry about that. I put the wrong box in there. Ace had threw that empty box in the car. I was running late for practice when I dropped them off, so I didn't even notice. I still got the other box in my car." His hand ran down his face and he blew out a heavy breath. "Momma was real pissed, huh?" He asked and I nodded. "Damn, I'mma have to tell her."

My arms folded under my chest and I laughed. "Oh, she already knows. Nigga, yo momma is not fuckin' dumb… well not all the times, she ain't. She figured that shit out quick as hell, maybe five minutes after you left, she pieced that shit together." I let out a few chuckles before I got serious. "Lil B, don't go losing yo fuckin' focus over these little ass girls. They ass gon' always be here, yo gotdamn career ain't. Once you fuck up that opportunity yo ass can't get that shit back. I done told you that. You hear me?"

Blake nodded his head while his arms folded over his chest. "Yeah, I hear you. I remember the talk you gave me when I was eight." He laughed. "Dad, I'm focused. You don't have to worry about that."

I looked at his little friend. "Make sure she knows where yo focus is at. I'ight?"

"She knows where it's at." He reassured me.

I smiled at my son. Whenever I looked at Blake, I saw myself in him. I was happy but that shit also scared me because I didn't know just how much he was like me. "I'ight. Gon' take that girl home."

Blake started laughing. "Dude, her name is Janae." He reminded me while walking backwards toward her.

My brow raised. "I don't give a fuck what her name is. I'll call her ass, *That Girl* or *Ghetto Blanket Girl* if I feel like it. Fuck out of here with that shit."

"Oh, my God, please don't call me that." She whined while covering her face.

Me and Blake started laughing at her reaction. "I'll think about it." I turned away from them and jogged over to the court where my niggas were.

Mac hit my shoulder and nodded behind me. Mariah stood there looking at me. Once she noticed that I had glanced her way, she rolled her eyes into her head and then went back to playing with her nephew.

Shrugging, I chuckled then started shooting the ball around.

***

"Babe, have you talked to Joseph?" Peaches asked as she walked into the bathroom.

"No, but he been blowing my damn phone up. I'll call him tomorrow." My eyes were closed as I laid in the tub.

Peaches splashed me with water before her hand ran over my chest. "Please do, he's been calling me nonstop for the past few days. Whatever it is, he says it's important." She kissed me.

I peeked at her out of one eye. "He didn't say what was important?"

She grabbed my towel, getting it soapy. Peaches started to wash my chest down. "No, he didn't tell me." She mumbled, distractedly.

"What's wrong with you?" My fingers tugged at the ties of her purple robe.

"Nothing... I missed you is all." She looked away from my chest and her eyes met with mine. Peaches hand grabbed my dick and she started to stroke me.

I pulled her ties undone and smiled. "You gon' get in with me?" I sat up and pushed her robe down her shoulders. She pulled it off then got in the tub. Peaches straddled my hips then kissed me.

My tongue slid into her mouth while I palmed her ass. Peaches hand slid between our body's, she grabbed my dick and started stroking it once again.

"Momma!" Brianna pounded on our bedroom door.

A groan left my mouth and my head fell back on the tub.

"Daddy!" She yelled, now in our room. "Daddy, are you in the bathroom? Momma, where you at?"

"What up Bri-Bri?" I called out to her.

"Daddy," She started sniffling.

"What's wrong with you?" Once I asked that question, she broke out crying. My head shook and Peaches got out of the tub. I could tell from the look on her face she was irritated. I felt the same damn way. While the kids were home with us, wasn't shit happening. If I wasn't in the tub, my dick wasn't getting wet at all. That was the only downside to having kids, they were some gotdamn cock blockers. It was no sex going on in the house.

I let the water out and stood up. Peaches threw my dry towel in my face before she pulled on her robe and walked out the bathroom. Now I had to deal with her gotdamn attitude.

"What's wrong with you, Brianna?" Peaches asked her. Bri, didn't answer her just cried.

I dried myself off then pulled on my basketball shorts. Once I walked out the bathroom Brianna moved from Peaches and came to me. "What's wrong with you?"

"BJ broke my doll and threw it out his window. I don't like him." Her arms went around my neck and she laid her head on my shoulder. "Can I sleep in here tonight?"

I looked at Peaches and her head shook, *no*.

"How about I lay in your bed until you fall asleep? That sound cool?" I asked her.

"I wanna sleep in here, please?" Her bottom lip started to quiver, and she sniffled.

Peaches was going to kill me, but she was my baby girl and telling her no was hard as hell. "You can stay in here until you fall asleep. I'ight?"

"Okay, I love you, daddy."

"I love you too, Bria." She gave me a kiss, then got down. Brianna climbed in our bed, going to the middle and getting under the covers. "I'm about to go talk to BJ." I left out our room and went to BJ's. He sat at the foot of his bed playing the game. "BJ, why you break her doll?" Brianna was my baby girl, but her ass wasn't innocent. She was sneaky as hell and always messed with him. BJ was like me to a certain extent. We didn't mess with folks unless provoked.

"She threw it at me, and I didn't even break it for real. She such a crybaby." He paused his game and reached on the side of the bed. "Here." He tossed the doll to me.

The doll wasn't broken just like he said.

"You wanna play?" BJ asked, holding out his remote.

I toss Brianna's doll on his bed, then sat down. "Yeah, I'll play for a minute." I pushed him off the bed and onto the floor.

"Dad, come on, man." He laughed then grabbed the other controller. "You gotda watch my back. Don't let me get killed." He warned as he put Call Of Duty on two players and we started playing.

I could admit that, although Peaches and I weren't having sex as often as we once had, because of our kids. I loved my badass, cock blocking children. It wasn't a better feeling to me than being a father and having a relationship with all three of my shorties.

I loved being a family man.

Chapter 5

Blake

I walked into my moms' room and flopped down across her bed. My dad left to take the twins to school, so it was only the two of us there.

"What's up, Blake?" My mom went to her dresser and started combing her hair.

Sitting up on the bed, my hand rubbed the back of my head. "Ma, the condoms in Dad's office wasn't his. I put them in there." Even though, she already knew that I felt it was best I brought it up first. That way I could ease into the whole sex thing with her.

"Why would you put an empty box in there?" She sat her comb down and faced me.

"Ace was playing around and threw the empty box at me through my window. I went to drop Dad's condoms off before I went to practice and grabbed the wrong box. I was rushing." I explained to her.

My momma let out a loud sigh. "But why would you be bringing your Dad condoms?"

I felt the muscles in my face loosen as I stared at her. She knew exactly why. I guess I wasn't the only one playing the dumb role. "Because…" I let out a small laugh and looked away from her. I wasn't ready to have that damn talk with her. It was so easy to talk to my Dad about sex, my momma was a whole different story.

"Because you wanna start having sex?" She asked me.

My hand rubbed over my mouth. "Yeah, that's what it was."

"Blake, why do you wanna have sex? You're only sixteen. I thought you only wanted to play basketball and box?"

I shrugged. "Honestly, it was just something I wanted to do—"

"But why? Were the dudes at school messing with you because of it? Did some girl pressure you into wanting to have sex?" She questioned while walking closer to me.

Her last question had me wanting to laugh because she should've known couldn't nobody pressure me to do shit. Then again, I wasn't surprise that she would think something like that. Hell, my momma was emotional and dramatic as hell when it came to me.

"No, wasn't nobody clowning me, and no chick pressured me either. It was me, something I wanted to do." I explained.

"And your Dad buys you condoms?" She asked.

"No, he doesn't. I mean, yeah, when I first told him I wanted to have sex, he did. Plus, the Lot ain't that far from the school. So, it was easy to go to his office to get a condom then going to the store." I shrugged like it was nothing.

"Why wouldn't you want to talk to me about sex. You know I used to be a RN, right?" She questioned.

I broke out laughing. "That's exactly why I didn't come to you. Ma, you would've done a search of all type of STD's and probably would've printed out pictures, then showed them to me so I wouldn't have sex. And like I said, I wanted to do it. So, it was easier talking to pops than you." I told her honestly.

She let out a heavy sigh. "I guess it's time I start to realize you're not my baby anymore. You're growing up." Her eyes got glossy as they started to water.

That was another reason I didn't want to tell her. Hell, my momma just couldn't see me growing up at all. My arm went around her shoulder and I pulled her against my side. "Ma, I'mma always be yo baby, regardless of how old I get. But I'm not gon' stay that same little boy."

"I know you aren't. I just wasn't ready for it to happen this soon. I thought you would've been at least thirty before this conversation came up. But I understand." She stood up and wiped her eyes. "Rashad, just don't grow up to fast on me. Okay?" She wiped her eyes again.

"I won't. So, don't cry." One thing I hated was to see my momma cry. I didn't like that shit at all. "Ma, stop crying."

She waved me off. "I can cry for a minute. I have to accept that you're growing up, is all. So just let me cry." She sniffled then turned back to her mirror.

My text notifications went off and I pulled my phone out my pocket. The message was from Janae.

A Love Like Ours: *The Carter Family*

Janae: *Babe can you pick me up this morning? My car is still in the shop.*

Me: *Yeah. Janae be ready.*

Janae: *I am ready now.*

After reading her message, I put my phone in my pocket. "Ma, I gotda go. Janae need a ride to school. Her car is still in the shop."

My momma turned to face me with a thoughtful expression. "Blake, is Janae your girlfriend?"

I got off her bed and stretched. "Yeah when we're together she's my girl. But when I'm alone..." I stared at myself in the mirror. Biting into my bottom lip, I traced my beard. "I'm everybody's man."

She grabbed my dad's belt so damn fast and raised it, about to whack me. Laughing, I quickly grabbed the belt.

"I know yo ass better be playing, Rashad!" She snatched the belt out my hand and hit me.

I jumped back away from her. "I am. Dang. I'm only playing. Why you so serious though?"

My momma glared hard at me. "That's not funny nor cute. Be honest with me Blake. Is she your girlfriend?"

I let out a groan. "No, she ain't my girl. We just real cool." I shrugged as if it was nothing.

"Sooo... Have you and her—"

I already knew what her next question was going to be, and I wasn't about to answer it. Hell, I couldn't because I was going to lie, and she would call my bullshit instantly.

"Ma, I gotda go. I'mma be late for school. Love you." I kissed her forehead, then ran out her room. Hell, I ran my ass all the way to the front door and then out the house. I wasn't about to give her a chance to stop me.

I had just told her I was having sex. She wasn't about to start asking who I was fuckin'. *Hell no!* My momma would've probably started crying again.

I didn't wanna have to deal with that shit. It was too early in the morning.

***

I pulled in front of Janae's house and blew the horn twice. The front door opened, and Janae's momma walked out with three different bags in her hands, including a purse. She was having trouble closing the front door.

I hopped out my car and jogged up to her. "Do you need help with your bags?" I asked her politely.

She stopped fumbling with her bags and looked at me. Her eyes slanted slightly before she looked at my car. "You're the one out here blowing?"

I scratched the back of my head and let out a nervous laugh. "Yes, ma'am."

"And you're here for Janae?" She questioned.

"Yes, ma'am. She asked me to give her a ride to school." I had never met a chick's parent before. So, I was nervous as hell talking to her.

"Yeah, you can take my bags to the car. You can sit it on the front seat, thanks." She handed me her bags.

"No problem."

"I'll tell Janae you're here. What's your name?" She asked opening the door.

"I'm Blake." I held my hand out for her.

She looked at it then gave me a slight smile. Taking hold of my hand, she shook it. "I'm Tameka. You are so polite. Let me go get Janae." She turned and walked back into the house.

I took her bags to the car, putting them in the front like she asked. Once done, I went and leaned against my car, waiting for Janae to come out.

After a few seconds, Janae walked out the house with an attitude. She and her mom passed words for a second before she walked off. Janae came to the car and I opened her door.

"Thanks," she stood on her tippy toes and tried to kiss me.

I pulled away from her. "Man, yo momma standing right there looking dead at me. I am not about to kiss you. Get in the car." I said as I opened the door wider.

Janae started laughing. "You're so scary, Blake." She told me once I got in the car.

I shook my head at her. "No, I'm not scared of shit. It's a respect thing with me, something yo disrespectful ass don't know shit about. I ain't even been introduce to yo moms as yo dude, so what I look like kissing you in front of her?" When she didn't say anything, I laughed. "You might think I act like an ass but I'm very respectful when it comes to some adults." Hell, I didn't have a choice but to be.

My momma didn't play when it came to disrespecting adults. Plus, if shit ever got out of

104

hand with an adult, my momma would take care of it, with no problems.

Janae turned in her seat to stare at me as a questioningly look covered her face.

Mentally, I sighed, knowing I had opened a door for some shit without even realizing it. "What?" I asked her as I pulled away from her house.

"Would you want me to introduce you to my mom as my man?" She asked.

I shrugged. "Shid, that's up to you, for real. I mean, are you my girl?" I glanced over at her as I rubbed my mouth.

Janae lips popped and she rolled her eyes at me. "I'm being serious, Blake."

"I know you are. Now answer my question." I stopped at a red light and looked at her.

She rolled her eyes again, then smiled. "Yeah, I'm yo girl."

"Okay then, so if you wanna introduce me as yo dude or yo friend is all up to you." I shrugged as I started driving again.

Janae leaned over to me and kissed my cheek. She then grabbed my chin and turned my face towards hers, bringing our lips together. "I love you." She mumbled, kissing me once more before she sat back in her seat smiling.

I shook my head at her as I drove us to school.

***

I stood at my locker talking to my boy Patrick about the game we had later that night. "Yo ass just make sho' you don't trip over yo gotdamn feet. You clumsy sonofabitch." I clowned him as I closed my locker.

"Nigga, fuck you, I ain't clumsy that nigga tripped my ass." He pushed me, laughing.

"Yeah, i'ight, nigga. Don't let that shit happen again." I thought about the game we almost lost three days ago. We were three games into the season, and we've won all of them. I wasn't trying to lose over no fuck ups. Especially, not because a nigga gets clumsy when it's only a few minutes left on the clock.

"Yeah, yeah, yeah. I'll remember to elbow the nigga when I'm falling next time." He stated sarcastically.

That made me laugh and I shrugged. "If that'll help then do that shit."

"Fuck you, Blake." He chuckled, closing his locker. "There go yo girl." He pointed behind me. "Hey, Ashley." He spoke to her once she reached us.

"What's up, Patrick." Ashley waved to him before looking at me. "Hey, Blake." She spoke, smiling hard.

"What's up." I nodded towards her. Ashley was a chick I'd known since middle school. She had been flirting with me since we met, I just wasn't interested though. Shorty was to out there for me, I mean, she wasn't afraid to throw her pussy at no nigga. I wasn't the type to just jump into any chick willingly. If I was desperate then maybe I'll try to hit her, but I haven't gotten to that level yet.

"So, Blake, when you gon' ask me out. I'm getting tired of waiting." She stood in front of me with her arms folded.

My brows raised at her. "What make you think I'mma ask you out?" I was curious as hell to know how she figured I wanted too. Hell, I barely talked to that damn girl, so I know I've never gave her any impression that I was going to hook up with her.

She rolled her eyes and let out a breath. "Don't front Blake. I see how you be looking at me, and it's okay—"

I broke out laughing at her ass. "Yo, you bugging hard. I don't look at yo ass no type of way. I ain't gotda front about shit, if I like something, I go for it. I don't front sweetheart." I shrugged. Ashley was a cute brown skinned chick, but she just wasn't my type. "Patrick, I'll catch up with you later. I'm about to be late for my fourth hour." I shook up with him, then walked off.

"Blake!" Ashley called behind me.

I threw up two fingers and kept on going.

"Blake, really?" Ashley asked, catching up to me.

I looked down at her and laughed. "You ran after me, just to say, *really?*" I asked her.

Again, she rolled her eyes. "No, well yeah, and we have next hour together." She pointed out.

I hummed, then shrugged. I didn't know we had a class together. "Oh, okay."

She walked in front of me and pressed her hand to my chest. "Serious question, why don't you like me, Blake? What's your problem with me, huh?"

I moved around her. "I don't have a problem with you. I mean, you cool, I guess—"

"You know that's not what I mean. Why wouldn't you want to date me? What's wrong with me?" She questioned.

I looked her up and shrugged. "Shid, personally I don't know you. Even so, from what

I've heard about you it really don't make me wanna know yo ass either. I mean if you gon' throw yo pussy to any nigga that talk to you. What's the point in me trying when I know what I'mma get?" I explained to her straight up.

She glared at me hard. "I'm not a hoe—"

Laughing, I rubbed the back of my neck. "I didn't say that. You must think so though." I shrugged, then opened the classroom door for her. "We're late." I nodded for her to walk in first.

She bumped into me, walking in, then stomped to the back of the classroom. Laughing, I followed behind her and went to my seat in the front row.

***

"Hey, babe." Janae ran over to me and jumped on my back.

I looked over my shoulder at her. "What's up? What you so happy about?"

She kissed my cheek then got down. "Because I get to see you. I missed you all morning." She whined out. "It suck that we don't have any morning classes together." Janae stood in front of me, wrapping her arms around my waist.

"Nah, that's a good thing we don't. Shid, I'll be distracted all morning if we had classes together." I told her and she laughed at me.

"Yeah, you're about right. I know I would be." She kissed me again then licked my chin.

"Man, stop that shit, damn. Why the fuck you slobbing on me." I wiped my chin. Janae ass never been all over me like that. Especially not in the school hallways. I didn't know what the fuck was going on with her, but I wasn't with her ass licking all on me. That was the first time she's ever done that shit.

"Ugh, what's wrong with you?" Her face screwed up as she looked me over.

My head shook as I went to my locker. "It ain't shit."

Janae popped her lips and crossed her arms as she leaned against the locker next to mine. "It's something if you're snapping at me. Especially, when I haven't done anything to you." Her hand came to the back of my head and she rubbed it. "Blake, what's wrong?" She questioned.

"It ain't shit—"

"Hey Blake." Some chick spoke and waved at me.

"What's up." I nodded slightly at her and Janae smacked her lips. I shook my head at her attitude as I put my morning books in my locker.

"Good luck on your game tonight." The girl said.

"Thanks, sweetheart." I responded to her, then look down at Janae to see her eyes rolling at ol' girl. "Why the fuck you doing all that for?" I laughed at her.

"That bitch seen us talking and she just interrupted us, with her rude ass." Janae stated while mugging the chick hard as hell.

"No, I actually didn't see y'all talking and if y'all were he ain't seem to have a problem with answering back. So, bitch—"

"Man, get on with that bullshit." I told ol' girl. Janae didn't have to get mad, but shit, she was right though. "Ain't no point in you standing here arguing with her. Sweetheart, gon' about yours." I waved ol' girl off before I muffed Janae head to the side. "Stop staring at her. Why you doing that for? All she said was good luck." Laughing, my head shook. Janae ass could be jealous as hell at times.

"I don't care, Blake. We were talking and you should've ignored her ugly ass. She was flirting with you and yo ass ain't make it better by calling her sweetheart." Janae hands went to

111

my chest and she pushed me hard. She then turned to walk away.

Groaning, I closed my locker and leaned against it as I watched her walk off. "Janae!" I yelled after her. She ignored me and kept on walking. "Janae, man bring yo ass here." Her paced picked up as she continued going, without a second look back. "That fuckin' girl, man." My hand rubbed over my head and I watched her go around a corner.

"She wants you to go after her." I heard someone say from behind me.

"I know that." I turned around to see the same chick that was at the courts talking to my dad. "What the fuck you doing up here? I know yo ass too old for high school."

"I came to pick my cousin up for lunch. And I ain't that old. I just left high school, about, umm…" She hummed, her words trailing off. "Six years ago."

I shrugged. "Nah, that ain't to bad. Well you go have fun finding yo cousin through all of this." I pointed to all the people that now crowded the hallways.

She let out a groan. "That's why I told her ass to meet me outside, but no she insisted I came in." She pulled out her cellphone and started dialing on it.

I turned away from her and started walking off to find Janae dramatic ass.

"Aye!" She called out to me before grabbing my arm.

I looked down at her, then the hand on my arm. "What? Man, get yo fuckin' hands off me." I pulled my arm from her grip.

"There's no need to be rude." She glared at me, but the look quickly went away as another expression crossed her features. "You were just going to walk away and not offer to help me find her?" She asked with slanted eyes.

I shrugged again uncaringly. I didn't know what was up with chicks and they damn attitudes. "Shid, I ain't gotda offer shit. That ain't my place. Now I'll give you a suggestion. Go to the office and have them call her for you. Bet?" I pointed behind her. "Go down those stairs and the office is on the right."

"You're a rude ass little boy?" She snapped at me.

"You're an irritating ass bitch. Yo ass was just in my dad's face, now you in mine tryna make conversation. Sweetheart, I ain't got shit for yo ass. Now gon' find yo people." I walked away from her and made my way towards Janae's locker where I knew her stubborn ass was at. Once I rounded the corner, I saw Janae talking to her cousin, Shantell.

Shantell saw me first and pointed in my direction, causing Janae to look back. She rolled her eyes and started putting her stuff in her locker.

"Mariah!" Shantell suddenly yelled, waving in my direction.

I looked back to see ol' girl I had been talking to walking over towards her. She looked at me, then rolled her eyes. We reached them at the same time. I walked up behind Janae. "So, you ain't hear me calling you?"

"Nope." Janae pushed her books into her locker.

I could hear the attitude in her voice. "Why the fuck you lying? What the hell is yo damn problem now?"

She slammed the locker shut, then picked up her bag. Janae turned towards her cousin ignoring me completely. "Shantell, you ready—"

"Man, what the fuck is yo problem?" I turned her to face me.

"I don't have a problem. I said I didn't hear you." She stated, pulling away from me. "Now I was talking to Shantell before you rudely walked

114

up interrupting us." She exclaimed with a roll of her eyes. She looked over at Shantell as if dismissing me.

My brows raised and I looked at Shantell, then back to her. "I don't give a fuck who you were talking to, fuck her." I grabbed her chin and turned her face so that she was looking at me. "What the fuck is wrong with you?" Again, her eyes rolled, and I laughed. "Yo ass gonna act like this because some bitch told me good luck? Man, check that mothafuckin' attitude before I knock yo ass out."

"Hey, Blake." Some girl spoke as she walked pass us.

"What's up." I spoke, not bothering to look back to see who it was. Janae smacked her lips and pushed me away from her. I started laughing as she got mad. "What the fuck I just say about that attitude?"

"Yo ass laughing and that shit ain't even funny. You act like you don't know how to ignore these bitches. You get on my damn nerves." She fussed, pushing me once more but harder that time.

That pissed me off. I grabbed the front of her shirt and pushed her into the locker. "Don't push me no fuckin' more. I said lose that gotdamn attitude. Yo dumbass acting like I'm fuckin' these mothafuckas. Saying what's up ain't shit,

115

so shut the fuck up with that dumb ass shit man."
Her lips popped and she rolled her eyes. I
grabbed her jaw and brought my face closer to
hers. "What I just say?" My lips pressed into
hers and I felt them form into a slight pout.

"Let my face go." Her arms wrapped around
my waist and she pulled me into her.

"You gon' make me knock yo ass out about
that gotdamn attitude." I warned as my lips
pressed into hers again.

Janae, let out a sigh. "I'm sorry. They just be
so irritating." She groaned out, wrapping her
arms around my neck, and pressing her lips into
mine, kissing me.

I pulled my head backwards, away from her.
My arms went around her waist. "Yo ass irritate
me every gotdamn day but you don't hear me
bitchin' at you." My hands slid down to her ass
and I picked her up.

"Aah! Blake, put me down before you get us
in trouble." Janae laughed but didn't let me go.

My head went into the side of her neck and I
bit at the skin. "We ain't gon' get in trouble.
Ain't nobody even out here."

"Janae, are you coming with us?" Shantell
asked her.

Shantell talking brought my attention back to them. I looked over to her only to have my eyes lock with ol' girl Mariah's. She was staring at me hard as hell. I watched as her eyes roamed over me and my head shook at her. I put Janae down.

"Babe, you have to meet with the coach in the gym, right?" Janae asked and I nodded my head. "You know how long it's gonna be? If it's not too long I can wait for you." She offered.

"Nah, gon' head with her. Coach can talk his ass off, and we have a game tonight. He about to take up this whole damn hour." I told her as I reached into my pocket and grabbed my money. I pulled out a fifty and handed it to her.

"Thanks, babe, I'll bring you something back." She stood on her tiptoes and kissed my chin.

"I'ight, I gotda go. He about to chew my ass because I'm late. Tryna chase after yo stubborn, jealous ass." I laughed at her and she popped her lips.

"I don't care, they get on my nerves. They ass be doing that shit on purpose and you don't be helping it. You need to start ignoring them—"

"Janae!" Some dude called her name.

"Oh, hey Max. I almost forgot." She turned away from me and went back to her locker.

Shaking my head at her, I turned and walked away.

"Blake!" She called to me.

"I'll talk to you later. I'm already late." I took off running towards the gym. I already knew the coach was going to go off on my ass. Once I made it to the gym the team was already in there and sitting on the bleachers.

"Mr. Carter how nice is it for you to finally join us!" He yelled at me.

"Sorry, I'm late. It won't happen again." I assured him as I went and sat down.

***

"Pat! Stay on that dude. Just like he be on yo ass when you got the ball, stick him just like that." I told Patrick as we walked back on the court. The ref passed me the ball and I took it out. He then blew his whistle signaling that start of the third quarter.

I passed the ball to my teammate, Lee and he threw it back. I dribbled down the court while signaling for them to get in position so we could run the play. Cam, a player from the other team was guarding the hell out of me, riding my ass hard.

Bouncing the ball between my legs, I faked right then left before I went right. I saw the player on Nelly leave him and come towards me, leaving him opened. I tossed the ball to Nelly, he pulled back and shot, making an easy three.

I looked at Cam, who I had just shook and Johnny, laughing. "Good shot, baby." My shoulder bumped with Nelly's, who was grinning widely at the opposing team.

Cam took the ball out and I pointed to Patrick to stay on his man, Mitchell. Cam threw the ball and Patrick smacked it out of Mitchell's hand. He then tossed it to me. I played the ball down the court and once again, Cam was on me hard, trying to get the ball.

One thing I hated while balling was for a nigga to hold on to me, and Cam was holding the hell out of my gotdamn jersey. I went to shake him, but his grip didn't let up.

"Yo, let me the fuck go." I snapped, jerking away from him. Turning, I tossed the ball to Lee who came running in front of me. Once I gave him the ball I turned around to Cam, pushing him off me. "Stop fuckin' grabbing on me." I moved around him and got back into the game.

Lee threw me the ball back and I shot it…

***

We had ten seconds left in the game, my team had seventy points while the other had sixty-nine. The game was close as hell.

Johnny took the ball out and Patrick was on him. He tossed it out to Mitchell and Lee stole the ball. I pushed Cam off me, then ran around Johnny. Lee tossed me the ball and I threw it to Mike. He tossed the ball to Patrick who threw it back to me. I shook Cam, then shot the ball. It bounced on the rim, then dropped in just as the bell went off. The crowd went crazy. I could hear both the excited and angry folks yelling.

We ignored the pissed off team's crowd as we made our way towards the locker room. I was hot as hell and sweating bad, so I used the bottom of my jersey and wiped my face as I turned the corner.

"You weren't bad out there." Mariah said as she leaned against the locker room's door.

"I know that. Why you back here?" My brows furrowed at her in confusion. I didn't even know she came to the game.

"I came to congratulate you." She pushed off the wall and came closer to me. I couldn't front, Mariah was sexy as hell. She stood five foot five, pretty, smooth brown skin, nice wide hips and her titties were big. "Congrats on your win." Her arms went around my neck and she hugged me.

"Thanks, you can let me go now. I don't want my girl to walk back here and get the wrong idea." I grabbed her arms and pulled them away from me.

Mariah rolled her eyes. "Let me start off by saying this, I love Janae... but... why are you even with that little girl. You're too much for her. She don't know what to do with you." Her finger traced down my chest.

"Is that the same thing you told my dad about my momma?" I licked my lips as I raised a questioning brow at her.

That made her laugh. "No, I didn't. Your dad's sexy and all but I only mess with him to piss off your mom. I don't like that bitch—"

My hand went to her neck and I pushed her hard into the wall, squeezing tight. Immediately her eyes widened. "Watch your fuckin' mouth. Don't ever disrespect my momma. I'll snap yo gotdamn neck." My eyes slanted as I glared hard at Mariah.

One thing I didn't play about was my momma. I'll beat the hell out of anybody for talking about her. "If you're smart, you'll leave her and my dad alone. I see you lack a few brain cells so I'm warning yo ass now. Sweetheart be smart and leave them the fuck alone." I warned her. "You understand me?"

Mariah's nails clawed into my hand as her eyes watered. Even so, she managed to nod her head no less. I let her go and she started choking while rubbing her neck.

"Thanks for the congrats." I told her then walked off and went into the locker room with the team.

It was obvious Mariah wasn't working with a full deck of cards. If that babe thought, she could fuck with my momma by going through me. She had another thing coming.

Chapter 6

Blaze

"D amn, why is it so hard to get in touch with you?" Joseph chuckled as he pulled me into a one arm hug. "What's up, Blake?" He turned to Blake and gave him the same hug.

"Not too much of nothing." Blake told him as he sat down on his couch.

Joseph looked back to me and nodded his head. "What's been up with you, son?"

Since I let Joseph back into my life, well since I've acknowledged him as my father once again, we've been hitting it off decently. On top of that, my kids loved the nigga like crazy, and that made the relationship we had a bit stronger.

"Shit, working as usual, you know. Now what's this important thing you need to holla at me about?" I asked getting right to the point. I figured it had to be something serious given he was hitting my wife up hard trying to get with me and he didn't want to talk about it over the phone.

He looked at Blake and I waved him off. "Lil B good. Speak yo mind, Joseph."

He let out a heavy sigh and rubbed his head.

"Oh shit." Blake suddenly said as the both of us sat up straight on the couch.

I laughed at his words because I was just about to say that. Joseph's heavy sigh and the rub to his head told that it was some shit he was about to tell me. "Joseph, what's up?" My head shook as I got ready to hear the bullshit, he was about to tell me.

"A year after I got with your momma, I cheated. The female I messed around with ended up getting pregnant. I gave her money to get an abortion and that was it. I ain't never talked to her again." Joseph let out a little chuckle and rubbed the back of his neck.

He looked at me and shrugged. "She ain't get the abortion like I told her to. She had a son. I

124

didn't know about him until about two months ago. Of course, I denied he was mine. I didn't tell you at first because when he reached out to me, he was locked up. Anyways, when he was release about a month or so ago, we got a DNA test done. He's mine. He asked if he had any brothers or sisters, I told him about you and Brittany. He wanna meet y'all. That's why I been trying to get ahold of you these past few weeks. Britt will be cool with it if you are." Joseph looked stressed as hell.

"Man, you stretched the hell out that story." Blake laughed. "I'm thinking you about to tell him, you robbed a nigga or some shit." Blake's head shook as I glared at Joseph. I thought the same damn thing Blake had. "What's his name?" He asked him.

"Joshua McKnight. He's a real cool dude. Hell, he looks just like us to be honest, especially you Blaze. So, what you think about meeting him?" He asked me.

I shook my head. "No. I don't care to meet him. Shid, leave his ass were he's at." I told him and I could tell he wasn't expecting me to say that.

"Blaze, come on don't be like that. What could it hurt to meet with him? He's your brother." Joseph asked, seriously.

Blake let out a noise in the back of his throat. I looked at him and he shrugged.

"How you thought I was gonna be? Welcoming? I don't know that nigga and we really don't need to know him for real. Shid, that's yo son, Joseph, you gon' head and get to know that nigga. And if Brittany wanna meet him then cool, that's all up to her. That mothafucka grown as fuck. I ain't got no say in what she do." I told him straight up. I wasn't too fond of meeting new mothafuckas. Joseph's son was cool where the fuck he was at.

"You can meet him once, Blaze. I done told him all about you, and he really wanna meet you." He said as if that was going to change my mind.

I shrugged. "I don't know why you go telling that nigga shit about me. Especially when you ain't talked to me first. So now you gotda untell that mothafucka about me—"

Blake cut me off, laughing. "Pops, how he gon' untell that man some shit though?" He asked and again I shrugged.

"Shid, I don't know but I'm not meeting with him, period." I told him and I meant that shit. I didn't have the time to be meeting with him.

"Come on, one time ain't gon' hurt you. He's your brother and he wanna meet you." Joseph pushed.

I shook my head. "He's yo son. He need to get to know yo ass, not me. I'm done with this shit, ain't nothing else to say." I didn't know that man and wasn't trying to get to know him.

Joseph then turned his focus to Blake. "What you think about this? You think yo daddy should meet Joshua?" He asked.

Blake shrugged. "Shid, I don't know, Joseph. Why dude all of a sudden pop up though. I mean, ain't nan one of y'all hard to find. What took him so long to reach out? And being locked up ain't no excuse if the nigga got in touch with you while he was in jail." Blake pointed out to him and to be honest that was some smart ass thinking.

Hell, that ain't even cross my mind not once. "And that's exactly why I don't wanna meet him." I added because those were good reasons.

Blake looked at me and started laughing. "Yeah, that's what it is."

"Shut yo ass up! Man, let's go. Joseph, we out, we got some shit to do before Peaches and the twins get home." I nodded at Blake and he got up.

"I'ight, Blaze, Blake." He gave Blake a one-armed hug. "Blaze, think about it, for me at least." He said, giving me the same hug.

"I already told you where I was at with that. Leave it alone." I told him as we walked to the front door.

Once we got outside, I got in the passenger side of Blake's ride. He got in and started up the car. When Blake pulled away from the house, he glanced at me and started laughing. "You got a brother that was locked up. I bet his ass just like you. Then again, maybe not because his ass actually wanna meet you."

"That shit ain't funny. Shid, I don't even know why Joseph told that nigga shit about me. Hell, I ain't even wanna fuck with Joseph's ass but yo baldheaded ass momma practically forced me too."

"Yo, watch yoself, don't be talking about my damn momma, and I don't remember her forcing you to do shit." He pointed out.

Looking at him, I smiled. "Yo moms' persuasive as fuck, yo. And you ain't hear that convo because you don't share a room with us—"

"Dad, come on, damn, I don't wanna hear that shit. It's some shit you don't supposed to say in front of me and that's number one, for real." He shook his head.

Laughing, I hit him. "You told yo moms' you fuckin'?" I asked him and he broke out laughing.

"Hell yeah, man. And her ass started crying. Then she gon' turn around and ask if I was fuckin' Janae." He stopped at a red light, laughing.

"Oh, shit. Yo ass lied, didn't you?" I asked, chuckling.

He shook his head. "Hell no, I took off running on her ass. She would've known I lied."

I broke out laughing because I could picture him running away from Peaches crybaby ass. Hell, if he had of said yeah, she would've no doubt started crying again. My baby was dramatic at heart so she couldn't help that shit, for real.

"So, you like that dirty ass girl?" I asked him.

He shrugged. "I mean, she cool. Man, I think she trying to be on some forever type shit right now. And I ain't thinking about nothing like that, you know?" He explained and I nodded.

"Yeah, now yo dumb ass fuck'd up by bringing her to the house. If you ain't tryna date that babe don't bring her ass around yo family. Shid, her dirty ass was to comfortable when she came to the house—"

"Why you keep calling her dirty, though?" He asked, laughing. "Shid, she's clean as hell for real, though."

"When I met her, she was dirty. What the fuck you mean? That damn girl was in a blanket and house shoes…" My words trailed off when I noticed he got off the highway. "Hold up, where the fuck you taking me?" We went nowhere near Magic.

"Oh, I told you I had to pick up Ace." He lied.

"Yo lying ass ain't said shit about picking him up! I told yo ass I had shit to do!" I snapped at him. I had business to handle and his ass knew that shit.

"Man, its right around the block from Magic."

"Pull the fuck over. Nigga, Magic in Gary, yo ass got me in Schererville. Wait, that nigga don't even live out this way."

"Why you bugging? His girl lives out here. And why you want me to pull over? You gon' get out and walk to Magic?" He laughed while pulling in front of a red house.

"What I look like walking? I was gon' put yo ass out. Where the fuck his car at?" I asked, looking at the house. I saw Ace walk out with a dark skinned chick behind him.

"It's in the shop. Vicky caught him cheating and busted all his windows out." Blake explained, laughing.

I stared at ol' girl. "She fuck'd his shit up and he back over here? Hell no, I'm glad I ain't have no crazy ass chick like that."

"Hold up, didn't momma shoot out yo windows a couple of times, though?" He asked.

I shrugged. "That was different, it wasn't over me cheating though. I had just pissed her off." It wasn't until after that left my mouth, I realized how fuck'd up that sounded. "Yo damn momma was fuckin' crazy." I said, laughing. We both had done some fuck'd up shit back then.

"Yeah, y'all was doing too much. Just like this nigga. That's too much drama for me." He rolled the window down while blowing the horn. "Man, let's go!" Blake yelled at Ace.

The girl looked our way and started waving. "Hey, Blake." She spoke.

"What's up, Ashanti." He said then rolled up the window.

"I thought you said her name was Vicky?" I asked.

"Nah, Vicky was his main girl before she broke up with his ass. Ashanti's the chick he was messing with on the side. She's the reason his car got fuck'd up." He explained and I started laughing.

I didn't miss that bullshit at all. Once Ace got in the car, Blake pulled off.

"What's up, Blaze?" Ace spoke.

"Man, shit." I shrugged.

"Was Squeaky there?" Blake asked him, smiling.

"She just left before you got there with her worrisome ass. She still talking about why you ain't called her back. I told her ass you didn't want her for real, she was just a run through." Ace said and Blake broke out laughing.

"Hell no, why the fuck you tell her that? Squeaky cool, it wasn't even like that with her." Blake shook his head at Ace before he laughed.

"What the fuck is a run through?" I asked them. I didn't want to say what I thought it was and be wrong.

"Something he just wanted to run through, no attachments. He just wanted to hit her ass and be through." Ace explained what I thought.

132

"Hell fuckin' nah! Yo ass bet not be doing these little ass girls like that." I snapped at him. Blake ass got him some pussy and done lost his gotdamn mind.

"His ass lying, and I don't mess with little girls. Squeaky eighteen, she's grown." Blake corrected and I jumped at his ass, making him flinch. "Pop's, what the fuck? You see I'm driving. You gon' make me kill us."

"That shit ain't funny. Wait, nigga yo ass sixteen, you shouldn't be fuckin' with no eighteen-year-old."

"I don't look sixteen though. Plus, I'm about to be seventeen in a couple of months. Besides, I like older girls." Blake shrugged.

My head nodded at what he said. "Like them mothafuckas all you want. But you get one of these little bitches pregnant I'm fuckin' you up. Then I'mma go to her crib and beat her ass in front of her folks. Keep fuckin' around, Blake I'mma fuck yo ass up. I promise you that shit, my nigga." If Blake ass brought a girl to the crib talking about, she was pregnant I was going to dog the fuck out of his ass.

Firstly, his ass was too young to be having a baby, and secondly, I wasn't about to get into it with Peaches ass over some Blake shit. I knew for sure her black ass was going to blame me for him getting some girl pregnant.

"Dad, chill, damn. You always gotda go overboard with shit. I ain't gon' get nobody pregnant. I ain't stupid, damn." Looking at me, he shook his head.

"Yo ass bet not be stupid." I told his ass.

Blake smacked his lips in irritation. "Man, whatever." He mumbled, then turned the radio up.

***

"Blake, go grab a case of Heineken and Red Stripe from the back." I instructed as I restocked the shelves at Magic.

"I didn't come here to work. I just wanted to play pool." He complained while sitting the pool stick on the table.

Blake was a lazy ass little nigga. If it didn't have anything to do with basketball, his ass didn't want to do shit. Peaches had his ass spoiled as fuck. When I was his age all I thought about was money.

"You think it's a coincidence I made yo ass drive me today. Yo ass cost to live, so yo black ass is going to work." I told him before I started counting the bottles of alcohol I had on the shelves.

"Blaze." Mac called when he walked into the club.

"What's up?" I shook up with him once he reached me.

"I got this dude out front looking to get some shit from you." He handed me a piece of paper. My brow raised in confusion and he shrugged. "When I pulled up, he was standing out there. He gave me this saying give it to you. I asked what it was he said an order. That was it." Mac explained.

I opened the paper, and it was most definitely a fuckin' order.

"Dad, that's it?" Blake asked, sitting the cases of beers down.

"Yeah. That's good." I balled the paper up. Once Blake walked off to the pool table with Ace. I grabbed my gun from the back of my jeans. Taking it off safety, I cocked it, then slid it at my side. Seeing me, Mac did the same.

"You don't know who the fuck would be bringing you an order?" He asked.

"Nigga, no! How the hell would I know some shit like that? But I got my son up here and some random mothafucka pop up, dropping off a mothafuckin' order." I was pissed off, the shit the person wanted I didn't even sell anymore. I came from behind the bar and headed for the front door. When we stepped outside wasn't nobody out there.

"That nigga was standing right by the door. I'm telling you." Mac pointed to the right of the door before he jogged on the side of the building. I did the same going on the opposite side and meeting him in the back. "Yo, I'm telling you that mothafucka was just out here." Mac glanced around the area.

"Well that mothafucka ain't here now. What did he look like?" I asked as we walked back around the front.

"Um, shid, about my height, six, one…um… Damn, B, I ain't get a good look at his face. He had on a hoodie and like I said, he just told me to give that to you. When I asked what it was, shid I was walking in here when he told me. That mothafucka couldn't have gotten far, I mean, it wasn't no other cars out here. That mothafucka had to take off on foot. I'll go hit a few blocks—"

I stopped him before he could go to his truck. "Nah, don't worry about it. My son here and whoever it was will show up again sooner or later. I'm about to go look at these tapes though."

"What was the order?" He asked and I handed him the paper as we walked back inside the club. "Damn." He whistled out.

"That's why I went out there. On top of that, the nigga asked for some cherries and it's not too many mothafuckas that know I sell those. But for that mothafucka to come here, is what's fuckin' with me. I ain't sold shit out this bitch since we moved back here and that was what? Eight years ago? So why come here now?" I voiced more to myself than to Mac because I knew he didn't know.

"Dad, you still gon' let me have my party here?" Blake came over to the bar, sitting on a barstool and getting my attention.

His question had me confused as hell because I didn't remember him asking me that. "When did you ask if you can have a party here?"

"Now." He said.

"Man, get yo ass out my damn face. Go stack them shelves. Everything gotda be ready before the club open. Mac, come on." I nodded towards my office so that we could watch the video. "Aye, don't open that door for nobody. Ace, get yo ass over there and help him stock them shelves. Make sho' y'all wipe the bar down, clean the pool tables and vacuum the floors." I instructed before walking to the back.

Mac laughed behind me. "You know they in there talking shit, right?"

I shrugged. "I don't give a fuck. Blake ass always in my damn pockets wanting some shit and Ace ol' hungry ass always at the crib eating. They just working that shit off." I told him as I pulled up the cameras.

***

We stood in front of the monitors watching the video for over thirty minutes and beside us, nobody else showed up on the video. Whoever it was knew to steer clear of the cameras around the club because we didn't get a glimpse of anybody.

"That mothafucka a ghost, yo, Boss. His ass was standing right by the door. Dude had to have walked by either the front or side camera to get to that bitch…" His words trailed off and his confusion covered his face. "He couldn't have dodged those mothafuckas." Mac rewind the tape again.

"You see just like me that nigga ain't there." I told him as I turned the video off.

Mac turned to face me. "What the fuck you done got yoself in?"

My brow raised at that. "What make you think I'm into some shit?" I was kind of offended at his assumption.

138

"A ghost shows up on yo damn doorstep, put in an order and then vanishes. I mean, this nigga came to a place you ain't sold no work out of in years. That ain't coincidental, B. Now, either yo hands ain't as clean as you making it seem. Or… shid I don't know what his intentions could be for coming at you with this." He pointed out and I shrugged.

"With all the shit I done did, my hands ain't never gon' be clean. But I ain't sold no damn work out this bitch in a minute and besides my cherry's I don't be selling shit really—"

"Yo boy's storage spot that y'all used to keep all yo shit in, is it empty?" He asked.

When he asked that question, I grabbed my phone and called Sam to see if anyone had popped up on him or stopped by the storage unit. With the way dude approached, it wasn't normal, especially if he didn't know us.

After everything happened so many years back, I slow down with a lot the shit I was doing. Which consisted of dropping old clients. Yeah, occasionally, some old, dumb ass customer would check to see if I gotten back in the business. Even then, none of them has ever came to me directly or popped up at any of my businesses. They would always hit Sam up first, knowing I would snap the fuck off.

After the third ring, Sam answered. "What's up, B?"

"Aye, everything over at Roxy's good? Ain't nobody been around there fuckin' with her, have they?" I asked him about the storage unit. I didn't trust phonelines rather it was a landline or cellphone. It was too much high-tech shit around nowadays and anybody could be listening.

"No, she's good and haven't nobody been around that I know of… let me double check right fast." Sam had a security system at the place, and he could access the cameras from anywhere. "Why you didn't call and ask her?" He replied.

I let out a laugh. "I didn't feel like talking to her, plus, I know how close you two are that's why I called you to check on her. I might stop through there later though."

"You should do that. We still balling later?" He asked.

I looked at the time to see that it had just turned four-thirty. "Shit, we might have to cancel. Damn, I gotda hit you back, I was supposed to meet Peaches at four."

"She gon' kill yo ass." He laughed into the line. "I'll get up with you later."

"I'ight," I ended the call, then dialed Peaches number. "Mac, go make sho' those two ain't fuckin' up my club."

"I'ight." He walked out my office, closing the door behind him.

"Where you at?"

The little high-pitched, demanding voice that answered the call surprised me, so much so, I pulled the phone from my ear and looked at it. "Little girl, where yo momma at. I ain't call for you." I laughed at Brianna's little grown ass.

"She in the living room talking to Nana and Auntie Britt. Daddy, where you at? Can you come get me? I'm so bored over here." She complained with a whine.

"I can't come get you, I'm working right now. If you bored go play with BJ or ride yo bike." I told her and she groaned.

"BJ don't wanna do nothing but play that stupid game. I wish I could just go over De'Asia's house, which is right across the street, but momma said no when she knows that's my best friend." Brianna let out a heavy breath.

I didn't say shit, hell, I couldn't say shit because I knew my ass was going to laugh. I simply held the phone to my ear as I tried not to chuckle.

"Hello? Daddy?"

"Yeah, Bria."

"So, you not gonna say something?" Her tone was serious as she asked that.

"Brianna, what you want me to say, sweetheart?' I chuckled into the line.

"Tell momma I can go over De'Asia's house for a little while—"

"Hell no, Brianna. If yo momma said you can't go, then that's it. I done told yo ass about doing that shit. I'm not about to go against yo momma. I ain't there so what yo momma say goes." I fussed at her.

Brianna's little ass had that shit bad trying to play me against Peaches. On some shit, I do give Brianna what she wanted, which always cause me and Peaches to get into it behind that shit.

"Hhuh," she let out a heavy breath. "Okay, hold on." There was ruffling in the background before I heard Brianna stomping down the stairs.

I started laughing because I knew she was pissed. "Bri-Bri, you mad?" I asked but didn't get a reply.

"Momma, here, daddy on the phone." I heard her say.

"Ugh, what's wrong with you?" Peaches asked Bria.

"Nothing." The attitude in her voice could be heard.

"Hey, babe. What did you say to Brianna?" She asked me.

"I didn't do shit. That's all on you, sweetheart. So, what's up? Why you still at my momma's house? We were supposed to meet a half hour ago?" I played it cool like I hadn't forgot.

"Oh, my God, babe! I completely forgot, damn. Sitting over talking to yo momma and Britt's ass. I forgot, I'm so sorry." She apologized sincerely.

I knew the moment Brianna said they was over there, that Peaches forgot about meeting me at the mall so that we could get the kids clothes and shoes.

"Don't worry about it. How long you gon' be over there?" I asked as I locked up my office.

"I'm about to get out of here now. Otherwise I'mma hurt yo damn daughter. She's mad because I won't let her go to her friend's house." Peaches told me.

I walked into the club area to see Mac, Blake, and Ace by the pool table. Snapping my fingers at them, they looked at me and I pointed to the door. The pair nodded, seeming relieved that they didn't have to work no more.

"I'mma get up with you later." I shook up with Mac, leaving him there since he was now managing Magic. He tossed up two fingers my way, then closed and locked the door behind me.

"Where you at?" Peaches asked, sounding like Brianna's ass.

"Not meeting you at the mall apparently." I laughed. "But why you ain't let her go over that girl house?"

Peaches smacked her lips. "Because De'Asia's daddy was there and like I told her, I don't know that man so she couldn't go. Her momma wasn't even there, so I'm not thinking about Brianna's ass."

"Oh, shid, i'ight." I shrugged. That was a good ass reason to me.

"Blaze, did you talk to Joseph? You said you was going to." She questioned.

"I did talk to him this morning, why?" I asked.

"Then why is he calling me? Let me see what he wants, I'll see you at home. BJ, Bria, let's go!" She yelled before the line went quiet.

"Peaches—" She had hung up on my ass. I tried to call her back but didn't get an answer.

I already knew Joseph was on some bullshit which was why he had called Peaches. I didn't give a fuck what he said to her ass, I wasn't meeting with his fuckin' son.

Chapter 7

Peaches

"No, Joseph. Don't bring me into y'all stuff. That's between you and Blaze." My eyes rolled hard as I thought about hanging up on him. I was not their damn mediator.

"Peaches, please? Just talk to him about meeting with Joshua. If anybody could get through to Blaze, it's you. So just ask him to meet with us. Or you can meet Joshua first—"

That man had lost his damn mind. Blaze would kill my ass if I went behind his back and talked to someone he had already said no to meeting.

146

"I'm not going to meet him first. I am not about to get into it with Blaze for going behind his back. Sorry, Joseph but I won't do that." I didn't know why Blaze didn't want to meet with that Joshua character, but it had to be a good reason behind it.

"You right, I shouldn't have asked that of you, but, Peaches, Joshua don't have anybody. Before you and Blaze came into my life, I was where he's at now. When I told him that he had a brother and sister, he was excited to meet them, and I thought they would at least meet him once. Blaze shut it down and Brittany isn't going to do it unless he agrees to meet him. I can't go back to Joshua and tell him they don't want to meet him. He has no other family now that his mom died, Peaches." Joseph stressed, pleading with me.

I heavy sigh left my mouth before I groaned. "Okay, I'll talk to Blaze, but I'm not going to push him into doing it. I'll just talk to him and if he say no, then that's it." I told him truthfully.

"Thank you, Peaches, that's all I'm asking. Maybe we could all go out to dinner this weekend." Joseph suggested. His ass was really trying hard.

"Let me talk to Blaze first and we'll see, okay?" I told him.

"Ma! Can I get in the pool!" Brianna yelled from her room.

"Hold on." I responded to her before returning to my call. "Joseph, I'll talk to him when he gets here, and don't go making plans until you've talked to me." I told him as I walked into my room.

"Okay, thanks again, Peaches. I hear that little girl in the background. Gon' head and attend to them. Tell the kids I said hey and I love them." I could hear the smile in his voice. Joseph loved the hell out of his grandkids.

"Okay, I will. Bye." We ended the call. I sat on my bed and let out a heavy sigh. Joseph having a son he didn't know about was crazy. It did leave me to wonder what he was like and if he was anything like Blaze.

Then again, he probably wasn't because he actually wanted to meet Blaze and Brittany. Hell, Blaze ass didn't care to meet new people, family or not.

"Ma, can I get in the pool?" Brianna walked into my room with her swimming suit on. She came and sat on the bed beside me. "What's the matter with you? You look sad."

"I'm not sad, I was just thinking about something. Where BJ at?"

"He outside playing basketball."

I got up and Brianna stood on my bed. "Girl, if you don't get down—" My words were cut off when she pulled me to her. Brianna then proceeded to wrap her arms and legs around my neck and waist. I glared at her and she smiled before kissing my cheek.

"I love you, mommy." She kissed my cheek again then laid her head on my shoulder.

My head shook at her. "I love you too, Bria. But you ain't slick, little girl, I am not yo daddy. You're not going to have me carrying you around the house." I told her as I held her securely.

Once we made it in the backyard, Brianna got down then ran and jumped in the pool. Rolling my eyes at her, I went over to BJ, where he stood shooting the ball into the net.

Getting the ball, I shot it. "You wanna play me?" I asked, getting the ball once again.

BJ stared at me with a raised brow, looking just like Blaze ass. "No, I don't wanna beat you too bad, but you can shoot around with me." He played me.

"Really? That's how you gon' do me, BJ?" I asked, laughing at my son.

He shrugged nonchalantly. "What? I'm just saying, I don't want to beat you."

My eyes rolled at him as I dribbled the ball. He wanted to be so much like Blake by playing basketball. I thought it was cute how dedicated he was about playing the sport like both his daddy and brother. "Let's make a bet. If I win, you have to wash my car every weekend for two months. If you do, then, I'll clean your room for a week." I offered a bet.

BJ broke out laughing. "You already clean my room so I'm not getting nothing out of it." He pointed out and I glared at him. "What? I'm saying, that's not a good bet. How about… if I win you get me that mini motorcycle like dad got."

I looked at him like he was crazy. "I'll get you a video game."

"Two games and we got a deal."

I started laughing at him. "Deal. I got the ball first." I took the ball out.

***

"Bria, let me go. Ma, y'all cheating!" BJ yelled as Bria held him back so that I could shoot.

"How you gon' hold him though, Brianna?" Blake laughed as him, Blaze and Ace walked into the backyard.

150

"Shut up, Blake. He was beating momma, so I had to help her." Brianna laughed, pushing BJ, then Blake before she ran to Blaze.

"He was not beating me. I was taking it easy on him." I lied.

"Like you used to take it easy on me?" Blake claimed, laughing. "BJ, what I tell you about playing her? She's a cheater. You can't play fair with momma. You gotda keep your distance and shoot far out." Blake said and I hit him.

"I was doing that. Then she started holding me, slamming me down and stuff." BJ told on me.

The boys broke out laughing.

"That's not funny and BJ shut up. His ass was doing too much damn running around for me, so I had to play streetball." I wasn't as young as I once was. I may could run around for a while, but I didn't have the energy of a seven-year-old kid, shit. He had my ass tired.

"You mean cheat ball. That wasn't streetball." BJ clowned me.

"Forget you, punk." I rolled my eyes at him, then laughed. Blaze walked over to me, wrapping his arm around my waist.

"Why yo ass out here cheating?" He asked as he leaned down and kissed me.

"Maybe you should teach your son to let girls win." I said looking at BJ who shook his head at me.

"Why I'mma teach him that for? Yo ass wanted to play so it's only right that he played fair and hard, with yo cheating ass." He laughed while smiling down at me.

Turning towards him, I wrapped my arms around his waist. I stood on my tiptoes and bit at his bottom lip. "So… you wouldn't let me beat you." The tip of my tongue licked at the corner of his mouth before I kissed the spot.

Blaze bit into his bottom lip then looked behind me. When he did, I sucked on his neck.

"Ma, come on, you're cheating now." BJ yelled.

My lips pressed into Blaze neck as I started laughing.

"On everything her ass cheating like a mothafucka." Blaze agreed. "But she won that one." He laughed, looking down at me. "You dirty as hell for that."

"I love you though." I kissed his chin, then pulled away from him. "Bria, don't be in that pool to long." I told her as I walked to the back door. "Ace, are you staying for dinner.

"Yup, you already know I am." He responded.

When I got in the house, I went to the freezer and took out the ground beef, deciding to make tacos for dinner. I had just taken the pot out when arms wrapped around my waist. A smile came to my lips as Blaze kissed my neck.

"Yo ass was wrong for that shit. I don't know why you wanna play with me like that?" His hand slid into the front of my shorts, into my panties.

"Blaze—"

He pushed my legs apart and pressed two fingers through my slit, parting my lips. "Don't, Blaze. Shit." His fingers pushed inside of my pussy, making me moan.

"Blaze, stop, the kids could walk in—"

"I locked the door and Blake out there. He'll keep them occupied for a minute." He whispered into my ear as his fingers continued to move inside of me.

Blaze removed his hands from my shorts and turned me around. My arms wrapped around his neck and I pulled his head down, bringing his lips to mine. My tongue slid into his mouth as he grabbed a handful of my ass and picked me up. He took us to our bedroom, once inside, he pressed me against the door, locking it.

I unwrapped myself from him and he place me back on my feet. I tugged his shirt off, then undid his jeans. My lips pressed against the center of his chest and I kissed my way down to his pelvis.

Pushing his jeans and boxers down his hips, I took hold of his dick, and my mouth wrapped around his tip, sucking as I stroked up and down his shaft. Pulling back, I spat on his thick, lengthy soldier as my hand began to stroke him once more as I sucked his balls into my mouth, moaning.

"Gotdamn, Peaches, fuck!" Blaze pulled my hair tie out and grabbed a fistful of my hair. "Hold up." He pulled me away from his dick. Blaze made quick work to undressed me. He then laid on the bed, stroking his dick. "Come here," he beckoned me to him as he licked his lips.

Immediately my knees buckled at the sight of him. He was just so gotdamn sexy. Just looking at my baby naked, watching him jerk his dick had my body weak and caused my pussy to throb hungrily for him.

"You gon' let me taste her while you suck my dick." He licked his lips again. "Come here and let me tongue kiss yo pussy, Peaches."

My inner walls pulsed fast with anticipation as I got on the bed. I stood over him, then lowered myself down to him.

Blaze grabbed hold of my thighs and brought me to him. His tongue ran through my fold, toying with my clit. His hand then came down hard on my ass as he sucked the swollen pearl into his mouth.

"Oh, my God!" I moaned as my forehead fell against his pelvis. My hips rolled as I started to grind against his mouth. "Oh, shit, baby, mmm, yes, papa bear, suck my pussy." I moaned as my teeth bit at his pelvis. Blaze slapped my ass again as his tongue thrust inside my love box.

Taking hold of his dick, my tongue swirled around the tip before I took him deep into my throat. My head bobbed on his man as I massaged his sack.

Blaze suddenly thrust two fingers into my pussy.

I moaned around his dick, then pulled back. "Ooh, God!" I cried out pleasurably as my forehead pressed against his pelvis. "Blaze, ooh, I'm about to cum! Ooh, shit!" My hips gyrated against his mouth as his fingers continued to fuck me while his mouth sucked on my clit.

Blaze's hand hit hard on my ass. "Sit up." He slapped my ass again, and I rolled off him. He went to sit up, but I pushed him back down. Turning around, I straddled his hips. Blaze bit into his bottom lip as he stared at me sexily.

Taking hold of his dick, I brought it to my throbbing tunnel. Slowly, I slid down on him until he filled me completely. My eyes closed as I panted. "Ooh, shit." He felt so gotdamn good.

"Damn! You sexy as fuck." He complimented as his eyes roamed over me. Blaze took hold of my breast, squeezing them. Sitting up, he pulled my right nipple into his mouth, sucking on it.

My hand held the back of his neck as I grind my hips into him. Pushing him down on the bed, my nails dug into his chest and I started to bounce on his dick faster, feeling my orgasm reaching its peak.

Blaze turned us over, then flipped me on my stomach. Raising my ass up, he thrust inside of my soaking tunnel and began to pound into me.

"Oh, my fuckin', ooh!" I cried out as I came hard. My body shook and I collapsed on the bed.

"Nuh uh, I'm not done yet, toot that ass back up here, Peaches." Blaze demanded.

Panting, I pushed my ass back up on my shaking legs. The moment he started to thrust inside me, my shake shook from him hitting my sweet spot repeatedly.

"Blaze, ooh, fuck, papa bear. I can't! Oh, my God!" My hand went to his stomach and I tried to push him back. Blaze grabbed my wrist and pinned it to my back. "Aah, shit! Baby, ooh…" My face pressed into the mattress trying to quiet myself down.

Blaze let my arm go and grabbed my hair, pulling my head back as his hand slapped down on my ass hard. "Don't get quiet on me, Peaches. Let me hear you, baby." His hand came down on my ass once again. My pussy contracted around him as I moaned out. "Come on, Peach. Fuck this dick, mama. Make that pussy suck this dick." His pelvis pushed into my ass and he grind his hips against me.

Blaze was so gotdamn sexy when he talked like that. On top of that, it turned me on terribly. My inner walls squeezed around him as I slowly moved my ass along his thick, long dick. I simply loved the feel of him.

"Damn, Peach, you feel good as fuck!" He grunted as his movement became frantic. Holding onto my waist, his hips jerked, pushing into me as he released his nut. "Aah, shit!" He groaned, collapsing on the side of me. Blaze kissed my shoulder, then wrapped his arm around my waist and pulled me into him.

I rolled over so that I was facing him. "You can't keep doing me like that. I'm not young no more." Laughing, I stretched my neck up and kissed him.

Blaze laughed as his hand slid down to my ass. "You most definitely ain't young no more and you still fuck me up. Shit!" He grunted out. "You're better than you were when yo ass was younger." Blaze complimented.

A smile came to my face and I kissed him again. "I love you."

He rolled over on his back, then pulled me on top of him. "Love you too, Peaches." His hand squeezed my ass before his teeth grabbed my bottom lip.

My head tilted to the side and my lips parted, allowing Blaze's tongue to slide into my mouth. A moan slipped from my throat as I started to lose myself into his kiss.

I was so in love with Blaze it didn't make any sense at all. "Eep!" I squeaked out loudly as he suddenly rolled us over. He pulled back from the kiss and moved down to my right breast. Blaze sucked on my nipple before his tongue started to play with the little nub.

My hand caressed the back of his neck as a light sigh left my mouth. "You wanna take a bath with me?"

Blaze let out a groan and laid his head on my chest. "I can't. I need to get back to work. I came home to get my truck."

"I thought you was just checking the books at the club?" I asked, trying to look down at him.

He blew out a breath, then rolled off me. He sat on the edge of the bed, rubbing his head. Sitting up, I got behind him, wrapping my arms around his neck. I kissed the side of his head, then behind his ear.

"I was but something came up while we were at the club. So, I had Blake bring us here, I told Mac I'll be back within an hour." He informed me. "I can run you a bath though." Blaze head turned in my direction.

Leaning forward, I kissed his lips. "No, don't worry about it. I'll do it. You go shower and I'll get you some fresh clothes out." I let him go then got off the bed, however, before I could walk away completely, Blaze pulled me back to him. I fell into his lap and he wrapped his arms around me. "You better stop or I'mma make you stay here." My hand reached down, and I grabbed his soft dick. "You know I can always get him up again." I pushed his soft tip through my slit.

Blaze grunted and I laughed. "I'ight, damn, I quit." He let me go.

"That's what I thought." I stood, then pulled him up. "I'm not mad. I know shit comes up on your end, so I can't be mad about that. Now go handle your business. Just be careful." I was far from an idiot when it came to Blaze. I knew that man probably more than he knew himself.

I knew something serious happened at work and when he was ready to tell me about it, he would.

"I wasn't even gon' ask if you were mad." He lied. I glanced at him over my shoulder and he laughed. "Shut the hell up." Light chuckles left his mouth. "You really not mad though?" He asked more serious now.

After I grabbed his black jeans and seafoam green polo shirt out the closet, I went and laid it on the bed. "No, I'm not mad, B, it's just a bath. Which you can always make up for. Now go shower." I picked his shirt up off the floor and slipped it on.

"I'ight, I don't wanna hear no dumb shit later, Peaches. I'm not bullshittin' either." He exclaimed, making me laugh.

"I swear I'm not gonna start anything later. Especially not after the sex you just gave me. I have no reason to bitch at you. Not until tomorrow."

160

Looking at me, again he laughed. "Yo ass crazy man."

"I'm being so serious, B. Shid, papa bear, you put it down—"

Blaze broke out laughing again. "Peaches, shut yo stupid ass up man."

I hit him. "Don't tell me to shut up. Hell, I'm being serious." I laughed while following him into the bathroom. "Hey, babe, have you talked to Joseph?" I asked the dumb question, remembering to late that he had been by Joseph's place earlier that day.

Blaze stopped at the shower and looked at me. "You already know I talked to him, that's why yo ass asked that shit." He snapped at me.

My eyes rolled at him. "Don't talk to me like that. I forgot you already told me that you had. Babe, I think that maybe—" The glare he shot my way had me shutting up.

"Peaches, stay out of it." He warned.

My lips popped as I went to the tub and ran my water. When I didn't say anything else, Blaze got into the shower. I wasn't about to argue with him behind Joseph's ass. Regardless of that, if Blaze had a brother, I did kind of feel like he should at least meet the dude.

I knew that was wishful thinking though. My husband was just so gotdamn untrusting and antisocial he simply didn't care about meeting anybody, family or otherwise, there was no limitation, hell.

Once the tub was full, I took off Blaze's shirt and got in. I sunk into the warm water and sighed as I pushed Joseph's issue to the back of my mind.

My eyes closed as I made myself comfortable. It wasn't long after I heard the shower turn off.

"Peach, stop talking to Joseph." Blaze said. Licking my lips, I laughed lightly but didn't say anything. "Peaches, I'm serious. I done already told his ass what's up. I'mma cuss his ass out for calling you about the bullshit. That's his gotdamn son, if he wanna make that nigga his family, cool. But leave me and mine out of it." Blaze stated, sounding pissed off.

"Babe, calm down. If you don't want to meet him, fine. I won't say nothing else about it." I could feel Blaze still standing over me. I peeked at him out of my right eye. "I'mma stay out of it. If I don't then you have my permission to spank me."

His head shook and he chuckled. "I'll call you when I'm on my way back." He leaned down and kissed me.

"Okay, love you."

"Love you, too, Peach." He kissed me once more. "Don't talk to Joseph." He warned again before he walked away, leaving out the bathroom.

My eyes rolled at him, but I didn't say anything. Sighing, I got relaxed as I enjoyed the peace and quietness I was having.

Chapter 8

Peaches

"**I**'m telling y'all I'mma fuck around and lose my job because of that little bitch. I swear." I told Kim and Ebony while I mugged Mariah as she walked by our table.

"Blaze not entertaining her ass though, so Peach don't worry about that hoe." Kim waved her hand in Mariah's direction.

"I'm with Kim on this one, Peaches. Besides Blaze crazy ass will check that bitch without yo help." Ebony chimed in.

"I know he will, and he has but that bitch still be coming for him. Girl, she gon' make the ratchet side of me pop out on that ass." My eyes rolled hard as she glanced my way. She returned the action before focusing back on her group. "Fuck her." I waved my hand while pushing Mariah to the back of my mind.

"Bitches! Look who I found." Missy called out excited, with Angel on her arm.

"Ang!" The girls and I squealed. Getting up, the three of us went over hugging her.

I was truly excited to see her. It had been months since we last seem her, given all our busy working schedules. Missy was the only one who could visit her as much as she pleased. Regardless of that, we continued to have our daily group calls and text messages.

"Why you didn't tell me you were coming down here?" I questioned, sitting back down in my chair.

"It was a last minute thing. Parker didn't tell me until this morning that he was coming down. I wasn't going to come because I didn't feel like lugging them kids with me. Them my babies and I love they ass, but Lord!" She laughed. "Having to be stuck in the truck and dealing with their fighting on top of Parker's mean ass. I didn't want to do it. Meka came through for me though." She explained, making us laugh.

Angel only had the three kids, Parker Jr., Antoine and their baby girl, Parisa.

I had to say, I loved the hell out of my niece and nephews, but they were in fact bad as all hell. Ant was a little monster, with his grown ass. Parisa was a flat out diva and Peewee, he was more like Parker, pretty laid back and he had no gotdamn filter whatsoever.

"Girl, yo ass could've brought them kids." I told her and she waved me off.

"I could've, but me and Parker needed some alone time. He been in a funky mood lately." She expressed with a roll of her eyes.

We laughed at her action.

"You better leave my boy alone. What you done did to him?" Missy glared at Angel.

Angel laughed and shrugged. "It's not me. His ass mad because he wants another baby. He saying the kids are getting older and he want some more babies." She groaned. "He says that shit because he ain't pushing them out. Hell, my damn body still recovering from the three I had back to back."

We broke out laughing at her.

"Y'all laughing and I'm for real. Peewee is fourteen now, Ant's thirteen and my Lil Pixie just turned eleven. My body still tired as shit."

Angel eyes fell on me, her finger jabbed in my direction. "The twins are seven now, if Blaze came to you asking to have another baby. What would you do?"

I laughed at the question. "He already asked and we're trying. Blaze's ass want a bunch of kids, which he's always said. My papa bear, has been patient enough to hold off until I got into my career field. Now that I have for the past several years, his ass ready." I laughed.

Angel groaned. "Bitch, yo ass ain't no help. Well your opinion doesn't count. Parker ass better leave me the fuck alone." She rolled her eyes hard before she laughed.

Kim waved her off. "Bitch, stop fronting. Yo ass probably pregnant now if not you're going to be soon."

I had to agree with Kimmy. Angel ass knew she was just talking shit. "How long y'all here for?" I asked her.

"A few days. We have to be back Friday because Peewee and Ant got a basketball game. You know I don't miss no games." Angel was a full out sports mom. She had her boys in all sports and put Pixie in gymnastics. Angel's little girl Parisa was so damn gorgeous, that she looked like a little chocolate doll, which was how she got the nickname Pixie.

My hands clamped together. "Why the hell Joseph ass pops up and tell Blaze he got a damn brother. The man came from out of nowhere."

"Oh, hell no! Two of those crazy mothafuckas." Ebony chimed in while looking up at the ceiling. "Lawd, why? Why?" She asked.

Kim hit her, laughing. "Yo ass so damn stupid."

I glared at Ebony. "Bitch, don't do my baby like that. He ain't even all that bad anymore." Her lips pursed together as she gave me a blank stare. "Fuck you." I stuck up my middle finger at her.

Ebony laughed at me. "You married to him so of course you're going to say that. I'm playing, he has calmed down a lot. So, what's the brother like?"

I shrugged. "I don't know. Blaze don't want to meet him. I'm kind of curious to know though, I'm not going to lie but I'm not about to fight with him over it. He told me to leave it alone so that's what I'm going to do."

Missy shook her head. "That's not a surprise with Blaze. He don't wanna meet no damn body. Hell, his ass doesn't like people. I think he just started liking me." She looked at me and broke out laughing. "That mothafucka could hold a

168

grudge. I kissed yo funky ass twice and he didn't like me." She exclaimed, causing the girls to laugh.

"I swear he didn't like you, Lips." Angel jumped in clowning.

Missy glared at her. "Okay, Black." She shot back and we all fell out laughing.

"Y'all gonna leave my husband the fuck alone. He's bad with names—"

"No, the fuck he ain't. That nigga just don't care to learn them. He gives you some shit he gonna remember. But that's my boy, though. Blaze just kind of grow on you." Kim threw in her two cents.

My eyes rolled at all of them hard. They better get off of my damn baby I know that much.

"Peaches ass sitting over there mad as hell." Ebony pointed at me, cracking up.

"Fuck all y'all asses!" I started laughing. Angel's sudden tilt to the side grabbed my attention. My brows furrowed at her as she started to wave. "Ang?"

Angel pointed behind me. "Ol' girl right there mugging over here hard as hell. So, I waved at her."

I looked behind me to see Mariah. "That's some young bitch that want my husband. I wanna whoop her ass. These young bitches is straight triflin' and just don't give a damn about fucking a married man. These little hoes fucking with the wrong one, I kill for mine." I snapped, looking dead at Mariah as I talked to Angel. Mariah started laughing, she said something to her friends as she nodded toward us.

"Oh, we can still stomp a bitch real quick. We might have grown but we can still get down. You a good one. I wish a bitch would attempt to try me with Parker, I'mma drag the hoe. I don't give a fuck." Angel went off glaring hard at Mariah. "Peach, if you wanna get that bitch we can start some shit."

"Oh, God! Peach, don't get Angel started. This right up her alley." Missy's head shook before she glanced back to see Mariah. "That bitch look young, but if y'all wanna pop off I'm down."

My girls would never fucking change, and I loved the hell out of them for that. Their asses was always down to ride no matter what.

"Fuck her, she don't want no problems for real. Blaze ain't thinking about that damn girl. So, she ain't even worth it." I told them trying to spare the little hoe. I glanced back at her once again and the little smirk that was on her face left.

"Ma." Blake called out.

My eyes quickly found him. "Hey, baby." I waved him over to us. Since my car was in the shop, Blake was my little driver for the day.

"Hey, Aunties." Blake leaned down and kissed each one of the girls on their foreheads. "What y'all over here gossiping about?" He grabbed a chair from a table and pulled it up, sitting down next to me.

"Boy, shut up. We don't gossip." I muffed his head to the side.

He snorted loudly. "Yeah, okay. Y'all just talk about people, huh?" He shot back smartly.

The girls started laughing at him. "Boy shut yo ass up. Go make you something to eat. Gon' now." I waved him off.

Blake laughed, then kissed my cheek before he went up to the buffet to get him some food.

"He gets on my damn nerves. Acting just like his damn daddy." I rolled my eyes thinking about Blake smart remark.

The girls and I sat there making small talk. We had to stop our little gossiping since Blake came. I didn't need him to know every little thing we talked about.

The clearing of a throat grabbed our attention and I looked to see Mariah standing beside me.

"Little girl, don't come over here with no bullshit. I swear to God I would love to fuck you up if you do." Angel told her as she sat her drink down.

Blake started laughing. "I bet you a hundred bucks you won't lay her ass the fuck out—ah shit!"

Kim slapped the shit out of Blake in the back of his head. "You better watch yo gotdamn mouth, I know that shit. Blake, don't try to act grown now." She fussed at him.

"Thank you. I was just about to deck his ass in the mouth." I told her as I looked at Blake like he was crazy. He had lost his damn mind cussing like he had.

"Fuck all that. Give me the hundred." Angel held out her hand, making Blake laugh.

"Shorty, what you want?" Blake asked Mariah.

She rolled her eyes at them then looked to me. "Peaches, I wanted to apologize for how I'd came off, being a total bitch and all that. The whole thing with Blaze, I could admit I was wrong for doing that and I only did it to get under your skin. I'm sorry for that. You have a good man that loves you. My actions were very childish, and I don't want to beef with you, Peaches. I know it'll take some time but hopefully you can one day forgive me." She explained and seemed genuine about what she had said.

I didn't know what to think about that damn apology. Mariah had been flirting with Blaze for a whole damn year and now she suddenly realized how trifling she had been.

"That's all I wanted to say. You ladies have a nice lunch." She gave a faint smile, then walked back to her group.

"I don't trust her ass." Ebony exclaimed. "Her ass up to something, I promise." She shook her head. "I done saw a lot of bitches like her before. That bitch up to something."

The girls agreed with her and I laughed. She was probably right but I wasn't going to sweat her little ass because I knew Blaze wasn't stupid enough to fuck with her. I'll kill the both of their ass if he did.

Blake hummed and shrugged, uncaringly. He glanced at Mariah for a second before he went back to eating his food.

***

"Ma, John just texted me and said your car is finished." Blake said looking down at his phone. "I can take you there to pick it up."

"Okay, we can go there when we leave here." I told him then looked at the girls. "Y'all coming back to my place, right. I just have to pick up the twins from Mom B's that's it."

"Man, I'm trying to go get fuck'd!" Angel explained. "It's hard as hell to get some with kids at home—"

"That's my cue to bounce. I'll be back." Blake's face twisted up as he stood from his seat.

Angel's mouth formed into an *O*. "Baby, I'm sorry. I have to remember to watch my mouth." She apologized to him.

Blake waved her off. "You good, Auntie." He walked off while laughing at her.

"Why y'all didn't stop me from saying that in front of him?" She asked us and we started laughing at her embarrassing groans.

Chapter 9

Blake

"They ass crazy as shit." I mumbled to myself as I walked to the bathroom. I had just made it inside when my phone started ringing. Seeing Janae's name, I answered it. "What's up?"

"Hey, babe." From the tone of her voice, I knew something was wrong. She let out a heavy breath. "Blake, I don't want to get an abortion. I know we're young and not ready yet, believe me I know this. But I can't go through with it. I also don't want to be selfish and have this baby which could possibly put both of our lives on hold. Baby, I'm sorry, I can't make that decision." She began to sob into the phone.

My hand rubbed over my head. I was fuck'd. I wasn't trying to have no shorties right now. I had hoped—no, prayed like hell that she would get an abortion.

"Damn." I blew out a heavy breath. Shorty was crying hard as fuck. "Nae, stop crying. Why yo ass ain't just call me over there and we could've talked about this in person?" I wasn't mad with myself about her decision, I couldn't be pissed at her for that. I felt bad that she was sobbing hard, and I wasn't there with her.

"Blake, I know you don't want me to have this baby. You know where I stand on this, but I don't want to hold you back either. I'm going to let you decide and whatever you choose to do, I'll go with it."

She was letting me finalize the decision. "Fuck." My hand rubbed over my mouth. "Look, I'm about to drop my moms' off. When I do, I'll be over there, and we'll talk. Bet?"

She sniffled into the phone. "Okay."

"I'ight, man." I hung up the phone. "Fuck!" I hit the stall door hard. I knew I wasn't ready, hell we weren't ready for a shorty period. We were to fucking young. I wasn't even one hundred percent committed to Janae.

For her to leave that decision up to me was fuck'd up. I knew what I was going to tell her was going to hurt, but I didn't have a choice. I couldn't lie to her.

"You don't look happy." Mariah said.

A laugh left my mouth and I turned to face her. "I knew you was going to follow me back here." I leaned against the sink, folding my arms over my chest. I had felt Mariah staring a hole into me since I walked into the restaurant.

A smile came to her lips. "So, you came back here intentionally?" She asked and I nodded.

"With the way yo ass was staring at me, it was obvious you wanted something. So, what's up?" Mariah locked the bathroom door and I laughed. I pushed myself off the sink and walked over to her. "Ain't no need for all that." I flipped the lock.

"You heard what I said to your momma." She stated and I nodded. "Aren't you going to say something about that?" She questioned.

I shook my head. "No. I mean, what the fuck you want me to say? You made the best decision with the options you had. What? Did you expect a *thank you* from me?"

She looked at me like I was crazy. "Yes! That's exactly what I expect. You choked the hell out of me—"

I pushed her against the door. "That smart ass mouth of yours is the reason I choked yo ass. You got disrespectful so that was your own fault. If anything, I think you should give me an apology."

She scoffed and rolled her eyes hard. "Apologize to you? Little boy, you done lost your fuckin' mind. What I look like apologizing to you. I done already told your mom sorry—"

"You don't think she deserved that apology?" My brows raised at her. "You were mad disrespectful to her and my dad. Yo ass seem to be missing that whole part. Plus, it's not like I'm making you do shit, never once did I tell you to apologize. I just said stop fuckin' with her. You did this all on your own." I pointed out factual to her.

"Little boy—" She began to say but I cut her off.

I laughed at her words. "I can be a little boy." Licking my lips, I nodded my head then I pointed to her. "That ain't stopping yo ass from being all in my shit and you steady following my little ass around, Mariah."

She popped her lips. "I wasn't following you. How was I to know you'd be here?" She asked and I shrugged. "You know what? Forget the apology, I don't want it. Point is, you choked the hell out of me and that wasn't cool, period. I was nice about it the first time, but don't ever put yo fuckin' hands on me again. Do you understand me, Blake?"

I laughed at the seriousness in her voice. My hand rubbed the back of my head and I chuckled before my hand went around her neck, pushing her into the door more.

I smiled as she gasped out. My head lower toward hers and she looked at my lips. I licked them. "Then stay in your place and I won't have to." Her eyes snapped to mine. "You thought I was about to kiss you?" I laughed at her. "You want my little ass to kiss you?"

"No, now let me go." She breathed breathlessly.

I did as she said, releasing my grip from her neck. My thumb rubbed over her bottom lip. I then pushed down on it. "Open it." She looked taken back by my request. "Don't tell me you're shy, Mariah. Open your mouth."

Her lips popped. "I'm not shy—"

"See you talk to damn much, shut the fuck up and open your damn mouth." I snapped at her. She smacked her lips but opened her mouth no less. My middle and ring finger pushed down on her tongue before I slid them to the back of her throat.

Mariah's mouth closed around my fingers and she sucked on them. I felt her swallow when my fingers touched the back of her throat.

"Damn, you got a deep throat." Without another word, I pulled her into a stall. Grabbing her shoulders, I pushed her down to her knees. I then undid my pants, pulling my dick out.

Without having to be told what to do, Mariah immediately started playing with my dick until it got hard.

My phone started ringing. "Open your mouth." I told her. Getting my phone out, I answered it not bothering to look at the screen. "Yeah?"

"Blake, what are you doing? We're ready to go." My momma asked.

I grabbed the back of Mariah's head, pushing it down on the full length of my dick until her lips were kissing my pelvis.

"Man, that food fuck'd up my stomach. I'll be out there in a minute. I'ight? Ah shit." I grunted out as Mariah swallowed my dick.

"Blake—" My momma started to say something.

"I'll be out there in a minute." I hung up on her. Once I put my phone away, I grabbed a handful of her hair and started to fuck her face.

"Ah fuck! Damn, shorty." I groaned out as she took my dick down her throat and moaned.

Her head was bobbing as she slurped and sucked on my shit. My hand left her head and it leaned against the stall as I watched Mariah do her thang.

"Yeah, swallow that shit. Suck that dick, fuck!" That bitch had my toes curling. My hand went back into her head as I felt my nut coming. I held her head to my pelvis as I shot nut down her throat. "Gotdamn!" I blew out a breath. Mariah had sucked every little drop out my shit. "Damn, shorty." I looked down at her. "That mouth of yours is gifted. Shit." I laughed as I left out the stall. I went to the sink and grabbed some wet towel paper then cleaned my dick before putting it back in my jeans.

"This was fun." She came up behind me, wrapping her arms around my waist.

"It most definitely was." I moved her arms from my body. "I gotda go." I headed for the bathroom door.

"Wait. We could at least exchange numbers." She exclaimed, walking over to me.

My hand rubbed over my mouth. "We could." I licked my lips as I pulled out my phone. "Let me gon' head and put this out there." I unlocked my phone. "You can suck a mean dick no doubt about that, sweetheart, but I'm not interested in having shit with you for real. What you just did for me, wasn't shit. I mean, I was stressing, and you helped me relieve that, but ain't shit happening between us." I told her.

A look of confusion came to her face. "Are you being serious?"

My eyes landed on her full size breast. "Dead ass serious." I pulled out a twenty-dollar bill and slipped it in between her cleavage. My finger ran over her breast. "I don't want you to feel used." I licked my lips again, before smiling at her. "Don't pout, sweetheart. I mean, what the fuck would you want with a little boy like me?" I grinned at her then left out the bathroom.

***

Once I pulled up in front of Janae's house, I shot her a text letting her know I was outside. After a few minutes, she ran out to my car.

Once inside, she leaned over and kissed me. Looking at Janae, her eyes were red as was her nose. That told me she had still been crying. I felt like shit, but I had to make the better choice for us in that moment.

I pulled away from her house. I didn't have a destination in mind, I was just driving. We rode around for a few minutes in complete silence.

"Nae, if the circumstances were different then I would say we could do this, and you should keep it. Right now, though, I'm just thinking about the future and who know where we're gonna be in a few years? Who's to say we're going to still be together? The shit is just fuck'd up, for real. It's a hard decision all around, but the best one right now is for you to get an abortion." It was fuck'd up as I had said but I wasn't ready to have no kid. She wasn't even ready, and I didn't want to put that responsibility on our folks at the end of the day.

After a while of driving, Janae still hadn't responded to what I said. Although I knew she was taking in my words, the car was too damn quiet. Spotting a playground, I drove over to it and parked.

Janae nodded her head as tears ran down her cheeks. "I figured you were going to say that. I've been hearing you and I understand where you're coming from, but, Blake, it's a baby, my baby. I don't want to kill it."

My hand rubbed down my face. "I don't know what else you want me to say, Janae. I ain't gonna change what the fuck I'm saying. It's no point in keep going back and forth with this shit. I'm steady telling you what I want and ain't shit changing. If you wanna keep the mothafucka keep it, Nae, damn! Just don't keep asking me the same shit. At the end of the day my decision is for you to get an abortion. What you choose to do is whatever you do, but my response ain't gonna fuckin' change. So, stop asking me the same shit over and over again."

She was pissing me the fuck off. I had made the decision she asked me to, and I wasn't going to lie to her just to spare her feelings. The whole back and forth thing was fucking dead.

"You don't have to be fucking insensitive and snap at me, Blake! You're acting like we're talking about throwing away trash. It's a fuckin' baby, Blake, our fuckin' baby and you're just fine with killing it? Something that's a part of you?" She snapped while reaching across the seat and pushing me.

"Man, keep yo gotdamn hands off me before I knock the fuck outda you, real shit. I ain't insensitive. I told yo stupid ass the decision wasn't fuckin' easy, but I'm not about to pretend I'm ready for this shit when I ain't. On top of that bullshit, my momma just met yo ass and the second time y'all see each other it's gonna be with me telling her yo ass pregnant—"

"Is that what's this all about? You don't want yo momma to know her perfect little golden boy ain't so gotdamn perfect?" She spat out at me. "So, you'd rather kill our baby instead of you facing your momma?" She muffed me hard.

I rubbed my bottom lip. "I ain't got no problem telling my momma shit. I'm just not ready for no fuckin' baby. You told me I could decide, and I did. If you wanna keep the fuckin' shorty, then do that shit, man that's your choice, regardless I'mma still be here. So, yo ass yelling and doing all that extra bullshit you're doing ain't gonna change how I feel." I shrugged being honest with her.

"You wanted to play grown up when we were fuckin'. Now that it resulted in me being pregnant you ain't ready?" Janae continue to yell and fuss.

My hand once again rubbed over my head. She was so damn emotional and because of that, I wasn't trying to be pissed at her. "You're acting like I meant for this shit to happen, Janae. We were both fuck'd up the night yo dumbass got pregnant. Hell no, I ain't ready for no mothafuckin' kid. Regardless of that, if you choose to have it, I'mma take care of my shorty. Stop acting dumb as fuck—"

"Fuck you, Blake. This shit ain't easy!"

"Man, shut the fuck up. We already said that shit. Do what the fuck you want. I don't give a fuck. So, don't fuckin' ask me no more." I started up the car. I was done talking to her ass about this shit. Driving away from the park, I headed back toward her crib.

"So that's it? You don't care." She asked me.

I didn't bother to respond. She was pregnant and emotional. It wasn't a point in talking to her. I was done with it. I turned up the radio, shutting her ass up.

***

I pulled in front of her house and Janae stayed in the car. She didn't make any attempt to get out. My head shook at her. "You just gon' sit there?" I questioned and she didn't say anything. "Man, go in the fuckin' house and clean yo damn face and shit."

The palms of her hands wiped at her cheeks, that was it. She didn't say anything nor did her ass move.

"Janae, get the fuck out. Yo ass starting to get on my gotdamn nerves, for real. Go in the house." I reached over and pushed her door open. She pulled it right back shut. I was about to snap at her when my phone started ringing.

"Yeah, what's up?" I answered as I stared at Janae, I was contemplating on slapping the fuck outda her ass.

"What yo ass into?" Ace asked me.

I shrugged, rubbing a hand over my head. "Shit right now. I'm dropping Janae off at the crib. Why? What's up?"

"Shit, bored as fuck. Ashanti on some bullshit, so I was calling to see what you was tryna get into."

"My Aunties all here so they at the crib. I know my dad and Unc about to be there. So, I'm about to chill with their asses. Shit, come through. I'll be there in about ten minutes. Bet?"

"I'ight. Aye, you think yo momma would trip if I brought Ashanti over?" He asked.

"No, she won't. Gon' head and bring her. My momma gonna be too busy with my Aunties to probably even notice shorty being there." I told him, then ended the call. I hope he didn't have shit else to say. "Janae, yo ass being childish as fuck. Get out." I snapped at her, pushing her toward the door.

"Keep your hands off of me, Blake." She fussed.

"Yo ass got a lot of shit to think about. Now go in the crib and clean yourself up. I'll talk to you later." She didn't say shit. "I'm about to drag yo ass out this car."

"I don't care do it. That's the only way I'm getting out and I don't care about you being pissed at me. It's hard to just—"

"Man, I told you, I don't wanna hear that shit. Do what you feel, for real. I'm over it, yo. This whole back and forth bullshit, Nae, I'm done. I don't give a fuck. Now get out, I got shit to do." I didn't want to be mean or a dick but shit, it was only so many ways to say the same gotdamn thing only to have her get pissed the fuck off. I was tired of talking about the shit.

I was already stressed behind the bullshit. Now I didn't even give a fuck what she decided to do. I knew I shouldn't have felt like that, but she was pissing me off.

I reached over to push the door opened and Janae whacked the fuck out of me. Before I knew it, I had her damn face against the window.

"Keep yo fuckin' hands off me. Yo, you trippin' hard as fuck." I let her go not wanting to hurt her. "Man, go in the fuckin' house. You gonna make me hurt yo stupid ass for real."

"I'm not getting out this fuckin' car. I'm going wherever you go. I swear to God you are so damn insensitive. Like you just don't give a fuck. I swear to God, man." Her hands roughly wiped at her cheeks, brushing the tears away.

"Crazy ass bitch, man." I mumbled to myself as I pulled away from her house. "I ain't bringing yo stupid ass back home." I told her and she shrugged. Janae sniffled as she pulled her knees up to her chest and laid her head on them.

I didn't say shit else to her the whole ride to the crib.

***

When we made it to my house, everybody was there. My Unc, Mac, Sam, Bell, Parker, Chris, my Aunties, even the twins, Kyree and Khalil were there.

They were all out back, playing music, talking and laughing, just having a good time like only they could do.

"So, y'all decided to have a party. Huh?" I asked coming into the backyard.

"That was yo momma." My dad said, slapping hands with me. "You brought your girlfriend to meet the family?" He laughed, nodding toward Janae.

"If that's what you wanna say." I shrugged. "What's up, Parker, Chris." I shook up with the both of them.

"Ain't shit." Chris said, then pointed at me. "You gon' make me beat yo ass." He threatened. I immediately started laughing.

"What he do?" My dad asked him.

"He be fuckin' with Tiana, well his little ass been trying to anyways. She said he always tryna holla at her, be all in her inbox—"

"Yo chill out. I just be bullshittin' with her, man. I only check up on her that's it for real. Christiana is cute as hell though, but I just be joking with her. I got a girl." My eyes pointed to the side, which they followed.

Parker started laughing. "Damn, you fuckin' up buddy's game and shit. Sweetheart, we just bullshittin'." Parker told Janae and Chris snorted, causing Parker to hit him.

Chris laughed and he looked at Janae again. His eyes squinted as he stared at her harder. "What's wrong with her? Shorty look like she's been crying." He pointed out, causing both my pops and Parker to look closer at her.

"She straight, ain't shit wrong with her." I shrugged then glanced back to her. Janae's eyes and face was red as hell.

"Sweetheart, if he got you crying, he ain't even worth yo time." Chris told her.

I looked at Chris' ass like he was crazy. "Why the fuck would you tell her some shit like that? Chris, yo ass trippin'. Man, come on." I grabbed Janae by the arm and pulled her into the house. Once we were in my room, I push her into the bathroom. "Man, clean yo damn face. Yo ass out there crying and shit. Yo ass should've stayed at home if you was gonna come over here with that shit."

"For real, Blake, you ain't even got to be a fuckin' asshole about this either. Do you not understand the decision I have to make? You wanna act an ass and be pissed at me because of that?" She snapped, pushing me. "Like, you're really showing me what you about, for real. You dead ass acting like this because I care and don't want to kill my baby?" Janae was pissed, tears were flowing heavily from her eyes.

My hand rubbed over my head. I didn't want to have that gotdamn conversation at my house. I didn't know what the fuck she wanted me to do or say. "Man, not once did I say you shouldn't care. I said this shit was gonna be hard. Ain't nothing about this easy, but I'm not gon' sit around and cry about this shit either. That's not gon' do a gotdamn thing for me." My hand rubbed over my mouth as I calmed myself down. I just didn't know what she was looking for me to say or do. "You know what? Keep the shorty,

Janae. I don't care what you decide to do at this point."

Janae arms folded over her chest and she nodded her head. "You're right, Blake. I shouldn't have it."

"Yo! Blake!" Ace called banging on my room door.

I opened a drawer and grabbed a face towel. "Clean yourself up before you come back out there." She didn't reach to take it, she stood there mugging me hard. I sat the towel down, then left out the bathroom. "What's up?" I shook up with Ace.

"Shit, I told yo ass that." Ace got that dumbass smirk on his face and I knew it was something crazy.

"What the fuck you done did?" I leaned against the wall with my arms crossed over my chest waiting to hear the shit.

Ace started laughing. "I ain't even did shit this time though." That nigga looked like he was lying. He nodded toward the front, then walked off.

I followed him to the living room. I knew it was stupid shit. "Man." My hand rubbed over my mouth and I looked back toward my room. I was hoping like hell Janae didn't walk out.

"It's glad to see that you're alive." Squeaky shot out sarcastically.

I looked at Ace again only to find him grinning like a gotdamn idiot. "Why the fuck you bring her here?" I asked him.

He shrugged. "Shid, she was at Ashanti's crib and we couldn't leave her there, then she asked about you, and since we were coming here, I brought her."

"You left out the whole part about her being with y'all to begin with." I snapped at him.

"I didn't think it was going to be a problem though." Squeaky chimed in.

Of course, her ass wouldn't think that. I had been dodging her clingy ass for a minute and she still didn't catch on.

"If I had of known you were with him then you would have." I told her, then looked back at Ace. "Janae's here."

"Oh, shit. I thought you dropped her off. Damn." He said, realizing the fuck up he made.

"Who is Janae?" Ashanti and Squeaky questioned.

"My friend." Squeaky lips popped and her eyes rolled at my words. "Man, chill out with that shit. Ain't you still with buddy ass?" I couldn't think of her dude name, then again, I didn't care to know it for real.

Again, her lips popped. "Ain't nobody gonna say shit to yo *friend*." She walked closer to me. "At least now I got my explanation. You could've told me you have a girl." She laughed. "Don't worry, I can keep a secret. Now that we got that out of the way. Can I get a proper greeting?" Her arms went around my neck and she hugged me.

I returned the hug. Squeaky kissed the side of my neck before she let me go. I laughed at her ass. "Let's go outside." I led them through the kitchen, then out into the backyard.

"Hey, Kimmy." Ace smiled and waved at her. His eyes roamed over Kim's full figure. "Man, she need to stop playing and let me turn her ass into a cougar, real shit." He bit into his bottom lip as he rubbed his stomach.

"Hey, Ace." Kim waved as she made it to us. Ace didn't hesitate to pull her into a tight hug. She laughed at him. "Boy, let me go with your crazy ass."

"I ain't been no boy for a long time now. I'm telling you, Kimmy, you should try me out. I'll make you real happy, for real." His hand reached out and he thumbed her chin.

"Yo ass is to fuckin' much. Yo young ass wouldn't even know what to do with me if you had a chance. I'll have you sucking yo damn thumb, boy move." She smacked his hand away from her. "Hey, ladies." She spoke to Ashanti and Squeaky.

"Hello." They responded politely.

"Excuse me." Auntie Kim moved around us and continued on her way. As she did Ace eyes followed her.

His head shook. "I just want a day to be in that shit."

Ashanti slapped him in his back. "Really, Ace? You acting like I'm not even right here? Yo ass disrespectful as fuck, I swear."

Ace started laughing. "I'm sorry, baby. When it comes to Kim, you gotda make an exception. I've been in love with her since I was five. That shit ain't going away."

"You know she got a man though." I reminded him.

Ace shrugged. "So? He ain't got shit to do with nothing. Don't tell me you ain't never thought about hitting one of their asses."

I looked at his ass like he was crazy. "Hell no, never. Nigga they family. Man, get yo ass away from me." I laughed at him and went to the court.

They followed and we started playing around, shooting the ball. Squeaky ass was slick as fuck with her shit, whenever she got the chance, she was on me. Her booty was rubbing on me, she was on my back managing to kiss my neck or she was slipping her hands under my shirt.

My momma and dad was enjoying their guest and wasn't paying us no attention. They were laughing and talking loud as hell.

I shot the ball up then fell back on the ground as the ball went in. "Oh shit. I wasn't even trying to hit that mothafucka for real." I laughed.

Ace dropped down on the side of me and Ashanti sat on his lap.

I looked at Squeaky. "You wanna sit on me too?

"Your momma and them standing right over there. I ain't crazy." She laughed while shaking her head.

I shrugged. "They ain't paying us no attention."

"And your girl sitting there looking at us." She pointed dead at Janae.

For a minute I had forgotten all about her. When she came back outside, she didn't say shit to me. Janae found her a chair and just sat there.

"What you do to her. She looks pissed. Janae don't never just sit there quiet like that." Ace commented.

I sat up and looked over at her. She was on her phone doing something. "I didn't do anything to her."

"Peaches over there talking to her now." Ace nodded in their direction.

My hand rubbed the back of my neck and I blew out a breath. I wasn't about to let Janae moody ass get to me. She wanted to fucking argue, and I wasn't trying to do all that. Her ass was confused and frustrated about the situation we were in and she was channeling her anger toward me.

She wanted me to agree with her to have a baby either of us was ready for. If she wanted to keep it, then that was her choice. I was going to take care of my responsibility regardless.

Even so, us going back and forth, arguing about the different decisions wasn't going to help shit. That's why she should've gone the fuck home so she could figure out what she wanted. I wasn't going to mope around with her ass.

"They're coming over here." Ace mumbled.

"Man, shut up. I see them." When they finally reached us, Janae's eyes had rolled up in her head. That gotdamn baby had her sensitive as fuck.

"Blake, what's going on?" My mom pointed to Janae. "Why do you have her sitting by herself?"

My brows raised at her accusation. "I don't have her doing nothing. I didn't tell her to stay over there. She sat there because it was what she wanted."

"It doesn't matter, you left her over there. Yo ass could've sat with her. She's your guest—"

"He didn't have to, Ms. Peaches. I wanted to sit there, I needed to think." Janae chimed in to explain. She looked at her phone as it dinged and started texting on it.

"See." I pointed to Janae and my momma glared at me. "I'm just saying. You walked over here straight about to go off on me for nothing."

"It wasn't for nothing. I don't care if she wanted to sit by herself or not. She is still your guest and you've been ignoring her since y'all got here. That bullshit ain't cool, Rashad." She continued to go off on me. "Do you want him to take you home?" My momma offered.

"I ain't taking her home. She should've gone home when I tried to drop her off. She better find her own way there." My momma looked like she was ready to slap the shit out of me.

"Boy…" She bit into her bottom lip.

"It's cool, Ms. Peaches, he don't have to take me anywhere. I found a ride. He don't ever have to worry about me." She made a point to say.

My mom's lips pursed together, and she hummed. "Okay then." She looked at me and shook her head.

I didn't pay her reaction any attention. My focus was on Janae. "Why you gotda be so damn dramatic?" I asked her. She rolled her eyes at me and continued to text away on her phone. "Don't have yo cousin come over here."

"How are they going to come and get her then, Blake? Huh?" My momma asked me.

I wasn't tryna hear shit she was saying. Janae didn't say anything, she simply turned and walked away. I got up to follow her.

"Blake—" my momma grabbed my arm. "Now you're concerned about what she's gonna do? Leave her alone and continue to play with that one." She pointed to Squeaky.

I pulled my arm from hers. "Janae!" I quickly caught up to her as she made it to the living room. "Man, slow yo ass down. You heard me calling you."

She pulled away from me. "Don't grab me. Go back out there with that bitch and keep playing with your hoe acting like I'm not even here. Fuck you, Blake, for real." She looked at her phone as it dinged.

"I just told you not to have yo cousin come over here—"

"I heard you the first time you said it. My cousin not picking me up and my ride not coming here, I'm going to walk to the gas station." Janae pushed me away as her phone started ringing. I snatched the phone from her. "Blake, stop fucking playing. Damn. Give me my fuckin' phone." She punched me in my back.

"Hit me again, I'mma knock the shit outda yo ass, watch." I warned her as I looked down at the phone screen. "Eric? That's who you called to pick you up?" As bad as I wanted to be pissed. I couldn't because that was what she wanted. That's the only reason she called that nigga out of everybody her ass knew. I let out a laugh. "Here," I handed her the phone back. "Gon' head and meet your friend so he can drop you off." I wasn't going to chase her ass. We were only going to end up arguing and I wasn't trying to do that shit with her ass.

"I swear you is so fucking stupid. I promise you won't have to worry about me bothering you no more." She claimed.

I was about to walk away until she said that. "What the fuck does that mean? This the second time you done said that shit. Nae, don't throw no subliminal ass message at me. Shid, tell me what it is straight up." I told her, but she didn't say anything. "Man, don't get quiet, you done already said the shit. You done fuckin' with me? Is that what you're trying to say?"

Janae's phone started ringing again and she answered it. "Hey, Eric—"

"So, you're going to ignore me?" I grabbed the phone from her. "Aye, you ain't gotda pick her up." I ended the call with that. "Come on, I'll drop yo ass off. If you done fucking with me, Janae that's your choice."

"That's your problem, you don't care about shit—" She began to yell at me. Taking hold of her arm, I pulled her into my room. "Let me go!" She snapped, pulling away from me.

"Not once did I say I didn't care—"

"You didn't have to. Your actions is showing me that. I'm not asking you to cry about this, Blake. But you don't have to be mean and insensitive toward me. You don't have to shed not one mothafuckin' tear, but the least you can do is try to be here for me. This decision is hard, and it hurts. You acting like this right now only shows me how you'll be if I had this baby that you don't want."

"Nae, if you had the baby nothing would change between us and that's a promise. How many times do I have to fuckin' say that? Damn! Yeah, I've been a dick. I'm sorry for that, I don't know what you want me to say. I tell you how I feel about the situation, explain why. Only to have you get pissed. So, I don't want to talk about it because I don't wanna fight with you."

"Okay, Blake. I get it and we won't talk about it." She shrugged. "Can you take me home now?"

"You still mad?" I could see it on her face she was pissed off. I didn't know what the fuck she wanted, and I wasn't trying to be mean to her. Hell, it was the both of our fuck up that created a problem.

"I was never mad." She lied while walking around me. Janae opened the door and I closed it right back. Picking her up, I went to my bed. "No, Blake, for real gone. I'm not even in the mood for you right now. The way you just acted. Man, hell n'all." She tried to push me off of her.

"Nae, stop that shit. I'mma take yo ass home, just chill." I sat her in my lap, putting my arms around her. "If this was a few years later, there

202

wouldn't be a question on if you're keeping it or not. That's just my thoughts on it. If you wanna keep the shorty, then we can. I'mma be here with you regardless of your decision. I got frustrated today and was an ass, I'm sorry, i'ight?"

She licked her lips and sighed. "Okay, Blake." Janae attitude could be heard heavy in her tone. "I'll call and make the appointment." She tried to get up. "Can we go now?"

"I'ight man." I let her go and she wasted no time walking out my room. "That fuckin' girl and her attitude." I got up and left out, catching up to her.

We hopped in my car and I took her home. The entire ride there she was silent. I quit trying to talk to her ass. She was ignoring the fuck out of me and that shit had started to piss me off. So, I just shut the fuck up.

When I pulled in front of her house. She hopped out the gotdamn car before I could even put that bitch in park. So, shid, I kept on going. I wasn't about to kiss her stubborn ass. Yeah, I was wrong for how I acted, but I apologized. Her ass was acting like that ain't mean shit.

I knew she was just hormonal or some shit. I was going to let her cool down before I tried to talk to her again. Otherwise I was going to fuck around and choke her ass.

Chapter 10

Peaches

"Joseph, no, leave me alone with this. I'm not about to argue with that man because of you. Yo ass know how ignorant Blaze get. He told me to stay out of it and that's what I'm doing." He had lost his mind to think I was going to meet with his son behind Blaze's back. If I went along with that and Blaze later found out, he was bound to kill the both of us.

"Peaches, it'll only be for a minute. You can meet him, get a feel of his personality and if you think he's cool then you tell Blaze that—"

"No! Why couldn't you trick Blaze into something like this?" I fussed at him. Joseph had called me out for lunch, giving me the impression that he simply wanted to catch up. But, no, it was to meet his damn son.

Joseph looked at me like I was crazy. "He would probably kick my ass then walk out on us."

He was right about that. Shaking my head, I pulled out my phone and called Blaze. After the second ring, he answered.

"What's up, baby?" He asked through the line.

"Hey, babe. Look, Joseph is really working my damn nerves about you meeting his son. His ass done tricked me into coming to lunch and meeting the man—"

Joseph eyes grew wide as he looked surprised that I had told Blaze. He was crazy if he thought I wasn't. Given the shit we had been through in the past, I didn't trust new people and if Blaze told me to stay away from someone, I did.

"That's a stupid ass mothafucka. Where the fuck you at now?" He snapped, pissed off.

"We at B-dubs now. He haven't gotten here yet, but I ordered my food and I'm hungry for my wings." If it wasn't for the fact I was starving, I probably would've just left.

"Which one?" He asked.

"On 30." I informed him.

"I'll be there in a minute and fuck them wings. Get yo ass up out of there. Tell Joseph I'm on my way up there, and I'm smacking the shit out of his old ass." He threatened and I laughed. Knowing Blaze ass, he would most definitely try to smack Joseph.

"Okay. I'm about to have them wrap my wings to go. Alright babe, love you." I told him as I flagged down a waiter.

"I'ight, love you too. Now hurry the fuck up and leave. I don't want you nowhere around that nigga."

"I know. And I'm about to go once my wings come. You should've came home earlier and took me out—"

"Peaches, shut the hell up. Don't start that shit just because yo ass off today and bored. Now get yo ass from up there." He fussed, then hung up on my ass.

I glared at my phone and started texting him talking mad shit. He had lost his mind, going to hang up on me. "Ol' funky black ass."

"Why would you tell him? You know he's crazy as hell." Joseph glared at me.

My eyes rolled. "That's exactly why I told him. If I would've went along with this and he later found out. He would be on my ass and like I said, I'm not about to fight with that man, my husband, over you. I got him here like you wanted me too. You didn't say how to do it, but you wanted him to meet your son. Now he's coming." I shrugged as if that was my plan all along. Hell, that was just quick thinking.

"I don't know why you're acting. You know Blaze is scared of you and would do anything you ask him to do." Joseph guessed, sounding serious.

I snorted. "You must be out yo mind. Who told you that? Blaze don't do a damn thing I tell him if he doesn't want to. I don't know why you would want me to meet him anyways. Yo ass know how Blaze is when it comes to new people."

Joseph blew out a heavy breath before he rubbed a hand over his head. He looked so stressed out and I didn't blame him. I couldn't begin to imagine how that introduction was going to go. Hell, I doubt Blaze was going to be open to the idea of getting to know that man, his brother or not. Blaze simply didn't care for people.

If they weren't making him money or wasn't family, he didn't give a fuck about nobody.

"Hey, Mrs. Carter." A small cheerful voice spoke.

I glanced to my side to see Blake's little friend, Janae. I gave her a smile. "Hey, sweetie." I stood up and gave her a hug. "And I told you to call me Peaches. I've actually been wanting to talk to you. Do you have a second?"

She looked nervous but nodded no less. "Um, yeah, sure. My cousin haven't gotten here yet so you can come to my table." Janae offered.

I grabbed my purse, then glanced at Joseph. "I'll be right back." I told him, then followed Janae to her table. Once we sat down, I gave her a friendly smile. "I wanted to talk to you about Blake."

The last time I saw Janae was at the gathering we had at the house. I knew she was upset about something and Blake didn't make it better because he practically ignored the poor girl the entire time.

Seeing him do that, reminded me so much of Blaze and how nonchalant he was when it came to me and my feelings. I hated to see Blake has gotten that from his dad. He probably didn't even realize his ways and how they could affect a person.

208

"Saturday when you were at the house. I noticed you and Blake weren't so good. Seeing that look on your face, reminded me so much of myself. Blake is so much like his dad and he don't even realize it. I can tell that you genuinely like him. The way you stare at him tells me that. Blake on the other hand, he's just so nonchalant about everything. He doesn't know how..." I trailed off as I tried to figure out how to word what I wanted to say.

"He's not good with emotions, really. You could express how you may feel about something, hell, even cry to him about it, and he'll give you a response that'll make you feel as if he doesn't care. Regardless of his ways, I know he really likes you, Janae." I explained to her.

Janae's head shook and her eyes rolled into her head. She bit into her bottom lip as her eyes got glossy.

Was she about to cry? *What the hell did I say?* I was so lost. I didn't think I said anything to make her cry. I grabbed some napkins and handed them to her. "Why are you crying?"

"I'm sorry." She wiped her eyes. "I broke up with him the day after I left your house. I just don't know what to think when it comes to Blake. A part of me feel like he cares but then it's like he really doesn't. It's hard to explain really. I just don't know. How you know he likes me?" She questioned.

"You're the first girl he has ever brought home. Expression isn't one of his key points and to be honest, I don't know when it'll be. I've been with his dad for about thirteen years now and he's still insensitive as hell." I laughed and she smiled. "But one thing about those Carter men is that, if they truly care for you, then they'll always find a way to show you that. It'll take some time though, so if you really care for Blake, be patient with my baby, please."

Damn, I was sounding like Bianca's ass.

"I don't know if I can. I don't like the way it makes me feel. Like, I really love Blake. We've been together for a year and I've never felt this way about a guy before. And given the time we've been together I would've expected him to be more..." She groaned.

"Sensitive?" I asked her.

"I guess. Even when we're alone he can't be that. I shouldn't have to get mad at him to get the feeling that he cares. It's hard and I don't want to continue to have to guess what he's feeling. I just hate how uncaring he is." Janae wiped her eyes once more.

Those damn Carter men. They just didn't know the damage they could cause a woman.

"Then don't feel like that. Blake is my son and I love him deeply. But I was once in your place and what you're feeling I felt for years with Blaze. So, I get it. But let me say this. If my son really cares for you." I started laughing as so many memories came to me. "He's not going to let you go. And the way he went after you that day, says so much. He might leave you alone for a minute, but if he's anything like his dad, he'll be back."

Janae head shook and she shrugged. "It's no point now. I can't do this with Blake—"

"Janae…" A brown skinned girl called walking over to us. She looked at Janae then glanced at me. "You okay?" The girl asked her.

"Yeah. Ms. Peaches this my cousin Shantell, Shanny, this is Blake's mom." Janae introduced us.

The girls mouth formed into an *O*. "Oh okay, hey." She waved.

"Hey," I returned her gesture then slid out the booth. "It was nice talking to you Janae and if you want to talk about anything at all, give me a call. I can put my number in your phone." I offered. Hell, I was married to a Carter, so I knew how she felt.

"Yeah sure, I'd like that." She handed me her phone and I quickly added my number into her contacts.

"Shanny—Peaches?" Mariah called coming to the table. "What's going on over here?" She asked.

"Nothing, this is Blake's mom, we were just talking." Janae told her.

Hearing her damn voice just irritated the hell out of me. "I'll see you later, Janae."

She stood up and gave me a hug. "Thanks for talking to me."

"No problem." I waved at her and walked off, going back to Joseph's table.

"This is your food. Joshua is on his way up here, so you should get out of here." Joseph informed me, while handing me the bag on the table.

"Okay, see you Joseph. Remind your son, not to be offended by Blaze. That's just how he is." I gave him a hug then kissed his cheek.

"Shit, I hope he will be cool."

Hell, I did too. With a final wave, I left out the restaurant.

"Peaches!" Mariah called from behind me.

"Girl, leave me alone. We are not friends so pretend like you don't see me." I called out as I continued walking.

"It's about Blake." She yelled.

That got my attention and I stopped walking. I turned around to face her. "What about my son?"

"Look, Peaches, I know you don't like me, and I can't blame you. I was a serious bitch to you for no reason. My apology was sincere. Like, I am truly sorry—"

"Mariah, I heard you the first time you apologized and okay, you apologized but that still don't change the fact that you came after my husband. What you want me to say? Huh? You want me to tell you it's cool? No! I won't do that because it's not. Bitch we have a whole ass family and you wanted to ruin that. Yo ass lucky I'm not beating your mothafuckin' head into the hood of my car. So, if you ain't got shit to tell me about Blake, then leave me the fuck alone." It was taking everything in me not to start swinging on her ass.

"You know what? I'll let him tell you. Peaches, I hope you can someday look past all that. I really want you to like me. Especially since we have to see each other every day." She waved to me then turned around and walked away.

I glared at her back as I pulled out my phone. I didn't trust her ass one bit. Something wasn't right with the fuckin' girl. How she gonna flirt with Blaze for damn near a year, then suddenly she wants to be friends. Something was off.

"What's up, ma?" Blake answered the phone.

"Baby, Rashad—"

A loud groan came through the line. "Whatever it is I didn't do it. Dad or the twins did it. I haven't even been home yet." Blake began to explain.

"Boy, shut up. I don't know what the hell you're talking about." I looked at my phone screen. That damn boy was crazy.

"Oh, well you said Rashad, so I figured something happened. What's up?" He questioned, sounding relaxed.

I laughed at my baby. "Do you remember that slut from my job who tried to talk to your dad?"

He hummed into the line. "Yeah, Mariah. What about her?"

"Well she said it was something she needed to tell me about you. Then she turned around and said, she'll let you tell me. What's going on?" I asked him as I slid in my car.

214

Blake started laughing. "Man, that girl crazy. She was probably going to tell you that I choked her ass."

My mouth dropped opened and I felt my eyes widen. "What? When? Why would you choke her?"

"Man, she was being disrespectful..." Blake began relaying what she said about me. I rubbed my forehead as I listened to my oldest baby talk.

He was most definitely his damn daddy's son.

Chapter 11

Blaze

"**W**hy the fuck would you try to get Peaches to meet with that mothafucka? After I told yo black ass I was straight on seeing yo damn son, Joseph?" I was ready to smash his damn head into the table.

Joseph's hand rubbed over his face. "Blaze, I want you to meet him. I heard what you said, but come on man, he's your brother and I thought Peaches could talk you into meeting up with us. I figured if she met and liked him, you'll give him a chance." Joseph ass looked like he had aged ten years older from stress.

I glared at him. "I don't give a fuck for your reason, Joseph. Make this yo last time dragging my wife into some shit like this. We don't know this nigga. That's what you not understanding. Just because a mothafucka claim to be yo son don't mean he can be trusted. That's why you don't bring my family into that shit. Make this yo last mothafuckin' time doing some bullshit like this. Next time I'mma kill yo ass. You understand me?" I stared him dead in the eyes letting him know I was serious as fuck. I wouldn't have a problem killing his ass if he put my family in danger.

"Alright, son, I hear you. That wasn't my intentions though, Blaze. You know that." Joseph exclaimed and he seemed sincere.

I didn't give a fuck though, pops or not. I would kill his mothafuckin' ass. "I don't give a fuck. I didn't want Peaches around yo ass. It took a minute for that to happen. So why would this nigga be any different?"

"It's a good thing they warned me about your ways before we met." The chair on the side of me pulled out and a brown skinned nigga, that resembled Joseph, sat down. He was a stocky as mothafucka too. The nigga definitely had that prison build to his ass.

"Well it's a good thing you overheard me. So now I don't have to repeat myself. You this nigga's son, that's who your relationship should me with. You don't know shit about me, and I'll like to keep it that way." I told his ass straight up and I didn't give a fuck for how he felt about it.

Joshua laughed. "I know a lot about you actually. It's not too many Blaze's around this way and nigga's talk. I've heard crazy stories about a cat name Blaze running shit in Gary while I was locked up. When Joseph told me that I had a brother named Blaze. Shid, no lie, I was excited to meet with you."

My hand rubbed my mouth as I listened to what he had said. My head nodded. I wasn't surprised to hear it, though. Nigga spoke on me a lot and didn't really know shit about me. "I'm sure whatever you heard wasn't true."

"Oh, most definitely not. I don't listen to what other niggas say. Personally, I don't give a fuck what you done. My only thing is to meet with the family I never knew I had. I'm just telling you, for years I heard your name and respected it before I knew we were related." He shrugged uncaringly. "If you need time to come around, you got it, bruh. Either way, I ain't gonna kiss yo ass for you to get to know me. Shid after this it's your choice to do what the fuck you wanna. You feel me?"

I glanced at Joseph and he looked away from me, wiping his mouth. That nigga thought some shit was funny. Even so, I had to give it to dude though, he didn't sound like a bitch made nigga, for real. "I feel you." I stood up.

"Blaze, come on, son. You can stay and chill for an hour." Joseph grabbed my arm and nodded toward the chair.

My hand rubbed over my head and I sighed. "I'ight." I sat back down. I looked at Joseph and his eyes slid to Joshua. That mothafucka was pushing it. I knew once I got home Peaches ass was gonna be down my neck asking what happened. "Tell me, what you done heard about me?" Hell, that was what I wanted to know.

Joshua laughed and looking around us. I did the same. "Now ain't the time or the place to be talking about what I done heard. It's eyes and ears everywhere, you hear me." The way he said it was more of warning. "Just know, I done heard some shit."

After he said that, my mind was made. I didn't like that mothafucka. Regardless, I was going to feel him out. "I hear you. Shid, you know about me and I don't know shit about you. Well other than you're his son. So, what yo life been like?"

He laughed at that. "I'mma need more than just some wings and a beer to go into that." When he saw that I wasn't laughing, he stopped. "I guess that was a bad joke, huh?"

"I didn't know you were trying to be funny. So, what yo life been like?" I repeated my question.

Joshua shrugged. "Before I got booked it was good. I had the normal childhood, you know. Shit was good until I got caught up in the fast money. I wasn't on your level of shit, but I put in that work—"

I started laughing at what he was saying. "Yo, you're sounding like a clown right now. Look, Joshua, you don't seem like the type of mothafucka they try to sale himself for some shit. And you damn sho' don't seem like the type of nigga that want to meet with a pops' he doesn't know. I just don't get that from you. Now if you looking to put in some work and hit the streets again, then my nigga, I ain't the brother you need to be looking for. You hear me?" I got up out my seat. "I'm out Joseph. Joshua, I'll catch you around." With that I headed out the restaurant.

"Yo, Blaze!" Joshua called out before he caught up to me. "Look, I ain't tryna sell myself to you. Yeah, I'm tryna sound impressive. Maybe I did it the wrong way. I'm not looking for shit or tryna get back into these streets. And you right, once upon a time, I wouldn't have gave a fuck about meeting Joseph and that was because I didn't know shit about him. When my momma was dying is when I learned about him.

I was curious about the nigga, so, yeah, here I am. I'm the only child from my moms', yo. To find out I got a brother and sister, I'm curious about y'all. Like I said, I heard shit about you when I was locked up. Which only piqued my curiosity about you, yo upbringing, Brittany. That's it." He explained.

My phone went off with a message from Mac telling me he was on his way to the courts. My head nodded at him. "I'ight, cool. You ball?" I turned around and started walking to my truck.

"I'm pretty nice, why?" He followed behind me.

"Let's ball, then."

"What about Joseph?"

"What about him? This was what he wanted. He'll be good." I hopped in the truck. Joshua looked hesitant at first and I rolled the window down. "I'm about to pull off, you either riding or you're staying here?" I threw the truck in reverse.

"I'ight." He jogged around to the passenger side and out in. "I'll let him know I rode off with you." He stated while pulling out his phone and calling Joseph.

I shrugged, then pulled off, driving to the court.

***

"Nigga it's about time yo ass showed up. What the fuck took you so damn long?" King fussed as he shook up with me.

"I had to take care of some shit." I pointed to Joshua. "This Joseph's son, Joshua."

"Yeah, he looks like him. What's up homie." King bumped fist with him. "Now, let's ball. I hope yo ass can play."

"Yo B, let me holla at you." Mac nodded to the side. I walked over to him. "I found this at the club this morning." He handed me a piece of paper. It was the same order as before, the only difference was that time, whoever left a number for me to call once I had everything.

"Did you call the number?" I asked him.

"Yeah, but it's a nonworking number." He told me.

My head nodded as I stared at the paper. "If you can remember dude from the club. Was he about his height and built?" I glanced at Mac as he looked at Joshua.

222

"No, that nigga big as hell. Dude from the club was my size. We gon' figure out whoever it is soon, the nigga seem to really want some shit from you." Mac claimed.

I tore the paper into tiny pieces and put it in my pocket. "Whoever the fuck it is ain't gon' get a gotdamn thing from me because I don't have shit they can buy. On the other hand, even if I did, the mothafucka still ain't getting shit. They doing too much. Fuck'em, let's ball."

"Aye, did you talk to Lil' B about having his party at the club?" Mac asked as we walked to the truck.

"Hell no. But I'mma let him have it at the Shack, though." I hopped in the backseat of the truck and changed into my basketball shorts. Once I was dressed, I went back to the court.

"It's about time yo ass decided to come play, nigga damn. We got this big mothafucka right here." King said pointing to Joshua. "Y'all get Sam's nonplaying ass." He waved Sam off.

"Damn that's fuck'd up, King. That nigga probably don't know how to play." Sam pushed King and took the ball from him.

"I can ball, shid, when you on the yard that's all we did was ball. Don't start talking shit if you can't hoop." Joshua snatched the ball from Sam, turned toward the court and shot. "I'm not a

223

bragging type of nigga though. So, ball up." He told him before he jogged off to my truck.

"Yeah, he on our team." Bell chimed in. "So that's yo brother, huh? Who the oldest?"

I pushed him away from me. "That's Joseph's first son. I don't know the nigga, honestly, so I ain't claiming shit." I shrugged. "Yo, Joshua! Bring yo ass on! We tryna get this game going." I yelled over to him.

"I'ight! Chill the fuck out, I'm coming!" He yelled back.

King laughed as he bounced the ball. "Shid, he look just like y'all ass. You, Blake and Joseph. What Peaches say when she met him?" He asked while shooting the ball.

"Shit, because she ain't met him yet. I don't know that nigga, so I ain't about to bring his ass around my family. Fuck all that." I stole the ball from him and shot.

"I hear that, real shit. You gon' keep yo eye on him?" Bell questioned.

"Hell yeah, why you think he here? The nigga said he been hearing about me while he was locked up. I don't know what the fuck this cat mind done cooked up, so I'mma keep an eye on him." I told them straight up. I didn't trust niggas which they knew and by Joshua wanna come around I was going to be cautious as fuck.

Joshua had changed into a pair of basketball shorts he must have had on under his jeans. I didn't say shit about it.

I tossed Mac the ball and he took it out.

***

"Game bitch!" Joshua called out as he dunked the ball.

"I don't like that mothafucka." Both Sam and Mac claimed, making me laugh.

"How the fuck y'all ass gon' feel that type of way when B act the same mothafuckin' way. Man, you long face bitches. Y'all niggas just mad because we won with y'all weak asses." King clowned as he shook up with Bellow who was cracking the fuck up.

"Man, shut the fuck up. You bitches got lucky, so fuckin' what! King and yo cheating ass can't say shit because those two mothafuckas got all the shots. Old ass mothafucka!" I snapped at him and his ass fell out laughing.

"Nigga, fuck all that bullshit, run that two hunnit." He rubbed his fingers together.

"Fuck you. Sam, pay his ass." I nodded to King.

Sam ran off the court and got the money from his car. When he returned, he slapped the money in his hand. "Fuck ass nigga."

King dished the money out between them.

"What y'all niggas about to get into?" Bell asked looking down at his phone.

"Shit, going straight home. I got work in the morning." Sam told him and I agreed with him.

"Man, I'm about to take my ass to the crib. I gotda be at the Lot early in the morning amongst other shit." I wasn't about to hang out tonight. Hell, I was trying to get my ass to the crib so I could get some. But I wasn't about to tell those niggas that. I didn't need to be reminded that I was whipped over Peaches' ass.

"I got a few moves to make tonight." King shrugged as he tossed his jeans over his shoulder.

"My ass about to go find me some pussy to bury inside of." Mac stated serious as hell making us laugh.

"I'm on that same shit, no lie." Bellow shook up with Mac. "It's certain days I can get the pussy too, and today one of them, nigga I'm about to speed all the way to shorty. A nigga feel like a mothafuckin' addict, real shit. Man, I can taste that shit already." He grunted out and we broke out laughing.

"Boss, I feel you, nigga." I knew exactly how he felt.

"Josh, what you about to get into." King asked him.

"Man, shit, go to the crib and figure out my next move on the job front, you feel me." Joshua told him as he pulled on his jeans.

Everybody nodded to what he said.

"I'ight, we out. I'll get up with y'all later." I shook up with all of them and Joshua did the same. We then parted ways. "Where am I dropping you off at?"

"You can take me to Joseph's he told me to come by there once we were done balling."

Nodding, I turned up the radio and drove to Joseph's house.

***

I pulled in front of Joseph's crib and parked. "Yo, if you serious about being legit with the job, then I can get you in one of my spots. But I'mma tell you now, I don't like lazy ass workers. That's the quickest way to get fired with me, real shit."

"Man, I'm dead serious. I ain't tryna hit these streets no more. So, if you're offering a job, I want it." He sounded serious.

I grabbed my wallet and took a business card out, handing it to him. "Call me on this line in the morning, and we'll go from there."

"I'ight, bet. I appreciate it."

I nodded at him. "Gon' head."

Joshua chuckled then got out the truck. Once he was inside, I pulled off going to the crib.

Chapter 12

Blake

I glanced at Janae to see her nervously chewing on her lip. We sat in the waiting area at Planned Parenthood. She had decided to go through with the abortion, I knew she was only doing it because of me. We had been there for a good fifteen minutes and not once did she say a word to me. She simply sat there, with her leg shaking while biting her lip.

I was a dick to her, I knew that. I tried to apologize but she wasn't trying to hear anything I had to say. Janae was pissed, she ended the relationship and everything. Which I guess I brought on myself.

She suddenly let out a loud breath before standing up. She started pacing. I grabbed her hand and she pulled away from me. "Don't okay." She snapped, then sat back down. "I think I'm about to be sick." She quickly got up and took off toward the bathroom.

I rubbed my head, then grabbed her purse and went to the bathroom. Janae's hands were on the sink, she stood there taking deep breaths.

"I'm okay, you didn't have to come in here." She grabbed a piece of paper towel, wet it then wiped her face.

"Janae—"

"I'm fine, Blake. I'm just ready to get this over with." She sniffled then wiped her eyes.

"Look, you don't have to do this, Janae—"

"Look, just don't, okay. I know what I have to do, Blake. I don't want to abort my baby, but I don't want to trap you with a kid either. You were right, we're not ready for this responsibility. An abortion is the better choice for the both of us." She let out a deep breath and nodded at her reflection in the mirror as if reassuring herself.

I knew she was only telling me that and going along with the abortion because that was what I wanted. Grabbing her arm, I tried to pull her to me, but she snatched away.

"Janae, man stop that shit, damn." My arms went around her waist and I pressed my forehead to hers. "Just know this shit ain't easy for me either." I kissed her forehead and she pushed away from me.

"Yeah, I know." She snatched her purse off the counter then walked out the bathroom.

My hand rubbed over my head before I followed her out. She probably hated my ass for the decision she made because I wasn't ready for a kid. That was something I was going to have to live with. I was going to do what I could until I made it up to her somehow. Regardless of the choice that was made, I wasn't ready for our relationship to end. I really cared for Janae a lot and I wasn't ready to let her go. By the time I made it to the front they had called Janae to the back.

"You're not going to leave, are you?" She asked me.

I pulled her to me once more. "No, I'll be here." I kissed her on the forehead then her lips. Janae's body was literally trembling, that's how nervous she was. That made me feel even more like shit because I couldn't say fuck it and pull her out the clinic. The abortion had to be done, even so, I wanted to ease her and make sure she knew I wasn't leaving her. "I'm not going nowhere, I promise. I love you, Nae." I kissed her forehead and she hugged me tight.

"I love you too, Blake." She kissed me once more then let me go. Turning around, she followed the lady into the back.

Groaning, I went back to my seat. As I sat there waiting, my phone started ringing. Taking the phone out of my pocket, I answered it. "Yeah?" My hand rubbed my forehead as I let out a heavy breath.

"You don't sound to happy. Is there anything I can do to help cheer you up?" The feminine voice spoke sexually through the line.

I caught onto the voice immediately. Pulling the phone from my ear, I glanced at it. My brows furrowed. "Hello?" I stated trying to make sure I heard right.

"Now you sound surprised." She chuckled through the line.

"Mariah, how the fuck you get my number?" I knew damn well I didn't give it to her crazy ass.

"I got it from a friend. It's not that important how I got it though." She stated uncaringly. "So, what has you sulking this morning?"

"Man, why the fuck are you calling me? What do you want?" Mariah wasn't my gotdamn friend, hell, to be honest I had every mind to hang up on her ass because I didn't have no conversation for her.

She smacked her lips loudly into the phone. "I swear you are so gotdamn rude." She let out a heavy sigh. "I haven't talked to you since that day at the restaurant and I wanted to reach out to you. Shanny told me about Janae and the abortion today. I figured this had to be hard on you, so I just wanted to see how you were."

"Shantell ass talk too gotdamn much. She need to learn how to keep her fuckin' mouth shut." I don't know why Janae told that big mouth bitch shit.

"Blake, don't be mad at her. Tell me how you are— better yet, come outside. I just parked next to your car." Mariah informed me.

Again, I glanced at the phone. "You here? Man, yo ass on some bullshit. Mariah, yo ass better leave before my girl done. I ain't fuckin' with you, real shit." That babe was crazy as fuck. Why the hell would she come to an abortion clinic?

"From what I hear, y'all not even together anymore. Janae told me that herself. Blake, just come out here and talk to me for a minute. You're not going to miss anything. Look, if you

233

don't come out here, I'mma come in there where it's a room full of people. Matter of fact, I'm on my way in there."

Quickly getting out of my seat, I left out the clinic. As soon as I made it to the parking lot, Mariah had just got out of her car, and true enough she parked right beside me. That bitch was crazy as fuck.

Once she saw me a wide smile came to her lips. "You didn't have to come out here. I would've came in there and sat with you." Mariah jumped on me, wrapping her arms and legs around my body and kissed me.

Yanking her head back, I pushed her off me. "What the fuck is wrong with you?" My face contorted into a mean mug as I wiped my lips.

Mariah laughed as her thumb wiped the corner of her mouth. "What's wrong with me?" She pointed to herself then shook her head. "You are what's wrong with me. I don't know what it is about you, but ever since we've met, I can't keep you off my mind." She bit into her lower lip. "Then when I tasted you…" Mariah let out a breath as she ran a finger down my cheek.

"When you tasted me? Remember I'm just a little ass boy that you shouldn't be tasting." I pointed out to her as I leaned up against my car with my arms folded over my chest.

She let out another sigh, then ran a hand through her hair. "Look, Blake, I know this ain't right. The attraction I have for you shouldn't exist given our age difference. But I can't help that I'm attracted to you. Regardless of that, it doesn't mean you get to treat me like shit either."

A small laugh left my mouth, and I shook my head at her. "I'm at the clinic with my girl who's getting an abortion and you here confessing your feelings? Man, I ain't tryna here that bullshit, Mariah. Real shit though, I don't like you. I let you suck my dick to relieve my stress at that moment. That's all it was. On top of that shit, you and my girl hang out, hell n'all, man. Sweetheart ain't shit gonna happen between us—"

"Why? Because of Janae? Really, Blake? You two are over. She doesn't want anything to do with you—"

Grabbing Mariah by her shirt, I jerked her to me. "Stop saying that stupid shit. What make you think I'll believe shit yo ass say? Especially after you just stood here saying how you wanted me?"

Mariah glared at me then smacked my hands off her. "Don't flatter yo damn self that much. I'm a lot of things but a liar I am not. Blake, I'm not just saying this because I want you. It's the fuckin' truth. She told me and Shanny that once she gets this abortion, she's done with you. The way you acted toward her because she couldn't decide on what to do, Janae didn't like that." She explained.

I knew she wasn't lying about her ending statement. Hell, she had already broken up with me. I just wasn't ready to accept it. I didn't want to let her go.

"That's why she agreed to have this abortion so she wouldn't have any more ties to you when she officially end things. Believe me or don't, that's your choice." Mariah's hands moved up my chest, then around my neck. She looked hesitant as she stood on her tiptoes. Her hands massaged the nape of my neck. "I promise I'm not lying to you. When you see that I'm not. I'll be here for you… if you need me that is. Maybe I can relieve your stress once again…" She pulled my head down and hesitantly kissed me.

I wasn't lying when I said I didn't want a relationship with Mariah. However, I was a sucker for a sexy ass female and that was her. Not to forget, she swallowed the fuck out of my dick, so if the opportunity presented itself once again, I was definitely going to let her suck me off.

When I didn't pull back, Mariah's head moved back slightly. A smile came to her lips and she kissed me again.

Not once did I kiss her back though. My head pulled back and I moved her arms from my neck, then wiped my lips. "Regardless of how Janae feels right now, she's gonna always be my girl and I'm not looking for anyone to take her place. So, I don't give a fuck what Janae told y'all, she ain't going nowhere." I meant what I said. A part of me found it crazy, hell, funny that since Janae had called it quits, I wasn't trying to let her go. Then again, I never planned on ending what we had going on.

Mariah smiled and laughed before she shrugged. "If you say so." She walked around me, heading for the clinic.

"Where the fuck are you going?" I grabbed her arm, stopping her.

She pulled away from me. "Don't worry, Janae isn't going to find out about us." Mariah smiled and continued to walk inside. "And you're not the reason I'm here, Blake, so relax. I was never here for you." With that she went to the front desk and began talking to the receptionist.

A heavy sigh left my mouth and went to my seat. That damn girl was crazy as shit. I didn't care why she was there and I damn sure wasn't about to ask her ass.

***

When Janae finally came out, I just hugged her as she sobbed hard into my chest. To see her break down the way she had, tore at my heart, that shit really hurt me.

"Nae, baby, don't cry." That was the only thing I thought to say in that moment.

"Janae…" Mariah called out to her. Janae pulled away from me, looked at her and wiped her eyes. "Aw, baby." Mariah walked over and pulled Janae into her arms. "I'm so sorry you have to go through this, babe." She told her as she began to cry with Janae.

"Can we get out of here, please?" Janae asked as she continued to cry.

"Yeah, come on let's go." My hand grabbed hers and she pulled away from me.

"I'm not talking to you. Blake, I wasn't playing, I'm done with you. I swear you don't ever have to worry about me again. Mariah, let's go." Janae shook her head at me then walked out.

I followed behind them. "So, what was the fuckin' point of me even being here if this was your plan all along?" Grabbing her arm, I stopped her from walking to Mariah's car. "What was the fuckin' point, Janae? Huh?" I snapped at her. I was pissed off that she was choosing to end it that way.

"Don't fuckin' touch me! What did you think was going to happen between us, Blake? What? You thought once I had the abortion things were gonna go back to the way they were, huh?" She snapped, pushing me away from her. "It's not. You acted like a straight bitch toward me, so I don't want to be with you. I'm done. Now you can go out and fuck with that bitch Squeaky and any other hoe you want to. The baby was the only tie I had left to you. Now I don't have it anymore, so I'm going to move on like it never happened. I'm pretty sure that's easy for you to do."

My hand rubbed over my mouth and I nodded at what she said. It was taking everything inside me not to choke the fuck out of her ass at that moment. "That's how you feel, cool." I shrugged, then went to my car and got in. I only walked away because I knew if I stood there looking at her for too long, I was going to snap, and it was no telling what the fuck would've left my mouth, but I knew my words was going to hurt her ass no doubt. I couldn't do her like that, she was hurting enough from having the abortion. That was the only reason I was going to let her walk off for the time being.

Once my car was started my phone dinged with a text notification. Reading the message, I laughed.

I can relieve your stress if you want me to. You can come to my apartment if you want. If so… all you have to do is ask for my address.

I knew it was from Mariah's ass. That was some fuck'd up shit. Janae sitting in the car with that bitch and she was texting me.

That was her whole reason for coming up to the clinic in the first fuckin' place. I still didn't get why the fuck Janae stupid ass had me up there if she was going to have that hoe pick her up. Even though I did plan on being there for her to begin with.

I was pissed off that she played the fuck out of my ass. Fuck her stupid ass. I replied to Mariah telling her to send me her address. After that, I called up Ace.

The phone rung three times before he answered. "Yeah, what's good?"

"Shit, just leaving the clinic with Janae. Where the fuck you at?"

240

"At my pops crib. You about to slide through?" He questioned while yawning into the phone.

"Yeah, I'll be there in a minute." I ended the call and made my way to Jerron's house.

***

"She called Mariah to come pick her up?" Ace questioned as he shot the ball up.

Catching it, I tossed the ball back to him. "Shid apparently so. Man, that shit crazy as fuck though. Fuck'd up thing about it, I told that stupid mothafucka I loved her ass. She said it back only to have Mariah ass come up there. I feel dumb as fuck about that shit, for real."

Ace started laughing as he air balled. Grabbing the ball, I went to the line and shot. "I told yo dumb ass to let the mothafucka keep that damn baby. Nigga, she wanted that mothafucka even though y'all ass ain't ready for no gotdamn kid. But I blame yo stupid ass for even getting in that situation—"

"Man, shut the fuck up ain't nobody trying to hear that shit." I shot the ball, and he threw it back at me.

"Because yo ass know you fuck'd up. I don't give a fuck how drunk yo ass were when you fuck'd that babe, you shouldn't have ran in her ass raw, period. None of this shit would have happened if yo ass didn't get reckless while fuckin' with shorty. And yo ass was trippin' off on her about the whole abortion—"

"We weren't ready for no mothafuckin' baby. I was trippin' on her ass? How was me telling her that shit wrong? I don't want no gotdamn kids right now. I can't afford to have no damn baby. And I damn sho' ain't tryna have my folks help raise my kid either. I fuck'd up once, I mean, shit happens." I shot the ball and hit.

"That's true but still, B, yo ass can't be fuckin' up like that. What you need to do is get these bitches out yo head for the time being and focus on your gotdamn future. That way this slip up won't happen again."

My brows furrowed, my head tilted, and I stopped bouncing the ball. I just stared at his ass. "Nigga, shut the fuck up! You run in every bitch you see, and Ashanti ass done had how many abortions? Nigga, get the fuck outda here tryna lecture me on my shit and yo ass worse than me."

"Oh, that's some fuck'd up shit to say to me. Regardless of my shit, what I'm saying to you, is true which yo ass know. Ashanti ass had those abortions because that's what she wanted to do.

242

I didn't tell her ass to do that shit, but this not about me. Point is, Blake, be careful out here fuckin' these bitches. That's how niggas fuck up because of a mistake and then blame it on being drunk. Don't fuck around and raw dick a crazy bitch and she end up pregnant. She might not be like Janae and get rid of the kid."

He was right, but I was always careful. Hell, I wasn't fuckin' with too many females other than Janae and Squeaky. But it was mainly just Janae.

"I may seem calm right now, but I'm pissed off. I wanna choke the shit out of Janae ass." I threw the ball at the backboard and missed.

Ace chuckled. "Yeah, because you love her, for real and you just now realizing the shit. Just give her time, maybe she'll come around and if she don't then fuck her." He threw his arm over my shoulder and pushed the ball into my chest. "Don't let this thing with Janae get you down. At the end of the day you made the better decision for the both of you. If she can't see that then it's her loss." He shrugged. "Besides, if she doesn't want you, I know Sienna would love to have yo ass."

Looking over at him, I broke out laughing at the mention of Squeaky.

"Nigga, you laughing and I'm serious as hell. Squeaky crazy about yo ass. All she talks about is you. Man, you should've seen her when you and Janae showed up. Squeaky feelings were hurt." He chuckled throwing the ball toward the rim.

My hand rubbed my head and I shrugged. I wasn't really thinking about Squeaky ass, she had a nigga on top of that she was already clingy as hell.

"Blake, what I tell yo ass about parking in my gotdamn spot?" Jerron yelled from the back door.

"I told yo ass he was gonna bitch at you." Ace laughed as he walked toward the back door.

"My fault, Ron, I keep forgetting." Going up to him, we shook up and he pulled me into a one armed hug.

"You say that shit every damn time. Now go move yo damn car and park my truck." He tossed me his keys, then popped Ace on the back of his head. "Why you ain't tell his ass not to park there?" He questioned him as we walked into the house.

"I told his ass, but shid, he ain't listen." We walked into the kitchen and Ace grabbed some plates. "Blake, you eating?" He asked, motioning toward the Chinese food and fried chicken.

"Hell yeah." I went to the counter and grabbed a plate.

"If y'all don't go wash yo damn hands." Ron snatch the bag from Ace. "Y'all ass know better. Go and Blake yo ass bet not forget to park my truck."

"I got you, Jerron." Chuckling, I jogged off to the bathroom and washed my hands.

Once I finished my phone dinged with a notification. Pulling it from my pocket, I looked at it and shook my head.

Am I going to see you tonight? I really want to see you.

Mariah's text read.

Me: *I don't know yet. I'll let you know.*

Mariah: *Well I hope I'll see you.*

I chose not to respond back to her. Instead I texted Janae asking if I could come over and talk to her. After a few seconds it showed that the message was read. One thing I wasn't gonna do was harass or beg her ass to talk to me. If that was how she chose to end it then so be it.

Fuck her.

Chapter 13

Blaze

I sat in my office at the Lot waiting on Peaches ass to come through. It had just turned twelve o'clock and I was horny as fuck waiting on her ass to get there. I was seconds away from telling her we could meet halfway.

I was becoming impatient as hell waiting for her ass. It seemed like she was taking her sweet ass time driving. Pulling out my phone, I called her.

"Hello—" She began to say after the first ring.

I cut her words off the moment I heard her voice. "Man, where the fuck you at?" The line got quiet and I laughed. "Yeah I'm talking to yo short yellow ass. Baby, where you at though, for real?"

"I'll be there in about fifteen minutes—"

"Fifteen minutes? Really? Hell no. Yo ass can't talk all that shit, get me worked up then take forever to get here. Yo black ass on some straight bullshit. I could've made it to yo ass in about five minutes. My damn balls heavy and my dick hurt, I'm so gotdamn hard."

Peaches broke out laughing. "Babe, seriously? Yo ass wouldn't have made it to me in no gotdamn five minutes. Papa Bear, you're acting kind of thirsty for some pussy right now—"

I looked at the phone with a raised brow. "The fuck you mean kinda? I'm over here desperate as fuck." I grunted out before I laughed. "Man, Peach, why yo ass had to tease me like that? You know yo ass can't be talking that good shit to me."

"Babe, I wasn't teasing you. I promise we're gonna tear that office up as soon as I get there." Peaches stated, but I kind of tuned her out as I heard voices in front of my office door.

"Peach, hold on…" I didn't wait to hear her reply as I muted the phone. I then got up and went to the door, opening it. A tall dark-skinned man dressed down in an all black suit stood in the hall with Lisa, my front assistant.

"What the hell is y'all doing back here?" My arms folded over my chest as I glared at the pair.

Lisa looked shocked before she immediately began to explain. "Mr. Carter, I tried to stop him from coming back here but he insisted on speaking with you and walked back here on his own."

My office area was restricted from everyone. If they needed me in the front, I was simply to be called. My eyes slid to the man in the suit. "I don't know what it is you want with me and personally I don't give a fuck. If you're here to purchase a car which I doubt, but cars are out front a sales associate will help you." I told him as I started to walk back into my office.

"Blaze, I'm not here to get a car—"

"I assumed you weren't but that's not my business. If a car ain't what you're here for, then you have no business here with me. Now, if you have a particular car in mind that you want to discuss privately, then Lisa will set up a meeting and we can discuss that specific automobile." I nodded toward Lisa and she gave me a faint smile. "Now, if you'll excuse me, I have a meeting I need to attend." I walked back into my office and closed the door behind me. Grabbing my phone, I sat back down in my chair just as my office door came opened and the dude with the suit walked in and closed the door behind him.

"Hey, the meeting we had, I have to cancel. I'll call you later to reschedule." I told Peaches.

"What? Why?" I heard her say before I ended the call. Once I did, I sent her a text telling her not to come to the Lot.

"Mr. Carter—" Lisa called as she busted into the room.

"A few weeks ago, you received an order…" The man began saying as he came to the chair in front of my desk.

"I tried to stop him, but he wouldn't listen. Do you want me to call the police?" Lisa asked.

I waved her off. "No, don't. I got this you can get back to work." Once she closed the door, I waited for a minute to make sure she was gone before my eyes slid to the man. "If you wanted to meet me this bad, why not come here sooner instead of sending dumb ass notes and nonworking fuckin' numbers and shit?"

He pointed to the chair he stood in front of. "You don't mind if I sit, do you?" He pulled the seat back while unbuttoning his suit jacket.

"I personally don't want yo ass in my office, but that ain't stop yo ass from coming in this bitch, did it?" I pointed out as I made myself comfortable in my seat.

He sat down as a chuckle left his mouth. "I knew I was going to like you. But, first, let me apologize for the way you were approached to begin with. At the time I knew nothing about him putting in an order, or you receiving a number from him until after the fact. One of my partners was trying to do some underhanded shit behind my back, by trying to do business with you, not caring that you were no longer in the game. Because of his actions I decided to come to you myself, a sign of good faith, you know?" He exclaimed with a faint smirk.

I shrugged at the short story he told me. The fact that he mentioned I was no longer in the game, didn't sit right with me. Humming, I sat up straight in my chair. "What's yo reason for really being here?"

He was quiet for minute, then mimicked my actions, sitting up as well. "I want you to come work for me—"

"Get the fuck out of here." My head shook, and I laughed.

"I'm serious, Blaze. I think we can make a lot of money together. I know you've been out of the game for years and I must admit, I'm

250

impressed by the work you've achieved. I've done my homework on you and learned that you're well calculated and smart with the shit you do. I admire your work ethics and I think you'll be good for my business. If you decide to come work for me, you can run the shit how you see fit—"

"Look, whoever the fuck you are, I'm not interested. Shid, to be honest I'm lost as to what the fuck you even talking about. Whatever has you impressed by me lose that infatuation because I'm not working for you or with you." Dude was a straight clown to even approach me with that dumb shit. What the fuck did I look like working for another mothafucka?

"Let me explain this to you so that yo ass understand me clearly. I've been working for myself since I was damn near eleven, so if you've really done your homework as you claim, then you know how I've done for myself. Knowing that, why the fuck would I want to go off and work for another nigga?" I laughed at him as I got out of my seat. "Man, get yo clown ass the fuck out my gotdamn office and don't bring yo dumb ass back here. The next time I'm not gon' be this fuckin' nice. Stupid mothafucka." I went to the door and opened it.

"You're making a mistake, Blaze. We could make a lot of money together, and you don't have to look at it as you're working for me but instead with me. Don't give me an answer now, think on it. You'll make a lot of money with me, Blaze. By the way, I'm—"

"I don't need to know your name. I never saw you before and this talk never happened." I nodded toward the door.

He let out a chuckle. "I'll be in touch." With a head nod, he walked out of my office.

I closed the door behind him, then went to the security monitors to see what type of car he got in. He walked to a black and gold Rolls Royce. Before he got into the driver's seat, he looked up at the camera that was pointed directly in front of his car. Putting two fingers to the side of his head he gave a slight salute with a smirk, then hopped in his car.

Nodding, I let out a laugh then went back to my desk. I then texted Mac, telling him to meet me at the club in an hour. After I sent that message, I called Peaches.

She answered the phone on the first ring and let out a heavy breath. "I'm on my way back to work now and I'm not turning around." The attitude in her voice couldn't be mistaken.

I laughed at her snappy ass. "Something came up at the last minute—"

"For real, Blaze I don't even care. I drove all the way from Hobart to yo raggedy ass Lot only

to be turned around. Man, hell no, fuck you—"
a small chuckle left my mouth. "You always
think some shit funny when it's not."

"Peach, it wasn't my fault. Hold the fuck up,
now when I was calling yo ass to hurry up and
get here, yo black ass thought the shit was
fuckin' funny. Now that shit done changed you
wanna be pissed off at me? That's some bullshit.
Yo ass better sit in yo car and play with yo
pussy—"

"Fuck you, Blaze—"

I broke out laughing, Peaches was pissed the
fuck off. My baby really wanted some dick.

"Ain't shit funny for real, Blaze. Man, fuck
you." She snapped at me.

The line went quiet and I looked at the phone
to see that she had hung up on my ass. That
mothafucka was mad because she couldn't get
no dick for real. I called her back, but she sent
me to voicemail. I then sent her a text message.

*Yo ass done lost yo gotdamn mind. You
really gon' hang up on me? Let me call yo
baldheaded ass one more time and you don't
answer.*

Once I saw that she read the message, I
called her back and just like before she sent me
to voicemail. My head nodded as I sent her
another text while leaving my office.

253

I'm fuckin' yo black ass up. That's a promise Peaches.

***

"So, this nigga just showed up and ask you to work for him?" Mac asked, laughing. I nodded. "You should have at least seen what the fuck he was talking about."

"Why the fuck should I have entertained that bullshit? Mac, what the fuck I look like working for another nigga? Especially not with a mothafucka I don't even know. If I wanna slang some work or whatever, I'll do that shit on my own." Mac leaned back in his chair and smiled at me. I started laughing. "Nigga, I ain't saying I'mma start back. I'm just saying if I wanted to—"

"Aye, big homie you don't have to explain shit to me. I know what you meant but answer me this. Tell me you don't miss it." A smirk came to his face as he kicked his feet up on my desk.

I looked down at his shoes, then to him. "Get yo gotdamn feet down." He let out a groan, then moved his feet. "Yo ass acting like Blake black ass."

"Man, answer the gotdamn question. Do you miss it? Back then yo ass was on top of shit out here. You the only mothafucka I know who done made it out this shit alive and you gone tell me you don't have that itch to do some more shit, B?" Mac pulled a blunt from his ear, then lit it.

My hand rubbed over my head and I shrugged. "It was work that I'm good at. I got out the shit because I decided to become a family man. So no I don't miss it." I was done with the game because I had more to life now than just that high; I got when I was hustling. Peaches and my kids was what I needed. Hell, with the money I made from slanging we had more than enough to live off for life. Not only that, but my clubs and car lot was doing good as fuck.

"Nigga, don't give me the answer you'll give yo wife. Hell, I miss the shit sometimes, real shit." Mac admitted, and I shrugged.

"That's because yo ass don't have a wife or kids. You don't really have shit serious, so of course you'll miss it. These streets were yo only main bitch for years and until you find someone to replace that with," again, I shrugged. "You'll always have that itch to run back to yo main bitch. You feel me?"

Mac poured himself a shot and tossed it back. "Nigga, fuck all that. If I get that shit, then I'll just turn these streets into my side bitch—"

"Yo shut the fuck up!" I was cracking up at his dumbass.

"Real shit though, B, this nigga might not go away that easily." He pointed out.

Taking a square from my desk, I lit it. Inhaling the smoke, I then released it. "I don't expect him to. He wants something and for him to come to me himself, he'll definitely be back. When he do, I'll deal with him—"

"We'll deal with that shit." Mac corrected as he lit a blunt. His hand came out and I shook up with him.

"Definitely." I agreed. After how Mac went on a killing rampage when he thought I was dead. It was without a doubt I could trust him. He was my little nigga. That was why I brought him under my wing and looked out for him.

***

For the next few hours, we continued to put smoke in the air. We were high as hell when the buzzer rung, informing us that somebody was out front. I pulled up the cameras to see a Bentley parked by my truck. Mac stood, grabbing his gun.

"Nigga, sit yo high ass down. It ain't gonna be none of that bullshit in here." Even though I said that I took the safety off my gun, just in case.

We left out my office and went to the front. As soon as I opened the door, Mac pulled out his gun aiming it.

"Ah!" Britt yelled as she raised her hands. "It's just me!" She hollered.

"Oh shit. Man, yo ass better call next time. The fuck is wrong with you." Mac snapped, before grabbing her arm and pulling her inside.

"I didn't know I was supposed to call. What the hell is going on?" Britt asked Mac confused.

I was leaned against the wall cracking the fuck up. My nigga was high as fuck and paranoid like a mothafucka.

"Why are you laughing, Blaze? What's wrong with y'all?" She questioned.

I pointed to Mac, still laughing. "That mothafucka high as fuck, yo. He trippin', Britt. You good, man. Who car is that you driving?" I pointed toward the door.

"Dude, let me go." She pulled away from Mac, then looked at me smiling. "My friend. He said I can use it since mine is in the shop."

My brows raised at that. "Who the fuck is yo damn friend? Britt, don't get yo baldheaded ass fuck'd up, talkin' 'bout yo damn friend. I'll knock yo ass out."

Britt eyes rolled at me. "Don't start with me Blaze, I'm grown as hell and can have male friends—"

"She fuckin' that nigga, B, ain't no friend gon' let her whip a Benz if ain't no pussy involved, and that bitch clean as fuck too. He fuckin' the shit out of her ass." Mac pointed out while standing in the door, looking at the royal blue Benz.

Brittany turned and glared at Mac before muffing his head to the side. "Shut the fuck up. Like I said, I'm grown as fuck. Don't get mad and jealous and start telling shit because I didn't wanna take yo shit for a drive." She snapped at him. "Now tell that shit."

I glared at Mac. "You tried to fuck with my sister?"

He shrugged. "I was tryna get on some you and Peaches' type shit. Wife the homie sister… I wasn't doing shit yo ass didn't do. Didn't King tell you not to fuck with his sister—" I jumped at his ass and he bounced back swinging. "B, don't make me knock yo old ass out. I ain't tryna fuck with yo sister no more. Nigga that was about seven years ago when I first met her ugly ass. I don't know why she's bringing up old shit." He stated before looking at Britt.

I knew Mac was a hoe when it came to women, so him fuckin' with Britt was out of the question. I would've had to beat his ass if some shit went down between them, but learning it was years ago and Britt ain't go for his shit, I was cool. I knew Britany only threw that shit out there so I wouldn't be on her ass about the nigga she was seeing.

"Who the fuck is this nigga though?" I questioned while nodding to Mac. "Go get that plate number and shit. Make sure that bitch ain't stolen." He laughed and walked out the club.

Brittany's lips smacked, and she walked off to the bar. "You don't even have to do all that Blaze. It's not stolen, and his name is Kordell, we've been dating for a year and he's so sweet to me. He treats me so good. I've been wanting you to meet him, but I know how you are, and I don't want you to scare him off." She whined out.

I laughed at her. "You sound dumb as hell man. If that nigga like you he ain't gone let no mothafucka scare him off. If he does," I shrugged. "Then he a bitch and you need to find a new nigga, simple as that. You hear me?" If a nigga wasn't worth her time, I was going to let her know.

"I understand all that, but Blaze... you're... you. I mean first off, you're not the nicest person at all, you're mean as hell. I want you to meet him... but... I don't know man especially because I really like him." She looked stressed out as she spoke.

I didn't know what to tell her to ease her mind. "If you really like him, I'll meet him for you, and I'll be myself."

Brittany broke out laughing. "You're so damn helpless. You missed my whole point. I don't want you to be yourself when you meet him. I've told him all about you though and he really wants to meet you." She stated but still seemed conflicted on what to do.

I didn't care anymore Brittany was grown and could do what she wanted. Plus, it really was best if I didn't meet the dude. I dropped the topic. "What brought yo ass here. I know it ain't to show off that damn car or talk to me about that nigga. What's up Britt?"

She blew out a breath as her eyes rolled. "Have you talked to Joshua? Joseph keep on bugging me to meet that man, but I don't know. So… I wanted to see if you met with him and what was your vibe of him?"

I pulled a square from my pocket and I lit it. "He straight. I gave him a job at the garage and shit. I don't know too much about him, but shid don't go off my vibe of a mothafucka, feel him out for yoself." Hell, Joshua was straight, but I didn't plan on hanging with the nigga, brother or not.

"Well that's something if you got him a job. He might not be all that off then. What Peaches think about him?" She questioned, and I shrugged.

"She hasn't met the nigga yet."

She nodded. "Well I'll think about meeting him, it probably won't be too bad to have another brother, hopefully he's nicer." She glanced at me with a little smile, which made me laugh. "Anyway, I was thinking that maybe I should let Peaches meet Kordell first because if she likes him, she could probably get you to be nice." She explained.

I laughed at that. I didn't know why mothafuckas thought going through Peaches first would make a difference with me. "If she like the mothafucka that's not gonna change how I feel. On a serious tip, don't go telling niggas about me. Nobody needs to know yo ass my sister, for real, Britt, keep that shit between us."

Her lips popped, and she pushed away from me, going to the pool table. "Don't nobody know I'm yo damn sister. You so damn irritating I swear. Maybe I should meet Joshua, he's probably a better brother than yo ass."

"Aye, B, I got to make a run right quick. I'll get up with you later." Mac called from the door.

I tossed two fingers at him and he left out the club once again.

"Let's get a game." Brittany tossed me a pool stick. "I'll break." She pushed me out of her way and went to the front of the table.

"You gon' make me fuck yo ass up, keep playing with me." I told her as I pulled out my phone as it vibrated. Looking at the message from Peaches I laughed.

Wifey: *I hope yo ass is horny tonight. Just know I'll be knocked out and you bet not wake me up either. You on your own for dinner tonight.*

That mothafucka was for real pissed because she couldn't get no dick. Laughing I put my phone away and started playing pool with Brittany.

Chapter 14

Peaches

"Ooh, Blaze, fuck baby." I moaned before biting into the pillow. Blaze hand gripped tight into my hair and he jerked my head back. His hips thrust fast and hard into me from behind. Blaze hand soon came down on my ass. "Ooh, baby, you feel so damn good."

With his grip tight on my hair, his hand came down on my ass, causing my pussy to suck around him faster. His hand came down again before he gripped my shoulder, his dick stroking deep into my love box.

"Ooh, shit, I love you so much!" I cried out in pleasure as my body shook.

Blaze pulled me up to his chest by my hair. Turning my head to the side, he kissed me deeply as his fingers toyed with my swollen pearl. My pussy was throbbing rapidly as my orgasm reached its peak.

He pushed me back down and slapped my ass hard. "Fuck that dick, Peaches." He popped my booty again before he started moving it on his thick hard shaft.

"Aah, shit." I moaned.

"Fuck that shit, Peach, this yo dick remember, take that shit." Blaze shook my ass before slapping both cheeks hard.

I started throwing my ass back, bouncing on his dick at a rapid pace.

"Ah, fuck. Get that shit." His hands gripped my hips, his pelvis pushed against my ass as he released his nut inside me. "Ah, shit…" He grunted out. "Fuck, Peach. Damn." He continued to groan.

My ass slowly rolled on him as I laid on the pillow.

"Gotdamn…" His hand squeezed my ass before he slapped it. Leaning over me, he kissed the center of my back. "You keep fuckin' me like that, I'mma have to marry yo ass again." He groaned against my back.

I let out a breathless laugh. "You so stupid."

Blaze finally pulled out, then laid on the side of me. "I'm serious as fuck, Peach." His hand came down on my ass.

"B, stop. Stupid ass." I snapped at him and he hit me again.

"Shut the fuck up. You don't be saying stop when I'm smacking that shit while we fuckin'." He slapped my ass once more.

Laughing again, I rolled over cuddling next to him. "That's different. It feels good then."

Taking hold of my chin, he tilted my head back and kissed me. "You felt good. Yo shit still got a nigga sprung after all these damn years." Smiling, I kissed him back. "That's why I be telling bitches, I'm a happily married man because yo ass can handle this dick."

My lips pursed together, and my eyes rolled. "Nigga, don't make it seem like you're only with me because I can please you sexually. Nigga, yo ass is in love with me."

Blaze shrugged. "Shid, that's why we stayed together for so long is because of the sex—"

Sitting up, I punched him in the chest. "Keep fuckin' playing with me, Blaze."

"Damn, Peach, I was just bullshittin'." He laughed while holding his chest. He looked down at the spot I punched then glared at me. "Yo baldheaded ass hit me like that again, I'mma choke the fuck out of you." He threatened.

Again, my eyes rolled. "You shouldn't play with me like that then. Ugly ass." I snapped while placing my leg over his. My arm then went around his waist and I kissed his chest. I felt Blaze looking at me and I laughed. "Don't you say shit."

He moved my leg and arm from his body. "Fuck all that. Get yo ass up. How you gone talk shit and then try to get comfortable? Get the fuck up."

Laughing, I held on to him tighter. "Stop, Blaze, I'm sorry."

"That's what the fuck I thought. Yo ass happy now that you got some dick?" He chuckled, and I did the same.

"Yup. Happy and satisfied. I don't know why you be playing with me." I kissed his chest once more before rolling on top of him. "You never told me what came up though." Biting his chest, I kissed the skin before looking up at him.

He let out a groan, then rubbed a hand down his face. My eyes rolled at the action and I sat up sighing. I knew it was some bullshit. Hell, I knew Blaze well enough to know his movement gestures.

"Man, lay the fuck down. It ain't shit." He grabbed my arms and pulled me back on his chest. "Some nigga just popped up at the Lot and offered me a job." He stated nonchalantly with a shrug.

From his actions, I thought it was some bullshit, but not that. Why would someone come to his place of business and offer him a job? That didn't make sense to me. I sat up and stared down at him.

"Babe, that don't make sense. What type of job was it?"

Blaze looked away from me and licked his lips. He then shrugged as his hand rubbed over his head. I punched him in the chest. "If you gonna lie then don't tell me shit." With an attitude, I started to get off him.

He grabbed my arm, stopping me. "Man, you better chill the fuck out. I ain't even say shit yet, so how the fuck am I lying?" He snapped at me.

I pulled my arm from him. "B, I been with yo ass long enough to know when you're thinking about lying to me. Like don't play with me, B, I know you more than you know yo damn self. You were about to lie. Now lie and say you wasn't." I scowled him waiting for him to tell me otherwise.

He glared at me for a second before he laughed. "What I just tell yo ass? Chill the fuck out. I wasn't about to lie…entirely." He added as he placed his hands behind his head. "I didn't know the nigga, so I wasn't really up for much of a conversation." He shrugged again. "But the nigga apparently wanted me to sell some work for him. He admired my previous hustle and wanted me to push some shit for him."

I was even more confused. "Why would he think to come to you out of all people? Especially when you don't hustle anymore?" I stared at him trying to see if he was going to make any gestures regarding my ending statement.

"Fuck if I know. I told his ass I wasn't interested. I been working for myself since I was eleven. What the fuck I look like pushing weight for another mothafucka?" He made a good point.

"So… that was it? He just left?" I didn't see the man's point in reaching out to Blaze at all. Why would he think someone like Blaze would work for him?

"He said he'll be in touch, but I ain't worried about it. It's crazy though, for real because I've never seen that nigga before." He stated.

"What was his name?" Blaze shrugged again, and I started laughing. "Only you would not get the name of the nigga that came looking for you—ah!" I screamed out as he rolled us over.

"Because I'm not worried about no unknown nigga. All I care about right now is getting in them guts..." He growled while wrapping my legs around his waist.

"Daddy!" Brianna pounded on the door.

Blaze groaned out of irritation. "Man, yo fuckin' kid." He whispered while glancing at the door, he then looked back to me and pressed his fingers to my lips. "She'll probably leave." He whispered.

My lips pressed together tightly as I tried my hardest not to laugh at him.

"Daddy!" She banged harder on the door. "I can't sleep. Can I come in?"

Blaze head shook at her question. The doorknob soon started twisting. But she couldn't get in because the door was locked.

"Daddy, please—"

"Brianna, take yo ass to sleep, making all that damn noise." Blake snapped at her.

"Shut up talking to me, Blake. Stupid ugly little self. Mommy!" She continued to bang on the door. Brianna ass was worrisome as hell. "Mommy, please? I can't sleep." Brianna whined.

Blaze head dropped, and he sighed as if defeated. I glared at him. "You better fuckin' not. She'll go away."

"She gon' stand there until we open the door. You know that shit." He was saying as he tried to get up.

My legs immediately tightened around him so he couldn't move. "Well, let her stay out there. We not finished here—"

"Daddy, I'm scared. I keep hearing noises." She sniffled.

"Bria!" Blake yelled.

"Shut up, Blake! That's why I'm telling mommy you about to leave—aah!" She started screaming before we heard loud footsteps pounding as they ran.

"Yo fuckin' kids' man, damn." Blaze pried my legs from his waist and got out the bed. "Peach, change the sheets."

My lips popped, and I rolled my eyes at him. "I ain't changing shit. You do it." I got out the bed and went into the bathroom, slamming the door behind me. I was pissed. Blaze was such a damn sucker when it came to Brianna's ass.

Hell, I wanted to be able to sleep in my bed, with my husband naked as hell all damn night. That little girl was such a damn cock blocker.

I was beyond irritated with them, so I decided to take a nice warm bath and relax myself. All the while hoping Blaze was smart to bring his ass into the bathroom and get in with me.

Of course, he didn't come, Bri-Bri had his full attention.

***

I laid in the bed with a glass of wine and the first book my best friend, Angel ever published, titled *Syn*. I was so proud of my girl. I never knew how true the events were that took place in her life and to learn that Blaze had once helped her out so much. I knew I had one of the best men in the world.

Sighing, I glanced at Brianna who laid between me and Blaze. I then looked at him, only to find his eyes on me. My eyes rolled at him and I took another sip of my wine.

"You really sitting over there with an attitude? Let's go in the bathroom and I'll make it up to you." He bit into his bottom lip with a smirk on his face.

"Why should I go into the bathroom when I have a whole ass bed and room..." My words trailed off as Bria turned over, throwing her legs across mine. "You get on my damn nerves. She gone have to start sleeping in her own damn room at some point." I finished off my wine, then sat the empty glass down. I was really pissed at him and Briana.

"I'll go put Bri-Bri in her bed." He stated. When I rolled my eyes again. He got out the bed and picked up Bria, then left out the room.

Blaze thought I was playing with his ass. I closed my book, turned off my nightlight then made myself comfortable under the covers. I had just closed my eyes when the bedroom door closed. I pulled the covers tighter over me.

He slid in behind me, wrapping his arm around my waist. I shrugged my shoulder pushing his face off it. "Move, B, I'm trying to go to sleep. I'm tired." I claimed.

His teeth scraped along my shoulder as he gripped the hem of my nightgown, raising it above my thighs. "She ain't gon' sleep in here no more, bet?" Grabbing my breast, he squeezed it while pinching my erect nipple.

Again, I shrugged. "I'm going to bed."

His hips pushed into my ass, causing his thick hard dick to push between my cheeks. Instinctively, my ass pushed back. Even though I was mad at him, I was also weak when it came to that man. I simply loved having sex with him. It was amazing point-blank period.

Blaze raised my leg, his hips moved, pushing his man through my fold. "You gon' let him eat, Peach?" His tip pushed into my pussy and I bit into my bottom lip so that I wouldn't moan out. "Fuck, you wet…" Blaze grunted as his tip continued to push in and out of my pussy.

"Mmm, shit." I finally let the moan I'd been holding in, out. That was all Blaze needed to hear as he thrust, filling me completely.

Chapter 15

Blake

H appy birthday, Blake!" The loud screams that filled my bedroom, and somebody jumping on my damn bed, immediately woke me up. Groaning, I pulled the cover over my head.

"Get up, Blake!" Brianna yelled, jumping on my bed. She then flopped on the side of me and started yanking the covers from my head.

"Bria, I'mma knock yo ass out. Stop!" I pushed her off me.

"Stop, stupid!" Her hand whacked hard as hell over my head three times.

274

"I'm about to beat yo ass." I pushed the covers off me.

"Aah! Daddy!" She screamed then ran out my room.

"Stupid ass little girl." I snapped as I sat up.

"Leave that damn girl alone." Ace laughed as he yanked the covers the rest of the way off me. "Get yo ass up birthday boy." He tossed the balled up cover on me.

"He gon' beat yo ass next Ace." BJ told him as he sat beside me. "Happy birthday, bro." He handed me a card.

"Thanks." His hand came out and he shook up with me.

"Come on, mommy made breakfast." BJ got off the bed and ran out my room.

"What time is it?" I asked, leaning against the headboard. I was tired as fuck. I didn't get in until after one messing with Janae stuck up ass. Ever since she had the abortion, Janae was dead set on not fucking with me or seeing my ass. After I brought my birthday in with Ace and a few friends from school.

I was wasted as fuck and turned into a gotdamn stalker. I had blown Janae's phone up as I sat outside her crib. She still didn't answer the phone or text me back. I thought since we went to school together seeing and talking to her would've been easier. Nope. The plus for Janae on the school front was that we had no classes together. Shorty was like a damn ghost to me.

"It's ten o'clock. Now get yo ass up. We got shit to do birthday boy. Come on." Ace urged.

Groaning, I threw my legs on the side of the bed and grabbed my phone. "I'll be out there in a minute. Close my door." I told him, and he left out my room. My attention went back to my phone.

Janae: *Happy birthday. Hope you enjoy your day.*

Mariah: *Happy birthday Blake. Hope I get to see you tonight.*

Squeaky: *Happy B-day baby. See you tonight.*

Unlocking my phone, I replied to Janae's message. *Thanks. You'll be at the party tonight?*

Once I saw the message was read, I waited for her response. After a few minutes, I tossed my phone to the side then went and hopped in the shower.

***

"Happy birthday, baby." My momma kissed my cheek. "You've grown up to damn fast. You're seventeen." Her head shook as she hugged me tight.

Laughing, I kissed the top of her head. "Thanks, Ma. What you get me though?" I asked.

She pushed me away from her as she laughed. "Not a damn thing but these seventeen hits."

My dad came over and shook up with me. "You ready for yo present?"

My hands rubbed together. "Yeah, give it to me." He jogged out the living room.

"Here." Brianna gave me a card then sat in my lap. "Open it." She urged. Doing as she said, inside of the card was a pink lollipop and a twenty-dollar bill just like BJ's card. "You like it?"

"Yeah, thanks, Bri-Bri." Hugging her, I kissed her cheek.

"You welcome. You gonna take me to the store and by me something?" She asked, taking the taped sucker from the card. "You gon' eat this?" She questioned.

Brianna was irritating as hell and talked to damn much. But she made it hard not to love her ass. "Yeah, I'mma eat it." Taking the sucker from her, I opened it and put it in my mouth. "It's good too."

She rolled her eyes at me. "That was my only sucker. I shouldn't have given it to you. Ugly butt." My brows raised at her. How she gonna talk shit to me and be sitting on my lap. I tried to push her off me. "Stop! I was just playing!" Her arms wrapped around my neck and she held onto me tight.

"That don't make no sense how spoiled that damn girl is." Ace shook his head.

"My dad got her like this." As I said that my dad walked back into the room.

"Brianna, move." He told her, and she groaned before getting off my lap. "Here." My dad handed me a silver case.

Smiling, I took it from him excited and opened it. "Damn. Yo…" Inside the case was a gold desert eagle .50AE with a black handle. The bitch was beautiful as fuck. "Thanks." Getting up I pulled him into a hug.

"Let's see how she shoot." He stated.

"Hell yeah. Ace, you got yo gun?" I questioned, and he pulled out a black berretta. "Let's go. BJ!" I yelled.

He ran back into the living room where we were. "What's up?"

"We about to go to the shed—"

"I'm coming. Let me get my shoes." He took off running to his room.

"Just meet us out there." I told him as we headed out the back.

***

We were in the soundproof shed shooting for a couple hours. My momma and Brianna came out as well. Brianna was handling a Ruger SR22 and BJ had a 9mm. I had just emptied my clip when my dad tapped my arm. He nodded toward the door for me to follow him out.

"Happy birthday, Blake." Sha'Keema hugged me.

"Thanks, Sha." Once I let her go, she walked over to Ace. "What's up Unc." We slapped hands, shaking up.

"What's up. Happy birthday boy. Are we hitting the strip joint tonight?" He asked.

"No!" My momma said from behind me. "He ain't old enough to be in no damn strip club." She snapped while rolling her eyes. "King, don't make me hurt you."

He looked at me and winked. "My crib." He stated, and I started laughing.

"Blake, let's go." My dad yelled at me as he headed to the front yard.

While following him, I took out my phone checking my messages.

Mariah: *So, you're just going to ignore my message?*

That wasn't the message I was looking for. I clicked on Janae message and she still hadn't replied.

Me: *Yo ass actin stupid as fuck Janae real shit. Now when I stop reaching out to yo retarded ass I don't wanna hear shit. Stupid actin' mothafucka for real. Yo ass starting to piss me off.*

A few seconds later it showed she read the message. I came out the message and replied to Mariah.

Me: *Thanks.*

Once I made it to the front, I started laughing. "Damn!" I made my way over to the silver, black and blue Ducati Monster 797 motorcycle. Guns, old school cars and motorcycle was something I loved because of my dad. I had been saying for the longest that I wanted a new bike, but I didn't think he was gonna get it. Then again, pretty much anything I wanted my dad and mom went out the way to get.

"This mothafucka is a beauty." I complimented while running my fingers alongside the body of the bike.

My pops tossed me the key to it. "You wanna take her for a ride?"

"Hell yeah, let's go." I hopped on the bike, not needing to be asked twice.

"Yo Ace! Bring yo ass on." My dad had four motorcycles, so he was going to let Ace hop on one.

Even though Janae was on some bullshit, I was enjoying my birthday so far. I just couldn't wait for the party.

***

The party was in full swing and I was buzzed off the Henny, but I wasn't fuck'd up like I wanted to be. The party was cool, it was packed in the club, and everybody was really showing me hella love… my mind wasn't there entirely because Janae ass was still on that bullshit. She was pissing me off. I hadn't texted her since earlier but the fact that her ass read the message and wasn't responding had me pissed off.

"Let's dance." Squeaky grabbed my arm and pulled me into the crowd of people. Squeaky was starting to piss me off too. The bitch kept clinging to me like I was her gotdamn nigga. Plus, I didn't want Janae to pop up and see me with Squeaky's ass.

As Squeaky grinded on me, arms wrapped around my waist from behind. I glanced down to see Mariah. My head fell back, and I laughed. She was like an irritating ass gnat that kept coming back. The bitch didn't get the hint when I never showed up at her crib or when I was ignoring her calls and shit.

I turned away from Squeaky and faced her. "Yo ass just don't know when to quit."

Mariah shrugged as her hands moved up my chest. "Not when it something I want." She yelled into my ear before sucking the earlobe into her mouth.

"Where Janae at?" I asked her.

She moved back, then grabbed my hand, pulling me from the dance floor and into the back hallway. The music wasn't as loud where we stood. I searched through the crowd of people for Squeaky but couldn't spot her. I knew she was going to be pissed once she realized I was gone.

"Where Janae at?" I repeated, that was who I wanted to see.

"She didn't want to come, she told me and Shanny to go head." Mariah moved closer to me. "Look, I tried to warn you, Blake. Janae is done with you. I tried to tell her she was being foolish to let you go like that, especially since you were telling her right, I mean y'all weren't ready for a baby just yet. If she can't see that Blake, you shouldn't be wasting your time on her..."

Standing on her tiptoes she kissed my chin as her hand went to the button on my jeans. "Give me a chance..." Her tongue flicked over my lower lip. "I promise you won't be disappointed." She sucked my lip into her mouth as she stroked my dick. When I didn't pull away from her, she slid her tongue into my mouth.

Once my dick got hard, I said fuck it and kissed her back. Janae was on some bullshit and I would've ended up fuckin' Squeaky's ass at the end of the night. Mariah might've been a stalker, but she was sexy as hell and she could swallow a dick. I could only imagine how she was gon' fuck one.

Palming her ass tight, I picked her up and went into Mac's office. Once inside, I dropped her on the couch. Undoing my jeans, I pulled my dick out and grabbed the condom from my back pocket. Before I could open it, Mariah was on her knees in front of me.

"Can I taste it first?" She questioned as her eyes stared up at me sexily. She licked her lips, causing her tongue to rub my tip. Grabbing a handful of her hair, I brought her face to my dick.

Mariah wasted no time wrapping her lips around my tip, sucking. Her tongue swirled around the mushroom head before she moved down my full length.

Shorty, sucked, spit and slobber sloppily on my dick, all the while massaging my balls.

Shorty sucked the fuck out of my dick. "Fuck…" My head dropped back, and I groaned as my tip hit the back of her throat. Mariah swallowed, the contraction around my dick caused me to grunt. She then moaned, sending a vibration from the tip of my dick to the base. Once my legs stiffened, my hand tightened in her hair and I tried to pull her off my shit, but she held my pelvis, sucking my dick until I exploded in her mouth. "Shit!"

Mariah pulled back smiling and licking her lips as if satisfied with what she had done. "How was that?"

Chuckling, I rubbed her chin. "Sweetheart, yo fuckin' mouth is gifted, shit." I went to straighten up, but she stopped me.

Grabbing my arm, she pulled me back to her. "I'm not done yet." She took hold of my dick and started sucking on it again. Mariah did that for a few minutes until I became erect again.

"Get on the couch." I told her as I slid the condom on. Mariah went to pull off her short black dress, but I stopped her. "Nah, leave it on, just bend over." She took off her panties and got on all fours. When I got behind her, she tensed up a bit.

"Let me do it." Mariah took hold of my dick and brought it to her pussy. She eased back as I pushed forward. "Sss. Ah…" she moaned as my tip went into her soaking pussy. She continued to ease back until I filled her completely. "Ooh shit, baby." Mariah groaned as she slowly began to throw her ass back. Mariah's pussy squeezed around my dick as her pace picked up.

"Gotdamn…" My hands gripped her ass tight slowing her down.

Mariah was tight which I wasn't expecting her to be. Hell, with how hard she was coming at me, I knew her ass had to have been loose with no real grip. I was wrong. The way her inner walls gripped and sucked on my dick felt amazing.

Truthfully, I only planned on getting a quick nut off but the feel of her had my movement slow at first just enjoying the feeling.

Pulling out, I pushed back in and Mariah moved up while moaning. I repeated that action several times, holding her hips so that she couldn't move.

"Fuck." My hand slapped her ass as I grunted.

"Ah, my, God." She cried as my pace picked up. "Ooh, fuck, Blake, baby."

My pelvis slapped against her ass as she tried to keep up and meet my thrust. The gushy sound of her soaking wet box filled the room as I continued to pound into her.

"Aah, Blake, wait. Oh, my God. Fuck!" Her hand reached back, and she pushed at my stomach. "Wait, wait, wait. fuck." She moaned.

My pace slowed, I then leaned back on my back legs. My hand came down on her ass and it jiggled. Squeezing her cheeks, I started moving her down my shaft.

"Oooh, shit, baby." She moaned as her pussy pulsed around me. Mariah was panting hard as her hands gripped the pillow on the sofa.

My hand came down on her ass at the same time, I pushed deep into her pussy, filling her.

"Ah, Blake, fuck. You feel so damn good." She cried from pleasure as her body moved up. Mariah moaned, letting her face fall on the couch cushions.

"Fuck it." I slapped her ass. She groaned as I pulled out, then pushed back inside her.

"Ooh shit, okay." She panted breathlessly.

My hand tangled into her hair and I pulled her up causing my dick to fill her. Once I did, she groaned out and her hands gripped my thighs.

"This what you wanted, shorty. Fuck my dick, Mariah." My fingers went to her clit and started playing with it.

Mariah's body twitched but her ass started to bounce on my dick. She glanced over her shoulder at me through hooded eyes. The look on her face was one of pure ecstasy. Her arm hooked around the nape of my neck and she pulled my face down to hers. She rolled her hips into me as she licked my bottom lip.

"Make me cum again." She panted out a moan as her bouncing picked up.

Moving her arm, I pushed her down. "Push yo ass up." She did as I said, arching her back.

My hands gripped her lower back and I started to thrust, fast and hard into her pussy.

The muscles in my lower body tightened, my legs stiffening as my balls throbbed.

"Oh, my God. Blake!" She cried out loudly. "Ah, fuck, baby, I'm cumming." She moaned as her ass dropped flat on the couch.

I pulled out of her, whacking my dick as I nutted into the condom. "Fuck." I grunted breathlessly while leaning against the arm of the couch. "Gotdamn." My hand held my stomach as I squeezed the last of my nut into the condom. I glanced over to Mariah. She laid there panting heavily. "Come on, we got to get back in there. I know yo cousin probably looking for yo ass."

"We don't have to go back right now." She whined, reaching for my hand.

"Man, get yo ass up." Pulling the condom off, I went into the bathroom and flushed it. Grabbing some towel paper, I wet it and then cleaned myself up. Once I was done, I went back into the office and Mariah's ass was still laid out.

I went over to the couch and squatted in front of her. "Come on, shorty, you got to get up. I don't need Mac catching me in his office with you."

"Okay, just give me a minute, I'll get cleaned up and come right out." She let out a light sigh before a lazy smile came to her lips. Taking hold of the front of my shirt, she lifted up, then kissed me. "You were amazing." She kissed me again.

My brows raised, and I laughed, standing up. "I know that. Now get yo ass up." I slapped her on the ass. "I got to get back out there. So, hurry up." I hit her ass again, then walked out the room. Once I made it to the main room, the party was still going hard.

I weaved through the crowd of people and made my way to the bar.

"Where the fuck you been?" Ace came to the bar and got two shots of Henny and two beers.

Grabbing one shot, I tossed it back then took a beer. "Shit, had to get some air." He didn't need to know I fuck'd Mariah. That was going to be a story for another day if it ever came up.

"Some air? Nigga that took you damn near an hour?" He questioned, and I shrugged. "Janae still got yo head twisted?"

I glanced at him before taking another swig of the beer. "Nah, fuck Janae ass, man. I'm not about to trip over her dumb ass no more." I shrugged before reaching over the bar and grabbed the bottle of Henny.

"Hey, Janae. He ain't mean that shit." Ace stated.

I laughed as I tilted the bottle back. Chuckling, I nodded. "Yeah the fuck I do." Glancing at Ace, he nodded to my side. My gaze fell on Janae watching a sheepish look cover her face.

"I guess I deserve that." She chewed on her inner jaw before biting into her bottom lip and looking down at the floor.

My brows raised at her. "What the fuck you doin' here?"

Her mouth moved in the motion of a fish before she bit into her bottom lip. "It's your birthday, I couldn't miss it." She got quiet for a minute then her head fell back. "Can we talk, please?" She grabbed my hand and I allowed her to pull me through the crowd of people and outside.

"What's up?" I let her hand go and leaned against the building waiting for her to talk.

"I was upset with you, to be honest, I still am a little. Blake, I understood where you were coming from. You just didn't seem to care for what I was really going through emotionally…" Her words trailed off.

My hand ran down my face and I let out an irritated breath. "Look, yo ass had days, weeks to come and talk to me about this. I ain't tryna hear this bullshit right now, not on my fuckin' birthday. I'm trying to get fuck'd up to the point I don't remember this mothafuckin' day. Not stand out here and be emotional with yo ass, man, fuck that shit. If that's why yo ass came here, you might as well bounce."

She would pick my fuckin' birthday party of all places and times to bring up the fuckin' abortion. If she wanted to talk about that shit, we should've done that after it happened, but she didn't want that. She hopped her stupid ass in the car with Mariah and jetted on my ass.

"Is that why the fuck yo ass came here to talk about the abortion?" I asked her.

She shook her head. "No, I really didn't, Blake, I promise, but when I saw you, I felt like I needed to say that."

"So why are you here, Janae?"

Janae's teeth grabbed her bottom lip and she looked away from me. Even so, she moved closer to me and I could see the blush fill her cheeks from the light we stood up under.

Mentally I chuckled because I already knew what was up. The anger I felt moments ago quickly dissolved as I watched her closely. "You not saying nothing."

She must have caught onto my look because she rolled her eyes and blushed harder. "Blake, I came to be with you on your birthday because

I realized that regardless of everything else, I still love you."

My arm snaked around her waist and I pulled her to me. "You what?" I moved my ear closer to her mouth. "I ain't hear that. You what me now?"

Janae giggled softly into my ear. "I said, I love you, Blake Rashad Carter." Turning my face toward her, she kissed me. "I really am sorry, Blake."

My hand grasped the nape of her neck and I kissed her back, slipping my tongue into her mouth. Pulling back, my forehead laid against hers. "Me too. I'm sorry." I felt the was the right thing to say. The way I went about the situation was probably harsh to her, which I wasn't trying to be.

"Ah!" She screamed in my ear as I picked her up. Janae wrapped her arms and legs around me. "I missed you." Her lips pressed against mine once again. "I was so miserable being without you." She bit my bottom lip, then licked my top before she started kissing me again.

"Janae…" We heard as the club doors burst opened. Pulling away from her, I glanced to the side and saw Shantell standing there. She looked around before her eyes fell on us. "There you go. Don't go disappearing like that." Shantell fussed at her as she walked over to us.

"I told you I was about to talk with Blake." Nae told her.

"Okay, I was going to walk with you. Bitch, don't be going off on your own like that. I'm in there freaking out until Ace told me y'all came out here." She continued to go off.

"Man, calm yo ass down. She good. I ain't gon' let shit happen to her." I told Shanny.

She glanced at me and rolled her eyes. "I didn't say you would. Which is why I'm not talking to you. When she got here, I walked her in and I plan on walking her ass out too. I have to know where she's at." She snapped at me.

"Bitch—" Janae's hand slapped over my mouth.

"I'm sorry, cuz, I didn't mean to make you worry. I'm straight, though. I swear the next time I'll make sure you walk with me to Blake." Janae promised.

That made Shantell smile. "That's all I ask."

The club door opened again, grabbing our attention. Mariah walked out, looking around before spotting us. "Bitch, where the fuck you been? Yo ass ducked off the moment we got here." Shantell snapped at Mariah.

Mariah looked at Janae then to me. My head fell back because I had really fuck'd up. "Nae, what you doing here? I thought you weren't coming?" She asked instead of answering Shantell.

Janae kissed my chin, then tilted my head down and pressed her lips to mine. "I couldn't miss his birthday regardless of how I felt. I would've regretted it, and I just couldn't do him like that." She kissed me again.

I was nervous as fuck and prayed like hell Mariah didn't say shit. I glanced at Mariah and my eyes squinted at her, she looked hurt.

"So y'all about to try and work a relationship out?" She asked.

"Now yo ass know, Janae wasn't about to let his ugly ass go too far. She loves his funky ass draws." Shantell exclaimed and Janae broke out laughing.

"Damn, Shanny some shit ain't meant to be said in front of him." She looked at me and chuckled. "But Blake know I love him and wasn't going nowhere to far."

"I ain't know shit." I put her down. She smacked her lips at that, and I shrugged. "Let's go back inside. I'm tryna get fuck'd up." I started to walk off and Janae grabbed my hand.

"Nae, stay close to Blake or us because that Squeaky hoe in there and I don't trust that bitch." Shantell told her.

Reaching over to Shantell, I muffed her. "Man, shut the fuck up ain't shit gon' pop off."

"Blake, don't make me beat yo ass." She threatened while pushing me. "All I'm saying is, keep yo groupies in check." She linked her arm through Mariah's. "Come on, you have to watch my back. I'mma about to see if I can take Ace from his hoe tonight." Shantell stated making Mariah and Janae laugh. "I don't know why y'all laughing, that man is fine."

I laughed at that. "Ashanti gon' knot yo shit the fuck up if you go for her nigga. Janae yo ass bet not jump in that shit when she gets her ass stomped the fuck out. You or Mariah's ass." The pair looked at me and rolled their eyes.

"That's my mothafuckin' cousin, if she swings, I swing, period." Both girls said at once. Looking at each other the trio broke out laughing.

"You just make sure yo groupie hoe don't try to jump in." Janae pointed out.

"Let's go." I pulled the door open for them to go inside first.

Shantell looked at Mariah as they walked in "Now where yo ass sneak off to?" She questioned, and Mariah glanced at me.

"I was playing pool." She told her while smiling.

295

"Let's go dance." Janae pulled me to the dance floor and for the rest of the night we dance as I got full off of Hennessey.

Chapter 16

Blake

"Man, I'm hungry as shit." I told Ace as I looked over B-Dub's menu.

"Babe, you say that all the time and always end up getting the same damn thing. A mix of hot buffalo and BBQ wings with water." Janae stated taking my menu.

"That's why I don't pay his ass no mind." Ace laughed grabbing his beer.

"So, what. Aye, did Janae tell you Shantell big head ass like you?" I took a drink of my water. Since I had practice early Saturday morning, I wasn't about to drink shit but water.

Hell, I drunk so much gotdamn Henny on my birthday, I was still pissing that shit out. I was fuck'd up and didn't remember shit after we went back inside. I think that was part of the reason Janae been hip riding my ass.

Whatever the reason was, she wasn't telling me. I thought maybe she knew about me and Mariah. But that thought was quickly pushed to the side because those two were still cool and I doubt Janae would still be fuckin' with me if she did.

Ace looked to Janae and laughed. "That's why her ass kept staring at me all night during the party?" His head shook. "Ashanti was ready to beat her shit in. On everything, I had to calm her ass down."

Janae rolled her eyes. "She wasn't going to do shit but be mad at her." She shrugged.

"I don't understand y'all mothafuckas. How the fuck y'all gon' be pissed at Ashanti when Shantell hoe ass tryna get with her nigga, though?" I questioned. I didn't get that shit. Females were all fuck'd up in the head.

"First off, watch your mouth. Second off, it's different because that's my cousin." She stated factually. "So, say this, Ace fuckin' with some other nigga chick, right?" She started off and we nodded. "Dude come and confront him, and it comes to blows. You just gon stand there?"

I looked at Ace then back to her. "Hell yeah, I'mma stand my ass there and watch those mothafuckas fight. The fuck kinda question is that? Ace ain't have no business fuckin' with that nigga bitch, period. Now if another mothafucka jump in that shit, then yeah, I got his ass, ain't no question about that. But what the fuck I look like helping him whoop that man's ass when he got the right to be pissed off. Hell, I'mma grab me a drink and root for that nigga."

Ace broke out laughing then hit me. "Nigga, fuck you. Yo ass ain't shit for that. On some real shit though, I feel you. Let me find out Ashanti fuckin' with somebody else. I'mma beat her ass then stomp that nigga out."

"Who you gon' stomp out, baby?" Ashanti asked coming up behind Ace. She leaned down, kissing his cheek then sat beside him.

Ace glared at her. "You and whatever nigga yo ass slick fuckin' with."

She popped her lips. "Ace, don't start with me. I'm not fuckin' with nobody. When do I have time to mess with any other nigga when I'm either with you or at work?" She asked him.

"I know that. Hypothetically speaking, I'm saying." He rephrased his words.

"Next time say *hypothetically* first." Ashanti looked at me and smiled. "Hey, little brother."

"What's up?" I nodded at her.

"Starving. Have y'all ordered yet?" She pulled off her jacket. She glanced at Janae for a split second, once she looked away, she pulled out her phone.

"Nope. You know Blake got to look over his menu ten times before he orders the same damn thing." Ace told her, and Janae laughed.

"I hate when he does that. I swear I thought he only did that to annoy me." She leaned into me and pressed her lips to mine. "I'll be back. If the waiter comes order for me." She kissed me again, then got up and went to the bathroom.

"Blake, why you keep on playing Squeaky like that? You know she like you, but yo ass just keep stringing her on." Ashanti glared at me.

I looked toward the bathroom where Janae just went. "I ain't stringing shit on. Squeaky knew I had a girl and know what it was between us. I ain't never told that damn girl I liked her ass or made her think we were gon' be together. So, kill that bullshit you talkin'. Plus, that damn girl got a whole ass nigga."

Her eyes formed into slits as she glared hard at me. "No, she doesn't, Squeaky broke up with him, but whatever, Blake. If that's the case, you shouldn't call, text her none of that shit." She snapped at me.

My brows furrowed at her. "This my mothafuckin' phone. I do what the fuck I want with it. How the fuck you gone tell me what I shouldn't be doing? Bitch, I ain't Ace, you better shut the fuck up and talk to him."

Ashanti mouth opened then closed. "I was just playing with you. There was no need for you to get rude and call me out my damn name. Ace, you better check yo boy." She snapped at him.

Ace shrugged. "I told yo ass to leave that shit alone. You can't force that nigga to be with Squeaky ass. He's cool with Janae. You and Squeaky need to dead that shit, man." His head shook. "He broke shorty off once with some dick now she wants a whole ass relationship." Ashanti pushed him, and he laughed. "I'm just saying." His arm went around her shoulder and she leaned into him.

"I'll leave it alone, but they'll be cute together and our double dates would be so much more fun." Her lip poked out and she kissed him just as the waiter came.

I waved the waiter to me and order mine and Janae's food.

***

"Hey cuz!" Shantell loud voice came from behind us. Janae's head perked up. "I told you that was her."

"Y'all come over here." Janae waved her over. I didn't bother looking back. Once they reached us, it's Shantell, Mariah and two dudes I've never seen before.

"Hey, excuse me!" Mariah called to the waiter. "Can we push these tables together?" She asked him.

He glanced around for a second. "Yeah." He pushed the tables together, then handed them four menus. After promising to be back, he walked off.

I hadn't seen Mariah or heard from her since my party. Staring her over, she wore a tight blue jean skirt that stopped mid-thigh and hugged her ass nicely, and an off the shoulder light blue sheer top with a pair of blue and white Jordan's. She looked good.

One of the dudes they were with brought his chair next to mine. I waved him off. "Nah, bruh, sit over there, I ain't tryna rub my elbows against another nigga's while I'm eating." I told him.

"Mariah, sit down." I pointed to the chair next to me.

"Mariah, y'all can sit over here." Shantell waved her and dude down.

"Blake, scoot down." Janae told me.

I shook my head. "Hell no, I ain't about to do all that. She can sit her ass down right there and dude can sit beside her. Y'all mothafuckas ain't about to rearrange the whole fuckin' table. Sit the fuck down." I pointed to the chair again.

"His ass is so irritating." Shantell mumbled.

"It's cool, I'll sit right here." Mariah sat beside me, and dude took his place next to her.

Janae's hand came to the nape of my neck massaging the skin. "You good?" She whispered into my ear before kissing behind it.

Licking my lips, I nodded. "I'm straight." Grabbing my water, I took a drink of it.

"Squeak!" Ashanti suddenly yelled excitedly. I glared at Ashanti then Janae. Those two mothafuckas called they asses. It wasn't a coincidence that they all were there.

Janae turned away from me to Shantell.

"Y'all mothafuckas childish. Why the fuck would you two mothafuckas call their asses?" Ace beat me to asking my own damn question.

303

"I didn't call nobody— Ace give me my damn phone." Ashanti snapped at him trying to grab the device back.

Ace pushed her back. "Sit the fuck down." She flopped back down then looked to Squeaky and glared at her. "I told yo ass not to even come up here." Ashanti was pissed that she hadn't listened to her.

"You ain't the boss of me nor do you pay my car note. I go where I wanna." Squeaky grabbed a chair and pulled it to the table. She glanced around the table, rolling her eyes at the girls. "Hey, Blake." She spoke and I nodded at her.

Janae turned toward me, her face dead in mine as if she was waiting on me to say something. Laughing, I muffed her. "Man, get the fuck back."

She hit my hand. "I'm just saying, don't play with me." Her eyes rolled hard.

All I could do was laugh at her ass. "Gon' with that shit. I ain't did or said shit."

"And you not gon' say shit." Janae had a whole attitude. Even so, she leaned in and kissed me.

"Don't try to act funny because yo girl here. Nigga, I said what's up." Squeaky stated in a playful manner.

Chicks was fuckin' ruthless when it came to a nigga they liked. Janae bit my bottom lip then top. "You coming back to the room with us? Shanny got a hotel for tonight and tomorrow." She kissed me again.

I pulled away from her. "Who all gon' be at the hotel?"

"Just us. Shanny, Zac, Pint and Mariah." Janae pointed out and my eyes looked at dude who sat next to Mariah.

I pointed to him. "That's yo nigga?" It shouldn't have bothered me, especially since she wasn't my girl, but I wanted to know. I glanced at dude again. He was just an average dark skinned nigga who was an inch or so taller than me.

"Yeah, she my girl." Pint announced. "Why is that a problem?" His arm draped over her shoulder, pulling Mariah into his side.

Janae suddenly nudge me. "Why are you staring at him like that?" She laughed.

I didn't realize I was glaring at the nigga until she said something. Ignoring Janae, I shrugged at dude question. "If it was a problem with me, you would know about it, because I would've knocked yo ass the fuck out." Again, I shrugged. "In fact, I don't remember asking yo ass shit, homie. If you ain't no bitch and yo name not Mariah, you shouldn't be talking to me."

Janae hit me again and grabbed my arm. "Blake, you don't even have to talk to him like that." I shrugged her off me.

"Nigga, who the fuck you talking to?" Dude snapped, glaring at me.

"Pint." I stated plainly.

Mariah started laughing. "Y'all need to chill out for real. Pint, calm down, yo ass not about to do nothing." She continued to laugh as if it was nothing.

"If that is her nigga what's it to you?" Squeaky asked. "What's yo problem with it?"

I glared at Squeaky then look to Mariah.

"That's what I wanna know too?" Ashanti chimed in and I glared at her.

"It ain't shit to me." I shrugged, grabbing my water and drinking from it.

"Come on." Janae grabbed my hand and tugged on it hard. I went to pull my hand from hers, but she squeezed it tight. "I said come on." She snapped, glaring at me. Realizing I had fuck'd up, I stood and allowed her to pull me outside. "What the fuck is wrong with you? Do you like Mariah?" She fussed as soon as we got outside.

306

"No, it ain't shit like that. I don't know why the fuck you invited them here. Y'all rude ass didn't introduce those niggas or shit, just invited them to sit the fuck down at our table, so I was asking a mothafuckin' question until dude said something. I was gon' ask Shantell the same damn thing." That was the first thing that popped in my head, so I rode with that. "If you was gon' have them come up here, it should've just been they asses."

Janae head fell back, and she groaned. "I didn't think it would've been a problem—"

My brows furrowed, and I looked at her like she was stupid. "The only reason you even called those mothafuckas was because of Ashanti ass. Yo ass childish as fuck, ain't nobody got time for that bullshit, damn."

"So, you not gon' say shit about her calling that bitch up here? The bitch you fuck'd?" She pushed me, mad.

"Whatever man." I went to walk pass her, but she got in my way. "I made a mistake and fuck'd that bitch one time. I ain't thought about hitting Squeaky ass again. So why the fuck should I feel any kind of way about her ass being here? You shouldn't give a fuck about none of their asses for real. If you gon' trip off a bitch at least let me give you a reason too. That shit with Squeaky old as fuck, the beginning of our relationship. So, fuck her, you hear me?" I caged her against the building, then kissed her.

Janae arms wrapped around my waist and she kissed me back. "I don't like her ass though and I want to beat the shit out of her. You too for fuckin' her to begin with." She fussed but continued to kiss me no less.

"You can try to beat my ass." My hand gripped her ass tight. "I can tag yo ass, though."

She laughed against my mouth. "Nasty ass. Move. Let's go back inside. Are you coming to the hotel?" She questioned.

"Hell no, and yo ass ain't going either. I don't know those mothafuckas so I ain't hanging with they ass. So, you might as well tell Shantell you ain't going." She smacked her lips and turned to walk away. Grabbing her hair, I pulled her back. "Did you hear what the fuck I said? Yo ass ain't going to no fuckin' hotel with her or those niggas, you hear me?"

Janae smacked my hand out of her hair. "I swear to God, don't be pulling my damn hair, Blake. Stupid ass—"

"Did you hear what I just said?" I repeated.

She glared at me as she fixed her ponytail. "Yeah, damn. Stupid ass." With an attitude she turned and went back inside thrusting the door back hard. I didn't give a fuck about her attitude.

She wasn't about to be at no hotel with niggas. As I went back inside, Mariah walked by going toward the bathrooms.

Jogging in that direction, I quickly grabbed her arm. When I did, she tried to jerk away. "Yo, chill." I pulled her around the corner.

"What?" She shrugged my hand off her.

My brows raised at her. "Lose the attitude. Who is dude?" I asked, getting straight to the point. "You knew I was here, so why the fuck you bring him up here?"

Her mouth opened then closed before she rolled her eyes. "Why should you care who I'm with? You with Nae—"

"I know who the fuck I'm with and it don't got shit to do with what I'm asking." I moved away from her and leaned against the wall waiting on a reply. When she didn't say anything right away, I glared hard at her.

Mariah sighed with a roll of her eyes. "I didn't think you would've cared. Especially since you're working shit out with Janae." She shrugged but the attitude was clear in her voice and body language.

"You keep saying Janae like it really matter to you. Last I checked you ain't give a fuck, you go after what you want, right?" That was how she'd been acting all along.

She looked away from me and folded her arms. "Well it should've. Now seeing y'all really trying to work shit out, I don't see no point in wanting you. You're clearly not going to let her go, right?" Her eyes locked with mine as a slight glare covered her face.

Licking my lips, I nodded. "You right, she got me." Pushing myself off the wall, I glanced around the corner. I had a clear shot of our table. Janae and Shantell was joking, laughing loudly with one another. Ducking back behind the corner, I went to Mariah. Tilting her head back, my hand went to her throat. "He the reason you ain't been texting or calling?"

"Blake, let me go. I'm not about to play this game with you. Plus, I'm not the only one who has a damn phone either." She snapped and tried to jerk away from me.

"Yo, chill out." I peeked around the corner once more to see that Janae and Shantell were still talking. Looking back to Mariah, I nodded at what she said. "You right, I could've hit you up. Answer my question, is dude the reason you stopped calling and texting?"

"Why does it even matter, Blake? You and Janae working shit out, right? So, me not reaching out shouldn't move you no way, right?" She spat out, rolling her eyes hard.

Rubbing my bottom lip, I chuckled and nodded again. "You right, and I'm not gonna bullshit around with you. I wanna fuck you again." Mariah looked surprise as hell by what I said. "I mean, if you not with it, then good, it is what it is." I glanced back over to our table to see everybody still going on with their conversations. "Look, we can't really talk right now, but I wanna see you later. Is it cool if I drop by your place tonight?" My hand that held her throat, stroked the skin. I knew I shouldn't be concerning myself with that babe, because I knew she was crazy as hell, but after I fuck'd shorty on my birthday, I wanted to hit her ass one more time.

She snatched my hand from her and pushed me away from her. "Fuck you, Blake, when I wanted something with you, yo ass couldn't be bothered but now that I've moved on, it's something? Fuck you. Go work on your relationship with Nae and be happy with her and leave me the fuck alone. You just want to fuck, seriously?" Once again that hurt look came to her eyes and she pushed me away from her, then turned about to walk off.

Grabbing her arm, I pulled her into the men's, bathroom, ignoring the other niggas that were in there. "Yo, chill with that mothafuckin' attitude, I'm tryna be nice to yo stupid ass. What the fuck you want me to do lie to you, Mariah?"

She opened her mouth to say something but stopped. "No, I don't, but still. Fuck you, Blake. Like you dead ass just want to have sex with me and that's it. You have unlimited pussy you can get from Janae. Go fuck her." She pushed away from me again. "Now I'll be fuckin' wrong if I went out there and let your bitch know how you're saying you wanna fuck me right? I'll be dead ass wrong, right?"

My hand went to her neck and I hemmed her against the wall. "Yo, lower yo mothafuckin' voice. You know what? Fuck it, that's my mistake for saying shit to yo ass, you right, I'm trying to work shit out with Nae. I'm cool on you." I let her go and stepped off.

Mariah quickly grabbed my arm. "No, I'm sorry. I shouldn't have snapped at you like that. My feelings are all over the place when it comes to you. I know I shouldn't like you and that it's wrong, but I can't help that I'm attracted to you." She brought her hands to my chest then slowly moved them up, bringing her arms around my neck. "I'm sorry for getting mad… forgive me?" Mariah pulled my head down and kissed me.

My head pulled back and I had to laugh, females were so gotdamn weird. "Look, now ain't the time to be talking about this. I'll see you later if that's cool."

She nodded and kissed me again. "Yeah, that's cool only because I really wanna be with you again too." Her hand slid down to my dick, grabbing it. "You felt so good that night, I haven't been able to stop thinking about you ever since."

Groaning, I grabbed her wrist, stopping the friction her hand was causing to my hardening dick. "Man, what the fuck did I just say? Stop that shit."

Mariah laughed, smiling wide before she bit my bottom lip. "I just had to make sure I was who you really wanted." She kissed me again, then pulled back. "Oh, shit, we can't tonight. I'm supposed to be going with Shanny to the room—"

"Don't take yo ass to that damn hotel with that mothafucka, I ain't bullshittin', Mariah. I'll be at yo crib at twelve and yo ass better be there." My hand tightened around her neck and I tilted her head back before kissing her.

Mariah's arms tightened around my neck and she started to kiss me back, but before shit could get to heavy, I pulled back. "Okay, I won't go to the hotel. You better be there at twelve, Blake, I'm not playing."

Nodding, I pulled back, removing her arms from me, then motioned toward the bathroom door. "Go…"

She looked hesitant for a second but headed to the door. "Blake, don't stand me up." She stated then left out the bathroom.

"Fuck!" My eyes fell on my dick that was brick in my pants. "What the fuck am I doing?" Going to the sink, I tossed some water on my face as if that was going to help me out of the fuck'd up situation that I was putting myself in. Even knowing it wasn't cool didn't change the fact that I wanted to fuck Mariah at least one last time.

After drying my face off, I left out the bathroom and went back to the table, only to see that Mariah hadn't returned.

"You okay? You've been gone for a while." Janae asked, rubbing my leg.

My arm went around her shoulder and I pulled her against my side while grabbing my phone out my pocket. "Yeah, I'm cool. My pops hit me up." I showed her my phone as if that was going to make what I said the truth.

"Is everything okay with him?" I nodded at her question while putting my phone away. Janae took hold of my chin and pulled my face down so that we were at eye level. "Are you sure you're straight?" She repeated, seeming not to believe me.

Hell, I was far from straight. "Yeah, I'm good."

Janae's head stretched up and she kissed me. "I love you, Blake…" Her words trailed off as she kissed me again. Janae hand moved up my leg and she grabbed my hard dick. She smiled against my lips then pulled back. "You wanna get out of here?"

"Hell no, he don't!" Ace cut in. "This ain't just a two of y'all fuckin' night. I invited yo ass." He told Janae and I broke out laughing.

"Damn, my nigga did you really just get pissed?" I laughed, noticing Mariah had returned to the table. I pulled out my phone and looked at the time to see that it was almost ten o'clock. "We ain't leaving no way. I got to head to the crib in about an hour and a half."

Ace brows rose at what I said, and I shook my head at him to not ask or say shit. Before I ran into Mariah, my plan was to stay the night at Ace crib. His head tilted, and I could hear him asking me, *what the fuck?* But again, I shook my head while looking down at my phone once more.

"I thought you were coming back to the house with us?" Ashanti asked confused.

When she said that, her eyes met with Squeaky and she shrugged. Janae pushed herself from under me catching the action Ashanti made.

I started laughing. "Man, y'all on some straight bullshit tonight, for real. Yo, don't do that dumb shit, Ashanti." I told her while shaking my head. I looked at Janae only to see her glaring at me. "Man, fix yo gotdamn face." I went to pull her back into my side, but she pushed away from me again.

"No, what the fuck is she talking about?" Janae snapped, pissed off. She looked like she was ready to swing on my ass.

"Don't do what?" Ashanti tried to play confused.

"Tryna make it seem like I'm going over there to fuck with Squeaky dumb ass. I ain't fuck'd that babe but once, and I haven't thought about hitting her ass again. Janae, if yo stupid ass wanna sit here and turn yo gotdamn face up and believe every fuckin' thing these two dumb bitches say instead of me, yo, fuck yo ass too, real shit. I ain't about to sit around tryna convince yo retarded ass of shit. Believe and think what the fuck you want. I'm out, Shanny can drop yo ass off." Pulling my wallet out, I toss the fifty-dollar bill to Ace. "That's for my shit and hers, I'll hit you up later."

"Blake—" Janae began to say, grabbing my arm.

I snatched away from her. "Man, I ain't tryna hear shit you about to say. Keep listening to those bitches like you doing." I glanced at Squeaky to see she was ready to snap off at me. "Yo, shut the fuck up, don't say shit because I'll knock the fuck out yo ass right now, real shit. Y'all mothafuckas play to many childish ass games. Bitch, you know we ain't fuck but once. Stupid ass girl, man." I was ready to get the fuck away from all their asses. I started to walk off but stop once I looked at Mariah. I glanced at Janae then grabbed another fifty. "That's for yo food." I tossed it beside Mariah, then looked at Pint. "That's to piss you off." I told him then pointed to Janae. "Don't take yo ass to that damn hotel either, I'm not fuckin' playing." I warned her. I didn't know those niggas and didn't trust their ass. "Matter fact, Ace, drop her ass at home." After giving one last glance to Janae and Mariah, I walked away from the table.

"How the fuck you gon' order mothafuckas around and just bounce like that?" Ace yelled from behind me, but I could hear the laughter in his voice. "Y'all females ignorant as fuck, and Janae you dumb. Blake don't want that gotdamn girl…" Ace's voice faded off as I walked further away, then out the door.

Chapter 17

Blaze

One Month Later

I pulled on the blunt hard, then exhaled the weed smoke. "Man, Peaches stupid ass got me going on this fuckin' date thing with Britt and her nigga." I told Mac as I hit the blunt once more.

"And yo ass can't tell Peaches, hell no. My nigga you need to get yo fuckin' nuts back from that babe." He started laughing through the line.

I pulled the phone from my ear and looked at it before putting it on speaker. "Nigga, yo ass met my wife. I ain't getting shit back, she gon' have those mothafuckas until I die. Peaches stupid ass gon' stop letting these mothafuckas use her to get to me." Again, his ass started laughing. "Nigga, fuck you. Did you pack up the Cherries?" I inhaled deeply, holding the smoke in before exhaling from my nose and mouth.

"Yeah, I got everything together. I'm about to drop the shit off at the club now. You heard shit else from dude though?" He questioned.

I shook my head as I pulled on the blunt again. "Hell nah, his ass will pop up soon though. He don't seem like the type of mothafucka to go away so easily." I shrugged while dumping the ashes into the tray.

"Damn, Blaze…" Peaches started choking as she opened the passenger side door. "Why the fuck do you have this damn truck smoky like this? Oh, my God."

I held up a finger to her. "Aye, I'll meet up with you tomorrow, Peaches big mouth ass out here now—"

"Yo ass ain't funny. I don't know why you would smoke this damn truck up like this. Especially knowing we're about to go to dinner." She continued to fuss.

"I'ight, B, we'll get up later." Mac laughed, and I ended the call.

"So now you can't hear?" She reached over and pushed me.

I tossed my phone into the cup holder then looked at her. "I can't help but hear yo loud ass, and you saw me on the phone. So, stop all that gotdamn yelling." My eyes finally landed on her as I inhaled on the blunt once more.

"We have to take my car I'm not trying to smell like a gotdamn smokehouse. I can't believe you." Peaches eyes formed into slits. She was pissed off and that made her look sexy as hell to me.

"You look sexy as fuck, Peach." She had on a sexy little purple and black dress that hugged her body like a second skin. It was just a plain dress, but she made that mothafucka look good. "Damn, baby, you wearing that mothafucka ain't you? Fuck." I rubbed my stomach while staring her over.

Peaches glare deepened before her eyes rolled into her head and she looked away from me. I watched as her lips pursed together.

"Peach, come give me a kiss." I beckoned her to me. "Come here."

She started laughing. "B, no, you play to damn much. Why would you get high like this, babe?" Peaches took the blunt from me and put it out.

"Yo ass making me go to this damn dinner, so I had to get high to meet this nigga." I grabbed the bottle of water I had and took a drink from it as I shrugged. "Peach, come give me a kiss, for real, I ain't even bullshittin'."

She stared at me for a second before she broke out laughing. "Man, I'm not about to deal with yo high ass."

I started up the truck and let the windows down, then opened my door. "Come on so we can go."

Her brows raised as she stared at me confused. "I have to come all the way over there to kiss you?" I nodded. "Blaze, lean yo ass over here and kiss me so we can go. I don't wanna be late."

Oh, we were about to be late like a mothafucka. I reclined my seat and leaned into it, getting comfortable. "If we're late it's yo damn fault." I shrugged.

"Blaze, I'm not about to play with you. It's bad enough we about to go in there smelling like weed. We're not about to be late. Come on!" She snapped at me. Shrugging, I turned up the radio then closed my eyes. She turned the radio off. "Oh, my God! You're so fuckin' irritating. I don't know why yo stupid ass had to get so high." She snapped before the truck door was slammed shut. Once she reached my side, she hit my leg. "Here."

I peaked at her through one eye. "My lips up here—ah fuck, Peaches!" I grunted as she punched me in the stomach. "Why the fuck you hit me?"

"Because you're playing. Now sit up and kiss me." She grabbed my arm and tried to pull me up.

I gave her hand a tug. "Get up here."

With a groan, she climbed in and leaned over me. "You could have at least lifted the seat up with your dumb high ass." She gave me a quick peck and pulled back. "Now let's go... Blaze, stoooop!" She dragged out with a whine as my arms went around her waist.

"Peaches, stop playing and give me a real kiss man." My hands moved to her ass and I squeezed both her cheeks.

"No, because I don't wanna be late... Blaze, stoooop..." She dragged out again as I sucked on her neck.

My left hand moved from her ass and tangled into her hair. I brought her lips down to mine. Peaches bit at my bottom lip before sucking it into her mouth. She then licked my top lip and my mouth opened, letting her tongue slide in.

When she moaned, my hand slid under her dress. Moving the thin thong string to the side, my fingers played with her clit. Once I felt her pussy contracting, I pushed two fingers into her soak box, and she moaned.

"Blaze, wait…mmm." She moaned, pushing down on my fingers.

My hand left her hair and went to her ass, slapping it hard. Peaches pussy muscles squeezed around my fingers once again.

"You gon' ride my dick, Peaches?" I asked as I undid my jeans and pulled my dick out.

"You get on my damn nerves. Irritating ass." She hit me, then reached between us and grabbed my dick.

"Hold up. Turn around, I wanna watch yo ass bounce on my dick."

"Blaze, you're so fuckin' aggravating." Peaches slid out the truck, then got back in. She closed my legs, putting hers on either side of mine.

I pushed her dress up to the middle of her back, then guided her ass down on my dick. "Fuck!" Peaches pushed down on my tip then moved up, she did that a few times, teasing my shit.

"Ooh, shit, Blaze." She moaned as she came down, taking my full length deep into her pussy. Peaches gripped the steer wheel tight and started bouncing. "Ah, God." Her head went back as her ass went up and down at a rapid pace.

"Fuck that mothafucka, Peach." My feet pushed hard against the floor as I thrust upward, into her.

"Ah, shit, Blaze. Ooh, baby fuck. Ooh…" Peaches left foot came to the seat, beside my thigh and her hand went to my pelvis. "Hold on…" She panted and slowly started moving down on my dick once more.

I turn on the lights in the truck, watching as my dick went in and out of her pussy. "Peach, you wet as fuck." I groaned, watching as her juices coated my dick beautifully.

Peaches sat on my lap and rolled her hips as her nails dug into my lower stomach. "Baby, you feel so good." Her hand pushed into my stomach and she started bouncing again. "Ooh, God, Blaze, baby."

"You love me, Peach?"

Peaches' low eyes stared into mine and she nodded. Her lips were parted as streams of moans left her mouth. "I do, baby, I do, so much.

Ooh, fuck, I love you, B." Her bouncing stopped, and she sat on my lap, grinding her hips into mine.

Grabbing hold of the thigh, she had propped up. "Bounce on this dick, fuck that shit, baby." She started bouncing as I began to thrust, pumping into her hard and fast. My feet pushed hard into the floor as my nuts tightened. "Ah fuck, Peaches." My hand tightened on her thigh, stopping her movement. I held her to me as I fuck'd her.

Peaches' pussy milked my dick rapidly as her body tightened. She moaned out loudly and leaned into the steering wheel, blowing the horn.

"Ah fuck!" My pelvis pushed into her ass and my arms held her tight around the waist as I nutted inside her. "Gotdamn, Peach." She rolled and grinded her ass on me as her pussy muscles continued to suck around me. "Take that shit." Sitting up, I kissed the middle of her back, then pulled her head to the side, bringing her lips to mine. "I love you too, Peach."

I kissed her once more, then grabbed the blunt and lighter from the ashtray. After turning off the lights, I fell back into my seat and lit the blunt. I took several pulls, then sat it down before grabbing the wipes out the backseat pocket.

Taking a couple out, I tapped Peaches. "Sit up." She groaned. "Man, come on." I slapped her ass, then grabbed the blunt and took a hard pull on it. Peaches whined before sitting up and my dick fell out of her. Seeing that shit, I started laughing. "Yo, that mothafucka dead. Yo pussy killed my shit—"

Peaches hit me and started laughing. "You so damn stupid, I swear." She jerked slightly as the cold wipe touched her pussy.

"You love me though." Sitting up, I bit her on the ass, then kissed her cheeks before I smacked her booty.

"Blaze, stop—"

I slapped her ass again. "Shut the fuck up!" I kissed her red ass again. "Climb over in yo seat so we can go." Once Peaches, was in her seat, I cleaned my dick off and tossed the wipes in a bag. I then pulled off, away from our house. I was glad our damn driveway was enclosed from prying eyes.

"Can you at least let the windows down if you're going to smoke that whole blunt?" Peaches let her window down then looked back to me.

Laughing at her, I let the windows down. "Happy?"

"No, because we're late—"

I shrugged. After pulling on the blunt, I pointed it at her. "That's yo fault. You wanted some dick—"

She reached over and hit me. "I swear I hate you." She laughed. "That was you're horny, high ass."

I pointed to her once more. "Again, yo fault. Shid ain't nobody tell yo ass to be that gotdamn sexy." Stopping at a light, my gaze fell on Peaches. Her lips were pursed together, and she was looking straight ahead. "Peach, give me a kiss."

Her eyes fell on me and she started laughing. "You lucky I love yo ugly ass." She leaned over and kissed me. "Now go." She pointed to the green light just as my phone rung. "You want me to get it?"

I nodded. "Yeah, put it on speaker." She answered and held the phone toward me. I looked at the screen to see Khyree's name. "Yeah?"

"What's up, B?" He questioned.

"Shit with the wife. You got something for me?" After dude showed up at my Lot, the only thing I had to go by on him was his plate number. I had Khyree to see what he could find out.

"The only thing I found led me to some dead dude. And seeing as yo guy still breathing, it's not him. B, I had to dig hard just to get that little shit. Whoever the fuck dude is, he smart. I emailed you everything. Now you wanna tell me what the fuck is going on?" He questioned.

I glanced at Peaches who brows were screwed up in confusion. I took the phone from her. "Nah, good lookin' though." I ended the call. I could feel Peaches eyes burning a hole into the side of my head.

"I'm not gonna ask you about what's going on again, Blaze. Just keep that bullshit from our home. If you can't do that, then you leave it—"

"Peaches, shut the fuck up—"

She reached over the seat and decked my ass hard in the chest. "No, you shut the fuck up. B, you can't fool me, I know something is going on. It's cool that you don't wanna tell me the details, but don't fuckin' lie to me either, Blaze! Now, like I said, I'm not gonna ask yo ass again, just keep it from our home. And if it's a possibility that whatever the fuck it is can follow yo ass home, leave our fuckin' home." With that she leaned over and turned up the radio before sitting back.

My hand rubbed the back of my neck and she smacked her lips loudly. "Stupid ass mothafucka, I swear." Peaches snatched my phone up from the cup holder and started dialing on it. "Hey Britt, we're running a few minutes behind, but we'll be there shortly… alright, babe." She ended the call.

Reaching over to her, I snatched my damn phone, then turned off the radio. "Yo ass hit me like that again, I'mma smack the fuck out of you, I promise yo ass that."

"And I'mma slap yo ass right back. Dumb ass can't even pretend to fuckin' lie."

I glared at her. "I wasn't lying to yo stupid ass. I just ain't tell you every fuckin' thing because I don't know, Peaches. Once I figure out every gotdamn thing, then yo dumb ass will know. Until then, I'm not about to have you all anxious when it could be nothing. So, chill the fuck out and cool it with that damn attitude."

Again, she smacked her lips. "Whatever, Blaze. Stupid ass…" Nodding, I slowed down, coming to a stop at another light. "Eep!" Peaches squeaked out as I grabbed a handful of her hair and snatched her head back.

"What the fuck did I just say, Peaches? Kill that mothafuckin' attitude. If I was tryna hide some shit from you, do yo ass think I would've let you answer the phone and listen to everything he said? Stupid ass don't think. Now fix yo damn attitude." The car behind me blew their horn. I rolled my window down. "Yo, fuck you. Sit yo ass there and wait."

"Blaze, let my fuckin' hair go!" Peaches snapped, trying to pry my hand open.

Letting her hair go, I pushed her back into the seat. "Yo' ass bet not hit me either." I pulled off just as the light turned red.

"You're an ignorant ass mothafucka! Gon' pull my gotdamn hair like that. Stupid ass." Peaches turned in her seat, glaring hard as hell at me. When her arms folded over her chest, I broke out laughing.

That mothafucka was pissed off and wanted to hit my ass, but she knew better. I was gonna slap the fuck out her if she did. Peaches ass hit like a straight nigga.

"I love you, Peach." I told her.

"Fuck you." She hit the middle console and I looked at her. "Fuck you, Blaze." She turned away from me.

Laughing, I continued to our destination.

Chapter 18

Blaze

"Peaches, where the fuck do you got me?" I pulled into a nice restaurant sure enough, but I had never heard of the place before. It looked pretty upscale, which I wasn't dressed for. That explained why Peaches didn't tell me where the fuck we were going because she knew I wouldn't have wanted to come.

"It's a restaurant where we eat at. Blaze, be nice and don't act an ass, please. Brittany really like this guy." Peaches stressed.

My hand rubbed over the back of my head and I let out a breath. "Fine, man, damn." I got out the truck before she could say anything else. I went to her side and opened the door.

"Babe, I'm serious, please try to be nice? She really likes him." She begged once again while getting out the truck. "And…" She trailed off, going to the hatchback, and opening the door. "Change your shirt. First impression is everything." She pulled out a suit jacket and a button down lavender shirt.

I looked down at the black polo shirt I had on, to my black jeans and matching forces. "Man, you better bring yo ass on. I'm not changing into shit. If what I got on ain't cool, we can bounce. Y'all mothafuckin' women do too much to impress a mothafucka." Shaking my head at her, I walked away from the truck. "Bring yo ass on, Peaches."

"I swear, no matter how old you get, you're going to always be the same ol' damn Blaze." Peaches claimed, laughing. "Babe, hold up." She grabbed my wrist, stopping me. Peaches walked in front of me and wrapped her arms around my waist. "Look, I'm sorry for snapping and hitting you. I was wrong. I just knew it was something you weren't telling me, and I didn't want to push you, then when I heard what the twin said, I snapped. What I said about not bringing it home, I was out of line because I know you would never do that." Grabbing my face, she pulled it down and kissed me. "I really wanted to let you know that. Forgive me?" Her lips pressed into mine once more.

"Always." Peaches had a nigga weak without a doubt. She was the only reason I stayed away from bullshit, such as dealing drugs and shit. Peaches was my heart and if anyone found that out, they would use her to get to me, same with my kids. But her, Peaches, she kept me sane and leveled. She was literally my everything, my lifeline.

"Come on, let's get this whack ass dinner over with so we can get back home and work on this fourth or sixth baby." My hand slid to her ass and I squeezed it, making her laugh.

"Let's go." Taking my hand, she led us inside the restaurant. "This is beautiful..." Peaches mumbled.

The place was alright, most definitely a romantic spot. Grabbing Peaches waist, I pulled her into my chest as we stood at the hostess stand. I glanced around the place and laughed. I was the only mothafucka in that bitch with jeans on. Everybody else were in dresses and suits.

"Their go Britt right there." I pointed to a private area at the back of the restaurant. I placed two fingers in my mouth.

"If you whistle, I'm going to slap the hell out of you. Just come on." Peaches head shook and she took my hand, leading us to the room. Once we were inside, the doors were closed behind us.

"Blaze, Peaches!" Brittany excited voice exclaimed once she saw us. She got out of her chair and hugged Peaches. "Thank you." She told her then looked to me. "I'm glad you came." Britt hugged me next.

I shrugged. "It ain't like I had a choice."

"Still… Anyways, Blaze, this is my baby, Kordell. Baby, this is my brother, Blaze." She introduced us.

"Hm…" I hummed, glaring at the same nigga that sat in my office over a month ago. My hand rubbed over my mouth.

"It's nice to finally meet you, Blaze." Kordell held his hand out for me to take.

I looked at Peaches who stared at me confused, then glanced to my sister, Brittany. "You been with this nigga for how long?" I nodded to dude but didn't take my eyes off Britt.

She moved closer to me. "Blaze, please don't start no mess. I really like him." She whispered.

"Yeah, I heard." I shot a quick glance to Peaches before turning my attention back to Britt. "What he do for a living?"

Britt blew out a breath. "He owns a few high-end clubs Downtown Chicago. Now can we please sit down and have a nice dinner?" She begged.

I sat down beside Peaches, ignoring his still outstretched hand. "So, you and my sister, huh?" Nodding, I looked to Brittany. "Britt, what you done told this nigga about me?" Peaches squeezed my thigh in a tight vice grip. I knew she was just trying to get my attention, but I simply ignored her and kept my focus on Brittany.

She opened her mouth to respond but closed it right back once Kordell hand grabbed hers. "I can assure you she hasn't told me anything aside from the fact that you're an overprotective dick who she didn't want me to meet. She fears you may scare me off." He looked at Britt with a smile before he brought her hand to his lips and kissed it. "But I assured her that could never happen."

"Hm…" Again, I nodded. "I told her that too. Let's go for a walk." I stood up and so did Peaches.

"How about we eat first, then go for a walk." Peaches suggested, giving Kordell a smile. Her gaze then landed on me and a glare covered her features. "B, you promised." She whispered to me. "Please, Blaze."

I kissed her forehead. "We're just gonna talk, I promise you that. Order our food, we'll be back. Kordell, let's go." I wasn't about to sit and eat with that mothafucka until I knew what the fuck he wanted. He wanted my attention so damn bad, now he had it.

I could hear him and Brittany passing words in their hush tones, but I couldn't make out what they were saying. However, from the whining tone of Britt's whispers, I knew she was begging him not to come with me.

"Man, I'm not gonna do shit to that nigga. We just gon' fuckin' talk. Damn! Y'all acting like I'mma kill that mothafucka."

"Blaze, please, I really like him." Britt pleaded again.

Who the fuck did they think I was?

"I'll be fine, so relax." Kordell kissed Britt, then led us down a hallway.

Once we walked out the back exit, I grabbed Kordell and threw him into the door we had just left out of. With my forearm pushed against his throat, I pulled my gun and pressed it to his chin. His eyes widened having been caught off guard.

"You think going through my sister to get to me was smart?" My forearm pushed harder into his throat. Kordell tried to pry my arm from his neck, but that only made me push harder.

"Nigga, that's the quickest way to get buried, you stupid mothafucka." I smacked him in the face with the butt of the gun. "You been playing a fuck'd up game with my sister." I hit him once more, then pushed into his neck harder before letting him go. My gun cocked.

"Hold…" He choked out. His hand raised, waving for me not to shoot him. "Hold the fuck up!"

I don't know why I paused, but I did. Even so, my gun was trained on him as I carefully watched his movement, waiting for him to make an off move so I could empty my clip into his ass.

He pulled the handkerchief from his breast pocket and wiped his cheek. "Look, I didn't know she was your fuckin' sister when we met." He spat out a wad of blood beside my foot. "Britt didn't tell me she had a brother until a month ago. I didn't find out it was you until after I killed one of my men for how they approached you." He explained, wiping his mouth once more.

"So, you want me to believe that yo ass approached me out of pure curiosity?" I questioned not buying it.

He raised his hand and stood up straight. "No. I've never been curious about you. I've always known who you were and what you did beforehand—well used to do. I wasn't coming to you as a threat, just business, Blaze. When I found out you were Brittany's brother, yeah, I thought we could make some shit happen. I'm all about business and making money. No other bullshit, trust me and I love yo sister…" He leaned to the side and spat again.

My brows furrowed at the look on his face. The gaze in his eyes, caused me to lower my gun. I knew that fuckin' look. Hell, I got it every time I was with Peaches. "You love my sister?" He nodded at the question and I looked him over. He was a well-dressed mothafucka. "You got to let her go. You heard of me and up until a few weeks ago, yo ass didn't know I had family. It's a reason no one knew that because my life— past life was to fuckin' dangerous. From the looks of shit, yo life ain't no different. If yo enemies—if you have any—find out about Britt, they'll go after her to get to you. Love ain't shit you can have in this game."

"I know that, and I won't let shit happen to Brittany. My personal and business life is two separate things—" He tried to explain.

It really wasn't a difference, no matter how hard you try to separate the two, personal and business always find a way to entwine and become one. I learned that shit the hard way years ago.

338

"Do Britt know what business you're into, aside from the clubs?" I asked but thought about it. "Don't even answer that because I know she don't. The shit yo ass into ain't for love my nigga. The best thing you can do for Brittany is to let her go. Now, with that shit being said, if yo ass don't and some shit happens to my sister, you won't have to worry about revenge because I'mma kill yo ass, then find the mothafuckas that hurt her. Trust me when I tell you, I'll enjoy killing yo ass." I told him straight up and honest. "We done talking." I stepped away from him and put my gun back in its place. "Now, go get yoself cleaned up. I don't want Brittany to think I hit you or some shit like that." I pointed to his face.

He looked at the blood on the handkerchief, then to me before he started laughing. Not bothering to say anything else, I went back inside the restaurant. When Peaches saw me, she stood up and walked over to me.

"Is he okay? You know him, don't you?" Even though she formed it as a question, she already knew the answer. "Just tell me you didn't kill him?"

My brows furrowed at her question. Laughing, my head shook at her. "Y'all mothafuckas act like I'm some type of psycho. I just talked to the nigga, damn." I pulled Peaches to me and wrapped my arms around her waist, immediately she started laughing, while trying to get out my arms. "You wanna come to the bathroom with me?" I kissed her mouth, then moved to her neck.

"Blaze, stop!" She laughed while taking my face between her hands and kissing me. "No, we're not going in the bathroom, so get that idea out yo nasty ass mind. Let's go back and I promise once we get home, I'll give my papa bear all the loving he wants." She licked my bottom lip, making me groan at the promise in her voice.

"I'mma hold you to that too." Kissing her once more, I let go of her and she led us back to the table. Once we sat down, my hand waved at Brittany as her mouth opened. "Yo boyfriend good. He had to go to the bathroom. How you meet this nigga?"

A wide smile came to Brittany's face. "I was leaving a club and kinda hit his car. He has this beautiful ice blue 69 Chevrolet Chevelle…" Britt's hand covered her mouth and she laughed.

"Oh, you think that shit funny?" Kordell asked, coming around the table.

My brows raised as I stared at him, confused. The nigga had changed his whole fuckin' outfit.

"Oh, my God, Kordell!" Brittany got up and grabbed his face. I picked up the cup of water that sat beside Peaches and took a drink of it. "Blaze, what the fuck?" She turned on me and Kordell grabbed her.

"Baby, I'm straight. Calm down, we don't need to cause a scene." He told Britt before kissing the side of her head.

Peaches hit me. "Blaze? What the hell?" She pointed to Kordell's face. His cheek was swollen, and the corner of his lip was split.

I shrugged. "That man gon' be alright." I then pointed to his face. "Shid, that was his fault. Now, if he wanna tell you why the fuck I hit his ass, he can. I'm done talking about the shit though." I told Brittany, then turned my attention to Peaches. "What you get me to eat? I'm hungry as fuck." Peaches face turned into a mean glare as she stared at me. Grabbing her chin, I leaned into Peaches, glaring at her. "What happened or whatever the fuck I talked to that nigga about, ain't got shit to do with you, for real. Fix yo damn face, and mind yo business." I wasn't with her mugging or hitting me behind some shit she ain't know anything about. It wasn't like I just went around hitting mothafuckas for no reason. "You hear me?" She smacked her lips and rolled her eyes, which only caused my grip on her chin to tighten.

"Whatever, Blaze." Again, her lips popped, but the glare she was rocking went away. "Now, let me the fuck go. Stupid ass." She jerked out of my hold and rubbed her chin.

I couldn't do shit but smile at her. She was most *definitely* made for me. "Give me a kiss." I mumbled while grabbing her thigh underneath the table. That caused her mean mug to come back and I started laughing.

"The shit ain't funny, for real. I really want to slap the hell out of you." She snapped at me, still glaring. I simply just stared, smiling at her. After a second, she leaned into me and roughly pressed her lips to mine. "You get on my nerves, with your high ass." She chuckled, then gave me a real kiss.

"Hm…" I hummed against her lips as my hand continued to move up her thigh.

"I'm glad y'all can laugh this off while my man is sitting here with a busted lip and—"

I pulled away from Peaches and glared at Brittany. "Yo, shut the hell up with all that gotdamn crying before I smack the shit outda you—"

"That's when we really gon' have a fuckin' problem." Kordell chimed in, cutting me off.

I leaned back in my seat and stared at him. "Nigga, I'll smack the fuck out of yo ass too. I ain't worried about having no mothafuckin' problems with yo ass, nigga. Yo, when it comes

342

to me and that one right there," I pointed to Brittany who looked like she wanted to be anywhere but there at that moment. "Shut the fuck up, because you ain't got a say and shouldn't have a reaction about shit. If I wanna slap the fuck out of her I'mma do that shit, period. That's all me, my nigga—"

"Peaches?" Brittany called to her then pointed to me.

"Why the hell you calling Peaches for? I'll smack fire from her ass too."

Peaches just shook her head. "Brittany, baby, you know how your brother is." She glanced at me and pursed her lips. "I'm sorry." Peaches started laughing, before her hand went to her mouth. "I don't mean to laugh, Britt and I'm sorry, but I knew how he was gonna act. I'm not even surprised and to be honest, he's better than what I really expected him to be. Brittany, you're his baby sister, hell, practically his child, I mean, how did you think he would be?"

Brittany glanced at me and groaned. "I don't know, but different, shit. Peaches, look what he did to his face—" she snapped, pointing at Kordell.

"I see it, but I also know Blaze. He's not going to hit some random dude for no reason— well sometimes he won't. Look, whatever the cause was for him to get hit isn't our business, leave that shit between them." She told Brittany who looked to Kordell. He nodded in agreement to what Peaches said and Britt sighed.

"I guess, you're right."

I knew I said some similar shit to what Peaches had spoken. My brows furrowed in confusion as to how the fuck Brittany could understand Peaches' words but not mine. "Hold the fuck up. I just said the exact same shit Peaches did."

Everybody at the table turned to look at me with thoughtful looks on their faces as if they were thinking about what I had said.

"No, you really didn't, Boon, you just started snapping for real." Brittany replied before sighing. "Boon, I really just want you to like him, because I'm in love with him. I need this from you. If you can't approve of him it's going to tarnish what I want to build with Kordell, because your acceptance means so much to me and it's only yours that I care about." She expressed with glossy eyes like she was on the verge of tears.

I glanced at Kordell, then back to Brittany, before I even realized it, my shoulders had shrugged and that made the tears start to fall down her eyes. I didn't really care for her tears because I knew what type of nigga Kordell was. He could have been a great nigga to her, but his profession was likely going to get her killed and that wasn't a chance or risk I was willing to take on my sister's life.

"Love is a dangerous thing, Britt. I can't give you that though. I don't know that nigga personally, and I don't care too. I could never approve of you being with somebody like him."

"You a cold mothafucka to say some shit like that to her. Real shit, I wanna—" Kordell started to say while glaring at me.

I quickly cut him off. I was tired of hearing that nigga talk. "Yo ass ain't gonna do shit, though. I don't know why the fuck you keep talkin' to me when I'm speaking to Brittany. Real shit, you're starting to piss me off and I'm ready to bring yo ass that fuckin' problem you spoke of. Now, regardless of how nan one of you mothafuckas feel, I don't want yo ass with her, period. And her fuckin' crying ain't gonna change that."

"Blaze—" Peaches began saying as Brittany pushed from the table.

"I really fuckin' hate you sometimes." With that she stormed off towards the restrooms.

Kordell glared murderously at me and I shrugged at him. Regardless of how Brittany felt at that moment, she would get over it eventually.

"Yo, that shit was fuck'd up. At this point, I don't wanna say shit to you, I really want to fuck you up—" Kordell stood and so did Peaches.

"No, you don't. Y'all done already caused enough of a fuckin' scene. I'll go check on Brittany. Kordell, you sit down." Peaches eyes shot toward me and if looks could kill, my ass would've been dead. "You wrong, Blaze."

"How the fuck I'm wrong? She said what she said, I told her how I felt." I pointed out and she rolled her eyes at me.

"Look, I'm not about to argue with you right here. I'm about to go check on Brittny before I do though." Her gaze fell on Kordell. "Kordell, listen, I don't know you, but I'mma give you the best advice that I can. Trust me; if you care for Brittany and really want to be with her. Fighting with this man, is going to be constant. I don't know if she told you how deep their bond truly is, but, B, is like her father, and right now, you're not talking to a big brother, it's her father you're dealing with. So, threatening to throw hands with this fool, ain't intimidating shit, because he's always ready to go no matter what and he's going to enjoy it win or lose."

"When it comes to him threatening to slap fire from her ass or whatever the case may be, baby, stay the fuck out of it. Because at the end of the day, he's going to trump anything, regardless of how pissed either of them may be. Now, I'm about to check on her, and I do expect y'all to act like fuckin' adults while I'm gone." She shot a pointed look at me like I was the only one she was talking to.

I waved her off, just as they brought the food out.

"The well done steak dinner is his." She informed the waiter while pointing to me, then she walked off. I knew from the hard sway of her hips that she was pissed off at me. But I didn't see what the hell I did wrong.

Once the waiter sat my food down, I grabbed my fork and started eating.

"You just made yo sister run out of here crying and yo ass dead sitting here like you don't give a fuck."

Cutting into my steak, I ate a piece then pointed my fork at him. "She's crying because I ain't giving her what she wants, which is you. I don't give a fuck how much she's in love with you, her feelings don't matter to me on this matter. I don't want my sister nowhere near this bullshit. I know what the fuck my wife went through all because of my line of work. I don't ever want my sister to go through that bullshit and if yo ass don't see where the fuck I'm coming from on that, then you don't love her like yo ass think you do." After taking a bite of my steak, my fork jabbed in his direction once again. "Would you quit your line of work to be with her?" I asked, not bothering to look at him as I ate my food.

Kordell was quiet for a long time, glancing up at him I nodded. "If you couldn't give me an instant *hell yeah*, then you don't need to be with her. Yo' young ass still in love with the hustle, money and power you got right now, which is cool, just leave Brittany out of it."

He let out a heavy breath, then ran a hand over his head. "Look, I hear what you're saying. But believe me when I tell you, I love the fuck out of that girl and I'm not gon' just walk away because you feel like I can't protect her. Mothafuckas know not to fuck with me and if they do, they know the consequence is death. Me continuing to do my work don't mean I love it more than her. I'm just confident that nobody is stupid enough to try me."

He explained, and he sound so sure of himself. However, I still laughed. "Look, I don't doubt you can't take care of her and you might think a mothafucka won't touch yo ass. But it's always somebody bigger and crazier than yo ass. If they want what you got, then they gon' try to take that shit period. And if a mothafucka know where your heart at, ain't no keeping that shit safe. You should know that bullshit. I'm sho' yo mothafuckin' hands ain't clean so you know just how grimy this shit can be." I pointed out what he should already know. "I'ight, I'm done talking about this shit, y'all both know how I feel, either you gonna listen or you don't. But just know, if my sister gets hurt behind yo lifestyle, I'm going to kill you. So, if the shit happens, be prepared for me. Aye!" I called to the waiter that was walking by. "Bring me two to-go boxes." I motioned to Peaches and Brittany's food.

"Brittany wasn't wrong about you. I see why she didn't want us to meet. Anyhow, I feel where you're coming from, but if I didn't think I couldn't protect her, then—"

I cut him off becoming pissed off. "Yo, you're not fuckin' hearing what I'm saying. I don't give a fuck what you feel yo ass can do. Nigga, I was the same way you are right now, had that same fuckin' mindset, until a mothafucka damn near killed my fuckin' wife. And believe me, my nigga I ain't never been pussy to kill a mothafucka, so I knew a mothafucka wouldn't try me, but it happened. So yo ass can't convince me of shit. I done already live this shit. Now, shut the fuck up about it. Damn." The woman came back with two boxes and bags. "Put Britt's food up." I nodded toward the box as I grabbed Peaches' plate and put her food in the container. After I had it in the bag, I got up and went to the bathroom where the girls had gone.

My knuckles rippled on the door before I pushed it opened. "Peach, Britt, y'all come on, it's time to go." I yelled inside and received several groans.

"We're coming." Peaches snapped, and I knew she was still pissed off at me from the sound of her voice.

I didn't say shit about her attitude because I wasn't trying to argue with her. I went to the wall and leaned against it. As I stood there, my phone pinged with a message. Taking it out my pocket, I looked at the screen to see Joshua's name and opened it.

Joshua: *Hey bro, can we meet up and have a drink?*

My brows furrowed at the question. The bathroom door opened, and I looked up into Peaches hard glaring face and quickly shot him a text back.

Me: *Yeah. I'll pick you up from Joseph's crib.*

From the look on Peaches face, I knew what the night was looking like and wasn't trying to fight with her ass at all. "I packed yo food up." I told her, holding up the to-go bag.

Peaches eyes quickly cut into slits. "You need to apologize to her, Blaze—"

"What the fuck for? I haven't done shit to her ass. She asked me something and I gave her a straight up answer, I wasn't going to lie to her. Gon' get the fuck out of here with that shit for real." My eyes slid to Brittany's puffy red face and I glared at her. She looked away from me. My attention was brought back to Peaches from the punch to my chest and I looked at her ass if she had lost her damn mind. "Why the fuck—"

"Because you're a damn asshole, Blaze. This is just like you and King's dumbass all over again. Look, B, I understand why you can't accept their relationship, but Brittany don't get it. Tone down all that fuckin' aggression and tell your sister why you don't want her to date someone like Kordell. If I thought it would've helped, I would've explained, but she needs to hear it from you."

Peaches had told me several times that I spoke to harshly to folks. I didn't see the shit, though. "I don't know what I need to tell her... I mean... shit—"

"At least tell me why you don't want me with him? Blaze, I really love Kordell. He is everything I want and need in a man. And to be honest, he kind of reminds me of you, like how you care and always want to protect me. I used

351

to watch you with Peaches and wanted someone to look at me the way you did her, fuss over me the way you were with her. Boon, out of the five relationships I've been in, no one has ever stared at me the way Kordell do or treated me like he does. You know what? Even if you don't approve of him, I'm still going to be with him, Blaze, but I want you to tell me why you don't want this for me?" Tears ran down her face rapidly as her lips quivered.

My hand rubbed over my head as I watched her cry. "Britt, it ain't that I don't want you happy or in love. It's just I don't want you with him because he's too much like me. All this shit I was doing at his age, he's doing it now and all I can see is you getting hurt like Peaches had. I don't want that shit, because then, I'mma have to kill his ass, then go after the mothafuckas that hurt you. Doing that is either going to get me killed or sent to jail, taking me away from my family, but I'mma still do that shit because its you, Brittany. Baby girl, you my heart so I'll have to do that shit."

Brittany's arms were around me in an instance. I glanced to Peaches to see her quickly wipe her eyes. "I don't know why you couldn't just explain that to me from the beginning, because I would've understood clearer." With a heavy sigh, she let go of me. "Boon, I'm not stupid or blind, I know what Kordell does for a living. Like I said, he reminds me of you in a lot of ways. He has no idea that I know, and I don't want him to. I want him to tell me himself which is why I haven't said anything. Knowing him, he probably thinks I'm going to leave him because of it. *But I'm not!*" She quickly tacked on.

"Brittany—"

"No, Booney, I'm not some little kid anymore that you can run. I'm a grown ass woman who can make her own choices, whether the results are good or bad, it's what I want. All I need for you to do is support me on this."

It was at that moment that I really saw Brittany. She wasn't that little teenage girl anymore she was in fact grown as fuck. I then looked to Peaches, she was right also, I wasn't trying to be like King.

"Fuck!" My hand rubbed over my mouth. I had to let her grow up and if she got hurt in the end… "You right, Britt, so I'mma step the fuck off and let you do as you wish." Brittany started smiling widely. "But I'mma say this, if yo ass get hurt behind his bullshit, I'm going to kill his ass and his death gonna be on you." Her smile immediately faded.

"Blaze!" Peaches hit me. "Yo ass always have to ruin a good moment, I fuckin' swear." Her head shook as she stared at me for a long second before she broke out laughing. "Yo ass get on my nerves. Brittany, take that with a wide ass smile because it wouldn't be true Blaze form if he didn't tack on that last bit." She came over to me and wrapped her arms around my waist. "You are so lucky that I'm in love with yo rude, mean ass." Standing on her tiptoes, she kissed me.

"I have to tell him this, Boon." Brittany's excitement was back in her voice as she pushed past us in a rush. No doubt she was running to Kordell.

"It don't make any sense how you still have that damn girl spoiled. I just pray to God Brianna don't turn out like her, Jesus. Do you know I had to remind her that she was grown?" Peaches' head once again shook.

I didn't hear shit but the comment she made about Brianna. "If Bria ass think about a nigga, I'm burying the mothafucka right off bat. Hell no! You know what the fuck men and women do? Hell no! I wish a mothafucka would—"

Peaches hollered out a laugh. "Oh, so it's cool for Blake to be running around getting his shit wet—"

My hand slapped over her mouth. "Yo, Peaches, real shit, don't even go there. I ain't tryna think about that shit for real. Let's get out of here."

354

She pushed my hand from her mouth. "Wait, how you gonna pack my food up and make me leave? I wanted to sit down and enjoy my meal. I did not get all fine just to come in here for a half hour and then leave. No, B, we're about to sit down and eat like we're on a date. It's not like we really go out on dates—"

"I'ight man, we can stay. Just don't start all that damn complaining. You should've just told me you wanted to go out and I would've taken yo ass on a date. We would've gone to a nice ass buffet—" She punched me in the stomach, and I laughed while pulling her to me. "I'm just bullshittin'." My hand went to the nape of her neck, grasping it, I kissed her.

"I love you so much, Blaze." Peaches mumbled against my mouth.

My arm snaked around her waist and I lifted her off her feet. "Love you too." I kissed her once more, then let her down. "Let's go—"

"Wait, tell me how you know him?" She questioned.

I shrugged. "The nigga stopped by the Lot and asked me to go into business with him." Peaches brows furrowed. "I wasn't doing that bullshit though, I'm out and I meant that shit." I told her before she could start overthinking shit.

"But why would he approach you to work for him though—"

"Peach, I don't know and don't give a fuck. Now come on." My arm went around her shoulder and I walked us from the back and went to the table were Brittany and her nigga sat, kissing.

"Ouch…" Peaches said, pushing at my hand that held her shoulder. It wasn't until then I realized my grip had tightened on her.

"Oh shit, my bad, Peach." I didn't know how I was going to get through the rest of the fuckin' night with the two of them. "Y'all can cut that bullshit out for real." I told them once I reached the table. Brittany pulled away smiling hard at me.

"So, you cool with us being together?" Kordell asked me.

My brows raised at his question. "Hell no. I don't want her with you at all—" Peaches hand hit my stomach. I coughed at the sudden hard hit, then cleared my throat as my jaw grew tight. "But Brittany's grown, she can fuck with whoever she wanna."

"So, I was thinking, once we finished up dinner, we could go out dancing or something. Just so we can get to know you more, Kordell." Peaches chimed in, smiling at him.

Now she was taking shit to fuckin' far. I wasn't trying to hang with my little sister, hell no. "Nah, we ain't doing that. I got shit to do later." Peaches head snapped toward me so fast and her mouth opened to start asking questions. "Don't ask no questions, Peaches. Eat your food." I nodded to the foam container and she glared at me.

"I can have them make you two a fresh meal." Kordell told Peaches and Brittany who smiled at him. He then called the waiter over, put their orders in and handed over the containers. The waiter left with a simple nod. I was ready for that shit to be over.

The girls and Kordell made small talk while I texted Joshua letting him know I was going to be late.

"Brittany, finish telling us how y'all met." Peaches said.

"Oh, I was leaving the club and smashed into his car. He was so pissed at first, going off. Then when I got out of my car apologizing, it was like he forgot all about the car and his anger. Instead his focus came on me and he was trying to make sure I was alright. Once he realized I was okay, he asked for my number. When I told him no, he then made me feel bad for damn near wrecking his car, so I caved and gave it to him. We've been pretty much inseparable since then. Now I just need for him to meet Mommy."

My eyes snapped to Brittany's instantly, but she was already looking at me as if expecting me to look at her. "You damn sho' ain't doing that shit. Whatever the hell you about to say, keep that bullshit to yo gotdamn self, because I don't give a fuck. If you want to introduce that nigga to somebody let his ass meet Joseph and yo other brother, Joshua. But leave my fuckin' momma away from this shit." If the nigga wasn't so deep into the drug shit, then maybe I'll go for it. But I wasn't chancing my momma's life behind Brittany or her nigga.

"I agree with Blaze on this one, Brittany, I'm sorry. Blaze has done good with keeping you and Mom B out of shit, I wouldn't want to chance it with this new breed of niggas, honestly. So, for her safety, wait." Peaches spoke evenly and surely of what she had said.

Brittany glanced at Kordell who shrugged, and she looked back to Peaches. "Maybe you're right."

I chuckled at how easy she was to accept what Peaches said than me, especially when we basically said the same fuckin' thing.

As if knowing what I was thinking, Brittany and Peaches laughed. "Babe, it's your delivery on what you say." Peaches explained what she's been telling me for years. I didn't see it though.

Once again, I shrugged as the waiter came with their food and I ordered myself a beer.

After the trio talked for over an hour and finished their food, we were ready to leave. Peaches and Brittany were walking slow as hell while talking as if they didn't have each other's number or some shit. Hell, those mothafuckas didn't talk like that in real life. Now all of a sudden, they had shit to discuss.

I walked ahead of them to get to the truck, but my fast movement slowed down, as I saw a black truck turn down the lane that we were in. Instinctively, I grabbed my gun. I wouldn't have taken notice had it not been for the fact that the headlights were off, and the truck was driving slowly.

"Peaches, cut through the cars—" I was telling her just as the window rolled down and a gun stuck out of it. Immediately, I started shooting.

"Ah!" I heard Brittany scream.

I quickly ran back and dodged behind a little ass car. "Peaches!" I yelled through the gunfire, while moving to the next car behind me. "Peaches!"

"I'm okay." She shouted back.

"Get under a fuckin' car, now! The both of y'all!" I told them as I gripped my Desert Eagle tightly, then started shooting again. I didn't know if Kordell was hit or not, but I hoped like fuck that mothafucka was.

Another scream rang out from behind me. I didn't know if it was Brittany or Peaches, nor did I care, I immediately took off running in that direction where I heard the screams. The car I ran past, window shattered, and I ducked behind the hood. After a second, I started shooting toward the trucks once again. The truck crashed into a car and the horn started blowing, just as a shot came from behind me and another deafening scream followed.

My fuckin' heart dropped at the sound.

Chapter 19

Blaze

"Peaches!" Fear struck me hard and it felt like I couldn't fuckin' breathe when I didn't get an answer. "Peaches—"

"I'm fine—"

I found Peaches three cars down, kneeling beside a body, with her gun gripped tightly in her hand. Brittany sat on the opposite side of her, leaned against the car and staring at the body in shock.

"He tried to grab Brittany and I shot him." Peaches explained, standing up.

Grabbing her, my eyes roamed over her body, looking for any marks, bruises anything, When I found none, I pulled her into my chest, hugging her hard. "Fuck." Thinking something had happened to her, scared the hell out of me.

"I'm alright, B, I promise. I'm not hurt, baby. He didn't even touch me." She reassured me. "I'm okay." She repeated then pointed to Brittany. "She's shaken, but she didn't get hurt."

I nodded before going over to Brittany. "You good?" Like I had done Peaches, my eyes roamed over her, making sure she was alright. When I didn't see any marks, I nodded as if okaying myself.

Brittany actions mirrored mine. Her eyes began to focus more as she gradually came out of her shocked state. She looked from me to Peaches then around us. She leaned up straight. "Where's Kordell?" She sat up fully.

"I don't know. Y'all stay right here." I told them, then got up and cautiously approached the truck. The passenger was slumped over into the driver's seat, whereas the driver lay on the steering wheel, causing the horn to blare, the pair of them were dead. Reaching inside, I pulled the driver off the horn.

"Mario, just keep everybody inside…" I heard Kordell's weak voice pant out.

A glare covered my face and I walked over toward the voice. A second later, I heard a muffled *pop* of a gun going off. I looked around a black truck to see Kordell on the ground and his gun muzzle pressed against some dude's head. When he heard me, he turned his gun in my direction.

"Oh, shit it's just you. Where's Brittany?" He asked, lowering his gun.

I paid his question no mind as my gun was trained on his head. Without a second thought, I pulled the trigger.

"Blaze, no!" Brittany screamed, pushing me at the same time my finger squeezed off the shot. The bullet went through the truck's back door, an inch from where Kordell's head was. "Oh, my God, are you alright?" She kneeled beside her dude, feeling over him.

"I thought I told yo ass to stay behind that fuckin' car?" I snapped at Brittany. I wanted to knock the shit out of her.

She turned around on me so fast. "What the fuck, Boon? You could've killed him!" She screamed at me.

"That's what the fuck I was trying to do. I told his ass if you got caught up in his shit, I was gonna kill him. That nigga back there just tried to fuckin' take you, Britt! If Peaches wasn't there, then his ass would've got yo retarded ass. As long as that mothafucka breathing they gon' keep coming after yo dumbass. The best thing to do is to kill that mothafucka." I snapped at her while pointing to Kordell.

A mean glare covered her face. "I don't care and you're not killing him—"

"He's right, Brittany, they'll keep coming for you, but it's not for the reason he thinks. They're after me because I killed Turk for coming to you the way he did." Kordell grunted as he pushed himself up off the ground. He pointed to the body that lay at his feet. "That's Slick, Turk's older brother. Now that he's dead, his people about to start some shit for real." He explained.

I watched his movement as he spoke, and he didn't seem to be lying. "So, because yo nigga went rogue and you offed his ass, now his brothers after you?"

Kordell shrugged. "That's exactly what I just said." He glared at me before his fist shot out and he punched me in the jaw. "You could've shot me in the fuckin' head. Yo, what the fuck is wrong with yo ass? You weren't even gon' ask me who the fuck they were or shit. Yo ass was just gon' fuckin' shoot me." Kordell snapped as he moved Brittany behind him.

364

My hand rubbed my jaw, before I punched his ass in the mouth.

"Okay, would y'all fuckin' stop it!" Peaches got in between us, pushing me back. "Y'all need to put all this bullshit to the fuckin' back burner and get this shit cleaned up before the gotdamn police show the fuck up here. Blaze, fuckin' stop!" She yelled at me. "I'mma take Brittany to the apartment, once y'all done with this shit, meet us there." Peaches waved Brittany to her. "Come on, so they can clean this shit up." Peaches looked at me then stood on her tiptoes and kissed me. "If you kill him, I'm going to be pissed off at you. Hurry up with this and come back to me." She kissed me again. "I love you."

I nodded at her because she was right. I needed to put the shit with him to the side and take care of business before the laws showed up. "We got this, gon' head. Leave my duffle out for me." Peaches gave me a faint smile and started to walk off. Stopping her, I pulled her back to me. "Go straight there and call me when you get in the parking lot. I'ight?"

Standing on her tiptoes, she kissed me again. "Promise. We'll be fine, just hurry up." Peaches lips pressed against mine once more, she then pulled away from me. She went to grab Britt's arm, but she ran over to Kordell.

"You be safe too. I love you." She kissed him.

"I love you too and I'll be straight," he kissed her again, then pulled away. "Now, gon' get out of here." He motioned toward Peaches.

Brittany's eyes came to mine. "If you hurt him, Boon—"

"Man, gon' on with that shit. I ain't gonna hurt yo little ass boyfriend." I waved her off.

"You just tried to shoot him in the face—" She started to yell.

"Brittany, I'll be good. Now get the fuck out of here." Kordell snapped at her. My brows raised at his demanding tone.

Brittany looked like she wanted to argue but thought better of it. "Fine, but if you die, I'm going to kill you, Kordell—"

"Girl, bring yo ass the fuck on. Damn!" Peaches finally snapped at her. She yanked Britt's wrist then started dragging her off to the truck.

I had to laugh to myself from Peaches tone. Brittany pissed her off with all that gotdamn whining and complaining her ass was doing. Once I saw the truck start and Peaches pull off, I turned to face Kordell.

"My boys inside gonna handle the police and shit. But we got to get these bodies out of here—"

"I'll take care of the bodies. Yo ass bleeding, I don't need you leaving a trail of that shit around. Go clean yoself up." I told him then walked off and grabbed the duffel bag Peaches sat out for me. I took out my gloves, slipped them on, then went to work.

I went over, grabbed Slick and tossed his heavy ass over my shoulder, then went to the truck they rode in and tossed his ass in the hatchback. I did the same to the dude Peaches shot and killed. After tossing the passenger and driver in the hatchback, I left the restaurant.

***

After I drenched the bodies in gasoline as well as the clothes I had on, I struck a match and tossed it inside the back of the truck. Immediately the bodies went up in flames. I then tossed a match in the front seat to get the fire blazing quicker. Once the whole truck was engulfed in flames, I grabbed my duffel, and took off running from the abandon street I was on.

It took me fifteen minutes to get to the location where King sat waiting for me in an abandon parking lot. Once I was inside his truck, I snatched off the black ski mask and let out a heavy breath. "Man, I'm getting to old for this bullshit." I told him while stuffing the mask and gloves I wore into a bag King held out for me, I then stripped my gun and Peaches' apart and started cleaning them. "Man, I liked those fuckin' guns."

"You'll get new ones. Now what the fuck is going on?" King glanced at me while pulling out the parking lot.

"I don't remember if I told you this, but a while back, some nigga stopped by the club and put in an order..." I began telling him what had went down.

King pulled on the blunt and exhaled heavily. "Damn, and the nigga fuckin' Brittany's ass. Fuck. So, we gon' kill this nigga or what?" He held the blunt out to me.

That was one of the main reasons King and I got along. The nigga was down for anything without any questions. "Man, I tried to kill that mothafucka, but Brittany stupid ass stopped me talkin' 'bout she love that mothafucka. That's the reason his ass ain't with me now. Nigga, I know myself, buddy ass would've been back there in that truck burning with those other niggas."

368

King started laughing. "Boss, I just thought that shit, I figured that's why the nigga wasn't with you."

I exhaled the weed smoke and nodded. "That's the only reason. I'mma have Mac stay close to his ass though until this shit is over with."

King shook his head. "Hell no, Mac a little hotheaded mothafucka too though. I can see him killing that nigga over something dumb." He pointed out and I nodded.

My shoulders shrugged as I handed him the blunt back. "Shid, if that's what he gotda do, then, aye, it is what it is. That nigga's death won't be on my hands."

Again, King started laughing. "That's fuck'd up. You gon' use Mac like that to kill yo sister's nigga?"

"Fuck that nigga." I grabbed the blunt from him and toked on it. "We gotda go by Bell's crib, I found iPhones on those niggas and I need him to get into them."

King nodded, then turned up the radio and jumped on the highway, heading to Bellow's house.

***

"All I'm saying is, if she was with me, none of this bullshit would be happening to her, period." Mac pointed out as he flopped down on the couch across from Brittany and Kordell.

Although I didn't think he meant that shit, and was only trying to piss Kordell off, I still glared at him. "Yo shut the fuck up. That bullshit don't matter right now, what does; is how the fuck we about to end this bullshit for real. I ain't about to stand around here waiting on no mothafuckin' niggas to pop up again and try to kill my sister. We need to dead this shit now. Kordell, you know where these niggas be?"

Kordell stared at me for a long second before he started laughing. "Blaze, you ain't about to run up on none of these niggas without them knowing. It's been a couple of hours since this shit went down and Slick ain't got back with his people yet, so they know all their asses are dead by now. They're about to be on high alert and gunning for my fuckin' head." He explained as he paced around the living room.

"Nigga, who the fuck you think you're talking too? I've been doing this shit before yo ass was born. Of course, they gonna be looking for yo stupid ass. But they won't expect none of us." I pointed out. "It's one particular spot they ass meet in at least twice a month. If we find that spot, we can end this shit quick. I'm hoping the phones I pulled from those niggas would tell me that."

A thoughtful look covered Kordell's face and his head bobbed as if he was thinking on what I said. "That's smart... we can definitely do that—"

"No shit, that's why he said the shit." Mac spat out as he glared at Kordell.

Kordell returned the look. "Nigga, fuck you and shut the fuck up."

Mac hopped off the couch quick and went at Kordell. King quickly grabbed Mac, restraining him. "Yo, let me the fuck go. Nigga, I'll fuck yo ass up, you bitch." Mac's sudden anger surprised the fuck out of me.

"Mac, seriously? What the fuck, you really going to try and fight him when there's bigger shit at state, like somebody tryna kidnap and kill me?" Brittany finally spoke, snapping at him.

Mac's glare turned on her so fast. "Oh, now you're worried about somebody trying to kill yo dumbass? What the fuck you thought was gonna happen, Britt? I done told yo ass for years not to get in bed with a nigga involved in this fuckin' lifestyle and yo stupid ass do the shit anyway." He went off on her.

As I watched the rage take hold of Mac, I realized his anger wasn't from jealousy or no shit like that, he was genuinely concerned for her life. Like I was. In my eyes, Mac was a pissed off brother wanting to kill his little sister for not listening to him.

"I think you should slap her ass." I told him and the pair of them looked at me. I shrugged. "I'm dead ass serious. I didn't warn her of this shit, I thought she was smart enough not to get involved with a nigga like me. Now her damn life in danger. So yeah, I think you should knock the fuck out her ass. And ain't nobody gon' do shit to you if yo ass do." I looked directly at Kordell. I was itching to beat his ass.

"If he touches her, I'll fuck the both of y'all up. Don't fuckin' try me." Kordell bit out.

"For fuck sake put y'all gotdamn dicks away. What's done is done, so stop dwelling on the shit that can't be changed. And Blaze, King thought the same thing about me when I got with you, so chill the fuck out, damn. Mac... Lord, you just like a mini fuckin' Blaze. Just stop. If y'all wanna fight do the shit after the niggas that wanna *kill*, *kidnap*, hell, *fuck*, Brittany, and Kordell's asses are dead." Peaches went off. "Damn. King, you can let him go, he's good. Mac, there's no fighting in here." She glared at him and he looked away from her.

Through the years, Peaches practically became like a mother to Mac. She had his ass wrapped around her damn finger like the rest of us. Mac loved and respected the hell out of Peaches. So, it didn't surprise me one bit when his ass went back to the couch, and flopped down like an angry kid who couldn't get their way.

Peaches pushed me down on the couch then sat in my lap, making herself comfortable. "I wish you would leave that damn girl alone and that dude. If King couldn't scare you away from me, what make yo ass think you're gonna scare him off? If anything, it's gonna make her want him more. I mean… that's kinda why I wanted you because King didn't want us together—"

"You a black ass lie!" King cut her off by saying. "You wanted his stupid ass because it's who you wanted to be with. Dumbass." He snapped at her.

She glared at him but didn't address what he said, instead she looked back at me. "My point is; you can't stop them from being together. So, let the shit drop. The both of you?" She shot a glare over to Mac. "Now since that's cleared up, Kordell, what can you tell us about them?"

Kordell looked over to me as if he weren't sure about talking in front of Peaches. "Gon' head and answer her question. My shorty good, you don't have to worry about her talking to nobody about shit." Peaches ass was a mothafuckin' rider by heart. A nigga could torture her ass and she still wouldn't fold, she would die before talking. "And it's your choice to speak in front of Brittany." She wanted to be a big girl and get involved with Kordell, then I wasn't going to say shit else to her about not dating that nigga.

"Well, I'm not leaving. Gon' head and talk." Brittany told Kordell.

"I can tell you about Turk and his brothers, but where they're meeting at," he shrugged. "I wouldn't know that, but I have somebody who could find out. She's pricey as fuck, but shorty good at what she does."

I nodded and watched as Peaches did the same. I found out that Turk was the dude who dropped the orders off at the club. "Well then call her and setup a meeting so we can meet her. Oh, and you can pay her pricey ass since you were the one who killed Turk. The sooner we can meet, the faster this bullshit will be over." Peaches seemed already tired of everything as she spoke to Kordell.

Kordell glanced at me once again and I glared at him. "You heard what the fuck she said. Why the fuck you keep looking at me for?"

The nigga started smiling hard at Peaches. "I like you. Are you sho' you're married to that mothafucka?" He asked her, and Peaches started laughing.

She showed him her ring. "Positive and happily."

"Hm…" He hummed as if he didn't understand it.

"I can't believe it sometimes myself. Alright, Kordell you gon' get in touch with your girl." She told him then looked to me. "You wanna go to bed?"

After the night I had, I didn't have to be asked twice. I needed to fuck the shit out of Peaches, to get my head together. Fear was a hell of a thing when it came to the person that held your heart. I stood up with Peaches in my arms. "I'ight, we're about to crash. Mac, you're staying here. King, we'll get up with you later." I tossed two fingers up at Brittany, then carried Peaches to our room.

Chapter 20

Blake

One Week Later

"Y'all mothafuckas be all on my fuckin' ass, gotdamn." I pushed Patrick off me, then tossed the ball to Ace. I ran around Pat, caught the ball Ace tossed back to me, midair and dunked it. "Ah!" I yelled as I landed on my feet. "Yo ass got to move quicker than that baby. Slow ass." I laughed while grabbing the ball.

"Nigga, fuck you. I let yo ass get that shit, so you would stop fuckin' whining." Patrick pushed me and took the ball.

"I think that little bitch mad, because he caught a mouthful of balls, Blake." Ace clowned Patrick.

"Nigga, fuck you too. I ain't mad. I let that nigga get that shit." Patrick snapped at him.

"Blake, yo ass fouled the fuck out of Pat though." Nelly pointed to Patrick. "You pushed the fuck out of him." He took the ball from Pat and started dribbling it.

"Man, shut the fuck up. I ain't foul that bitch, he was all on my fuckin' ass. That nigga always do that shit. So that ain't no gotdamn foul. Now, let's get this game going, so we can win you bitches money."

"Y'all ass ain't gon' win shit." Nelly bumped pass me and took the ball out.

***

"What the fuck I say?" I held my hand out towards Nelly. "Give me my fuckin' money, nigga."

"Nigga, suck my dick, fuck y'all mothafuckas. Y'all ass be fouling and shit." Pat complained.

Ace slapped Patrick on the back of the neck hard as fuck. "Bitch, shut the fuck up crying and pay us. Ain't nobody tryna hear that shit, yo. And yo bitch can suck my dick, nigga, just like yo ass been gargling Blake's nuts all game." Ace picked, pushing Patrick who got pissed off.

Patrick stepped to Ace. "Nigga, I'll fuck yo ass up. Keep playing with me, bitch." He spat out, ready to fight.

Ace smiled widely and I got in between them. I knew Ace all too well and that smile told it all. "Yo, chill the fuck out. Ace, leave that nigga alone, man, you always fuckin' with that mothafucka." I pushed Ace back and he laughed. "Pat, I'mma need that money up off yo whiny ass, for real though."

"Pat, yo ass gon' learn to stop balling with these niggas." Nelly said while slapping a fifty in my hand.

"Here, Ace…" I tried to hand him the fifty Nelly gave me.

"Nah, Patrick gonna pay me. Come on, baby, run me my shit." Ace loved fuckin' with that nigga. But Patrick didn't make shit better with all that damn whining and complaining. Shit, that was the only reason Ace did it. He like the anger Patrick showed, he fed off that shit. Ace was psychotic like that.

"Aye," Nelly called and nodded toward the parking lot. Janae, Shantell, Mariah and the two dudes from B-Dubs was with them. "Shanny's cousin sexy as fuck." Nelly commented.

"She out of yo league little nigga." Ace told him while slapping a hand on his shoulder. "Shorty look like she got the type of pussy they'll have yo ass sucking yo thumb and crying for yo moms afterwards. That bitch poison, so kids don't need to play with her." Ace smirked at Nelly before he looked at me.

I laughed at his logic, but I had to agree with him, she definitely had some good pussy. "That means yo ass can't play with her, Ace, you're the biggest fuckin' kid out here."

"Nigga, fuck you." He threw the ball at me.

I quickly jumped to the side before the ball could hit me. "Y'all down for another game or what?"

"I'm game." The trio replied just as Janae and them reached us.

"Can I play?" Mariah asked while dribbling the ball over.

"Sweetheart, give me that before you hurt yoself." Nelly told her as he went to take it, but she quickly sent it between her legs.

"I might hurt you, is what you meant." She told him as she shot the ball in. Mariah turned and looked at me with a smile. "Hey, Blake." She waved as her eyes ran over me.

After I left B-Dubs that night, I did go to Mariah's crib and fuck'd her, which I was regretting like hell. The idea of fuckin' her one last time was all good until the shit happened. Ever since that night, Mariah had been calling and texting my ass relentlessly. The texting would get worse when she knew I was with Janae. She just didn't give a fuck, even though I had made the shit perfectly clear that was going to be the last time we fuck'd.

"What's up." I tossed up two fingers at her, then turned back to my group. "Y'all figure that shit out." I told them before turning my attention to Janae who had walked off as she talked on the phone. I caught up with her and swooped her up bridal style. She let out a squeak before laughing.

"I'll send you the email when I get home. Bye." She ended her called. "Why you do that? You scared me."

"Who you on the phone with?" I asked instead of answering her question.

She looked at her phone and shrugged. "Nobody, so mind your business." Janae put the phone in her bra.

"Oh, it's like that?" Her lips pursed together, and she nodded. I returned the gesture before sticking my hand into her bra.

"Blake!" She yelled, grabbing my wrist. "Seriously? You gonna dig in my bra for my phone?"

My brow raised as I pinched her nipple. "Nah, I just wanted to touch yo tittie. What you do last night? I thought you was gonna stop by Ace's crib?"

Janae's arms went around my neck and she pulled my head down, kissing me. "I was helping my momma out and when I finished it was late. So, I just stayed in and called Shanny over. Her and Mariah kept me company."

"Hm... you couldn't call me and say that?"

She rolled her eyes at that. "I thought about it, but I know how you and Ace get when y'all together. Plus, Mariah, thought you should have a boy's night. Am I clingy?" She suddenly asked, seeming really curious.

Once again, my brows raised at her question. "What the fuck make you ask that?"

She shrugged before kissing me again. "Just something Mariah said, had me thinking that I could be. I mean, we do spend mostly everyday together and we're always together on the

weekends. You barely hang with your friends—
"

"Yo, why the fuck is you even listening to that fuckin' girl? If I had a problem with being with you so much, I'll tell yo ass that." What the fuck was Mariah doing by putting that shit in her head?

Janae sighed and laid her forehead against mine. "I thought you would too, but now I don't know. Maybe you just don't wanna hurt my feelings because of what we went through with the baby."

"That's what she told you?" She shrugged once again. I quickly put her down and headed toward Mariah, I was about to knock the fuck out of her.

"Shit! Babe, wait!" Janae ran in front of me, placing her hand on my chest and stopped me. "Blake, don't go over there all pissed off at her. In fact, don't say shit at all. See this why I don't be telling you shit now. You always just snap off. She just gave me some friendly advice that's it."

I glared at her, I wanted to slap her ass too. "That bitch ain't yo fuckin' friend, Nae, I bet that mothafucka told yo ass that shit to hurt yo dumbass feelings. Yo ass need to stop hanging with that bitch, Shanny stupid ass too! You a dumb mothafucka—"

Janae hand shot out and she slapped the fuck out of me. "I ain't gonna be to many dumb mothafuckas, Blake. You're not gonna keep talking to me like I ain't shit! How the fuck you gon' tell me who ain't my fuckin' friend? Mariah and Shanny was there for me through my abortion when yo stupid ass was acting like a fuckin' bitch—"

My hand went to her throat and choked the fuck out of her. "You better keep yo hands to yourself and watch yo fuckin' mouth. Call me another bitch and I'mma bust yo shit. You gon' call me that shit because I wasn't sitting around crying with yo dumbass all day? Get the fuck out of here with that bullshit, we didn't need no fuckin' baby. Just because I wasn't fuckin' crying don't mean I wasn't there. Bitch, I was with yo stupid ass through the whole fuckin' thing until you had the abortion." My finger jabbed in Mariah's direction. "That bitch ain't yo fuckin' friend either, she tryna get close to yo stupid ass so she could be in our shit. But yo dumb ass don't see that shit though."

"Blake, yo chill out—" Ace bumped into me. As he tried to slide between us.

Janae reached around Ace and slapped the shit out of me again. "Don't ever grab me like that again. You don't even fuckin' know her, so how the hell you gonna assume what her reasons are. Like I said, when I was going through everything before I had the fuckin' abortion that you wanted, Mariah and Shanny was there. You might've paid for the abortion and took me, but yo ass wasn't there, you were too busy fuckin' Squeaky and any other bitch willing."

My head nodded. "Yeah, including—" Ace's hand slapped over my mouth.

"B, chill the fuck out. You niggas dumb as fuck, like y'all dead ass doing that bullshit right here, in front of every fuckin' body." Ace snapped at me.

"It's not like we're saying shit everybody don't already fuckin' know." Janae shot back glaring at me.

"Bitch, shut the fuck up, ain't nobody know shit until yo dumb ass ran yo fuckin' mouth to Shanny hoe ass."

"I ain't know none of this shit until just now." My head fell back at the sound of my dad's voice.

"I second that. This all news to me." My Uncle King chimed in.

"Shid, don't stop talking because we're here. Gon' head and finish this shit." My dad said, and I looked back at him to see he had sat on a basketball. My Unc, Bellow and Sam had also sat down in the middle of the court, whereas

384

Joshua stood behind my pops, but they all were staring at us.

"I ain't got shit else to say." I shrugged. At that point I didn't even give a fuck. Whatever happened from there so be it.

"Hey, Mr. Carter." Janae spoke to my dad and he simply nodded at her. "Shanny, Mariah, let's go."

"That's fuck'd up how much his ass is yo son." Sam told my pops with a shake of his head.

"I have to question that shit sometimes. The boy dumb as fuck if you ask me. So, I don't know if he's mine or not." My dad saying that literally caused everybody to look at him.

"Nigga, it look like you birth that mothafucka yo gotdamn self. That nigga you straight through. Fuck is you talking about?" King asked him.

My dad stood up and brushed himself off. Picking up the ball, he threw it to Ace. "Ace, you gon' step in for me." He looked at me and shook his head. "Bring yo stupid ass on." His head jerked to the side for me to follow him. "What the fuck you mothafuckas looking at? Wasn't you just about to bounce?" He asked Janae, before looking at Mariah and Shanny.

Janae looked at me and my dad shook his head at her. "Don't worry about him. Gon' bout yo fuckin' business." He shooed her off. He walked past them and I followed him. Once we were on the other side of the court, he stopped and faced me. "So, yo stupid ass out here fuckin' these little bitches raw and knocking they ass up?"

My hand ran over my mouth and I shook my head at his question. "I fuck'd up once and I took care of it. She ain't pregnant no more."

"The bitch shouldn't have gotten pregnant in the first fuckin' place, Blake! What the fuck is wrong with you, nigga? Then you made her ass get an abortion? If yo ass ain't won't no mothafuckin' kids, yo dumb ass shouldn't be out here fuckin' raw. Yo ass about to fuck up everything for some fuckin' pussy?" He was pissed off.

Seeing how mad he was, I knew to be cautious with his ass. I could deal with my dad except for when the nigga was pissed off. The mothafucka had no sense and was unpredictable as fuck. I damn sure wasn't trying to be out there fighting with that big mothafucka.

My hand ran over my head and I took a step back. I just didn't know what to expect from him. I damn sure didn't want to be close enough that he could knock my ass out before I even realized what the hell happened.

"I fuck'd up one time, it was a mistake." I repeated, that was the only thing I could say.

"Ain't no fuckin' mistakes nigga, you were just being fuckin' reckless. Yo ass about to throw away a career because of a mistake, Blake? What if that girl didn't have the abortion, then what? Huh? Ain't no fuckin' basketball no more. I've been talking to yo ass about shit like this since you were eight years old. I done watch yo ass work hard for this shit, Blake, don't fuck this up behind no gotdamn pussy. I'm telling yo ass now, I ain't looking after no fuckin' kids, yo moms ain't either. You better start using yo damn brain and not yo fuckin' dick." His head shook at me before he laughed. "Yo ass telling yo momma this shit too."

My damn heart dropped into the pit of my stomach. "We don't have to tell her shit. I mean, she doesn't have to know especially since it's not gonna be a baby. She doesn't need to know." My momma was already dramatic as hell and I could only imagine how the hell she was going to react.

"Yeah the fuck she does. Especially since I know now, I can't keep that shit from yo moms. If she finds out I knew and didn't tell her…" his head shook. "I ain't about to be arguing with that mothafucka behind yo stupid ass. So, find yo fuckin' balls and tell her ass today, nigga. And while yo stupid ass at it, you better tell her ass about Mariah—"

"Mariah? What about Mariah." My brows arched at the mention of her. I didn't know why he even brought her up.

His head tilted as his eyes slanted. After a few seconds, he nodded, then rubbed his bottom lip. He socked the shit out of me in the mouth without warning.

"What about her? Nigga, do you think I'm fuckin' stupid, Blake? Huh? Nigga, I done heard every fuckin' thing y'all ass was saying. You fuck'd that bitch, now she in yo fuckin' girl's ear whispering in that bitch. Now, lie and tell me you ain't fuck that hoe?" He snapped, leaning in as if to make sure he heard what I said.

My tongue ran across my stinging lip, tasting the blood. Spitting the blood from my mouth, I wiped my lip. I had every fuckin' mind to knock him in his shit right back but I had to admit to myself, I deserved that shit. The shit with Mariah was dumb as hell, period.

My head fell back, and I groaned. "Yeah, the shit was stupid as fuck, I know. Shid, I surprised myself when I did it. That whole shit with Janae and the fuckin' abortion, really had me fuck'd up. The shit shouldn't have happened especially not after all the shit she was doing to you and momma—"

He waved that off. "She ain't did shit to us because I wasn't stupid enough to fall for her shit and fuck her. Blake, do you know how many chicks try to get at me daily, nigga? That hoe ain't no different. She might be cute as hell but she ain't fuckin' with yo moms. Don't apologize for fuckin' that bitch, just learn from this shit and do better, you hear me? Don't lose yoself in these fuckin' girls, is my point, Blake. Like I said, I've been telling yo ass this shit since you were eight, nigga, these damn girls gon' come and go forever, yo gotdamn career ain't, you got one chance with that shit. You understand me?"

I nodded because I did. That was part of the reason why I wanted her to get the abortion. We weren't ready for no damn kid at all. "Yeah, I hear you."

"Nigga, don't just be saying that, Blake, because you think that's what the fuck I wanna hear."

"I'm not doing that, I heard you, pops, I understand. I admitted I fuck'd up. Janae getting pregnant was a mistake, man, we were drinking—"

"Stop that shit, nigga, you gon' blame that shit on being drunk? That's a weak man's excuse, Blake, don't do that, own yo shit and learn from it. Don't use that—I was drunk— bullshit, yo ass wasn't to fuckin' wasted because

389

you wanted to fuck. So, don't give me that bullshit. Own yo shit and be careful out here before you slide into the wrong bitch that ain't gon' get an abortion like yo girl did. Got me?" His hand came out and he held it in front of me.

I nodded and took hold of it. "You right, pops." My dad pulled me to him, his hand went to the back of my head and he kissed the side of it. Affection was something my pops barely showed if it wasn't to my momma or Brianna. So, for him to kiss the side of my head, it kind of fuck'd me up. "You ain't pissed at me for getting her pregnant or for the abortion?" I asked once we parted.

He shrugged and shook his head. "No, I ain't pissed at you. Just be smart about the shit you do from here on out, that's it. Now, that's not to say yo moms ain't gonna be fuckin' ferocious, about the pregnancy, the abortion and you fuckin' that bitch." He started laughing as his arm went around my shoulder. "Yo ass shouldn't worry about me being pissed. It's yo fuckin' momma you need to worry about. She about to turn this bitch out and I ain't gon' be around when she does. Me and the twins going to yo nana's crib while you talk to her." His hand went to my head and he kissed the top of it. He pushed me away from him.

"Wait, you gon' leave me there with her by myself?" I wasn't trying to tell my momma about none of that shit let alone not by myself. I've seen my moms' temper and I didn't want to be on the other end of it.

His brows raised at me. "Hell yeah, that's between y'all. Nigga, you better man the fuck up, and own yo shit. Did you not hear me say that? This the start of it." He pointed ahead of us. "Yo little girlfriend still here. She probably thought I was gonna beat yo ass or something."

"Probably. Dad, I was there for her through everything, I just wasn't crying or shit like that. Shid, I don't know why the fuck she saying I wasn't there for her ass." I didn't want my dad to think I was some low life ass nigga that wasn't there for Janae. "And I told her, if she wanted to keep the baby she could have, I still would've been there for her."

He stopped walking and stared over at Janae. "Hmm…" He pointed to her. "That babe hurt. I believe you was there for her, but yo ass probably ain't give her that emotional support—"

My eyes slanted at him. "What the hell you know about emotional support?"

He started laughing again. "Peaches stupid ass told me that shit a few times. So, I'm guessing it's the same for you. Shid, females are emotional ass creatures, I still don't understand they asses. Real shit though, Blake, she 'bout only got that abortion because it was what you wanted, and she probably ain't wanna trap yo ass just in case you fell back. Shorty angry for real, but I think she actually like you though. Hell, she still wouldn't be around if she didn't."

I looked over at her and she caught my eyes. "I like her too and the abortion wasn't just about me, shid, she wouldn't be able to do shit either, her damn career would've been forgotten too. She understood that, but she wanted to keep it, and I didn't want to lose my career because of our recklessness, you know, and I didn't want to put that responsibility on nobody else."

"I understand. But shid, that's a new wound for her and it's gon' take time to heal, real shit. I know that from experience. Our situations may be different but losing a baby is still a loss and that shit ain't easy to get over, it took yo moms' years to get over it. That shit damn near tore us apart. If you care for her for real, just give her time. Obviously, her ass ain't going nowhere, regardless of how hurt she is." He nodded in her direction once again and she was staring at us. "Don't fuck that up for some pussy, Blake, especially if you care for her like you say. Oh, and tell her about Mariah—"

"What? Hell no." Even though I was going to tell Janae in the heat of my anger that I had fuck'd Mariah. I'm glad I didn't since I had time to cool down. That should would've probably killed her ass.

He shrugged. "Do it or don't, I don't give a fuck, but get that snake out her gotdamn ear, that bitch gon' fuck up everything. If Janae find out yo ass fuck'd that girl from somebody else, that shit gonna hurt her a million times worse. Take my word or don't, your choice."

I groaned. "Fuck!" When the hell did his ass become so damn insightful. "You must've put momma through some shit when y'all were younger, huh?"

A grim look covered his face before his hand ran over his mouth. "Lil B, this shit you got going on now is play, play, baby... Y'all shit wouldn't touch the beginning of the shit we been through."

"No, I'm talking about fuckin' different females." The look that covered his face had me cracking up. "Why the hell you look at me like that?"

"Have you met yo moms? that short mothafucka scares me sometimes." He laughed before he pointed to the ground and sat down. I did the same. "Real shit though, I never fuck'd another female while I was dating Peaches. I had one chick that sucked my dick, though on regular. Man, and that babe could swallow a dick, the shit should've been illegal. Anyways, when yo momma found out she beat the both of our asses." He laughed once again. "I was dumb back then and Peaches had my head all fuck'd up. Regardless though, I never fuck'd that girl. I couldn't hurt yo moms like that." He chuckled before a genuine smile came to his mouth. "That mothafucka right there, Peaches ass was definitely a rider."

"You can barely find a chick like that nowadays, but if yo ass just so happen to come across that rare shit," he pointed to Janae. "Do whatever the fuck you gotda to keep it. That babe naïve as fuck, but she reminds me of Peaches a little bit. Like when she slapped fire from yo ass." His head fell back, and he started cracking up.

I didn't find that shit funny though. "You always laughing at the wrong shit, for real."

"I'ight, that's enough sharing, the shit weird as fuck. Let's go ball." He hopped up off the ground. "Ace and you," he pointed to Patrick. "Y'all get out. Me and Blake in." He told them and we took their places and started playing.

Chapter 21

Blake

After we finished playing basketball, Janae and I stayed back at the courts because I wanted to talk to her. I waited until the area was clear before saying anything. From Janae's body language alone, I knew she was still mad about the fight earlier.

"I know you pissed at me for snapping at you. I can't apologize for that because I meant what I said. Mariah ain't yo damn friend—"

"Blake, I really don't wanna hear that right now. Like, I don't care who you think are my friends or not. If that's the only reason you asked to talk to me, I'mma go. I don't want to argue with you, I really don't wanna talk to be honest with you." Janae's eyes rolled before her arms crossed over her chest.

I thought about telling her about Mariah's ass but decided against it. Grabbing her forearm, I tugged on it, but she jerked away from me. "Nae, stop that stupid shit and chill out, damn."

"Blake, what do you wanna say? Would you just tell me and get it over with? I'm ready to go home." The attitude in her voice didn't go unnoticed.

Taking hold of her waist, I pulled her up and into my lap. "You really pissed at me because of what I said earlier about yo friends? Or is it something else? 'Cause yo ass japped out hard and that shit ain't even have to go that way, Nae."

She rolled her eyes and looked out at the empty courts. "It's not nothing else, I just knew you were about to start some pointless shit, then you started yelling which is why everything went left."

"I wasn't about to start shit, I wanted to know why the fuck she felt the need to put that shit in yo head. Yo ass snapped the fuck off. You dead ass feel like I wasn't there for you?" She let out a sigh and shrugged. "Nah man, yo ass had a whole fuckin' outburst about the shit, so now that we're alone, shid talk to me about it. Because I was there, and you dipped off on my ass to go with Mariah and that shit was planned before we even went there." I heard her sniffle and turned her face to me, but she jerked away from me, then wiped her cheeks. "Why the fuck is you crying?"

"Because I fuckin' want to, Blake! Damn! You're so gotdamn irritating. You know what? Yeah, I feel like you weren't there for me. Blake, while I was going through this, you were out here doing whatever you wanted while being mad at me. Yes, it was planned for Mariah to pick me up after I had the abortion. I felt that was probably what you wanted. The way you acted was like you wanted to be done with me and everything, so I was going to give you your space. The folks you claim aren't my friends, were there for me day and night after the abortion. You weren't, Blake. Not once did you ask, how was I feeling or anything—"

Hearing her say that pissed me off. "How the fuck—"

Janae jumped in my face and muffed my head back hard. "No, shut the fuck up and listen. You wanted to know what the hell my deal was, now I'm telling you so shut the hell up and listen!" She yelled as tears kept running down her face.

Seeing her crying was the only reason I didn't snap back at her. Licking my lips, I nodded and crossed my arms over my chest. "You got it."

She wiped her cheeks roughly and took in a deep breath. "I slept nights at Shanny's and Mariah's place for days, waiting to hear from you, Blake and nothing. Not even an—*are you breathing message*. Even after all that, like the dumb ass I am, I went to your party just to see you. Again, being the weak ass love struck girl that I am, we got back together. And even then, you still acted like nothing happened. You asked nothing about the procedure or the pains I had afterwards, absolutely nothing. So, yeah, Blake, I'm pissed off at you and at me for caring so much about you period. I'm so mad at you because I wanted you there, not Shanny or Mariah, but they were."

My hand rubbed over my mouth as I took in what she said. The shit really pissed me off more. Like her ass wanted me to do some impossible shit. "Janae, how was I supposed to ask yo ass any fuckin' thing when you were ignoring me? You weren't answering my fuckin' calls or text messages. So, tell me how the fuck was I supposed to do any of that shit, man? How the fuck was I supposed to be there for you if I couldn't even get ahold of yo ass. Explain that to me."

"Blake, I didn't get not one call or text from you. Don't you think I would've notice if you did? Like, did you not just hear me say I waited for both and didn't receive either?" She stared at me like I was lying.

"I don't give a fuck what you didn't see, I called and text yo ass for days after the fuckin' fact, until I just said fuck it. I wasn't about to keep reaching out to yo ass when you weren't tryna hear me. Yo ass acting like I just said fuck you, Nae, you know it ain't never been like that with you, man. Come on, Janae, you really think I ain't wanna be there for you man?" Grabbing her arms, I pulled her closer to me, then wiped her eyes. "Sweetheart, I don't know why you ain't get my texts or calls but I hit you up every fuckin' day up until my birthday, that was when I said fuck it. I knew how hard that decision was for you, so, yeah I wanted to be with you."

She pulled away from me and wiped her eyes. "Blake, don't do me like that. You can't keep playing with my emotions, especially when you know how I feel, that's not fair, man, I swear to God it's not cool." Her tears ran fast from her eyes as she started to get mad.

I didn't know what the fuck to do or say at that point. "I'ight, Janae. I can't change how you feel, and you obviously don't believe me." I laughed and shrugged. "Shid, I don't know. What I do know is that I ain't tryna be out here fighting with yo ass like this. Especially not in front of every fuckin' body, man, that shit ain't cool."

Janae sat down on the bench and put her face into her hands. "I don't wanna be fighting with you like that either. I just..." She looked at me and then looked away. "I know you don't be wanting to hear about it and I be trying so hard not to think about the abortion so I don't bring it up, but, Blake, I can't pretend it didn't happen. I can't get what I did out my head..."

"I never said I didn't want to hear about it, stop putting words in my mouth. Like stop thinking that shit period. If that's what you wanna talk about, baby, I'm all ears to listen. If you wanna cry that shit out, I'm here. And it's not just what you did, that whole decision is on us." I kneeled in front of her. "Come to the crib with me." I wiped her eyes again.

"To your house?" She questioned, seeming unsure. I nodded. "I don't think so, especially not with your dad. After today, I can't, and he heard everything we said and saw me hit you—"

I cut her off and laughed. "Yeah, he thought that shit was funny when you slapped my ass. You don't have to worry about my pops, he'll be cool, real shit."

"Janae, we need to go. Shanny's momma calling her for the car, which is at my house. So, we need to go right now and since you rode with me too, you need to come on." Mariah sounded irritated as hell as she spoke.

Janae cleaned her face and got up. "I'm going home with Blake, so y'all can go head. Tell Shanny, I'll call her tomorrow—never mind, I'll tell her, she has my phone." She told her.

"We can go then." I motioned for her to follow me to the parking lot.

Janae jogged over to Mariah's car and opened the passenger door. "Shanny, y'all can take off, I'mma ride with Blake. Hand me my phone so we can go, and I'll call you tomorrow." Janae told her.

"Okay, don't have too much fun." Shantell was saying as she searched her pockets. Her brows furrowed before she started checking her purse. "You sure you didn't take it? I remember you giving it to me…" She mumbled double checking herself and bag. "Mariah, have you seen Nae's phone?"

"No, I saw her give it to you, Shanny." Mariah explained then shot a glare over at me.

"Can you just check your stuff to make sure." She grabbed another purse that was in the front seat and started looking through it.

"Shanny, her phone isn't in my purse." She went to grab the bag.

"Ain't this it?" Shanny held up the iPhone with a pink heart case. The screen lit up and it was a picture of Mariah on it. "Oh, my bad, Nae got that same case.

Mariah made a sound which caused us to look at her. She pulled out a phone from her back pocket. "Janae, I'm sorry, I must have grabbed yours by mistake. I just saw the case and put it in my pocket. Shanny must've sat it down on the bench. I'm sorry." She gave Janae her phone.

"It's cool, it was a simple mistake, so don't stress it. I'll see y'all later." She waved to them.

"Call us if you need anything or want us to pick you up later on." Mariah told her.

"She's good, I got her. Nae, let's go." I glared at Mariah before walking over to my car. Janae was so damn naïve. Mariah ass took that damn phone on purpose and she got the same phone case as Janae's so that it didn't look suspicious if she was caught with it. I didn't trust that bitch at all.

***

"Janae, hey." My momma hugged her as we came through the door. "It's been a while since I've seen you. How you been?" My momma was smiling from ear to ear, she acted like she was so happy to see Janae.

"I've been okay. How about you?" Janae was smiling right back.

"BJ, Bri-Bri, bring y'all asses on!" My dad yelled as he walked from the back room. He stopped once he saw Janae. His brows furrowed before his eyes slid to me. "What she doing here?"

"Blaze!" My momma hit him. "Don't be an asshole. Blake invited her over, so be nice." She glared at him before she turned back to Janae smiling once again. "Janae, are you hungry or thirsty?"

"Man, I don't wanna go over Nana's house, I wanna finish playing my game. Why I can't stay here with momma?" BJ complained as he stomped into the living room.

"BJ, get yo little ass knocked the fuck out. Go back in yo damn room until I call you." My pops snapped at BJ and he took off running without another word.

"Is it okay that I'm here?" Janae suddenly asked, looking at my dad nervously.

"Yeah, it's fine. I'm glad he brought you back. Ignore my husband's yelling. You'll learn that he yells about any and everything. That's just how he talks, it's best to just ignore him. Come on and get you something to drink or eat, whatever you want." She motioned Janae in the direction of the kitchen before she turned and smiled at me.

Mentally I groaned at the thought of telling her ass everything. I didn't know how she was going to react, but I hated it already. However, I knew she was gonna cry. Then again, I would take crying over anything else.

"What the fuck yo ass think you doing?" My dad snapped as he dragged me further into the living room. "Wasn't yo ass supposed to tell yo moms everything today? I know I told you to do that shit today."

"I know and I was, then I started talking to Janae about everything and she started crying and shit, next thing I know I'm inviting her here. Pops, you ain't see her crying, that shit got to me. That whole abortion—"

"Nigga, shut the fuck up." He snapped before looking behind him to make sure my momma wasn't coming. "Don't even say that fuckin' word in this damn house, not while I'm in this bitch. I don't give a fuck about that babe crying, Blake. What the fuck I do care about is yo momma finding out I knew that damn girl was pregnant without telling her ass shit. Blake, you better tell her tomorrow otherwise I'mma fuck you up."

"I will, promise. Just don't say shit to her." I told him.

"Blake!" Brianna yelled, before she ran over to me. She stood on the couch then jumped on me, wrapping her arms and legs around my body. "Hey, brother, I missed you all day." She kissed my cheek.

I glared at Brianna. "What you do?"

She looked confused. "Nothing. I just missed you—okay, fine, can you take me to the store?"

Unwrapping her from me, I threw her on the couch. "Hell no, I just got in the house. I ain't going back out."

"Please!" She pleaded.

"No—"

"Pretty please, Blake?" She continued to beg.

"Brianna, gon' somewhere now, I said no." I waved her off.

Brianna punched me in the stomach, then took off running. "I swear you get on my nerves, stupid self. Momma! Blake cussing at me again and you told him not to do that no more." She yelled before running in the kitchen.

My dad sat on the couch laughing. "You could've taken her to the damn store. Why you gotda be so mean to her?"

Before I could say anything, Brianna ran back in the living room. "Give me your keys, Janae said she'll take me." She held her hands out for my keys. My momma and Janae walked back into the living room at that moment. "Janae, didn't you say you'll take me to the store?" Brianna asked her.

Janae laughed. "Yeah, I'll take you. You're so cute." Brianna smiled wide before hugging her.

"Get y'all kid. Bria ask yo momma or daddy, she ain't come over here to take you to no damn store." I got off the couch and stretched. "I'm about to go shower. Janae you can wait in my room, come on."

"Blake, I can run her to the store, it's literally right up the street. We'll be back before you're done with your shower." Janae stated.

"Yeah, we'll be real fast." Brianna chimed in.

Taking out my keys, I tossed them to her. I wasn't about to stand there going back and forth with them.

"Thank you, Blake!" Brianna hugged me. "BJ, Blake's girlfriend about to take me to the store. If you want something you better come on." She yelled while running to the back. Brianna ass was irritating, but funny as hell sometimes.

"Ugh, what's wrong with you, Blake?" My momma asked.

"Nothing, tired. I'm about to go get in the shower. Don't let y'all kids run her crazy." I left them in the hallway and went into my room.

***

When I got out the shower, Janae was laying in the middle of the bed watching tv. She looked at me and laughed. "Your little sister is so funny and cute."

"Wait until she starts irritating yo ass." I took the towel off and pulled on my basketball shorts. "You always give Shantell and Mariah yo phone?" I asked as I got in the bed next to her.

Janae shrugged. "If I don't have any pockets, then yeah. Why you ask?" Her arm went around my waist and she kissed my chest.

"I told yo ass I texted and called you. Let me see your phone." I wanted to check her message because if they didn't match mine, which I doubted, then Mariah had deleted the ones I sent her.

"I'm telling you I didn't get any messages." She got up and grabbed her phone off the dresser. "Am I staying a night over here?"

I looked down at my bare chest and basketball shorts. "Yeah, I ain't going back out until tomorrow. You can get a shirt out my drawer to sleep in... unless you wanna sleep naked, shid, I'm cool with you doing that."

Janae started laughing as she threw a pillow at me. "I'll get a shirt." She tossed me her phone then went and grabbed a t-shirt. "I'm about to hop in the shower, is that cool?"

I nodded. "Yeah. Look in the closet and get you a towel." I instructed as I unlocked her phone and went to the messages. I clicked on our chat box and started strolling up. We had sent to many fuckin' messages, I was about to give up until I found what I was looking for.

Sure enough, there was a big ass gap from the morning of the abortion until after my birthday. "Man, that scandalous ass bitch." I grabbed my phone and found all the damn messages that was missing and screenshot them all. I then texted Mariah.

Me: *Yo you a dirty ass bitch for real. Why the fuck you delete all the messages I sent to Janae. And don't fuckin' play stupid like you don't know what I'm talking about. Every fuckin' message I sent her after she got the abortion is gone.*

I was pissed off and I wanted to knock that bitch head off her shoulders. My phone pinged a few minutes later.

Mariah: *I'm so lost... what are you talking about Blake? Why would you even think I did that? Maybe she deleted them and lying about it. Have you thought about that?*

Me: *Yo stupid ass did that shit. Just like you were trying to steal her damn phone when you thought she was going with yo ass. Bitch you dirty as fuck.*

Mariah: *Blake I swear I don't know what you're talking about. I didn't delete any messages and I wasn't trying to steal her damn phone. It was clearly a mix up because we have the same damn case.*

Me: *Yeah i'ight.*

I left it at that because I knew she was lying. Same phone case or not, you couldn't mistake the phone because Janae's had our picture as her screen saver.

Mariah: *I really didn't delete any messages from Janae's phone. I wouldn't do no shit like that.*

I read the message she sent and then tossed my phone to the side. A few minutes later it went off again and I grabbed it.

Mariah: *I hope you're not mad at me. I really didn't do that.*

Mariah: *I miss you Blake. Can I see you tonight? No sex, I just wanna talk to you.*

Mariah: *Blake?!*

Mariah: *Look I'm sorry okay. Can I see you?*

Mariah: *You're so damn frustrating. I didn't delete that girl's fuckin' messages. She had to have done it. Ugh! God! I don't know why you even continue to deal with her ass. All she fuckin' do is cry and crowd you. I can see what it's doing to you Blake. Just leave that fuckin' girl alone. She's not mature for a relationship with you. I can't believe you're acting like this because of some damn messages.*

Mariah: *Can I see you? We need to talk.*

Me: *I don't wanna see yo ass or talk to you. Stop fuckin' texting me, I'm good.*

Mariah called my phone five times back to back and I ignored every call. When she couldn't get through, she started texting me again.

410

Mariah: *You don't wanna see me no more? Why not? I haven't even done shit! If you're serious about that you can tell me face to face not through a fuckin' text.*

Mariah: *You really going to end our relationship behind some fuckin' deleted messages? Are you fuckin' kidding me?*

Mariah: *I'm not accepting that. You can't break up with me.*

Reading that message had me sitting up straight and I texted her ass back quick as hell.

Me: *Break up? Bitch what the fuck are you talking about? We were never together. Look Janae here so stop fuckin' texting me.*

After that message was sent, she started blowing up my phone. After about the sixth or seventh missed call. Janae's phone started ringing and I rejected the call. A minute later a text came through.

Riah Riah: *Hey babe, I just wanted to check in on you to make sure that you're alright and if you made it home or needed a ride? Call me babe and let me know what's up.*

Mariah: *Blake why are you doing this? Why is she even over there? Call me please, I just want to talk.*

I turned off my text notifications and then put my phone on the nightstand. Janae's phone started ringing again.

"Who is that?" Janae walked out the bathroom with the towel hooked around her chest. "No, stop looking at me like that." She laughed as her phone went off again.

"I'm not looking at you no type of way. Shid, I think you beautiful as fuck though." Janae was sexy as fuck. I hopped off the bed and she jumped away from me.

"Blake, stop looking at me like that. You play too much." She laughed and grabbed her phone.

I went and locked my room door, then grabbed the lotion from the dresser. "I can look at yo ass however I wanna." I tossed the lotion on the bed then unhooked the towel from her chest.

"I'm not having sex with you, Blake." She pointed out before laying on the bed. "So, don't try nothing. You can start on my back." She tossed me the lotion then rolled over on her stomach.

Laughing, I spread her legs and got between them, I then slapped her ass cheeks. Janae's head snapped back so fast. "Shut the fuck up. Don't try to boss me around, when yo ass knew I was about to put the lotion on yo ass."

She chuckled and made herself comfortable. "Whatever, and don't hit me like that again. That shit be hurting, Blake, like you heavy handed as hell. Now my ass stinging, for real." She complained.

"That shit red too. Want me to kiss it?" I asked while rubbing lotion over her back.

"Yeah…" she pushed her ass up and I slapped her cheek again. "Blake, stop damn! I just told yo ass that shit hurt. That shit burn, got my ass feeling hot." She fussed.

"Watch yo damn tone, Janae. Don't forget who the hell you talkin' too." I popped her ass again, then kissed the sore cheek. "Feel better?" I kissed her ass twice before biting the top of her butt. My lips trailed up her spine until I reached the base of her neck.

Janae's hand went to the back of my head as I sucked on her shoulder, then her neck. Biting at the skin, Janae moaned and pushed her ass up until she felt my dick. "Blake, stop. I'm not playing with you." She mumbled breathlessly as her hips rolled.

I pulled my hips from her protruding ass. "That's yo little nasty ass. Talking about you ain't playing with me. When you pushing yo shit all on my damn dick. Shid, you giving me all the access I need… to slide into that shit." My fingers pushed into her pussy.

"Ah…" She pushed her ass back into my hand as her face went into the pillow. "Blake…"

"Damn, yo shit so fuckin' wet. You sho' you don't wanna fuck me?" I questioned as my fingers stroked inside her pussy. Janae grabbed my wrist and started grinding against my hand. Laughing, I slapped her ass, then pulled my fingers from her body.

She groaned. "Why are you playing with me…" Her words trailed off as her phone started going off again. "Who is that?"

Looking at the screen, I shook my head. "Shanny." The call ended, but it started ringing right back, but it was a Facetime call from Mariah. "These mothafuckas really don't want us together. They blowing yo ass up real shit. Mariah Facetiming you."

She groaned and held her hand out. "Give it here. They're gonna keep calling until I answer it. They just want to make sure I'm good."

"Turn over." I handed her the phone as she rolled over onto her back. "Don't be on that phone long. You talk to those mothafuckas every day."

Janae laughed as she answered the phone. "Y'all I'm good. I swear." She told them as I leaned over her, biting her bottom lip. Again, she laughed, kissing me. "Blake, stop, you're so rude."

"Fuck them, those two bitches rude as fuck." I kissed her again, then went to her nipple.

"His ass is so damn mean. Like he just be snapping for no fuckin' reason at all." Shanny said with an attitude.

Janae laughed as I bit her side. "Stop!" She pushed my head back, before returning to her call. While she did, I went back to her tittie, sucking on the right then the left.

"Girl, I don't think his ass can help it. His father be snapping off like that too. He scares me. Like you'll just be sitting there, and he'll start yelling, then he got that deep as voice— Blake, stop! Don't bite me no more." She snapped at me as I bit the shit out her tittie.

"Bitch, is you naked?" Shanny broke out laughing.

"Yeah, I just got out the shower when y'all called. Blake was putting lotion on me—" Janae's hand went to my forehead as I kissed her pelvis. She glared at me.

"You should get my name tatted right here. That shit would be sexy as fuck." I kissed just above her pelvis.

"I'll think about it." She smiled as her hand rubbed over my head.

"Are you sure you're good, Janae?" Mariah asked her.

"Seems like she's about to be real good in a minute." Shanny broke out laughing once again as did Janae.

"No, it's not like that. Nothing is going to happen. And yeah, Mariah I'm good. Honestly, I'm just happy to be here with him. Even though, he gets on my damn nerves, he's my baby. So, y'all don't ever have to worry about me when I'm with him."

"I was never worried. That was Mariah's ass all concerned and shit. I told her yo ass was straight and was probably about to get some dick." Shanny said. "You know how Mariah ass is though. She just has to make sure we're good no matter what."

"Mmhm, I know…"

I pushed Janae's leg up to her side, watching as her pussy lips parted, showing off that sexy ass pink glossy shine from her being so wet. Janae's eyes snapped to mine as I kissed her inner thigh.

416

"Hey, I'mma call y'all back in a minute." Janae told them.

"Wait! I'm bored as hell, let's meet up and go out to eat or something." Mariah insisted.

I continued to suck and bite at Janae's inner thighs, moving closer to her pussy. I chuckled as I watched her pussy pulse every time I moved passed it to go to the other thigh.

"I'm not making any promises, but I'll see if Zac wanna hang out. I doubt it though, he already in a funk. I'm trying to be on some lovely dovey shit, like Janae and Blake on. Blake, you good friend? Yo ass silent as hell."

"Ye…" Janae cleared her throat. "Yeah, he's good." Janae bit into her bottom lip as my tongue ran through her slit. Her hips raised and her hand went to my forehead as my tongue played with her clit. "Aye y'all—" Janae was trying to get off the phone, but they kept cutting her off.

I was fuckin' tired of waiting for them to get off the damn phone.

"I don't wanna be around Zac when he's pissed off. I don't have time for his damn attitude." Mariah said irritated. "Janae, how about I come pick you up and we can go out—"

"Oh, my god!" Janae's moan was loud as I pushed two fingers into her pussy while sucking her swollen pearl into my mouth. Janae's nails dug into the back of my neck as she grinded her pussy against my mouth. "Blake, ooh, baby." My tongue replaced my fingers, slipping into her pussy. She took hold of the sides of my head and started fuckin' my tongue. "Ooh, oooh!" She moaned as she came hard. I sucked on her pussy savoring her sweet nectar.

Moving her left leg on top of the right one, I kissed up the side of her body, biting at the side of her breast once I reached it.

Janae glanced back at me panting hard. She turned and wrapped her arm around my neck, kissing me. "I love you, Blake."

From the way she was staring at me, I knew she meant that shit wholeheartedly. Licking my lips, I nodded, then rolled over onto my back.

Janae laughed. "Don't get all closed off because I said I love you." She placed her leg on top of mine and brought her arm to my waist.

"I ain't closed off, yo ass got my heart for real, Janae. Don't ever think otherwise and don't play with that mothafucka either." I told her straight up.

A heavy sigh left her mouth, and she kissed my chest. "I would never play with your heart, like you do to mine. I know how that feels and wouldn't want you to hurt like that."

What the fuck was I supposed to say to that? "Yeah…" My hand rubbed over my mouth. "I've done some fuck'd up shit these past few months. That shit done with though. I'm sorry for hurting you, I ain't gon' do that shit no more, i'ight?"

Janae sat up and stared down at me for the longest time, her eyes searching mine. "I believe you mean it. I just hope you stick to it. I'm not always going to be so forgiving, in love or not, won't keep being your fool."

Nodding, I grabbed the back of her head, bringing it down, I kissed her. "I hear you." Janae definitely had my fuckin' heart because of that, it was no way in hell I could let her go or lose her behind Mariah's ass.

Chapter 22

Blake

"Oh, here." I pulled up the screenshots of our messages and handed her my phone. "I told yo ass I texted you."

Janae looked so confused as she read the messages. "Blake, I swear I didn't get these. If I had, I would've called or something." She said reading the messages. She went and grabbed her phone.

"They not there, I checked last night. Somebody deleted that shit hoping we wouldn't talk or get back together." I pointed out and grabbed my phone.

She still looked shocked. "But who would do that? I am so pissed. Dude, you don't even understand how much I had cried myself to sleep during all those damn days and you had been texting me the entire time. What the fuck?" Her confusion turned into anger as she glared at her phone. "Why would somebody wanna do that."

"I wish yo ass would stop saying *somebody* like you don't know who the fuck it was. It had to be either Shanny or Mariah's ass. Those are the only two mothafuckas you give yo damn phone to and who yo ass was hanging with when all this shit happened. I keep telling you they not yo damn friends."

Janae's brows furrowed. "But that don't make sense to me. Like, although you don't like Shanny, she's never really talks bad about you, unless I'm crying. And Mariah... I don't know, it's the same with her. They never bring you up unless I'm talking about you..." Her words trailed off and she sighed. "If one of them did, then maybe that's the reason for it. I was really hurt and said some stuff before and after I had the abortion about being completely done with you and everything, I said a bunch of shit, they could've taken that literally." She explained.

Walking up behind her, my arm snaked around her waist. "I don't give a fuck for their excuses, Nae, they shouldn't have done the shit period is my point. Ask they asses about it and see what happen. And yo ass better stop talking about me to those damn girls." My hand tangled in her hair and I jerked her head back, then kissed her neck.

"You better stop jerking me like that. You ain't gonna stop until I knock you out, for real." She turned her head sideways and pecked my lips before she turned back to the mirror. "So... I was thinking that maybe you would wanna have dinner with my mom and me, later today?" She chewed on her bottom lip as she stared at me through the mirror.

"I don't care, if that's what you wanna do." I was down to do anything if it meant putting off talking to my momma. Laying on my bed, I grabbed my phone and called my momma. I put her on speaker.

"Rashad, why are you calling me?" My momma answered with a laugh.

Janae looked back at me and did the same. "You did not just call her when she's right down the hallway." She came over and laid between my legs.

"Shut up." I muffed her. "Ma, I'm having dinner with Janae and her momma tonight—"

She quickly cut me off. "That's nice... why don't you just invite her over and we can all have dinner together? I wanna meet her—" My room

422

door opened, and Janae jumped hard. "Why you just didn't come in the living room and talk to me?"

Janae jumped up off the bed. I looked at her like she was crazy and my momma did too. "What the hell you jump like that for?"

"She popped up like she just got caught doing something she wasn't supposed too." My momma chuckled and grabbed the computer chair and sat down in it. She looked at Janae and waved her off. "You're fine, sweetie. Anyway, Janae, why don't you invite your momma over here for dinner. I would really like to meet her, that way we could all get acquainted. Plus, things seem to be getting serious between the two of y'all and I like you." She smiled at Janae. "I know it's short notice, but I could whip up a nice dinner or order something, whichever is fine. What do you think about that?"

Janae looked at me and I shook my head. My momma hit me. "Rashad, don't do that. Besides, I wasn't even talking to you. Janae?" She glared at me before looking back to Janae.

She laughed and sat back down on the bed. "Um, yeah, I think it'll be nice. And if it's to short of a notice for my momma, we could set another date. However, we do it I think it'll be nice."

"Great." My momma sounded so excited. "Now, I have to okay it with Blaze." She rolled her eyes before she got up and left out the room. "Babe!" She yelled.

"Your momma is so funny and sweet. I don't see how she's able to deal with your dad though. He just seems so mean." She laughed.

Groaning, my head fell back on the pillow. I shouldn't have told her ass shit and just went. "Lock my door." I told her. After she locked the door she came and straddled my lap and just stared down at me with a thoughtful look. "What?"

"Your mom doesn't know that I was pregnant, does she?" She questioned and I shook my head. "Why didn't your dad tell her?"

"Because he wants me to tell her. I was supposed to do it yesterday. I'mma tell her though." Again, I groaned.

"You don't have to do it by yourself. Do you want me here with you?" She offered, leaning down and kissing me. "I wanna be…"

My head shook, given everything I had to tell my moms, I didn't want Janae nowhere around. "No, I got to do that shit on my own. She's probably gonna cry. Shid, you ain't see her when she found out I was fuckin'. N'all, this is something I gotda do by myself."

She nodded in understanding. "Well, I'm here when you need me." She leaned down and kissed me. Grabbing the hem of her shirt, I pulled it over her head, making her laugh. "Your mom and dad is literally down the hall."

Rolling us over, I sat back and took off her shorts and panties. "So? If yo ass be quiet they won't hear shit." I had just pulled my basketball shorts down my hips when her phone rang. Janae looked at the dresser where her phone sat. "Man, fuck that phone."

She quickly rolled off the bed laughing. "It's probably my momma, hold on."

Groaning, I flopped down on the bed. I took off my shorts and grabbed my dick, stroking it. "Is it her?"

"No, it's Shanny." She rejected the call and sat the phone back down, but before she could walk away it started ringing again. That time she groaned.

"Man, fuck them and get over here." I told her as I continued to stroke my shit.

She laughed. "You just tryna get yo dick wet—"

"Hell yeah, so get yo ass over here and wet it for me." I beckoned her over to me. She smiled and came over to the bed.

Janae crawled between my legs and took hold of my dick. I watched as she leaned in and sucked my balls into her mouth while squeezing the tip of my dick. I groaned at the sensation that jolted through my dick. The sound caused her to look up at me, Janae smiled and licked up my dick. Her tongue swirled around the tip before she sucked it into her mouth.

"Fuck…" I grunted. "You sexy as fuck!"

Janae spat on my dick and started working the shaft as she sucked on the tip. She moaned around my tip and my hand went to the back of her head. "Stop." She slapped my hand from out her hair. "Touch my head again and I'll stop." Her hands went to my pelvis as her mouth slid down my dick until it touched the back of her throat. She moaned and squeezed my sack.

"Gotdamn! Fuck!" Her head bobbed in a rhythmic pace. "Suck that shit." My hand gripped her hair tight as I fuck'd her mouth. Feeling my nut build, I moved her off my dick. "Lay back." She quickly got on her back. Grabbing her legs, I pushed them up to her shoulders. My dick rubbed over her clit, playing with it before I pushed deep inside her pussy. "Fuck!"

"Ah!" Janae gasped from the penetration. "Ooh, shit!" Janae moaned as I stroked deep into her love box. My hips rolled and I pulled out only to push right back in, I did that twice before I started at a rhythmic pace. "Ah, Blake, ooh, baby."

The way her pussy sucked on my dick was like no other. The shit felt fuckin' amazing. I pulled out of her so that I wouldn't nut to quick. I toyed with her clit before sliding back into her warm slick tunnel.

Janae hands went to my ass, holding me to her. She leaned up and kissed my chest, then neck. "Ooh, I love you so much, Blake." She moaned my name.

My head dropped, bringing my lips to hers. She caught my tongue between her teeth and sucked on it, causing me to groan. Breaking the kiss, I widened her legs and picked up my pace and started pounding into her pussy faster.

"Oh, my God!" She gasped out and her hand quickly went to my pelvis. "Ooh, fuck! Blake, wait, wait, wait!" She said loudly and I quickly pulled out of her. She put her hand between her legs as the other held out toward me. "Wait…" She panted. "Oh, my God." She breathe out, then looked at the door.

I laughed at her ass. "Yo ass can't be getting that damn loud if you gon' get scared of somebody hearing you."

"You can't be doing all that then. It be too much when you go that fast and deep." She whined.

Laughing, I hit her leg. "I'ight, turn over." She groaned and got on all fours. I pressed on the center of her back and she dipped down. Leaning down, my tongue ran through her slit and she moaned. When she started to move her ass, I sat up and placed my dick at her entrance.

My hand came down on her booty as I pushed inside her. Janae's ass moved up as she gasped out before she sat up. "Wait, get a condom."

"Gotdamn, I'm really fuckin' up." I reached over into my nightstand and grabbed a rubber. I was glad as fuck I didn't nut in her ass. I wasn't trying to be back in the situation we had just got out of. After sliding the condom on, I slid back inside of her.

Janae grabbed the pillow and pushed her face into it as she bounced her ass back on my dick. Her head suddenly popped up and she let out a loud moan. "Ah, shit, baby, fuck! Blake!" Her pussy muscles contracted around my dick faster, milking my shit, as her body tensed shakily.

My hands gripped her ass tight as I released my nut. "Fuck!" That nut was hard as fuck. "Gotdamn." I pulled out of her and got off the bed. I took the condom off noticing it was wetter than usual. I laughed as I looked down at Janae's glistening pussy. "Yo shit was soaking. You must have really needed that nut, huh?" Not paying attention to the condom, I went into the bathroom and flushed it. "Man, damn." I got back in the bed beside Janae. She was still laying on her stomach. Licking my lips, I couldn't help myself as I slapped her ass.

Janae popped up so fast and punched the hell out of me in my chest. "Stop, you stupid ass bitch! Why the fuck would you hit me like that?" She hit me again.

I didn't mean to hit her ass that hard, and I knew she wasn't exaggerating because my damn palm stung like hell. "Damn, I ain't even mean to hit yo ass that hard. My bad, for real, dead ass." I pulled her on top of me and rubbed her booty.

"No, man, gon' for real. I keep telling yo stupid ass you heavy handed as hell. Like I wanna punch you in yo stupid ass face." She snapped while trying to get off me.

I rolled us over and she glared at me. "I'm sorry," I kissed her, and she popped her lips before rolling her eyes.

"Whatever. My ass sting." She complained.

"You want me to kiss it?" I asked while wrapping her legs around my waist.

She rolled her eyes again, before her lips twitched. "You get on my nerves, for real, Blake." She laughed.

I kissed her again, then moved down to her breasts, licking then sucking on her nipples. Janae's hand stroked the back of my head as I kissed my way down to her lower stomach. "I know I do, but you love me, though."

She laughed at that. "Whatever."

I bit at her stomach. "You should really get my name right here. With some cherries underneath." Biting my lip, I looked up at her.

Janae broke out laughing. "With some Cherries? Why of all thing's cherries? I don't even like cherries."

My brows raised at what she said. "It ain't got shit to do with you liking cherries—"

"Oh, my God!" She started cracking the hell up. "Blake, get off me, right now. You so damn nasty. Blake's cherry? Really?" She pushed my head back.

"Hell yeah, I'm dead ass serious." I wasn't bullshittin' at all.

"Why not peaches—"

"Hell fuckin' no. That shit nasty as fuck, my momma's name Peaches, hell n'all. Nae, don't fuck up my vision man." I sat up and she wrapped her legs around my waist, stopping me.

"If I get the tattoo you want, what do I get in return." Her nails ran up my chest, then snaked around my neck.

Leaning into her, I bit her bottom lip, then sucked on the top. "Whatever you want."

She smiled against my mouth, then kissed me again.

***

"Unc!" I shook up with my Uncle King.

"What's up, nephew. You coming shooting with us?" He asked palming a beautiful gold Tec.

I took the gun from him and held it. "This bitch sexy as fuck."

My Unc laughed at that. "Ain't she though? Bitch beautiful. Are you coming?"

I continued to handle the gun as I shook my head. "Nah, my shorty in the back. I got other shit I'm about to get into. I ain't even know y'all was going shooting. If I would've known sooner, shid, I would've come. I wanna take that bitch for a ride though. What the—" The hard slap to the back of my head had me glaring back.

"Blake, watch yo damn mouth. You ain't gonna keep cussing like I ain't around here." My momma snapped at me before she jumped at her brother, King.

"I didn't even see you." I laughed while rubbing my head.

"Because her ass wasn't in here. She just walked in. Short ass always talking shit." King muffed her head to the side.

"King, don't get fuck'd up." She hit him just as Janae walked in. My momma's whole demeanor changed. She went over to her and pulled her into the living room. "Janae, have you met Blake's uncle, King?"

Janae's head shook. "No, I haven't. Hey." She waved to him.

King tossed up two fingers. "What's up." He then cocked a brow at me. "Yo shorty?" His hand moved in a slapping motion.

Immediately I knew what he was referring too and mugged him hard. "Man, get on with all that." My hand rubbed at my cheek where Janae had slapped fire from my ass at the courts.

"King, don't be rude. Janae, I'm sorry, I have to apologize for him and Blaze, they can't

432

help themselves. So, please don't take their actions, attitudes, or tone of voice to heart. They're really sweet, their just assholes at heart." My mom explained.

Janae looked at me and her lips twitched. "Yeah, I'm learning that firsthand." She chuckled.

"Man, shut up. Don't get in front of my momma and do all that. Yo ass ain't seeing shit firsthand, so get on with that." Janae and my momma were getting to damn comfortable with one another.

"Rashad, get smacked in yo damn mouth, keep playing with me—ah!"

"What the hell you in here yelling about now?" My dad asked, chuckling as he bypassed her.

She ran behind him and punched him in the back. "Blaze, why the hell would you do that? Stupid ass play to damn much. When y'all leaving? Y'all need to hurry up and go, stupid ass."

My hand covered my mouth to stop myself from laughing. "Momma, you better stop all that cussing, for real." She turned around on me and my dad picked her up and slammed her on the couch.

"You better calm yo ass down. Yo short ass ain't scaring no damn body." He grabbed the pillow and pushed it in her face before he jumped away from her.

My momma got off the couch and was hot as fuck. "See... yo ass always fuckin' playing." She took off her gym shoe and threw it at his head. He ducked down quick and she ran and jumped on him.

Grabbing Janae, I moved her back and just leaned against the wall watching them. My dad caught my momma's arms and pinned them to her side, picked her up and slammed her back down on the couch.

"Peach, yo ass better chill out before I hurt yo ass, for real." He bit her cheek, then took his mouth to her ear.

The glare on her face deepened before she started laugh. "Blaze, get off me. I'm not playing. I'm about to knock the shit out of you. I don't know why you always playing with me."

"I'm sorry, i'ight?" He pressed his lips to hers and he kept doing it until she started laughing.

"You so damn childish sometimes. Get off me. Stupid ass." He let her up and she stood, fixing herself.

434

"King, you met Blake's dirty little girlfriend?" He pointed to Janae, making my uncle laugh.

"Huh? Me?" Janae pointed to herself surprised.

"No, Blake's other girl that's standing next to him." He stared at her like she was slow.

"Yeah, I met her…" He said as his phone started ringing. After looking at the screen, he walked outside and took the call.

My momma started laughing as she pushed him down on the couch. "Blaze, leave that girl alone. You always fuckin' with people." She rolled her eyes at him, then sat on his lap. "Janae, ignore him. And excuse everything you just saw. I'm not like this for real."

My pops laid back and kicked his right leg up on the couch. "Fuck if you ain't." He hit her thigh hard.

"Blaze." My momma snapped at him.

"Shut up." He hit her thigh again.

Janae turned around to face me. "You act just like him. Like, this is déjà vu right now." She whispered to me.

My brow cocked at that and I glanced at my dad. My head shook. "I don't see it." My arm went on her shoulder and I pulled her closer to me. "Pops, why you ain't tell me y'all was going shooting?"

"Shid, I forgot. You can still come. Ooh, I got a sweet new bitch I just bought too. That bitch sexy ass fuck. Yo unc shit ain't touching that hoe." He boosted, sounding excited.

"Let me see it. Y'all niggas bogus as fuck—hell. Why y'all ain't take me with y'all?"

My pops looked from behind my momma to me. "Nigga, didn't I just buy yo ass a new gun for yo birthday? Fuck is you talking about? You can hit that mothafucka up and get something new just like we did."

"We don't wanna hear y'all talk about no damn guns. Come on, Janae, let's go out back." My momma went to get up, but my dad pulled her back down.

"No, let them go. I need to holla at you right quick." He told her, slapping the side of her thigh again.

I started laughing because I already knew what was up with him. "Yeah, we out."

"Okay, will you be bringing Janae back?" My momma went to get up again, but my dad held her to him. She turned and glared at him. "Blaze, stop." She snapped at him. "Are you?" She asked me.

I shrugged. "That's up to her if she wanna come back. So, ask her."

Janae hit me in the stomach and my momma smiled at her. "You didn't have to say it like that." She turned her attention to my momma. "Yeah, I'll be back. Oh, and my mom said she's free to do it Wednesday or over the weekend if that's cool with you."

"Yeah, that's cool. Okay, y'all can go." She waved us off before looking back at my dad. "You're ridiculous, I swear." She broke out laughing as we walked out the house.

"Y'all out?" King asked.

"Yeah. I'll get up with you later. I'm serious about trying that baby out, Unc." I pointed to his gun.

He chuckled and nodded. "I got you, nephew." He slapped hands with me. "Bye, Janae. Y'all mothafuckas don't be holding up no fuckin' traffic."

I broke out laughing as I walked Janae to the car. "Yo ass ain't shit for that, Unc, I swear. Oh, and you might as well bounce too, my pops just dragged my momma to the room, you know they about to be a minute."

"Man, that nigga on some bullshit. I'ight. Good lookin'." He nodded at me, then went back into the house.

Once I got in the car, Janae turned to face me. "What was so funny when he said don't be holding up traffic? I don't get it." She said and again, I started laughing.

"Remember that last time you were riding my dick and driving when my Unc called me at that light?" I ran down the events to jog her memory.

She groaned, then laughed. "Yeah, I remember that shit."

I pointed in the direction of my house. "That was my uncle that called. His ass saw everything."

Her eyes damn near popped out of there sockets. "Oh, my God." She covered her mouth, then fell back into the seat. "He probably thinks I'm some type of freak hoe or something."

I broke out laughing. "Shid, he'll be right to think that shit. Yo ass is a freak for real."

She reached over and hit me before laughing. "I hate you sometimes man."

I looked down at my lap and smiled. "You wanna drive us to the mall?"

She bit into her bottom lip, then leaned over to me. She licked my lips while her hand slid between my legs and she grabbed my dick. Her lips pressed into mine. "No, I don't." She kissed

438

me again, then sat back down and put her seatbelt on.

"Yo, fuck you. That was messed up, dead ass." I laughed as I drove us to the mall.

***

"I can't believe I let you talk me into doing this." Janae whined as she laid on the tattoo bed. She squeezed my hand and pulled it over her eyes.

"I didn't make you do nothing. All I did was ask. She almost done though." I really didn't think her ass would go through with it, especially because she didn't have any tattoos.

"Mmm." She muttered and squeezed my hand tighter. "Oh, God!"

After a few more minutes her tattoo was done. I went and looked at it. My name was tattooed on her lower stomach and right under there, hanging from the cursive K in my name was a chain with a heart locket and key, that sat right on her pelvis. When we made it to the tattoo shop and I knew she was serious about getting the tattoo, I had changed my mind about the cherries because that tattoo was for life, I felt the locket and key was self-explanatory.

"Yo ass smiling way to damn hard." Janae said.

I didn't even realize that I was even smiling. "That mothafucka beautiful. Probably should've got a print of my tongue and put it on there." I joked, fuckin' with her.

She started laughing but stopped. "Don't make me laugh. You got the nerve to call me nasty."

"Yo ass is though. You said that shit as if I was lying." I took out my phone and took a picture of her tattoo. I then handed the phone to her. "Tell me that bitch ain't sexy?"

She rolled her eyes at me. "It's sexy, Liz, thank you." She told the woman.

"No, thank you. I agree though, it's sexy." Liz grabbed the black tattoo pad. "Are you done with pictures?" She asked me.

"Nae!" I heard Shantell loud ass yell.

I looked at Janae and glared at her. "Why the fuck you tell her we was here?"

She waved me off. "I didn't think she was going to come up here. She asked what I was doing, and I told her." She shrugged.

Shanny walked into the room. "Hey, Lizzie. When I heard you was tatting my boo, I had to pull up and see this shit for myself."

440

Liz laughed and pointed to Janae. "You know I did her right. I'm glad I was able to take her tattoo virginity."

"Thank you, Liz. I love it, for real." Janae told her, then looked at me.

After Liz covered the tattoo, I helped Janae up.

"It's cute or whatever. I mean, the lock and key sexy." Shanny glanced at me and rolled her eyes, before laughing. "I'm just playing, before you start yelling. Girl, he done put a claim on yo coochie, bitch." Shanny started cracking up. "Yo ass is real life in love."

Janae's face twisted up. "I love him sometimes."

"Yo ass love me all the time, ain't no damn sometimes. She don't realize her ass stuck with me for the rest of her life."

"Y'all are too cute." Shanny smiled at us.

There was a tap on the door that got our attention. I looked back to see Mariah's ass. I wasn't even surprised to see her. Wherever Shantell and Janae was she was never too far behind. She looked bad like she hadn't slept all night. Her eyes were red and puffy like she had been crying. She didn't look like herself.

"Come on, Blake, you're next." Liz patted the chair. I took off my shirt and sat down. "Where you want it?"

"Right here." I put the paper to the center of my chest by the left peck. Looking at the image through the mirror on the ceiling, I nodded. "Exactly like that." I put my headphones in and blasted the music as she started on my tattoo.

***

"Babe…" I heard Janae say before I felt her lips on mine seconds later. She brought her hand to the side of my face at the same time I grabbed the back of her head. Janae's mouth opened and my tongue slid in. My arm went around her waist and I pulled her closer to me, she broke the kiss, laughing.

"Why you playing with me?" I peeked at her from one eye.

She kissed me again, then sat up. "You were sleeping, and I tried waking you up, but yo ass was out. Kissing you was the only thing that got a reaction out of you."

Groaning, my eyes closed once more. "I'm tired as fuck because of you. Yo ass had me up all night."

Janae's hand went over my mouth. "Babe, we are not alone, shut up."

I pushed her hand off my mouth and opened my eyes again. The same folks were in the room. I wiped my face and got up.

"How you like it?" She pointed to the mirror.

Stretching, I went to the mirror. Seeing the tattoo, I couldn't stop the smile that came to my mouth. "Awe yeah, hell yeah." The tattoo was of Janae's name and her lips right underneath it. The shit looked good as hell and it was exactly where I wanted it, right at the top of my heart.

"So, it's safe to say you like it?" Liz smiled as she grabbed the pad.

"Hell yeah, that bitch look good. You outdid yoself with it. Good lookin', sweetheart."

Janae was all smiles too. "I didn't think it was going to turn out like that. I love it. Now that's sexy as fuck." She held out her phone and took a picture of it.

After Liz covered the tattoo, I put my shirt back on, paid her for our tatts then we left. Once we got outside to my car, I stopped Janae. I pointed to my chest. "Yo ass know this shit forever, right? You ain't going nowhere."

She stood on her tiptoes and kissed me. "I hope so, otherwise your name will be covered with a dozen roses."

"Yeah, that ain't gon' happen, believe that. Come on, let's go." I went and opened the door for her.

"Nae, we gon' follow y'all to the mall, then we can go get something to eat after, cool?" Shanny asked and Janae looked at me with her lip poked out.

"Man, y'all ass better keep the fuck up, 'cause we ain't waiting." I hopped in the car and pulled off.

"Thank you." Janae kissed my cheek. "Shanny really does like you, Blake, so you shouldn't be so mean to her..." Her words trailed off. "Then again, yo ass just like your daddy, so you can't even help it. You definitely got it honest. At least I know you're not just coldhearted."

My brows furrowed at the road in front of me. I decided to keep my thoughts to myself because I knew asking what was on my mind would open a door that we probably closed a long time ago.

Once we got to the mall, Janae took me all over the fuckin' place. We spend damn near thirty minutes to an hour in one gotdamn store.

"She looks really happy." Mariah flicked through the racks of clothes beside me. I nodded. "So, you really going to ignore me? Like we didn't have shit going on—"

I shrugged her hand off my arm. "Man, get the fuck on. We didn't have shit going on. We just fuck'd that's it. Mariah you good with what you can do with that mouth and yo pussy got a nice grip to it, I'll give you that, but…" I laughed before looking around for Janae. I pointed to her. "Yo ass ain't her. You weren't shit but a fuck, Mariah, that's it."

"Blake, why are you saying this to me? What we had didn't mean shit, not after how you acted at B-Dubs when you saw me with another nigga." She faced me, grabbing my hand. "You wanted me, Blake."

I pulled my hand from hers. I wiped my mouth as I thought on what she said. "Yeah, I wanted to fuck you again, that's it though, I didn't want no fuckin' relationship with yo ass, which I told you. And if I was gonna be fuckin' you, I didn't want no other nigga doing so, that's what that whole thing was about at B-Dubs. Shid, I hit yo ass once more after that, now you're free to go fuck whoever you please. Now go on." I picked up a leather skirt and was about to walk away but Mariah snatched on my arm.

"Don't walk away from me. Blake, I'm in love with you—"

I pushed her hard as hell and she fell to the floor. I kneeled beside her. "Are you fuckin' stupid? Bitch, two fucks doesn't equal love. I don't fuckin' love yo ass, I don't even fuckin' like you, Mariah. You were just a good fuck, yo, nothing else. Yo, stay the fuck away from me and don't say that bullshit again."

"Blake…" Janae's voice trailed off as she looked at us. My fuckin' heart dropped, and I hoped like fuck she didn't hear shit that was said. "What are y'all doing?" She questioned, looking between us.

I picked up the skirt I had dropped. "She fell, I was making sho' she was good." I got up and held the skirt out to her. "I was about to come show you this when her dumb ass tripped and busted her shit."

She glared at me. "You could've at least helped her up. Boy, I swear. Are you okay?" Janae reached down to help her up.

Mariah brushed Janae's hand off her. "Yeah, I'm good, thanks." She pushed passed me, then walked out the store.

Janae's eyes were right back glaring at me. "What you do to her?"

446

"Me?" I pointed to myself. "What the fuck make you think I did something?"

Janae's mean mug didn't fade. "Because I know you. You're always snapping at somebody. Shanny just told me that Mariah was crying all night, that's why her eyes were so red and puffed up." I shrugged and she hit me. "Don't be so mean."

"I'm not being mean. If she was crying that's her business, not mine. Shid, what you want me to say or do?"

"Don't be so mean. You just never know, what your actions could cause a hurt person to do. Regardless if you weren't the cause of their pain or not." She explained and from the tone of her voice I knew she felt sorry for that girl.

My arms went around her waist and I kissed her neck. "You too good to be friends with those chicks." I bit the skin on her neck, and she elbowed me. "Why was she crying, Janae?"

She let out a heavy breath as she checked the size on the leather skirt, I gave her. "Why do all girls cry?" She glanced up at me with pursed lips. "Over a man. I knew she liked someone, but I didn't think it was that serious, you know. She wouldn't tell us who she was, talking about, she didn't want to jinx anything and if everything went the way she planned then we would have all known." She shook her head. "Guess it didn't work out like she planned."

That fuckin' girl was crazy as shit. I don't get why the fuck she thought we was going to be together. The shit just didn't make sense to me. Had I known that babe had that many fuckin' bolts loose in her head, I wouldn't have fuck'd her at all.

"I feel so bad for her. Mariah was asking us to come and hang out and I wasn't there for her, like she had been for me." When I groaned, Janae smacked her lips. "Regardless of what you think about her, she really been there for me and I was down bad, Blake." Her head shook as if she was remembering it. "Oh, and she was the one who deleted your messages. I asked while you were getting your tattoo. When she admitted it, I was pissed off, so was Shanny. She said it was only because of how I was during that time and she thought seeing your messages would only make me feel worse. Mariah said, she felt bad for me and it hurt her to see me crying that much. She didn't want me to go through that again. She thought I needed time away from you."

Janae was so gotdamn naïve it didn't make any sense. I wanted to slap some sense into her.

"Don't go snapping at her about the messages, I already did it. So, let it go."

448

I chose not to say shit else about that damn girl. Mariah ass deleted that shit for herself. She probably thought if I stopped fuckin' with Janae then we could get together. Then again, it wasn't no fuckin' probably to it, that's what the hell she thought.

Feeling eyes on me, I looked at the entrance to see Mariah standing there staring at us. Yeah, that mothafucka was crazy as shit. I was definitely going to have to watch her ass.

Chapter 23

Blaze

"**B**, you should really talk to Rome especially if you want to sit on somebody. That nigga's patience level is a mothafucka. Little nigga smart as fuck too." Mac was saying as we got ready to meet up with Kordell and Brittany.

"That little angry mothafucka?" I looked away from my phone at him. He nodded and I shook my head. Mac and Rome had gotten cool as fuck out of the blue. Mac had really taken a liking to Jerome, but I saw aspects in him that I didn't like. What it was exactly, I didn't really know, and I didn't give a fuck to try to find out either. I just knew the nigga was a little angry mothafucka. "No, dude good where he at."

"B, I'm telling you, if yo ass gon' do this get him. I done watched this mothafucka, I'm tell you, Blaze, the mothafucka good. He might be angry, but his mothafuckin' patience, yo." Mac was really trying to sell that nigga skills.

Rubbing my bottom lip, I groaned and sat up. "I'ight, I'll see how he do. After we finish talking with this nigga, we'll meet up with yo boy."

"I'ight, bet. What's going on with the new brother?" He asked while texting on his phone.

"Not a gotdamn thing, for real. I mean aside from playing ball, I don't really see him. He wanna meet the fam, and aside from him meeting Blake at the courts, I don't want that nigga to know about Peaches and the twins just yet. I just don't know if he got some type of motive or not. You know how I am when it comes to those four and the nigga only met Blake because we were hooping, and I know my son can hold his own if need be."

Mac nodded in understanding. "I hear you. But the nigga could really just be looking for family too. Shid, step yo ass out there and give that nigga a chance to know you. Then judge his ass on how he moves with you. Yo ass can see a snake from a mile away. You far from a dumb mothafucka, real shit. Nigga you got pull, find out what you can about him, who he ran with while he was locked up."

Putting the blunt between my lips, I lit it. After inhaling, I pointed the blunt at Mac. "I'm having that done. Shid, in time we'll see what's up with him."

"Aye, if the nigga is on some bullshit, yo ass got a houseful of shooters in that bitch." He pointed out and I broke out laughing.

"Nigga, dead ass. Shid, even my baby girl a pro with that bitch." I laughed thinking about Brianna shooting skills. That little girl was my damn heart. She looked like both me and Peach, with her mommas' bad ass attitude. I loved the fuck out that little girl. "Peaches ass finally gonna give me another shorty. Now this shit coming up and a new brother and shit. Man, the shit got my head fuck'd up, just remembering all the bullshit we went through. Seeing Peaches ass in a shootout, scared the fuck out of me, man. I can't be having her dodging bullets. I've been thinking about sending her and the kids off until this shit with Brittany is over with." I dumped the ashes from the blunt and looked at Mac.

His face twisted up and he sat back in the chair. "Yeah, I don't see Peaches doing that. She'll send the kids off with yo moms, but she's not gonna be that far from yo ass, especially if mothafuckas gonna be shooting at you."

His ass had a point. Peaches wasn't one to hide, especially if I wasn't going with her. I pulled hard on the blunt, inhaling deeply. "Yeah, I don't see that shit either..." The smoke left my mouth as I spoke. "I haven't even had the chance to catch Blake up on the shit that's been going on. But that mothafucka got his own little bullshit going on for real. Nigga, I feel old as fuck."

Mac's brow cocked at that. "Nigga, yo ass is old as fuck, what you mean?" He laughed.

"Yo, fuck you." I handed him the blunt. "No, bullshit though..." My hand rubbed over my face as I felt the weed starting to kick in. "I haven't set a fire or popped a mothafucka in a minute... it's fuck'd up that I kinda miss that shit." I told him straight up. "Don't get me wrong, I wouldn't change where I'm at now for that shit again. That next level excitement is a mothafucka though."

Mac stared at me like I was crazy. "B, you burnt about what? Four bodies and that's some shit you miss? Yo ass crazy man."

I shrugged. "Shid, those mothafuckas was dead, they ain't feel the shit."

"Nigga, yo ass sick as fuck. Oh, so because they were already dead that make the shit cool?" He laughed.

"Mac, what the fuck is you talkin' about?" I asked as the doorbell rang. Mac lean back and kicked his legs up on the table. "Nigga, go open the fuckin' door. Fuck you gon' get comfortable for?"

Mac stopped mid puff on the blunt and looked at me then to the door. "This yo crib, by all means you can open up yo own gotdamn door." The apartment door came opened and Mac jumped up with his gun out.

"Y'all didn't hear the damn buzzer?" Peaches snapped, as she walked in with some bags.

"Why you didn't call before you came here?" I went over and grabbed the bags from her and took them in the kitchen.

"Didn't know I had to call, especially when I told you I was coming over once I got off work." She said with an attitude.

"What the fuck wrong with you?" I asked her.

Peaches blew out a breath and shook her head. "It's nothing, just work stuff."

"Come here." I beckoned her to me. Slowly she made her way to the other side of the kitchen where I stood. "Do I need to go to yo job and fuck everybody in that bitch up?" Peaches lips twisted to the side. "Do I? Shid, all you gotda do is say the word and that whole mothafuckin' hospital gone. Dead ass. So, what you want me to do?"

Peaches started laughing while wrapping her arms around my neck. "Exactly what you're doing. But it's nothing serious, I can handle this so don't worry about it. Besides, you have way more important things to worry about. I should be asking you all that." She pulled my head down and ran her tongue across my lips. "Is it something you need me to do? All you have to do is say the word." She exclaimed before licking from my bottom lip up to the top.

I groaned at the sexual submission in her tone. "Yo ass sexy as fuck, Peaches." My hand slapped her ass hard and she moaned while sucking on my bottom lip. Pulling back, I licked my lips. "Gon' take yo ass in the room then." She kissed me once more, then walked out the kitchen. "Man, that mothafucka sexy as fuck." My dick was hard as hell. I made quick work with putting the food and shit away then went back into the living room.

Mac was stretched out on the couch watching tv, looking bored as hell. I left his ass there and went into the room. Hearing the shower running, I pulled off my clothes and then went into the bathroom.

Peaches was in the shower with her head under the spray. Getting in, I went up behind her. My arm went across her chest, cupping her right breast as the other snaked down her body, going between her legs. My finger pushed through her slit, finding the jewel. I played with her clit while pinching her nipple and sucking on her neck.

She moaned as her head fell back on my shoulder. I pushed two fingers into her pussy, and she gasped and tightened her grip on my wrist. Peaches arm hooked around my neck, and she brought my lips to hers. My fingers moved faster inside her pussy, causing her moans to come out louder as she panted heavily.

Her mouth opened and her tongue twisted with mine. "Oooh, Blaze, baby, fuck me, please." She begged as her pussy squeezed around my fingers.

Turning her around, I grabbed a handful of her ass and lifted her up. Pressing her against the wall, I slid into her pussy. Peaches head fell back against the wall as she moaned out in pleasure.

My hands gripped her ass tight, my hips thrust upwards as I bounced her downwards onto my dick, pounding into her love box. Even after all the years we've been together her pussy never got old. The shit still felt like heaven to me. Every time I was inside her, it was fuckin' amazing, the shit was crazy as hell to me, but I loved the fuck out of it, out of her ass.

"Oh, my God, Blaze. Ooh, fuck, baby." She cried out as her nails bit into the back of my neck. "Ooh, baby, you feel so fuckin' good." Her head went to the side of mine and she bit the tip of my ear.

"Gotdamn, Peaches, fuck!" I grunted as her pussy squeezed my dick. I felt her body tense shakily as she came. My hips jerked upwards and I held her to me as I nutted inside her. "Fuck!"

Peaches panted heavily into my ear, before she pulled back and grabbed my face then kissed me. "God, I love you so much, papa bear." Her arms tightened around my neck as she continued to kiss me.

Tangling my hand in her wet hair, I pulled her head back. "I love you, too." I kissed the center of her chest, then went to her left nipple, sucking on it.

Peaches pulled my head from her tittie. "You gon' wash me up or take me in the room and let me fuck yo dick?" She ran her tongue over my bottom lip. I turned that water off so damn fast and Peaches started laughing. "Baby, I wasn't serious. Oh, my God."

I put her down. "Why the fuck you playing with me?"

"We couldn't go another round anyways, because Kordell and Brittany should be here soon." She stated and I honestly didn't give a fuck about none of that.

"Fuck them. I just need five minutes to let off this second nut, I promise." What I said probably wasn't true, but I meant that shit wholeheartedly. I didn't know if it was the weed or what the fuck, but I was horny as hell.

Peaches continued to laugh. "You ain't right, I swear and yo ass know you're not about to bust no nut in five damn minutes. You're not a— *in and out* type of man, baby." She said rinsing the soap off her body. "Wash up and come on." She pushed the towel into my chest and quickly got out the shower.

I looked down at my hardened dick. I shut off the water and got out. Peaches stood in the mirror, naked and combing through her wet hair. Walking up behind her, I placed my hands on the counter, watching her.

Peaches lips twitched as she tried hard not to look at me through the mirror. She moved back, pushing against my dick as she went into the drawer for a hair tie.

"You gon' do him like that? For real?" I asked as her booty bumped against my dick again.

"I don't know what you're talking about." She pushed her ass into me and bent down, going into the bottom drawer, she got out the blow dryer.

Laughing, my arms went around her waist. "I love the fuck out of yo ass, for real, Peach."

She finally looked at me through the mirror. "I know." She then bent over onto the counter. "Now are you gonna let me fuck yo dick or not?" She placed her leg on the countertop, then reached underneath herself and grabbed my dick, guiding it to her pussy. Peaches lips parted and her eyes closed as the tip pushed in. Her ass started to bounce slowly on my tip, fuckin' it.

"Fuck…" Licking my lips, I stared at her booty, watching as my dick slowly started to disappear into her pussy. "Gotdamn." I grunted, seeing her slick juices covering my shit. I bit into my bottom lip then squeezed her ass cheek. As bad as I wanted to thrust, I didn't. I let Peaches do her damn thing. I glanced back into the mirror to see that she too was biting her lower lip as she watched me.

Once our eyes locked in the mirror her pace quickened as she fuck'd my dick faster. Her lips parted and her breathing picked up. Before her head could drop on the counter, my hand tangled into her wet hair.

"No, this yo dick, take yo shit baby. Fuck yo dick." I pulled her head back at the same time, I pushed my dick deep inside her. "Take yo shit, Peach, fuck this mothafucka, don't stop."

I watched as her toes squeezed together and she pushed up off my dick. Reaching behind her, she pushed me back slightly then gripped that gotdamn counter and started fuckin' the hell out of my dick.

***

"What you find out?" I sat on the couch opposite Kordell. It had been a week since the shooting went down. That was more than enough time for his ass to find some shit out.

"Not much. Shit been quiet as hell since Slick and his niggas been gone. Their brother Saul haven't made a move yet, which I'm surprised." He stated before glancing around the room.

"How many brothers these niggas got and were they all in business together? Nigga, tell me what you know about the family in general.

460

Lay the bullshit all out there, that way we know who and what the fuck we're dealing with." I really didn't like that mothafuckin' nigga. He might've dressed like a nigga in business, but I saw a straight bitch in men clothing.

"It's been a fuckin' week and all you can tell us is that it's been fuckin' quiet. Yo ass ain't tried to find out why these mothafuckas been silent?" Mac was looking at that nigga like he was stupid.

"That's all the fuck I know. I got several businesses to run while looking into those niggas. I'm finding out as much as I can with the time I got. If those niggas ain't making a move and quiet as a fuckin' mouse, how am I supposed to find out shit exactly?" Kordell snapped right back at Mac.

Mac looked at me and pointed to Kordell. "Is this stupid mothafucka serious?"

I nodded. "I think he dead ass serious." I needed to smoke. I saw at that moment I couldn't talk to that mothafucka if I wasn't high otherwise, I would kill that stupid son of a bitch. "Mac, light a blunt and put some smoke up." I rubbed my forehead before I sat up. My arms rested on my knees as my thumbs rolled over one another. "I'm tryna make sho' I'm hearing yo ass right. Mothafuckas you know try to kill yo ass and yo ol' lady, the mothafucka you love and yo ass is at work?" I glanced up at him and the mothafucka was nodding. I let out a laugh.

"If I act any other way, they're gonna suspect something is up, I don't want that, you don't want that. I'm moving like everything is good. Blaze, you don't know me, but I know what I'm doing." Kordell pointed out and what he said made sense.

"I get all that, but yo ass don't know shit about them other than those mothafuckas are quiet. I don't know about yo ass, but a silent mothafucka worry me. It's the hushed mothafuckas you need to pay the most attention too, because they're always planning and watching in the backgrounds. I can guarantee yo ass they know where the fuck you are at this fuckin' moment. Now answer me this shit straight up. Do you have eyes on the other living brother or brothers? Can yo ass make a call right gotdamn now and tell me where any of those niggas are at?"

Kordell's hand rubbed over his head and he looked how I felt, frustrated as fuck. "You're not listening to me—"

"Because yo dumb ass ain't saying shit!" I barked out as I hopped off the couch. I was about to beat the shit out that mothafucka. "Now answer the fuckin' question, yes or fuckin no, don't give me no other explanation. I don't wanna hear they asses can't be reached or fuckin' touched."

The room had fallen quiet as hell, as the tension grew.

Kordell sat up and rubbed a hand over his mouth. He then cracked his knuckles before flexing his fingers. "No, I can't. Hear it or don't, they can't be touched. It's three other brothers, none of which is stupid, all of whom is crazy as fuck. Nobody can get to close to them or sit on them twenty-four fuckin' seven. I got hella fuckin' resources all through the city and nobody can get to them." He explained.

"B…" Mac held the blunt for me. I looked at the twisted brown paper before my eyes slid to the gun on the table. "Take the gotdamn blunt, Blaze." Mac thrust the blunt at me.

Grabbing the blunt, I sat back down on the couch. Once I did, Mac took his gun off the table and put it on his lap. I kicked my leg up on the couch and my mind started to run with what he said, the shit didn't make sense and if it didn't make sense to me, then it wasn't right. His ass wasn't right.

"What's up with that expensive chick you were talking about?" Mac questioned. I had forgotten all about that chick.

"She had another job to work." He stated. My head shook and I pulled on the blunt, inhaling deep.

"What you know about the other three brothers?" Mac asked Kordell.

"It's Saul, the oldest brother, he owns several strip clubs throughout the city, he got a club and two clothing stores he run with his middle brother Sean and the younger brother Tony. Slick was working with him until I killed Turk. Me and Turk was running a club together, we wanted to expand out here. That's when Turk's attention turned toward you," he nodded to me. "We wanted to do business with you. I mean, yo name moved through the streets out here and on top of that, you're a smart businessman. Like I said, I looked into you and who's better to run shit out here than you? That's what Turk was sent out here for, to talk business with you, not try to buy no fuckin' drugs, I didn't know shit about that until after the fact—"

Mac cut him off, waving his hand. "Yo, skip all that shit. We don't give a fuck about that no more. We just wanna know about the three brothers that's alive. Give us the name of the clubs, stores, whatever else they have and pictures of them. House addresses if you got that."

464

I continued to smoke on the blunt while listening to Kordell tell Mac the name and locations of the strip joints, the night club and the clothing stores the brothers owned.

"So, what's going on?" Peaches walked into the living room with a lavender dress on that hugged all her curves. During the years, Peaches had filled out, her hips had widened, ass was bigger, titties were fuller, and her stomach had a pudge to it. The shit was sexy as fuck on her. Hell, then again, any look would be sexy as hell on her. Peaches hair was pulled up into a ponytail. She walked over to me and sat on my lap. "What happened?"

Kordell's movement caused me to look at him. I watched as he brushed off his suit, then fixed his jacket. That mothafucka had to be dumb as hell. The nigga fixed himself up because Peaches walked in.

Peaches took the blunt from me and handed it to Mac. My head tilted as I looked at her. "I wasn't done with that. I need that shit." I shot a glare at Kordell thinking about the dumb shit he had said. "Brittany!" I yelled. She had been in the back ever since they got there.

Peaches hit me. "Don't yell like that in my ear. She'll be in here, I had her doing something, so just give her a few minutes. What happened?" She repeated.

I nodded to Kordell. "Tell her everything you told us, from the beginning. Gon' head and tell her." I instructed. He did, he jumped into the story of how they couldn't be touched and how resourceful he was, everything.

Peaches hand stroked the back of my head all the while, I knew she was really paying attention to what he was saying. Every so often she would bite on her bottom lip as her eyes squinted either in thought of what he was saying or confusion.

"Hm..." She hummed as her legs crossed. She was acting as if she was in a damn chair and not my lap, on my dick. "Maybe you're not as resourceful as you think." She told him straight up. "I mean, think about it, you're supposed to be this big time... *boss*, you got shooters at your beck and call, niggas watching your back or whatever... yet, they were still able to get at you when that shouldn't have been possible. Not only that, how is it impossible for you to have people sit on them, that doesn't make sense to me." Peaches looked confused as she spoke.

"Thank fuck it's not just me who thought that." I said, rubbing my forehead. "Either you're not the fuckin' boss yo ass pretending to be or the niggas on yo mothafuckin' team aren't as loyal to you as yo ass think they are." I told him.

466

"I ain't pretending to be shit. Nigga, what the fuck you ain't about to do is keep talking to me like you fuckin' stupid. We both men in this bitch, so you gon' talk to me like I'm one and not yo fuckin' child." Kordell spat, glaring at me.

I moved Peaches off me. "Nigga, fuck you. I don't see a fuckin' man, but a little as boy tryna play grown up and done got himself in a fuck'd up situation. *Little bitch nigga*, you walked yo ass in here with shit to give. You ain't no fuckin' boss with no gotdamn resources, but a little ass *bitch boy* that done came into some fuckin' money and done got way in over his fuckin' head. Yo ass playing in a mothafuckin' game you don't know shit about. Shid, I'm surprise yo stupid ass ain't fuckin' dead yet—"

"Blaze—" Peaches grabbed my arm.

I jerked away from her. "Yo, don't fuckin' touch me. Don't tell me to calm down or shit. This mothafucka gon' get everybody in this bitch killed because he tryna play some tough ass boss nigga. Where the fuck is yo people at? Man, where yo niggas at? You in this bitch with nobody at yo back, no information about the niggas that tried to kill you. Nigga, fuck you! Man, get the fuck out my house."

"Blaze, don't—" Peaches grabbed my arm again.

I jerked her off me. "Peaches, sit yo ass down and shut the fuck up, damn."

"What's going on?" Brittany asked, finally coming into the living room. She looked confused as she stared around at us. "Boon, what happened?"

I didn't give a fuck about anybody's feelings. Brittany wanted to be grown and in the middle of everything. It was about time I let her ass be grown. "Why the fuck is you still sitting there? Get out my shit before yo ass get dragged out."

"Wait, Blaze, what the hell is going on? Why are you putting him out? I thought—"

"You thought what? I was gonna help him? How the fuck can I help his ass when he can't help himself? This nigga at fuckin' work and ain't tryna do shit. Fuck a gotdamn job, if a nigga come after mine, everything is fuckin' forgotten except for the mothafuckin' target. And if I don't have no niggas behind me, my ass gonna still be out there doing that shit myself." I was pissed the fuck off.

"Brittany, you can stay if you wanna, and I got you without a fuckin' doubt, you know that. But this nigga got to go and can't come back around here. That mothafucka got a target on his head, and it's the same for everybody around him, including you. He can't be around me." I looked at Peaches. "I got too much to lose and I'm not putting his life above theirs period. Like I said, if you wanna stay, you can, but he can't be around. Now, if you wanna be with him, you got to go because I can't put your life above theirs either."

Wasn't nobody more important to me than Peaches and my kids. I wasn't about to jeopardize their lives for them. If I did shit their way, that's exactly what I'll be doing, and I wasn't walking into shit blind.

"What you gon' do, Britt?" I asked her.

She looked shocked while staring at me in disbelief. "Are you serious, Boon?" She asked as tears filled her eyes.

I nodded. "Dead ass serious. You ain't a kid any more Brittany, you're a grown ass woman. You can decide what you wanna do. His life ain't important to me and I'm not risking shit for him or you if you choose to be with him." I shrugged.

Brittany wiped her eyes and nodded. "Okay." Her tears were coming down faster, she stomped off into the back. she came back a few seconds later with her stuff. "Come on, Kordell."

I nodded at her decision and walked to the door and opened it for them. Brittany's lips quivered and she stomped out the apartment without a word.

"You really gon' do your sister like that?" Kordell asked. "It's not just me they want."

"She chose to go with you." I punched his ass in the mouth. "Remember what the fuck I said. If something happens to her, those niggas is gon' be the least of yo fuckin' problems. Yo ass better protect her with yo fuckin' life." I closed the door in his face.

The apartment was dead silent once that door was closed.

"You really just gon' let her go like that?" Mac questioned.

My hand rubbed over my head and I shrugged. "I couldn't make her stay. Shid, she's grown and was going to do what she wanted to." I looked at Peaches. She sat on the couch, elbows on her knees, head in her hands as her legs bounced frantically. "Peach—"

She was off that couch so gotdamn fast and kicking off her shoes. "You a stupid sonofabitch!" She yelled while throwing her flat shoes at me. She then grabbed the glass cups off the table.

"Peach, yo ass bet not—" I ducked just as the first cup came flying at my head. It smashed into the wall shattering. "Yo, what the fuck is wrong with you—"

"What the fuck is wrong with me? You're what's fuckin' wrong with me!" She threw another cup at me and I jumped out the way, causing it to shatter against the door. "Don't you ever fuckin' talk to me like that again. What the fuck is wrong with you? How you gonna put her out, Blaze? That's your fuckin' sister no matter who she wants to be with!" She screamed as she looked for something else to throw.

She looked at Mac and he hopped over the couch. When she couldn't find nothing else, she turned and glared at me.

"I'm so fuckin' pissed at you right now, that I'll stab yo ass in your sleep. Ugh!" She yelled. "I can't fuckin' believe you put her out!" Her hand waved before she stormed out the living room. A few seconds later the bedroom door was slammed shut.

"Yo, that babe scary as fuck when she's pissed off." Mac rubbed his head as he looked at the broken glass. "Damn. B, tell me you ain't washing yo hands with Britt?"

Laughing, I picked up Peaches shoe and threw it at him. "Mac, act like you know me. I'll never trust my sister's life in the hands of a nigga that can't protect himself." I walked over and gave him my phone, showing him the messages between me and Bellow. "Bell is tracking his car, using Britt's GPS to make sure nobody is following them, and they get there safe. If somebody is following them, Bell will tag that car and we go from there. But I couldn't do it, they probably already know about me because of Turk. And I couldn't let you do it, that shit would've been to obvious, plus I don't need you on their radar."

"So, while he was talking to Peaches, yo ass was texting Bellow?" Mac wiped his mouth before a look of relief hit him. "Man, next time text my ass and warn me about this shit. That fuck'd me up for a minute."

"It fuck'd Brittany up too. The shit had to be real for everyone to believe it. We don't know if Kordell's car is bugged or not. And the way my mind works, I have to believe everybody think like me, so I know how to move. So, if the car is bugged, they'll hear how I put my sister out and walked away from this shit." I told him as I got the broom.

"Damn, well shit, I wasn't thinking like that at all." He leaned against the wall watching me as I swept the floor. "Why the fuck you ain't tell Peaches that then?"

I looked at his ass like he was stupid, then pointed to the glass I was cleaning up. "It's not like that crazy mothafucka gave me a chance too." Peaches ass was crazy as fuck. I had every mind to go back there and slap the shit out of her, but I wasn't going to do that shit because she really thought I turned my back on Brittany's ass.

"Bellow said it's a car on them. He sent a picture and plate number. How the fuck he get a plate number when he driving? I knew it was something off about that nigga." Mac laughed while still looking at the phone.

It was no telling how Bell did half the shit he was able to. One thing I did know was that Bellow was a fuckin' tech genius, the nigga could hack any gotdamn thing.

"I need you to call up yo boy Rome. Once we get pictures of the brothers, I want him on the oldest one. See if he can find out where he lives and when he's by himself. If he down, I wanna meet up with him as soon as possible."

"I'ight. Here." He held his hand out. "I'll clean this up. Go talk to the wife. This time I believe she may just stab yo ass in yo sleep." He took the broom from me and nodded towards the rooms. "Gon' now."

I left out the living room and went to our room. When I walked in and didn't see Peaches on the bed, I went and checked the bathroom. She sat on the tub, looking at a white plastic stick. I walked over to her and looked at the test that read pregnant.

"You pregnant?"

Peaches stood up and slapped the thing into my chest. "This ain't mine. Next time you see your sister, if she's not dead, tell her congratulations." She snapped at me then walked out the bathroom.

I grabbed the stick before it could fall. I read the thing several times before rubbing my forehead. That's why her and Peaches was locked in the room for so long. She was taking a damn test. I tossed it on the counter, washed my hands, then went into the room.

"Blaze, I really don't feel like talking to or looking at you right now. Like, just get away from me because I want to hit you in your damn face right now." She was really pissed off.

"Peach—"

"No!" She yelled as tears filled her eyes. "Don't fuckin' Peaches me. No! You're fuckin' wrong, Blaze, period. It's no way in hell you should have turned your fuckin' back on her—"

I grabbed Peaches quick and pinned her arms to her side before she could try to swing on my ass. "Peaches, calm down, man, I didn't turn my back on her. You should know me better than that. I would never do no shit like that, especially

474

not to Brittany, no matter who she's with." I told her. Peaches didn't say anything or move for that matter, but I wasn't stupid to let her go. "Peach, you really think I'll do that too Brittany knowing somebody tried to take her?"

Peaches eyes rolled and she shook her head. "I didn't think you would—"

"Believe I wouldn't. Yo ass know how much family means to me. Baby, I didn't turn my back on my sister. I had Bellow hack her phone and track it through GPS. If I didn't have a plan, I would have never let her leave this fuckin' apartment. But I needed them to believe that I did just in case Kordell's truck was bugged."

Peaches eyes stared into mine for a long while searching them. I let her arms go and she punched in my chest. "Why you didn't tell me that. You sounded so serious. Hell, you looked serious. Oh, my God, Blaze!" She went to hit me again, but I grabbed her wrist. "Don't ever do no shit like that without telling me. I felt so bad for her. She was already in here crying when she found out she was pregnant. She was scared of what you would do or say and then you go and throw her out. Man, my damn heart hurt for her. You looked so serious."

"I had to be serious for them to believe me. That way if their car is bugged whoever's listening will think I'm out of it. They won't be expecting me to do shit, so they won't look into me, now you and the kids will be safe." My arms wrapped around her waist. "Making sure y'all straight is the most important thing to me. Know that my mind is always running with different ways to make sure of that. I was going to have y'all get out of town for a while, but Mac ass reminded me that you wouldn't leave with me still being here. So, I had to think of something else."

A smile came to her mouth and she laughed. "And I threw glass cups at you. I'm so sorry, I should've gone with my gut feeling instead of what I was hearing. B, you were so convincing. I can't believe you." Her hands went to the side of my face and she kissed me. "Baby, I'm sorry." She kissed me.

I picked her up and walked us to the bed. "You wanna make it up to me?"

Peaches broke out laughing. "You so damn nasty. Yeah, I'll suck yo dick."

I tossed her on the bed and pulled off my shirt. "Shid, you were gonna suck my dick anyways. That's not what I want though. I'm hungry as shit for real. You can go fry up that chicken, make some greens, macaroni and cornbread." I told her as I laid down beside her.

Peaches leaned over and kissed me. "I can do that for you." She kissed me again, then got off the bed, and left out the room.

Man, I loved that damn woman.

Chapter 24

Blaze

"After listening to Mac sell yo ass to me. I wanna hire you for a job." Jerome's brow shot up, and he glanced over at Mac. Previous to Mac saying anything about Rome doing the job for me, I had heard about the little nigga when he was first released from prison a while ago.

Not only was he an angry mothafucka, but his actions backed up his ways. The nigga wasn't afraid to kill a mothafucka and was clean as fuck with covering it up. Whatever his pops did to him when he was younger molded his ass to be the way he was.

"He sold me to you? What the fuck did he tell you?" Rome asked, turning his focus back on me.

"That you're patient and that's something we lack. I want you to sit on somebody for me. I need to know everything, where they go and for how long, when they're alone and for how long, how many niggas surround him and how good they pay attention…" My words trailed off as Jerome raised his hand. I glanced over at Mac, like what the fuck and he shrugged. "What's up?"

He sat up and grabbed the ash tray from the table, then took out a square and lit it. "Am I killing him?"

"No, not right now. Once I know what you've learned then we'll go from there until then don't kill him, Bet?"

He nodded. "Was just making sure. So, who is he and where he stay?"

Thanks to Sam we were able to get background on Saul, Sean, and Tony, from criminal records, to social media accounts. Funny shit about it was that the three loved the spotlight, those mothafuckas posted on social media daily.

"It's three of them, I want you on Saul," I slid the picture of the dark-skinned dude in front of him. His eyes squinted as he looked at the images. "But if he meets up with these two mothafuckas—"

"That's Tony…" He picked up the picture, his eyes slanted before his brow cocked. "What the fuck you niggas done got into and what Tony got to do with it?" He asked me.

"You know him?" I asked as Mac walked over to us.

Jerome face relaxed and his head tilted to the side. "Nah, I just know his name and want to know what he got to do with it."

I glared at him and pointed to the picture. "Nigga, don't get smart and tell me how you know Tony?"

He stabbed out his square, then reached over and grabbed the other pictures. He pulled out two others. "I know, Tony, Sean and Slick." He laid them out in order, pointing to each person as he said their names. "I was locked up with all three of them. The last time, Sean and Slick only stayed in for about two months. Tony did three years for assault with a deadly weapon, he was supposed to do more, but time got knocked off. If you ask me, he didn't do the shit," he pointed to Sean and Slick's picture. "He took that charge for one of them because they already had two strikes against them. That's how I know them." He pushed the pictures away and sat back down.

480

"Hm…" My fingers tapped on the desk as my mind started to roam. "How well you know them?"

"First tell me what this shit is all about." Rome said, motioning to the papers.

Shrugging, I ran down what happened with Turk, then I pointed to Slick. "That nigga and a couple of his boys, tried to take my sister because of the nigga she's fuckin' with. I don't give a fuck about the nigga, but the brothers coming for my family I ain't having that shit. You feel me?"

He groaned and sat up. He grabbed the picture of Saul. "I never met Saul, but I did a couple jobs for him while I was locked up and looked after his little brother. Tony ain't made for this lifestyle so the nigga couldn't survive in jail, which is why he asked me to look out for him. Some of the body's I dropped was for niggas fuckin' with him. Even took out a guard for that nigga. If you want to get close to him, I can help you. With the jobs I did for him, he promised to look out for me when I got out, I never hit him up or shit. I can do it now, though."

"Why?" No nigga did shit for free. It was always a price for something. "What you want?"

"Shid, from how I see it, I owe him." He pointed to Mac. "I'm cashing in here. If that babe yo sister, then it's his too. Plus, Saul has a whore house, if he was trying to take yo sister instead of killing her ass, there's no doubt that's where she would've ended up." Rome grabbed another square and laughed. "It's fuck'd up how much you learn about a nigga when you done pissed off yo' blood. Tony talked a lot about Saul, Sean, Slick and Turk. But don't shit happens unless Saul approves it. He run those boys, except with Turk, so I'm not surprised his ass dead. From the way you said he came at you tells me he did that shit on his own. Now the shit that went down with your sister and her nigga, yeah, that's Saul."

It was crazy how some shit just fell into our fuckin' laps. "Reach out to Tony and meet up with him, I'll give you a place and time if he agrees." He nodded but didn't move. "Gon' do that now. Mac will give you his info."

As Rome and Mac headed to the office I had in the apartment, my phone started ringing with Brianna's face popping up on the screen. "What's up baby girl?"

She let out a dramatic sigh into the phone. "Nothing. I'm bored and I miss you and mommy. What y'all doing?"

I chuckled as I made myself comfortable on the couch. "Shit, just working. How you bored, baby when you just got out of school?"

"I'm about to FaceTime you." A second later my phone rang again. I answered the call and Brianna sat on the porch of our house, with her elbow on her knee and chin in her palm. She looked bored. "It's nothing to do out here... Daddy where you at? You not at work. Can I come with you? Please? I don't wanna be here with BJ and Nana. All BJ do is play his game and Nana just watch her boring stories." She complained, whining. "Daddy, can you come get me, please?" She begged, pouting.

I had to admit, I missed my baby girl, it had been several days since we've been home with the kids, my momma and Blake had been looking after them for us. Brianna knew how to make me feel like shit without even knowing it.

"Baby, I can't come get you right now. I'm trying to hurry up and finish my work so I can get back to the crib. Why don't you go to that little nappy headed girl's house, down the street?"

Brianna rolled her eyes. "April's not at home. I went over there already. I'm the only kid out here and BJ don't wanna ride bikes and play with me. He just sits in his dirty room and play that dumb game." Her head fell into her lap. "I'm so bored! I'm gonna die of borvation—"

I broke out laughing at the word borvation. She was her fuckin' momma's child. Brianna was so gotdamn dramatic. "Borvation? Bri, that ain't no word sweetheart—"

"Daddy, it's not funny!" She snapped at me before falling back on the porch. "Please come home. I miss you so much."

I have never spent that many days away from the kids, since they were born, except for Blake. The twins though, I was always around them. "I miss you too, baby. I promise I'll be back in a few more days. Alright?" Brianna nodded as her face turned red, a second later her arm went over her eyes. "Yo momma will be home tonight, when she gets off, okay?" All she did was nod from behind her arm. "Baby, don't cry. Hold on right quick, okay?" When she nodded, I grabbed Mac's phone and called Sam, while muting the Facetime call.

"What's up?" He answered.

"Aye, what you about to get into?" I asked him while looking at Brianna cry.

"Shit, being lazy, today my off day. Why what's up?"

"I need a big favor. Where Linnea's bad ass at?" Linnea was Sam niece, his sister, Tishana's daughter. The bitch that set all that shit in motion between me and Peaches. Even though that bitch was dead, I still hated her with a passion, but I loved the fuck out of her daughter. While I was on the phone with Sam, I was texting King asking him what Keema ass was doing.

"In the room doing something. Why what's up?"

"You know all this bullshit going on, I ain't been at the crib with Brianna and she bored as fuck, crying and shit. You wanna go by the crib so she can hang out with Linnea and Keema? King gon' meet you at the house if you come through. That way you ain't there with them by yoself."

"Nigga, this sound like a setup." Sam groaned before he laughed. "Yeah, I'll swing over there. Tink!" He called for Linnea.

I laughed at the nickname because that damn girl looked just like a fairy doll. I heard her yell back in the background.

"Get some clothes on, Bri-Bri want you to come over there—"

"Can you take us to get our nails done? I promised her we would go the next time I came over there, please!" She begged him.

"How the hell you making promises and you don't drive?" Sam asked her as I laughed. I swear all our damn girls were spoiled as fuck and grown as hell. It was crazy how the three of our girls clicked together regardless of there age difference. Keema and Tink were about fourteen whereas Brianna was seven, but once those three got together you couldn't tell there was an age difference.

"That's why I have an amazing daddy like you for! Please, please, please with a cherry on top. I swear I'll love you forever. Please, daddy?" She continued to plead with him.

He groaned. "Man, go get ready!"

Linnea let out a loud squeak. "Thank you! I'm about to call her. Can Keema come too?" She asked.

"Tink, go get ready damn." He snapped at her. "I said that shit sounded like a gotdamn setup. Tell Bri-Bri to get ready and let King ass know we're going to the nail shop."

Laughing I sat up straight on the couch. "Thanks, man, I owe yo ass one for real."

"You fuckin' right you do." With that Sam ended the call.

I got back on with Brianna. "Hey, baby, go get your stuff together—"

"You coming to get me?" Brianna arm left her tear stained face as she got excited. "Hold on, daddy, Tink texting me." The screen paused and I waited like I was really on hold.

"Baby, what she's saying?"

"That's okay, daddy, you don't have to come get me no more. Tink gonna come get me and take me out. She said we're gonna get our nails done and go to the mall afterwards." The sadness in her voice was replaced with excitement.

I laughed at her change of attitude. "I'ight then, baby, gon' get ready and I'll talk to you later."

"Okay, I wish you could come, but I know you're busy. Bye, daddy, I love you." She blew a kiss at the screen.

"I love you too, baby." She waved then ended the call. I let out a heavy breath and laid back down. Brittany stupid ass just had to get into some shit with a dumb mothafucka. I was pissed off that I had to call my niggas to go spend time with my daughter because I couldn't. That shit was bothering the fuck out of me.

Mac and Rome came back into the living room. "Dude responded to Rome inbox on Instagram. B, I don't know about that Tony nigga, he seems a little sweet to me."

My brows cocked up. "Sweet? Like he's gay?" Mac nodded and I was confused. "I'm not understanding what you mean."

"He's saying the dude gay, what's not to understand when you just said it yourself." Rome pointed out.

"I don't understand what him being gay got to do with shit. What? Because the nigga like dick that supposed to make him less of a threat? What we supposed to let our guard down or some shit?" I was confused as fuck what sharing that information was gonna do for us.

"I ain't saying that. I just put out an observation." Mac said with a shrug.

I glared at him. "I don't give a fuck if his ass love dick or pussy, if yo fuckin' observation ain't to help end this shit today, I don't give a fuck about it, period. I'll get up with y'all niggas later." Grabbing my shit, I left the apartment. I had to clear my fuckin' head.

***

"Daddy!" Brianna screamed once she saw me. She had a little champagne glass in her hand with some orange juice in it. She looked around for a second, then handed her glass to the black woman who was about to start on her feet. I quickly made my way to her before she could run to me and bust her shit. Brianna jumped in my arms and threw her arms around my neck.

Once her little shoulders started to shake, I kissed the top of her head. "Sweetheart, don't cry." I kissed her again.

She sniffled and pulled back, wiping her eyes. "I didn't think you would come. I thought you had to work?" She was staring at me like she couldn't believe I was there.

"You know I had to come see my baby, I took a few hours off to be here with you."

Brianna grabbed the side of my face and kissed my lips. "I missed you so much." She hugged me once again.

"I missed you too, sweetheart." I kissed the side of her head again.

After snapping on Mac and Rome, I knew I had to come spend some time with my baby girl. Especially when I was sure nobody was on me. After seeing Brianna cry, I had to come see her. That little girl had me weak to the fuckin' bone, I would move mountains for her if I could.

"You brought me flowers?" She pointed to the three yellow roses in my hand.

"Of course, I had to bring my baby some roses."

She squeaked and gave me another kiss, then took the roses. "Thank you, daddy, they're beautiful. You know yellow is my favorite color." It wasn't until I heard a collective of awe, that I realized we had an audience. "Okay, daddy, put me down, I have to get my feet done." She instructed, laughing. I put her back in the chair she hopped out of. "You not about to leave, are you?" She quickly grabbed my hand.

"Nah, I'mma sit up front—"

"You can sit right here and get your feet done too. Loni, can my daddy sit here? He getting his feet done too."

Loni started laughing at Brianna. "Yeah, sweetie he can." The nail shop we were at was ran by a black chick Peaches and her girls knew. "You can sit next to her." She told me before handing Brianna her glass.

"Daddy, take off your shoes and sit down." She ordered. Rubbing my head, I then took off my shoes and sat down. The shit I did for that little ass girl was beyond me. Brianna looked at her glass then to me. "I don't think they have your drink, but you can get some orange juice." She told me. "Loni, can my daddy get something to drink?"

Loni broke out laughing. "Whatever you want, Diva."

"If you ain't call that shit right." I couldn't do shit but laugh at Brianna's grown ass. "What's up Tink and Keema."

"Hey, uncle Boon." They spoke at once while waving to me.

"Where y'all pops at?"

They pointed to the wall in front of us. "At the bar next door." Linnea stated.

"They said they didn't want to sit in here and listen to girls talk." Keema's eyes rolled. "You know how they are."

I looked at my shoes then to the wall, ready to get the fuck out of there my damn self.

"You coming to the mall with us?" Bria took a sip of her juice and looked away from her phone to me.

"Yeah, I'mma come with you."

"Okay, cool. Here, take this pic with me. Loni, can you take this picture of us?" She was so damn demanding, but the lady didn't seem to mind as she grabbed the phone. Bria held up two fingers and stuck out her tongue.

"Put yo damn tongue up." She popped her lips but put her tongue away. We took several pictures before the tub was filled and they started working on Brianna's feet then mine.

I sat there in disbelief that I was getting my gotdamn feet done. I felt so out of body in that moment. However, I didn't complain because it was what my baby girl wanted.

***

"Tell dude you'll meet him at the courts. That way he'll think it's really on some friendly shit. But aye, once I finish up with what I'm doing, I'll meet y'all back at the apartment. Aye, Mac, get up with Bell and see what he pulled off those phones."

"I'ight, B, I got you." Mac ended the call.

"So, who the fuck is this nigga Brittany ass dating? Where the fuck he come from?" King asked as we followed behind the girls in the mall.

I had been meaning to call King and catch him up on everything that was going on, but the shit kept slipping my mind. "Fuck if I know, King. From the way that nigga approached me, I thought he was about his business. Maybe even had niggas on his payroll. You know that bitch mothafucka sat in there and told me, those brothers couldn't be touched? On top of that, the dude couldn't get none of his niggas to sit on the brothers." I got pissed off all over again just thinking about that mothafucka.

"I don't know where the fuck these new niggas are bred from. These niggas ain't shit like we were. I think that mothafucka done got in over his head with this shit. Don't get me wrong, the nigga quick to pull the trigga, but his ass ain't like us."

King laughed and threw his arm over my shoulder. "Nigga, ain't nobody like us. Those niggas didn't have our guidance. what the fuck is you talking about?" He pushed me away from him. "Real shit though, anybody can be touched, you just got to know where and how. Yeah, that mothafucka lacking all type of sense."

"That's what I was trying to tell that mothafucka." I told him.

"It's always a way to draw them out. It's just what you do once their out and you got their attention." Sam added.

What he said hit me, causing different scenarios to run crazy in my head. "Sam, you think you can find out what each one of those niggas got out there in their names?"

He nodded. "Yeah, give me a few days to look into it."

"I'ight, bet. Bri-Bri you ain't getting no more damn shoes, yo ass got enough already." I told her as she started walking toward Footlocker.

"I'm not, I just want to see what they got." Linnea and Sha'Keema started laughing as Brianna mumbled something.

"Get yo ass knocked out, Brianna, don't play with me." I glared at her because I knew her ass said some smart shit. She was Peaches daughter, so she couldn't help her damn self.

She let out a sigh and came over to me. "I'm sorry, daddy." She hugged me. "Now, let's go find you some shoes." Brianna started, pulling me to the store.

"Bitch!" King stupid ass coughed out loudly from behind us.

"Nigga, fuck you." I stuck my middle finger up at him and went into the store. Once we were inside, Brianna let my hand go and went to her cousins.

King, Sam and I sat on the bench for damn near thirty minutes while the girls walked through the store.

"I know damn well they done saw every gotdamn shoe in this bitch. What the fuck is they looking for?" I was ready to fuckin' go. That was why I didn't go to the fuckin' stores, females took way too much time shopping. I looked over to the girls once again. Only to see the same little dude and his friends, looking at Tink and Keema. The little niggas couldn't have been no more than fourteen, fifteen or sixteen.

"Aye, what the fuck is you looking at? They don't look like no mothafuckin' shoes to me. Watch yo fuckin' eyes before they go missing. Yo, King, Sam, that nigga and his boys keep

looking at y'all daughters, like they want some."
I pointed to the nigga and his friends.

"Oh, my God." The girls groaned, covering
up their faces.

"Who the fuck looking at my daughter?"
King and Sam got up and the little niggas got
ghost quick as fuck.

I fell out, cracking the fuck up. "Yo."

"Uncle Boon, why would you do that? They
weren't even looking at us. Y'all so
embarrassing, I swear." Keema's eyes rolled
hard into her head.

"Keema, get yo damn head knocked off.
Don't fuckin' play with me, yo." King snapped
on Keema.

"Daddy, don't say nothing to me, because I
didn't do anything. I was just looking at the
shoes. Y'all can't be going off on us because of
what somebody else's eyes are doing. We're
minding our own business." Tink quickly
chimed in as Sam's eyes shot to her.

I had to admit she had a point. "She got a
point, Tink you smart. You tryna be in the law
field like yo pops."

"No!" Her lips twisted up at that. "I'mma be
an Instagram model." She said proudly.

"Make me break yo gotdamn neck, Linnea—"

"Daddy, I was just playing, dang, so calm down." She looked at Keema and Brianna and the trio broke out laughing as they went back to looking at shoes.

"I'mma murder that gotdamn girl, man." Sam hand ran over his mouth as he sat down.

"Janae!" Brianna yelled before running over to Blake's girl.

"Hey, Bria." She said hugging her. "Hey, Mr. Carter." She waved and I nodded at her.

"Bri-Bri, who is this?" Keema asked, looking Janae up.

"Oh, this Blake's little girlfriend. She's cool, though." Brianna told them.

Janae laughed at her before looking at Keema and Linnea. "Hey."

Keema waved at her. Tink looked her up then pursed her lips. "Hm. I think, I like these over here." Tink grabbed Keema's wrist and pulled her to a pair of shoes.

"She doesn't like new people, so don't worry about her." Brianna told Janae. "Who you up here with?"

"Yo ass nosey as shit, Brianna." That girl was too damn grown. "Man, leave that damn girl alone. What shoes you want so we can go?" I stood up off the bench and stretched.

"Blaze?" The bright skinned chick that called my name, I was all too familiar with. She smiled wide at me as if trying to see if I remembered her or not.

"What's up, Tameka."

She came up and hugged me. She fuck'd me up when she did that. I wasn't the hugging type, which she knew, and her ass was holding my ass tight. Tameka was suddenly pushed back, and a second later Brianna had her arms and legs wrapped around me. She glared at Tameka before her mug turned on me.

My hand raised. "I ain't did shit, so don't look at me like that." I told Brianna.

"She's so cute and protective." Tameka touched Brianna's arm.

Brianna jerked her arm back so fast like she had gotten burnt. "Don't touch me, I don't know you."

"Oops, I'm sorry." Tameka apologized but Brianna ignored her as she laid her head on my shoulder.

"Ma, you know Mr. Carter?"

"Ma?" I looked at Janae.

"Yeah, that's my mom, Tameka—well you knew that already. How do you two know each other?" Janae questioned.

I nodded to her momma. "She used to work at one of my shops back in the day—"

"More like ran the whole thing." Tameka chuckled. Licking her lips, she looked back to me before her eyes fell on Brianna. She cleared her throat. "How do you know Blaze, Nae?"

Janae looked like she was in an awkward situation. "Um, he's Blake's father."

Tameka's mouth dropped open. "Oh wow. When I saw him, I knew he looked so familiar I just couldn't place the face until now. Damn ain't this a small world."

Brianna got out my arms. "Daddy, I see some shoes I wanna get momma. Let's go get them. Bye, Janae, I'll see you later." She didn't wait for no reply as she pulled me off. "I don't like that woman. She lucky my momma wasn't here. I can't wait to tell her." Brianna went on. "Why would you let her hug you? I can't believe you." She sounded just like Peaches ass.

"I didn't let her hug me—"

"You didn't stop her either or push her off you. I so can't believe you right now." She continued to fuss. She suddenly stopped and whirled around on me. She waved her finger, beckoning me to her. I kneeled so that she was taller than me. "No girl is to hug you but me and momma. Do you understand me, Daddy? Don't let this happen again." She fussed at me.

My lips pursed together so that I wouldn't laugh in her face. Baby girl was so pissed and serious as fuck that I couldn't crush her little moment. Clearing my throat, I nodded. "It'll never happen again, swear."

"Okay, come on."

After buying Brianna and BJ two pairs of matching shoes, and Peaches a pair of new shoes, that Bria picked out, we left the store. With five pair of new shoes and a shit load of new clothes as well as Mall food, my baby girl was beat and ready to go home.

Chapter 25

Blaze

"What you find out?" I asked Mac as I flopped down on the couch.

Mac tossed me the unlocked iPhone. "What Rome said was right. They don't make a move unless Saul tell them too. He sent Slick after Kordell and he didn't know shit about you from what we could tell. He just knows Kordell killed his brother for going behind his back." He explained.

I opened the text messages. "All that shit in his text messages?"

"They were using some app to message each other from, and that bitch was locked, you needed a password to get in it. Bellow figured that shit out somehow. Oh, and Tony said he'll meet up with him Friday at the courts."

"I'ight, bet. Did he say anything about Brittany?" I asked getting up off the couch.

"Yeah, he said they good, he got somebody sitting on them. They've been at the house all day." I nodded as the buzzer rang. Mac looked at the door confused. "You expecting somebody."

"Yeah." I went and unlocked the door.

"Who?" Mac asked. I didn't say anything, I just waited at the door. A few seconds later, Joshua came up to the third floor, I whistled and waved him down. He jogged over to the apartment.

"What's up." He asked and I shook up with him.

"I was about to bounce, but do you need me to stay?" Mac eyes shifted between me and Joshua.

"We're good, gon' head. I'll hit you if something come up." I nodded to the open door for him to leave.

"I'ight." He shook up with me then left out.

Closing the door, I look back to see Joshua still standing up. "You can sit down." I walked into the kitchen and grabbed two glasses and the bottle of Henny, then went in the living room and sat down. "I don't know if you drink, or what you drink, but this the only thing I fuck with." I poured myself a glass then slid the bottle to him.

"I was surprise when you called, you've made it clear you ain't wanna have shit to do with me. So, don't get offended if I'm not too quick to reach for a drink." He stated straight up.

I nodded at that and took a drink from my glass. "Shid, I'm surprising myself, that's what the drink is for, it's more so for me than you." I told him before taking another drink. "I'mma be straight up with you. I don't know where I wanna go with you on this brother tip because I don't know. I'm not the welcoming type of nigga, especially to mothafuckas I don't know. Brother or not that ain't shit but a title to me. I done had mothafuckas I looked at as family turn on my ass. So, understand why I ain't so welcoming, I got too much to lose to let just anybody come around. Now, yo ass done popped up and I don't know what yo motives are. And understand, regardless of what comes out yo mouth, to me those are just words." I finished off my drink and went to grab the bottle again, but Joshua picked it up.

502

He filled up his cup, then mine. "I hear what you saying, but how can we get around that so you can get to know me and see that I don't have no motives? Look, Blaze, I don't want shit from you, Joseph, Brittany, but a chance to get to know y'all. I wouldn't even know what my motive would be toward you for real. Now that my moms' dead, I don't have no family. Shid, it ain't my fault or yours that we didn't know shit about each other…" His words faded as he took a drink from his cup.

That's something I didn't understand. "Why yo momma wait so long to tell you about Joseph?"

He stopped mid drink and furrowed his brows. "You want me to go dig her up and ask her that?"

I couldn't help but laugh at his response. "Nigga, fuck you. All yo ass had to say was that you didn't know." He also had a point that it wasn't our fault we didn't know each other either. "What yo momma tell you about Joseph?"

"No, but she basically told me, he was a mistake and that she was messing with him while he was with somebody, I'm guessing your mom. Joseph didn't want to have shit to do with her and when she found out she was pregnant, shid she took off, after he told her to get an abortion." He told me.

I filled up our glasses once more. "Shid, that was the best thing she did then." I told him, laughing. Grabbing a sack of weed from out the drawer, I twisted up a blunt. "Yo pops wasn't shit to grow up with. The nigga was a crackhead for most of my life, until several years back. So, you ain't miss shit with that nigga, yo moms would've been a single parent anyways. Mine was, to two of his kids." I lit the blunt and took a deep pull. "You smoke?"

"What made you decide to call me over to talk?" He reached for the blunt. I took another hit and handed it to him.

I held the smoke in my mouth for a second as I thought on his question. "Something my little nigga Mac said earlier had me thinking about some shit."

My instincts on a mothafucka was good as hell. That was why I survived for so damn long, trusting my fuckin' instincts. On top of that, I knew my family was some shooters. Peaches didn't have a problem dropping a body nor did Blake if it came to it. Same with my twins, they knew how to handle a gun and protect themselves, on top of that, Marcus was teaching them both how to box.

Joshua started choking and I took the blunt from him. "If yo ass don't know how to smoke, you shouldn't be smoking."

"Nigga, fuck you." He said between coughs. "So, you opened to getting to know me?"

I motioned around the apartment. "Yo ass here ain't you?" I looked at the blunt. "I know yo ass ain't high yet?" Dumping the ashes off the blunt, I put it back between my lips and inhaled. I then pointed the swisher at him. "But know this, if you try to fuck me, I'm going to kill you with no problem or hesitation. Understand me?" I took another hit of the blunt then passed it back to him.

He took the blunt and nodded. "I got you. Now in twenty years when I prove yo ass wrong, I want an apology."

I looked at that nigga like he was crazy. "Yo, fuck you, I ain't apologizing for being honest. Yeah, yo ass got to be high."

He looked at the blunt with furrowed brows. "I don't think I'm high, for real, though."

My head shook and I started laughing. That nigga was high, I knew that shit from the way his ass kept looking at that damn blunt.

For the next several hours we sat in the living room rotating blunts. We were so fuckin' high that we had two blunts rotating between the two of us. I'll hit that bitch a few times and hand him the blunt and he'll pass me the one he had. The Henny only added to that shit.

We were fuck'd up and talking about everything.

"Yo, so yo ass was fuckin' the momma and the daughter?" Joshua fell back on the couch as I nodded. "Damn that's fuck'd up."

"No, the fuck it wasn't. I was the shit period, I had both those hoes…" I was telling him as my phone started ringing. Peaches name popped up on the screen. "What's up, baby?" I was high as fuck.

"B, why aren't you here? You forgot about the dinner, huh?" Peaches voice came through the line.

"What?" It was like I heard her, but I didn't.

"Oh, my fuckin'—" The line got quiet. "Babe, the damn dinner with Janae and her momma." She snapped at me.

I passed the blunt to Joshua and took the one he held out for me. "Shid, I ain't got to be there. Y'all can handle that shit—"

"Yes, you have to be here. What the fuck? We're doing this for Blake—"

"Man, you doing that shit for you. Yo ass wanna meet that damn girl momma. Don't nobody wanna have fuckin' dinner with that damn girl or her momma. Shid, that's Blake's girl let his ass eat with them." I was fuck'd up.

"Blaze, you got fifteen minutes to get here. I'm not fuckin' playing with you." Peaches hung up on my ass.

It wasn't until after the call had ended that I realized I should've told Peaches who Janae's momma was. I tried to call her ass back five times, but she didn't answer. "Fuck!"

"What's up?" Joshua asked, passing me the blunt again.

My hand rubbed over my head. "The bitch I used to fuck back in the day, her daughter fuckin' with my son. Back then, she ain't like my wife and now her ass on the way to my crib. My wife don't know it's the bitch I used to fuck and her dumb ass ain't answering the fuckin' phone." I got up off the couch, grabbing my shit.

"Nigga, what the fuck you just say?" Joshua looked confused as fuck.

I was so fuck'd up I didn't remember what the fuck I said. "Man, just bring yo ass on." I grabbed the half bottle of Henny and made my way out the door.

***

"You used to fuck yo son's, daughter, momma? That don't sound right." Joshua was fuckin' wasted. The nigga just wasn't making no sense.

"Nigga, my son's girlfriend, momma. What the fuck? Yo ass don't drink or smoke no fuckin' more." I parked in front of the house and hopped out the truck. Joshua did the same. As I made it to the front door, I could hear Brianna yelling that I was there. "Oh, fuck, hold up." I left Joshua at the door and ran back to the truck to get my gun. I had just hit the lock on the truck when I heard the door open.

"Yo, what the fuck?" Joshua yelled.

"Oh, my God, I am so sorry, I thought you were Blaze." Peaches was saying as I made it to the porch.

"What happened?" I looked between the pair to see; Peaches looking shocked as hell and Joshua rubbing his jaw. I fell out laughing. "Yo ass was just gon' smack me without knowing why I was late or shit. That's real fuck'd up, Peaches." I pushed past them and walked into the house.

"I'm going to take a wild guess and say you're Joshua. I don't want to seem rude or anything but, Blaze what is he doing here?" Peaches asked me as I flopped down on the couch.

508

I shrugged. "Shid, if we're inviting mothafuckas over and into the fam, I might as well bring my brother, right? The kids can meet the uncle they never knew they had." Peaches stood in front of me glaring hard. Grabbing her waist, I pulled her closer to me. "Baby, don't trip, I done already ran shit down to him. He knows I'll put a bullet between his eyes if he fucks up." I kissed her clothes covered stomach. "Ain't no baby in there yet? I know I've been—"

"And you're completely drunk off your ass." Peaches slapped me on the side of my head. "I can't believe you, Blaze. You knew this dinner was important for us. I don't want the girl momma to think you're some type of drunk."

I sat up quickly remembering what I needed to tell her. "Oh, shit, Janae's momma is Tameka."

Peaches looked confused. "Am I supposed to know who that is? You're fuckin' drunk, I can't believe this shit." She looked back at Joshua. "You are too. So, what? Y'all decided to bond over fuckin' weed and Hennessy?"

"He called me." Joshua pointed to me. My brow cocked at him asking what the fuck? "I ain't no shit about the dinner. Yo, you slapped the fuck out of me. My shit stinging." He told her while rubbing his jaw.

"She's heavy handed as a bitch, yo. Look, that ain't the point. Peaches, you remember Tameka from the shop? The chick I used to fuck—"

Her hand raised. "Not the girl from the repair shop."

"Yeah, her ass. That's Janae's momma."

"How the fuck you know this?" She asked and I explained how we ran into her at the mall. After I told her everything, Peaches walked out the living room.

"She looks pissed." Joshua announced the obvious.

"Because she is. So, don't say shit to her." I told him. I didn't know what the fuck Peaches ass was about to do, but I knew not to follow her.

"Daddy!" Brianna halted in her tracks. She looked at Joshua confused. "Who are you?" She questioned before looking over at me. She smiled then came and jumped in my lap. "I thought you weren't coming home today, but in a few days. Don't worry about answering that, I'm glad you here." She hugged me. "Who is that man? He kinda look like you." She whispered in my ear.

I started laughing at her ass. "Yo ass to damn grown. Go get yo brother." I tapped her leg and she hopped up and ran out the living room. "Why you still standing there? Sit down."

Joshua's hand ran down his face and he looked around at the couches. "Man, I'm fuck'd up. I don't feel right being here like this." He brushed himself off and sat down. Fuck'd up thing about that, he looked serious as fuck.

"You good, as long as you don't have no crazy split personality thing going on, you good. Shid, just relax and be yoself, i'ight?"

He dusted himself off once more and nodded. "I'ight, I'm good."

BJ walked in the living room with Brianna on his back. "I'ight, now get down." He shook her off him. "What's up, dad." He came over and shook up with me. "Thanks for the new kicks." He sat down beside me. "How's work?"

I didn't know if it was because I was drunk and high that his statement seemed funny to me or what. My arm went over his shoulder and I pulled him into my side. I kissed the top of his head. "Work is work, stressful as hell. How you been in school?" I asked him and he shrugged. "BJ." I glared at him.

He shrugged again. "School is school, stressful as heck."

Joshua broke out laughing. "My bad, ignore me." He told us as he chuckled to himself.

BJ looked between the two of us. "Who is that?"

"That's Joseph's other son, Joshua." I told them and they looked him up.

"When he get another son?" Brianna asked.

"A long time ago, Bria." I answered her question. "Joshua, these my twins, Lil Blaze and Brianna."

"So, you my dad's brother." BJ stated with a nod of his head. "Cool. Who the oldest?" He questioned.

Joshua raised his hand. "I am."

BJ's head continued to nod before he got up off the couch. "Cool, so I'm yo nephew." His hand went out.

Joshua took his palm and shook it. "Yeah, I guess you are. I ain't never had a nephew before so be easy with me. I'm new to being an uncle."

BJ shrugged. "You'll get used to it. You like shooting?"

Joshua looked at me with a cocked brow. "Shooting?"

BJ stepped in his line of sight so that he was looking at him again. My lips pursed together so that I wouldn't laugh. "Yeah, shooting, like guns? Pow, pow, pow." While making the sounds, his hand raised, and it jerked as if he was actually shooting a gun.

"Um… yeah, I'm a pretty good shot." Joshua seemed to be uncomfortable as fuck.

"Do you have a gun on you—"

"BJ, leave that nigga alone, man." That little dude was crazy. He was his father's son, though. Just like me and Blake, BJ had a thing for guns, and he loved shooting.

"I'm not doing nothing but making conversation with him. Maybe, I'll take you shooting one day." BJ came back over and sat beside me.

Joshua broke out laughing. "I'mma hold you to that too, BJ. They like some little grown ass midgets."

"So, Joshua, do you have a girlfriend or kids, are you married?" Brianna questioned.

Joshua cleared his throat and laughed. The nigga rubbed his head then his mouth. "No, I'm not married, I don't have a girlfriend or kids either."

Brianna nodded at his answer. "Your eyes are really red. Are you sleepy?"

"Peaches! Come get yo damn kids, man. Y'all go find yo momma." I waved them off.

Joshua pointed to the kids as they ran out. "How old are they?" His head was shaking as he laughed.

"Seven, believe it or not. They'll be eight in a few months. Oh, and BJ serious as fuck about going shooting. He loves guns and shit. Little dude a great shot too, he loves showing that shit off." I couldn't help the proud smile that came to my mouth.

"Shid, I can tell from how he talks. That little girl grown as fuck." He sat all the way back on the couch, getting comfortable.

"Bria think she is. I hope she didn't say anything out of line, did she? Because her daddy isn't going to say anything to her if she did." Peaches was saying, coming into the living room. She had changed her whole outfit. Instead of the black and pink flower dress she had on before, she now wore some black leggings and a red crop top sweater with a pair of red Nikes'.

"No, she wasn't out of line. She was funny as hell, like I told Blaze they like some little ass adults." Joshua told her.

I watched as he talked to Peaches, his eyes didn't wonder all over her, even though she was showing a little skin. His sights stayed on her face the entire time. I liked that.

514

"Well, I'm glad he reached out to you like this. That's something he never does, so it's says and shows a lot even if you think it don't. Trust me, his process may be slow but it's always worth the ending result." Peaches was all smiles as she talked to him.

"I hope so. He was talking to me and I can see why he got his defenses up. I get it now. Shid, as long as I'm getting to know him and vice versa, then the long process don't matter to me." He explained to her.

Again, Peaches smiled at him. "I hope you mean that. I like you, Joshua. Oh, and I'm so sorry for slapping you. I was not expecting you. I thought he was going to walk through that door." She shot a glare at me.

Joshua rubbed his cheek as if he was feeling that slap again. "We're good. I should've ducked or some shit. That hit woke my ass up, though."

I broke out laughing. "She slapped fire from yo ass."

Peaches came over and sat on my lap. She placed her arm around my shoulder and slapped me on the back of the head. "That wasn't funny at all. I feel bad. You pissed me off because you weren't here, although I know it was for a good reason now." She tilted my head back and kissed me. "I'm glad you reached out to him. And you did it without me telling you too. I'm proud of you."

"Hm…" My arms went around her waist. "You proud? What my award gonna be?" My eyes roamed over her as I squeezed her thighs.

She muffed my head back and started laughing. "Leave me alone, Blaze, I'm still mad at you for getting high and drunk—" She looked at Joshua with a raised hand. "Although it was for a good reason, I'm mad at you."

"I ain't tryna hear all that shit. I need to come down some, you gon' help me out?" My grip on her thigh tightened as my hips pushed into her ass.

She chuckled. "No." Her lips pursed together, and she rolled her eyes at me.

I muffled her head to the side. "Fuck you. Get yo ass off me." I tried to push her off me, but her arm tightened around my neck.

"No! Stop, B, damn. Yo ugly ass play to damn much. I can sit here." She was really pissed off too.

"How the fuck you mad because I don't want yo ass on my lap? Get the fuck up!"

She started laughing. "No! And stop pushing me, for real." She leaned back into me, kissing

516

the side of my head. "I love you." She kissed alongside my face.

I chuckled and shook my head at her ass. She just deemed my lap as her chair. My arms went back around her waist and I heard Joshua laugh. "Fuck you, Joshua, her ass spoiled as fuck. Ol' baldheaded ass." Her lips stopped moving along my face. "Why the hell you change clothes for?" I asked before she could say something smart.

"I wanted to be comfortable." She sat up. "Joshua, you want something to drink?"

"Yeah, thanks, and y'all can call me Josh, Joshua seems so... I don't know—"

"Formal?" Peaches finished for him.

He nodded. "Yeah. So, Josh is cool."

"Okay, Josh, I'll be back with your drink. Blaze you can show him where the bathroom and guest room at."

"Who said he was spending a night here?" I know damn well I didn't give him that invitation.

"I did, now go." She waved me off then left out the living room.

"Fuck you, Peaches." She stuck up her middle finger as she kept walking. Josh's hand covered his mouth. "Fuck you laughing about?" I got up off the couch. "Come on."

"Guess I know who run shit around here." He pointed out.

"Nigga, fuck you. She don't run shit but her fuckin' mouth." Joshua barked out a laugh. "Nigga, fuck you." That was all I could say. We all knew Peaches ran shit around the house.

***

"Janae was telling me that you used to work for my pops back in the day." Blake said, looking at Tameka.

"Yeah she was the receptionist if I remember correctly." Peaches chimed in before Tameka could say anything.

Tameka laughed and nodded. "I was pretty much everything at that shop. I ran the whole place, while your dad was gone. That was my baby, the shop. It was actually your dad that help me decide to go back to school and get my business degree. He really helped me out a lot."

I looked over to Brianna to see her face twisted up, her eyes rolling and her mouth moving as Tameka spoke. It was safe to say she didn't like Tameka at all. Shid, neither did Peaches.

"That's what's up. Did you ever do anything with the degree?" Blake continued to ask her questions.

"Yeah, I opened several clothing stores out here, in Indy and Chicago. They've done pretty good. And you're going for basketball, right?" She asked him.

He nodded. "Yeah, that's the plan." He told her.

"Blaze, it is hard to believe that this is your son." Tameka chuckled, smiling at me.

"Nah, he don't have nothing to do with how I am. This all my momma." Blake told her before looking at Peaches and winking.

"So, Tameka." Bria twisted spaghetti on her fork and ate it before pointing the fork at Tameka. She was definitely Peaches daughter. "Are you married or dating somebody?"

"Brianna, why the hell you in that woman's business?" I asked her.

She rolled her eyes. "I'm just making conversation. She don't have to answer it." She stabbed the baked chicken with her fork.

"It's fine, I have no problem answering her questions. She is so cute." Tameka cooed, smiling at her. Brianna smiled sarcastically and it was gone a second later. "No, I'm not married and yes I'm single."

"Then you should go out with my new Uncle Joshua, he's not married, he's single with no kids." Immediately Josh started choking. "He's handsome like my daddy. You should smile at him." Brianna was fuckin' coldblooded.

Tameka broke out laughing. As she glanced at Joshua. "You're right he's very handsome. Thanks for the advice."

"You're welcome." Brianna said cheerfully.

I looked over at Peaches, her eyes were closed, and her lips were pursed together as her head slowly shook. Clearing her throat, she got herself together.

"I must admit, I would have never guessed that you were her mother. I really like Janae. You've done great with her. I can see how much my son really cares for her. That's why it was important that we all sat down and met." Peaches smiled at Blake and Janae.

"I can see that Janae really likes him too, and I'm kind of on the fence with that, even though it's not my decision on what they do or anything. I'm still cautious and I advise her to be guarded with herself because I'll hate for her to get hurt. Janae loves hard and with her whole heart, that's just her." Tameka glanced at her daughter and

Blake before her sights settled on Peaches. "So, you don't think this is just puppy love between them? That they won't grow out of this faze?"

Peaches sat her fork down and was quiet for a minute just looking at the couple. Finally, she shook her head. "I can't speak for Janae, but I know my son and rather he has admitted it to himself or her, but he loves her to the core of him."

Tameka laughed and Peaches glared at her. "You can't say that for sure."

"Actually, I can. Like I said, I know my son." Peaches looked at me. "Blake looks at Janae the same way Blaze looks at me, and we've been going strong for how many years now? I'm not saying Blake won't do some dumb shit, you can't say the same thing about Janae, but that's what people do. We do dumb shit, learn from it, and grow. Regardless of the stupid shit, that doesn't change the love a person has for you. So, yeah, I can say Blake's heart is in it. Regardless if they're together a year or five years from now, she has his heart plain and simple." Peaches broke that shit down and shut Tameka's ass up.

Biting my bottom lip, I stared at Peaches. No matter how much time has gone by that mothafucka always find ways to amaze me. I loved how she be quick to snap and shut some shit down over her kids.

"I guess you have a point." Tameka stated. "I can see you definitely did wonders for Blaze. I've never saw him becoming a family man."

"That's because he never met the right woman until me." Peaches smile was wide as hell.

"You fuckin' right and I wouldn't trade yo ass for nobody." Grabbing the back of her head, I pulled her face to mine, kissing the fuck out of her ass.

"Your parents are so cute together." Janae told Blake.

"Ain't we though?" I looked at her.

"Blaze, I didn't know you had a brother." Tameka cut in, glancing over at Josh who had been quiet the whole time.

"He didn't know either until a few months back." Josh spoke up before he pointed to his empty plate. "This was good as hell, Peaches. You threw down on this shit for real." He complimented. He had cleaned his damn plate. That's probably why his ass was so gotdamn quiet, he was fuckin' his food up.

Peaches laughed and pointed to the counter. "It some more over there if you want seconds."

"Thanks." Joshua got up quick as hell.

"You don't mind if I do too?" Tameka asked, pointing to her dish. She still had food on her plate, though.

Peaches shrugged. "Gon' head."

I watched as Tameka talked to Josh, she was trying hard to flirt with him, but he didn't seem interested at all. She touched his arm and the nigga smoothly moved it out of her way as he continued to pile food onto his plate.

"Hm…" My brows furrowed as I watched them. Dude showed no interest in her and Tameka wasn't ugly. Maybe she just wasn't his type. I shrugged the thought off as I turned my attention to Peaches. Reaching under the table my hand went to her thigh. "You wanna take me to bed?" My eyes dropped to her breast.

"When everybody leaves." She leaned in and kissed me then brought her mouth to my ear. "I really want to ride that sexy ass face of yours." She sucked my earlobe in her mouth.

"I'ight y'all it's time for bed—"

Peaches hand slapped over my mouth. "Y'all ignore him. He's playing." She laughed. "Yo ass don't have no damn sense, stop!" She kissed me still laughing against my lips. "Finish your food."

Shid, I wasn't even hungry no more, my damn dick was so fuckin' hard.

Chapter 26

Blaze

I knocked on Blake's room door, when I didn't get a reply, I walked in. Janae was in his bed passed out. I heard the shower going and went into his bathroom. "Blake."

His head peeked out the curtain and he looked at me. "What's up?"

"Why the fuck you ain't talked to yo momma yet? What the fuck are you waiting for?" I leaned on the counter, folding my arms over my chest.

"Pops, I'm going to tell her. I just need to figure out how to tell this shit to her. The whole Janae thing, I could talk to her about, this other shit though, man, I don't know how to do that." His head came from out the shower again. "Just give me a few more days and I promise I'll tell her everything."

"I'ight, Blake, if I got to come to yo ass again, I'mma dragging yo ass to her myself. Understand me?" He nodded then his head disappeared back into the shower.

I was pushing his ass to tell Peaches about that bitch Mariah because I didn't trust her ass. Mariah would fuck around and tell that shit to Peaches in a fuck'd up way and my baby ass would be locked the fuck up somewhere because she was going to snap. I think if she heard the shit from Blake, she wouldn't react to damn bad, she'll be pissed off, yeah but she wouldn't try to kill the bitch.

I left out his room and went to BJ's. I knocked on his door, then walked in. Once he had his shirt on, he looked back at me.

"What's up, Pops?" He sat on his bed and started putting on his socks and shoes.

"Shit, came to see if you were getting ready for school." I sat down in the computer chair by his desk.

"Yup, I'm ready to go." He tied up his shoes. "I'm trying out for the football team today, you gon' come?"

"Most definitely, you already know that. I'mma be up there early so we can run drills and shit. So, don't be surprise when I show up early. You nervous about it?"

"Yeah and no. I know I got this though, I just can't wait to get it over with." He shrugged.

"You a little cocky there ain't you?" My hand rubbed over his head.

"Man, come on, you gon' mess up my waves." He went and grabbed his brush. "You know I got to keep these babies nice, fresh and tight." He stood in the mirror, brushing his waves.

I started laughing at his little ass. "Nigga, yo damn waves ain't messed up. Come sit down and let me holla at you real quick." I motioned to the bed for him to sit on it. When he did, I moved the chair closer to him. "I just wanna let you know that I'm proud of you. Even though you act an ass at school, you smart and keep those grades tight. And the fact you out here playing sports, making that decision on yo own, and working hard to do that shit, I'm really proud of yo ass, BJ. Keep that shit up, man."

I wasn't really an affectionate mothafucka. It took me years to learn how to be that, given I didn't really have that growing up. The shit kind of fuck'd me up for years, so it was important for me to tell my kids that every so often. I didn't want them to be shit like I was. They needed to know that I was proud of their asses' period. So, their hard work and accomplishments didn't go unnoticed. The shit really made me proud to be the man that I had become.

BJ got up and hugged me tight. "Thanks, Pops." He let me go smiling hard. That look on his face was everything to me. "I love you, Dad."

I hugged him again, kissing the side of his head. "I love you too, Lil B. Now, let's get into these little girls at school."

BJ wiped himself down. "Man, I can't help it if these chicks on me. I'm cursed." He wiped his mouth as he looked in the mirror again. "I'm just a handsome mothafucka." He started brushing his hair once again.

I fell the fuck out laughing. The talk I was about to have with him, left my mind as I laughed hard. I couldn't help the shit. My son was a damn fool. He had that shit honest as fuck so I couldn't even be mad at him.

A Love Like Ours: *The Carter Family*

BJ had done good as hell at tryouts. His reward was that I'll take him shooting afterwards. He had insisted that Josh came along. That wasn't an issue because Joshua had been hanging with me all day. He went to the car lot and the clubs with me. He even helped me with BJ training. He was really a chilled dude to be honest. Although we had played ball together a couple of times, we never just hung out and talked.

"BJ, you ready to show him something?" I nodded to Josh who looked interested to see how BJ was going to do. BJ was grinning hard as he plugged his ears and aimed his gun at the target. He started shooting, emptying his clip.

"Let me see—" Josh went to bring the target back, but BJ stopped him.

"No, let's see how you do first." He told him while pointing to the second lane. "Gon' head." He said while ejecting the clip from his gun and pushing in another one. "Dad, give him your gun." His hands moved in a hurry up motion.

I gave Josh my gun. "Don't be mad if I'm a better shot then you." He picked at BJ.

"I ain't gon' be mad. Everything better be perfect since you wanna talk shit. Gon' head and shoot." BJ came and stood behind Joshua.

Laughing at my son, I put my arm around his shoulders, and we watched Joshua aim and empty the clip at the target. They brought their sheets back at the same time.

"Yeah, you pretty good. You might just be my uncle." BJ nodded his head as if he approved of Josh shooting. He patted him on the shoulder. "You did good, but not better than me." BJ pointed to his sheet.

"Dude, my shit damn near match yours." Josh pointed out. Theirs were close, except for four of Josh's shots were off.

"Damn near ain't a match. It's okay, I'll teach you." He patted his arm.

Joshua broke out laughing. "You a little asshole, you know that, right?"

BJ smiled while bowing. "Thank you."

"Can we join y'all?" Peaches and Brianna came into the room.

"Bri-Bri, come show this dude something, real quick." BJ grabbed Brianna and pulled her over to his lane. "Now watch my sister's shots be better than yours and she's just a girl."

"Hold up, what's that supposed to mean? She's just a girl? Like a girl can't out shoot a man or a little ass boy." Peaches glared at BJ waiting on his explanation. "Talk, Lil Blaze, I wanna hear this." Peaches turned and glared at me.

"Why the fuck you mugging me? I ain't say that stupid shit. Put that up with yo son." I moved away from them and sat on my stool. I didn't have shit to do with that shit BJ was talking.

"BJ?" Peaches turned back to him.

BJ mouth started moving as he motioned around his ears. "I can't hear you, it's too loud in here." He yelled.

Once again, I fell out cracking the fuck up. Wasn't nobody even shooting or shit, the room was quiet as we waited on his reply.

"Man, y'all funny as hell. I ain't laughed this damn hard in years." Joshua sat down on the stool looking at the twins and Peaches as they talked. "Blaze, you think Brittany will be down to meeting me?"

My hand rubbed over my head and I let out a breath. "I'll talk to her. It's gone take some time though, it ain't got shit to do with you, she just going through some personal shit. Once that's handled, she'll meet up with you."

"I'ight, thanks."

I nodded at him and went back to watching Peaches and the kids shoot.

***

"Mac, what the fuck you doing? Stay up on that nigga man, damn." I wanted to knock the shit out of him as Rome shook him.

"He was on me, that nigga just can't hold me, baby." Rome said, grinning from ear to ear.

"Nigga, fuck you." I wanted to knock his ass out too.

"Come on, baby, don't be mad. It's just a game." Rome continued smiling.

"Yo ass laugh at the wrong shit. Take the damn ball out." I threw him the ball. "I don't like that mothafucka." I said to no one in particular. That only made their asses laugh more.

"That nigga look like he ten seconds away from saying, *I'm about to call Blake*." Bellow clowned. "Yo little golden boy ain't here to help yo ass out."

"Fuck you, Bell. Nigga yo ass on my team bitch, we both losing, fuck is you talking about?" That shut his ass up quick as hell. "That's what the fuck I thought. Mac, stay on that mothafucka. Josh, get on King's ass."

We played ball for another hour before I called time out. I tossed the ball in the air and went to the cooler and grabbed a bottle of water. Mac, King, Bellow and Josh followed suit.

"Toss me one." Sam held his hand out and I threw him a bottle of water. Rome and his brother soon came over and grabbed one for themselves.

Josh stood up and took off his shirt, he wiped his face, then poured the cold water over his head.

"That's a sweet ass tattoo." Bellow pointed to the big ass Lion tatt on Josh's back. Of course, his ass would like that shit. He had a whole ass dragon on his fuckin' back.

Joshua's tattoo was of a lion roaring, the damn thing covered his whole back. The shit was nice. "The details in that bitch nice as fuck. But I couldn't get that shit. I don't trust no nigga behind my back for that long. Fuck that." I said and they all looked at me. "I'm dead ass serious."

"Nigga, we know you for real." Bellow said getting up. "Let's get back to this game."

"Hold up." Rome stopped Bellow. "Tony's here." Rome nodded toward the parking lot. "Let's chill here for a second."

"Aye, King." Mac suddenly called him.

"What?" King asked, covering his eyes from the sun.

"Don't get pissed, bet?" He told him.

"Why the fuck you say—" In the middle of King talking, Mac kicked the ball from under him, making King fall on his ass.

"Yo! What the fuck, Mac?" I asked, cracking the hell up.

"I'm about to kill yo stupid ass." King jumped up and went after Mac's ass.

"That was foul as fuck." Sam said, laughing with us. "I'll be right back." He got up and jogged off to his truck.

"Rome, what's good. It's been a long ass time." Tony finally reached us and shook up with Rome.

"Yeah, it has been for real." Rome finished off his water then tossed it in the trash.

Tony then glanced at the rest of us. "What's up." He nodded at us. Rome tapped his arm and nodded to the side and the pair walked off, talking.

"That nigga got a lot of balls to come out here by himself. Especially with the shit going on with his brothers." Bellow stated eyeing Tony.

"He don't know some shit is up with Rome, so he don't need a reason to be cautious." I told him while glancing at Rome and Tony. I did notice that every so often Tony would glance around the court as if he was expecting something to happen. But that didn't make sense to me, because if he felt like that, why come by himself?

Josh grabbed another water bottle and stood in front of me, blocking out the sun. "You a big ass mothafucka for real." Joshua was cocky as fuck, that prison weight stuck to his ass.

Josh flexed his muscles. "Shit look good as fuck, though and make that tatt look even better, so fuck you." Twisting the cap on his bottle he tossed it at me. "Watch my back." He threw his shirt at me then ran on the court.

"I'm going to knock his big ass the fuck out." I tossed his shirt on the cooler and glanced over to Rome and Tony. Jerome said something else to Tony causing him to chuckle. Dude glanced around once again until his focus was set on the court.

"B, pay attention." Joshua called out to me. He got the ball and bounced it. I glanced back to Tony and his eyes were locked on Josh. He bounced off his feet and took off toward the basket.

My brows shot up as I watched the tattoo on his back move with every motion of his arms. The nigga dunked hard and that mothafuckin' tattoo looked like it was really roaring.

"My shit does that too. But my dragon breathes out fire, bitch!" Bellow got up off the ground and took off his shirt.

"Nigga, you childish as fuck. Now you tryna flex yo shit too? Man, sit the fuck down." I laughed at his goofy ass.

I glanced back over to Tony only to see that his eyes were back on Joshua, watching as he jogged back over to us. Maybe that nigga really was gay. Tony caught my eyes and looked away.

"Aye, come sit here right quick." I told Josh motioning to the spot beside me. "Bell, give us a sec."

Bellow nodded and got up, taking the ball from Joshua he jogged to the court. Josh sat down beside me. "What's up?"

I nodded at Tony. "You know him?"

His head shook. "I've never seen him before. Why? What's up with him?" Josh looked over at Tony and dude eyes went back to Rome.

"I don't know for real; he keeps on staring at yo ass, though like he knows you or want some." I was convinced dude was probably gay at that

536

point from the way he kept staring at Joshua. It was like the nigga was sizing him up, probably hoping to try his ass out.

Josh brows shot up and there was no mistaking his confusion. "Want some? Nigga, what the fuck is you talking about? Say what the fuck you mean, I dead ass don't understand."

My hand wiped my mouth and I laughed. "Nigga, like he wants some of yo ass, Josh." He shrugged at what I said. "I think dude gay and he want some of yo ass."

"Oh, why the fuck you just ain't say that shit. Got me feeling like I'm fuckin' slow or some shit. What the fuck make you think that?" He asked, looking back over at Tony.

"He keeps looking yo ass up like you a meal or some shit." I pointed out. "For a second, I thought his ass was looking around out of paranoia. But now that I think about it, he just didn't want to make shit obvious."

Josh sat there quiet for several long ass minutes. His eyes were focused on the court, but I could tell he wasn't seeing shit. His ass was deep in thought. I knew that for a fact because I zoned out like that when my mind was processing shit.

"Answer me this. Why Blake ain't here balling with us and who are these two new niggas?" He nodded from Jerome and Jonell. "I saw Sam take off the moment dude showed up. So, tell me what the fuck is going on. Either you gon' trust me on some shit or don't. But don't have me in the middle of some bullshit blind."

His anger wasn't misplaced, shid, had the roles been reversed, I would've clocked his ass right off bat. Regardless, I was going to trust my instincts on him. I got up and brushed myself off. Josh's eyes followed me.

"Come walk with me." I held my hand out for him, he grabbed my wrist and I helped him up. I waited until we were in the middle of the field, away from everybody before I ran everything down to him.

Joshua stood there with his arms crossed. He said nothing, his brows only furrowed deeply when I spoke on Brittany and Peaches being in the middle of a shootout.

"That's what you meant by Brittany being held up." He stated as a fact instead of a question. I nodded. He looked back over to Rome and Tony. "I'ight. Come on." His head moved in the direction of the court, but he didn't say shit else.

"Hold up." I grabbed his arm stopping him. "Don't go over there fuckin' everything up—"

He pulled his arm from my grip. "From how I see it, they're part of the reason I can't meet my sister. So, I'm about to go over there and talk to his ass—"

That nigga had lost his fuckin' mind. "What the fuck you gonna say exactly, Josh? *You and yo brothers stopping me from meeting my sister?* Man, you got to fuckin' think and not just jump into the shit."

Joshua laughed. "I'm not about to do shit stupid, man trust me. You said, his ass looked like he was interested in me, so I'm about to talk to his ass." He shrugged as if it was that simple.

I was confused as fuck. "You know I think his ass gay, right? Like, he wanna fuck you."

Josh brows cocked as he stared at me like I was the slow one. "I heard what the fuck you said the first time that's why I'mma go talk to him and find out for sho'."

"So, if the nigga like yo ass then what?"

Josh hit my shoulder and let out a hard laugh. "Blaze, then I'm going to fuck him."

The reply that was going to leave my mouth got stuck as what he said hit me. For the first time in my life, my ass was speechless. My finger rubbed over my brow as my eyes squinted.

"Hm…" My arms crossed over my chest as I took him in. The nigga didn't look gay. Then again what did a gay mothafucka look like. "Hm." I repeated as shit started to make since. "Damn… so you like niggas?" That explained why he wasn't interested in Tameka's ass. Shid, I hit the nail on the head with that bitch, she dead ass wasn't his type.

He shrugged. "I'm bisexual, I fuck with both." He said that shit uncaringly and unashamed to admit it. Like he really didn't give a fuck about nobody knowing. "Is that gon' be a problem for you?"

"Shid, I don't give a fuck what you like or who you fuck, that's you. It explains a lot, though. You shutting down Tameka and yo ass wasn't staring at Peaches like a lot of niggas do."

"Tameka? What the fuck I look like fuckin' with yo ex bitch? I don't like hand-me-downs. As for Peaches, that's yo wife, I would never do no shit like that, period. She's cute as fuck, but checking her ass out, I ain't that damn disrespectful."

I chuckled at that. "Shid, as long as you keep that same mindset about my wife, we're good." My hand went out and he didn't hesitate to grab it. "I meant what I said too, I don't have a problem with it. I wish yo ass would've told me from jump, though. Shid, had I known sooner, I would've put yo ass on the nigga—"

He pushed me away from him. "Yo, fuck you, Blaze, real shit."

Had I known before; I most definitely would've had him bait that nigga. I shrugged. "I mean shid, it would've been for Britt though. It's no difference from what you're about to do now. Oh, so it's cool for you to hoe yoself out, but I can't? Yo, what sense does that make?"

"Do yo ass every hear the shit that comes out yo fuckin' mouth?" He asked seriously. "It's cool, though. Look, I'm not gon' enjoy this at all but play along. Bet?" He stated.

"What—" I ducked back as he suddenly swung on my ass. After that swing, we squared up. We were fuckin' around for a good minute, going blow for blow, until his ass switched it up and rushed my ass. He picked my ass up and slammed me on the grass. "Fuck!" I groaned. "Nigga, I'mma fuck yo ass up." I was getting to fuckin' old to be playing around like that.

"Come on, baby boy, get yo ass up." He held his hand out for me and I slapped it away.

"Fuck you." I pushed myself up and brushed the grass off me. Looking at Josh and seeing the blood run from the corner of his mouth. I started laughing. That mothafucka seemed just as twisted as I was. "You a cool mothafucka." After boxing with his ass, it seemed like some type of barrier was broken. Or maybe I was just growing the fuck up for real. "I fuck'd yo shit up." I pointed to his busted lip.

"It ain't shit, I got yo ass too, though so we even." He licked his lips, then spit. "Plus, I beat yo ass." He pushed me. Laughing, we talked a little more as we made it to the courts.

"Brotherly bonding?" Sam asked us.

I shrugged. "Something like that. I beat his ass, didn't I?"

"No, that shit was a tie, up until he slammed yo ass. I got it recorded if you wanna watch it." King said holding up his phone.

"Nigga, delete that shit. Why yo ass out here recording like a bitch." I glared at his ass.

"Fuck you, bitch." King laughed.

"Yo, fuck what he talkin' about, let me see that shit." Joshua said reaching out for King's phone.

"Man, let's finish this game up. I'm tryna win this money, fuck all that other shit." Mac dribbled the ball. Sam, Bellow, Jerome and Jonell all agreed with him.

"You ball?" Joshua cut through the talk and addressed Tony.

"Hell no, his ass suck if I can remember." Jerome chimed in shaking his head.

"Dude, how long ago was that? Fuck you, Jerome, I ball better than yo brother." Tony shot back.

"Yo, leave me the fuck out of that shit. Ball better than me or not, I can still beat yo ass." Jonell put his arm around Tony's shoulder, rubbing his head.

Tony pushed Jonell off him. "Fuck y'all niggas." He snapped at them before he rubbed his waves. I laughed at that thinking about BJ's ass.

"So, you ball or not?" Joshua asked him again, seeming bored of them playing.

"Yeah, I play." Tony replied.

Joshua nodded. "I'ight, you in. My little brother gon' sit this one out." My eyes snapped to his and that mothafucka glared at me.

"Yo, you can't do that, we got money on this game." Mac jumped, staring at Josh like he had lost his damn mind. I think he had.

"I'll take what money Blaze put up, which I'll give him back and Tony can take what I put up." He decided and everybody stared at his ass before they looked at me. "Tony, you over there, Sam come over here."

"Nigga, why would I do that and y'all losing?" Sam face twisted up into a mug.

"And why the fuck would we take him, and he suck?" Jerome asked him.

"Because you mothafuckas are, now come on. You bitches winning so you shouldn't be worried. Plus, we're taking y'all weakest player, so shut the fuck up, sounding like a bitch and take the damn ball out." Josh threw the ball at Jerome.

"I can wait this game out and play in the next one—" Tony chimed in, no doubt feeling the tension between everybody.

"Nah, you good, you're playing." Josh reassured him.

"Aye, let me holla at you right quick." I motioned for him to follow me over to the cooler. "What the fuck is you doing?"

Joshua grinned. "Trust me." That was all he said before running back on the court.

Everybody looked at me, I shrugged. "Gone play. I know we bet not fuckin' lose." Everybody looked disappointed as fuck but went on about the game anyways.

I sat on top of the cooler and watched the game. I was yelling like a sonofabitch from the sidelines. Jerome's team was up by five points.

For the first half of the game, Sam was sticking Tony, then Joshua switched up, putting Sam on Jonell while he took Tony. Shit got crazy from then. I didn't know what the hell Joshua was mumbling to Tony, but the little nigga just wasn't as focus as he once was.

Joshua was sticking his ass hard while saying some shit to him. I could tell whenever Joshua spoke because Tony mouth would twitch as he tried not to laugh or smile.

Jerome tossed Tony the ball and Joshua slapped it out his hand. "Tony, what the fuck is you doing? Nigga, pay attention. What the fuck?" Rome was pissed off because we had caught up with them once Josh got on Tony.

"I am paying attention, what the fuck is you talking about?" Tony snapped right back.

"I'll get on Josh." King said, pushing Tony out the way.

"Yo old ass think you can stay on me?" Joshua asked, pushing King.

King glared at him. "Bitch, you're older than me. How the fuck yo ass gon' call me old. Yo ass just try to keep up with me." He pushed Josh back. King was heated.

The game was entertaining as fuck once we caught up. Josh had all they're ass pissed off and ready to beat his ass. He kept shaking King's ass and finding his way to stick Tony.

"Hell no, that nigga cheated, fuck that shit." Jerome pointed to Joshua, pissed off.

"How the fuck I cheat? And don't say shit about Tony being on y'all team because that nigga plays better than Sam's ass." Josh pointed out. "Plus, y'all niggas were up. What? Five/six points? Man, kill that noise."

"Nigga, fuck you." Sam snapped at him.

Josh just shrugged at Sam. My ass was cracking up. I didn't give a fuck about shit they were talking about; I was happy we won. My eyes found Tony and he was off to the side, talking on his phone. Josh didn't miss that either and jogged over to him. Once he had, Tony ended the call.

"Man, this game was fuck'd up." Jerome came over and sat down beside me as everybody followed along.

"What Tony say to you?" I asked him instead of replying to what he was talking about.

Jerome groaned and took a drink of his water. "He was waiting on me to reach out to him. He didn't think it would've been this long, though. He said he was going to take care of me. Tony also said that; Saul was asking about me once he heard I was released from prison. Saying he wanted me to work for him. Tony don't want me to do, given the shit he was going to have me doing, which was probably going to be dropping bodies no doubt. Still he gave me his number just in case I wanted to holla at him." He was saying while messing around on his phone. "I texted Mac the number."

"I wanna know what the fuck he saying to that nigga?" King thought out loud as Tony barked out a laugh.

"Aye, B, is yo brother gay?" Mac asked seeming confused.

"Shid, he ain't really got no preference. He like them both." I told him, shrugging.

"That's why we fuckin' lost. He was whispering to that nigga like a bitch." Jerome snapped, making us laugh.

"Whatever the fuck he's saying, he got that mothafucka feeling him." King stated and I nodded.

"That nigga big as fuck, yo. I just can't see a nigga fuckin' him. His ass probably be fuckin' them niggas." Mac said and I turned and looked at him.

"Nigga, what the fuck is you talking about? Yo, why the fuck would you even be thinking about that shit?" I felt my face twist up.

"Real shit, I was thinking the same thing." Bellow broke out laughing.

"Y'all niggas weird as fuck, yo." My head shook at their asses. They continued to talk as I watched Josh and Tony. Josh motioned toward the parking lot and Tony glanced at his phone then nodded. Josh then jogged over to us and grabbed his shirt. "Why dude keep checking his phone?" I asked him.

"His brother blowing his shit up, and his ass keep ignoring the call. What's the closest bar around here?" He questioned, grinning.

We chuckled at that nigga. "I got a pool hall not too far from here. I'll text you the address."

"Bet." He shook up with me, then he took off. Tony led then to his car, they hopped in and pulled off.

"He about to have that little nigga in love and that shit gon' get his ass killed." Jerome shook his head.

"How so?" I got up off the ground and grabbed my shit.

"Saul controls everything that nigga do. Tony ain't made for the lifestyle his brothers live. I told you about that bid he did, he ain't do that shit. It's no doubt he took that shit for his brothers. Saul know Tony ain't made for this shit, that's why he had me look out for him." He explained.

"Dude need to get the fuck away from his brother then. But that's their family business." I shrugged. "Let's go."

Chapter 27

Blaze

"**W**hat the fuck is you doing here?" I asked Kordell as he stood at the door.

"Can we talk?" He questioned, motioning inside the apartment.

"Where my sister at?" I looked around him to see that she wasn't in sight.

He pointed behind him. "Out in the car. She told me I was wasting my time coming here. That you wouldn't talk to me." He explained.

I shrugged. "She wasn't wrong. I don't have shit to say to you."

"Then let me talk and you listen. Bet?" He insisted.

"Go tell Brittany to get her ass in here, then I'll listen to you." I closed the door in his face and went back into the living room and sat down. I was tired as fuck and wanted to pass the hell out, but I still had a lot of shit to do.

I was still waiting to hear back from Joshua. After him and Tony went out for drinks, I didn't hear shit else from him. However, I wasn't worried about him being on any foul shit. After kicking it with his ass for the past few days, I really believed he just wanted a family straight up.

Rubbing my face, I looked over the files Sam had gotten on Saul, Sean, and Tony. The younger two didn't really have shit aside from a nice ass crib, and some cars. Saul ass had everything, from houses, cars, clubs, and stores.

From the information I was given, I knew exactly how I wanted to go at Saul. He was the one I wanted. He was the king whereas the other two were just pawns. I knew once we took him out, Sean might step up and start running shit. If he would inherit all Saul's beef, though? I didn't know, only time would tell that. Tony's ass would probably leave altogether given; he didn't seem as if he wanted to have shit to do with Saul's businesses.

Nothing I thought of was for sure, everything was only wishful thinking at that moment. I wanted the shit to be over with so that Brittany was straight.

The apartment door swung opened and Brittany walked in. She glanced at me then stormed to the kitchen.

"Yo baldheaded ass better speak when you come in this mothafucka. Fuck wrong with you? Mothafucka gon' mug me in my shit." She had lost her gotdamn mind.

She came from the kitchen and stood in the entrance. "First of all, I didn't ask to come to yo shit, I was fuckin' brought here and I didn't want to come in here to see yo stupid ignorant ass either. I was forced to come in, so you can really shut the fuck up talking to me, Boon. I'm not in the fuckin' mood for yo ugly ass attitude." She went clean the fuck off, then walked back into the kitchen.

I hopped off the couch quick as fuck and went into the kitchen where she was. "Who the fuck yo ass think you talking too, Brittany?"

"Mothafucka, I'm talking to yo stupid—" Brittany's eyes went buck wide as my hand grasped her throat tight.

"I don't know what the fuck done got into yo mothafuckin' ass but you better calm the fuck

552

down and remember who the fuck yo ass talking too. You done lost yo fuckin' mind if you think it's cool to fuckin' talk to me like yo ass stupid. Grown or not, I will still beat yo mothafuckin ass, Britt, don't get out yo fuckin' body with me. So, calm yo ass the fuck down, walk yo ass out my shit and reenter this bitch like you got some mothafuckin' sense." As I let her go, I pushed her ass back. "Go!"

Brittany jumped hard while rubbing her throat. Tears filled her eyes and she walked out the kitchen, seconds later I heard the front door open and close. That mothafuckin' girl had lost her damn mind. I grabbed a beer out the fridge and went back into the living room, as I did, Brittany walked back in, closed, and locked the door.

Rage showed in her face as she stared at me. "Hi, Blaze."

I nodded at her and she stomped off into the kitchen like she was a damn kid. "Brittany, come here." I glanced up to see Kordell standing there mugging me. "Sit the fuck down, y'all mothafuckas came over here tripping hard as fuck. Britt, yo ass know better."

Brittany came into the living room with a cup and sat on the couch opposite me. "You started this mess when you put me out your place, knowing that somebody tried to take me and kill Kordell. You didn't even care, you just threw me out." She fussed as tears ran down her face.

"I didn't throw yo ass out, you walked out this bitch. I don't want that nigga around me because he would fuck around and get all our asses killed. I said his ass had to go and you chose to take off with his ass. That was yo fuckin' choice not mine. I'm not about to put my family at risk for no mothafuckin' body."

"Because he's my boyfriend, Blaze. What part of I love him don't you understand, I couldn't just leave him, Boon. If this was you and Peaches, she would've followed you to the end of the earth if that's where you was headed. She wouldn't have left you, no matter what. Yet you just expected me to leave him. What sense does that make?" Her tears flowed faster as her voice changed.

"I didn't expect you to do shit, but what you chose to, sweetheart and that was to follow him—"

"Boon, you're missing the point! You knew the situation and you just didn't care enough to help him for me." She snapped, crying harder.

"How the fuck you expect me to help a mothafucka who wasn't trying to help himself? This nigga would've fuck'd around and got all of us killed. What don't you understand about

554

that shit? Are you not hearing what the fuck I'm saying, Brittany? Regardless of how much you love that nigga, I'm not going to put his mothafuckin' life above my fuckin' family's—"

Brittany jumped off the couch quick. "I'm your fuckin' family too, Boon! We have the same gotdamn blood! Am I not your family? Do you not give a damn what happens to me even if you don't like Kordell?" She was straight bawling hard as hell.

"Yo ass know I do, but yo ass walked out with him. You made the choice to leave. When you made that decision, you should've been secure in the fact that yo nigga would protect you at all cost."

Brittany's hands went up and she flopped down on the couch, her face going in her hands. After a few minutes she wiped her eyes and looked at me, shaking her head.

"That's not the point, Boon. I am secure in Kordell, I know he'll do everything in his power to make sure I'm good, but that doesn't change the fact I wanted my brother with me. You just turned your back on me because he didn't have enough information for you."

Grabbing the half smoked blunt from the ashtray, I lit it. After taking several long deep pulls from the blunt and exhaling, I rubbed my forehead.

"I'm really trying not to walk over there and slap the fuck out yo stupid ass. I done looked after yo ass since you were a fuckin' baby, yo. Yo ass like my fuckin' child, you really think I'll turn my fuckin' back on yo dumb ass? Regardless of who the fuck you're in love with, do you really think I'll do that shit?" I dumped the ashes from the blunt, waiting on her to reply.

"I didn't think you would until you did." She snapped.

That pissed me off. "I never turned my fuckin' back on yo ass!" I jabbed the blunt at her before pointing it to Kordell. "I turned my back on him, never you! I've had eyes on yo stupid ass since you left this bitch! I've been working and making plans to end this bullshit for you, not me. I ain't got a fuckin' thing to do with none of this shit. But since a mothafucka came for yo dumb ass, I'm in the shit now." I motioned to the folders on the table.

"What the fuck you think all this shit is, Brittany? I've put in more work and figured out more shit than that mothafucka brought us, which was shit! I can make a fuckin' call and tell you were each one of those mothafuckas is at, putting my niggas at risk for yo dumb ass. Doing shit that mothafucka wasn't." I had never wanted to knock the shit out of Brittany so bad in my life. I wanted to choke the fuck out of her.

She opened a folder and glanced through it. "Boon, I didn't know, you looked so serious—"

"Because I was fuckin' serious, Brittany. I ain't doing shit for that nigga, I'm doing all this shit for you to make sho' yo ass is safe. Yo ass chose to walk out that fuckin' door." Brittany burst out crying, sobbing hard as hell. My hand rubbed my forehead once again. I looked over at Kordell who was just watching us. "What the fuck did you want?" I wasn't even going to address Brittany crying. I knew her ass was overly emotional because she was pregnant.

Kordell went over and sat by Brittany. His glare was still on me, but I didn't pay it no mind. I didn't give a fuck for his attitude. I saw the nigga wasn't that stupid because he didn't say a fuckin' word while I was snapping at Brittany's crybaby ass.

"Brittany, go in the fuckin' room with all that crying, man. I can't fuckin' think with all that damn noise." I didn't feel like hearing that bullshit. At twenty-nine, I would have thought her ass would've grown out that shit, but she didn't. Then again, I guess I had myself to blame for that shit.

"You don't have to be an asshole." She fussed before storming out the living room. Kordell got up to follow her.

"Let her ass go, she's straight. Yo ass crazy if you think you gon' walk around my crib for real. Now, what it is you wanna holla at me about?" I sat the blunt in the ashtray and started rolling another. I knew I was going to need that bitch if his ass had something to say.

"Yo ass don't have to handle her like that, brother or not that shit ain't cool."

The aggression in Kordell's tone didn't go unnoticed. Grabbing the blunt, I hit it twice, then blew the smoke in his face. "Fuck you. If yo ass don't like it, do something about it. I done already told yo ass, that's me right there, however I handle her ass ain't no concern of yours. Now either tell me what the fuck brought yo ass all the way out here, or bounce." I laid back on the couch and blew the smoke in the air. I could hear Kordell cracking his knuckles and that only made me smile because I knew he was pissed off. I hit the blunt twice, holding the smoke for a second before releasing it.

"What *yo wife* said to me made sense, and I looked into my people. She was right, niggas I thought were close to me was just being paid to watch me and had I not been so into my work, I would've seen that shit sooner." He explained what I already knew.

A Love Like Ours: *The Carter Family*

The fact that he said—*my wife made him realize that*—had me laughing. I thought I told his ass that before Peaches even said shit.

"Answer me this, how the fuck you get into this shit? Because from the way you move, yo ass wasn't born into it or grinded to get the shit. You ain't no complete bitch either, straight up, so how the fuck you get into this shit?"

"You just don't give a fuck how you talk to people?" He asked. "The fact that you're rude and disrespectful as a bitch, don't bother yo ass at all, do it?" His eyes slanted as he mugged me.

Shrugging, I released the smoke from my mouth. "Not at all. You're just a sensitive mothafucka. Now how the fuck you get into this shit? How you get yo clubs, restaurants, and shit? Don't lie either. I know yo ass didn't stand on a corner and hustle for the shit."

His thumb rubbed between his brows and he laugh. "I was born into it. My uncle ran the clubs and restaurants I have now, he taught me a lot before he was killed several years back. The older niggas that's with me now ran with him back then. So, shid, I never expected none of them to turn, because of their loyalty to him. To be honest, yo ass kind of remind me of him."

"Hm…" After inhaling deeply, I blew the smoke into the air. "He ain't teach you much. Just because some niggas was loyal to him don't mean that shit gon' be given to you. Shid, what have you done to show that yo ass deserve any type of loyalty aside from being that nigga's nephew? This shit was given to yo ass, you ain't earn a gotdamn thing. Shid, I'm not surprised niggas done turned on yo ass, real shit. Those mothafuckas worked with yo uncle and 'bout grinded with him for everything yo ass claiming is yours."

"They're doing all yo foot work while you're sitting behind a fuckin' desk. If yo ass want a clean business, let them niggas have that shit, and you start over. If you want the shit yo uncle had, get yo ass out there and grind for that shit. Be yo own front man, not have niggas you barely know doing it for yo dumb ass. You got to show mothafuckas yo ass can get dirty and you ain't shit to be played with." Hitting the blunt again, I sat up and stretched.

Exhaling, I pointed the blunt to him. "If yo uncle was like me, then every mothafuckin' nigga that went against me would be dead." I stabbed the blunt out and poured me a shot of Henny. After tossing it back, I sat the glass back down. I pointed to my blunt. "Don't smoke my shit." I told him before looking toward the back. "Brittany!"

"Aye, yo ass ain't even let me tell you what I found out." Kordell said.

"Shid, it can't be more than me. I don't wanna hear that shit. I already got shit set in motion. You just sit there and think on the free game I gave you." I told him before walking out the living room and going to find Brit. She was in the guest room sitting on the bed looking at her phone. When I pushed the door fully opened, she glanced at me and rolled her eyes. "Roll them again and I'll pop those bitches out."

"You should've told me you had a plan instead of having me think you wasn't going to help him." She moved over on the bed and pulled her knees up, bringing them to her chest.

"I shouldn't have told you shit. Some part of your brain should've told yo ass that. I didn't think yo ass was that damn dumb for real. Besides, I needed your reaction to be real. I didn't know if dude car was bugged or not."

Again, she rolled her eyes. "Only you would think somebody would bug a car—"

"Don't say it like that shit ain't possible. I was right about somebody following y'all ass. But don't worry about that shit and when you leave here don't go talking about it either, nowhere, the car, crib, bathroom nowhere, Brittany. I'mma tell his ass the same thing."

She nodded, still staring at me. "Boon, I really do love him."

I laughed at that. "No shit, I figured that much when you left with his ass."

"I want you to like him. I know he's not like you or your friends. But Boon he didn't have it easy either though. He lost his momma in a house fire when he was fourteen, then the only father he knew was his uncle who he lost a few years later. The man just disappeared. Now he just found out the people he trusted the most had set him up. That's how they knew where we were that night. He's really not handling that well. How would you feel if Sam or Mac, set you up and put the one person you love and swear to protect in danger? That's a serious head fuck, Boon."

She had a point, but shid, they would've been dead simple as that. Head fuck and all, everybody would've been dead family included. Nobody was spared when it came to mine.

"Then that's some shit he needs to handle ASAP before they get his ass."

Her head shook as if she was disappointed in my reply. "That's the same thing he said. I don't want him to, though. What if he dies? Blaze, I'm pregnant." Tears once again filled her eyes. "I don't want to raise my baby without him. I want our baby to know him, Boon."

"Britt, you can't stop that man from doing shit. It's that nigga's right to kill all those mothafuckas and if he dies in the process, that's an honorable death to me because he died trying to protect what's his. That's what the fuck you tell y'all kid. But if you're suggesting that nigga run and hide out. That's a bitch move and there's going to always be a fuckin' target on his head and yours."

Brittany's tears flowed faster, and her head shook once again. "I don't want him to."

As my shoulder shrugged, I knew I was the wrong mothafucka she needed to be talking too. "That's not your choice, sweetheart." I couldn't provide her with the right words of comfort to console her. I knew that's what she was looking for. Brittany's face went into her thighs and she started to sob hard as her body shook. My hand rubbed over my head as I stared at her for a second. Mentally groaning, I put my arm around her shoulder, and she leaned into me, wrapping her arms around my waist as she continued to bawl hard.

Chapter 28

Blaze

It was a little after seven at night when Joshua turned back up and from the sound of shit, him and Tony hit it off quick as hell. He also pointed out how Saul kept blowing the youngin' up. He felt like Rome did, Tony wasn't made for that lifestyle. Regardless of how he talked, he was soft.

"He said his brother be working him like crazy, but…" Joshua's hands rubbed together as he grinned.

"Man, tell me what."

He laughed. "He wanna meet back up at the bar in a couple days—"

My head was nodding as he spoke. "You can have a sleepover while we make that move on his brother…"

Joshua glared at me. "Nigga, how the fuck you gon' volunteer me to have a fuckin' sleepover?"

"You offered to be the whore in this situation. I'm going with yo plan remember." I hit his shoulder as Brittany and Kordell came from the back. Joshua pushed my hand off his shoulder and I laughed, but we didn't say shit else on the matter. "Brittany." I motioned for her to come to me. She kissed Kordell, whispering something to him before coming over to us.

Brittany and Kordell had been in the back when Joshua had showed up. I never told him that she was there. That was the first time the pair was meeting. "Britt, this Joshua, Joseph's son. Josh, Brittany. Y'all can talk and do whatever." I introduced them, then flopped down on the couch and started texting Peaches.

I hadn't seen Peaches ass since the day before and that was just to fuckin' long for me. I needed to have some face time with my wife, and some sex on top of that. Morning shower sex was routine for us since we had the kids. But, since I stayed the night at the apartment, I didn't have my fill of her, and my ass was going through withdrawals.

Me: *I'm dead ass having withdrawals. I ain't have my fill this morning. Send me a pic.*

Wifey: *Lol! I missed you too this morning. I had to get myself off this morning which sucked. I thought about making you a little video to show you what you were missing.*

I groaned as my dick twitched.

Me: *Yo ass should've made me a video if you were gonna be playing with my shit. Gon' send me a pic.*

Peaches thought her ass was being funny. She knew I couldn't beat my dick. I couldn't get off on that shit, I needed her pussy to bust in. My phone pinged a few minutes later. I laughed at the picture she sent. Brianna arms was wrapped around her waist and her little leg was thrown over Peaches'. BJ was on my side of the bed, knocked the fuck out.

Wifey: *If your daughter wasn't wrapped around me then I would. But I really don't want to wake her up.*

Me: *Don't. Then she'll be blowing my ass up.*

Wifey: *She misses you… I miss you. When are you coming home?*

As I was texting Peaches, I kept my eyes on Kordell as he paced around the room. His ass would glance at Brittany and Joshua talking, then to the door. He repeated that action several times. I knew his ass was going to cut out, he was just working up the nerves to do so.

Brittany ass really broke down and that was weighing on that nigga. But shid, he had to do what his ass had to.

Me: *Tomorrow. I miss yo ass too baby, real shit. I'm thinking about doing a quick drive by. You down for climbing out the window?*

Wifey: *CTFU! I will most def be jumping out the fuckin' window if you pull up.*

I laughed to myself as I read over the message. My eyes slid back to Kordell as he walked over to Brittany and whispered something in her ear. When she nodded, he kissed the side of her head and whispered something else before he left out the front door. No doubt he told her ass he loved her before taking off on that damn suicide mission.

Wifey: *Are you really gonna do a drive by? Babe I haven't seen you since yesterday morning. That's too damn long. I want a kiss… you gon' come give me one?*

Me: *Give me fifteen minutes.*

567

After I sent that message, I slid my phone in my pocket. Truth be told, I didn't want to be around when Brittany ass found out Kordell ass took off to go handle his business. I couldn't sit around with her while she cried especially if she was going to breakdown like she had earlier. I didn't want to snap at her ass because she didn't understand why it was important for him to do what he had to.

If the nigga survived that shit, he would have most definitely earned my respect, hell if the nigga died, it would've been the same thing.

After grabbing my keys, I left the apartment without a word.

***

When I got to the house, I texted Peaches letting her know I was outside. She hit right back telling me to go around back. Laughing, I put my phone away and got out the truck and went to the backyard. The security lights flashed on for a second before they were turned off and Peaches came out the sliding door. She only wore a t-shirt and a pair of socks.

She silently closed the sliding door, then ran over to me. Peaches jumped in my arms, giggling like a damn schoolgirl. "We have about an hour before Brianna start moving around and realize I'm gone." As she spoke her hands went between us and she undid my jeans, pushing them down my hips.

Peaches wasn't wasting any time. We knew how Brianna's ass was. That was her routine, every other night when me and Peaches would sneak off to the bathroom for a quickie, she would wake up knocking on the damn door. That little girl was a gotdamn cock blocker for real.

"We need to hurry up then and you can't be loud, don't want to wake the neighbors." With Peaches still in my arms, I sat down on the lounge chair. I kicked off my shoes then my pants and boxers.

"I make no promises." She whispered against my lips before taking my shirt off.

Grabbing the hem of her shirt, I pulled it over her head. I wasn't surprised that she was naked underneath. My hand slid to her pussy feeling how wet she already was. Before I could push two fingers into her soaking box, Peaches pushed my hands out of the way. Placing her feet at my side, she lifted herself up and handled my dick. Bringing it to her pussy, she slid down until our pelvis were kissing.

"Mmm, shit." She moaned, bouncing on my dick.

Lifting myself up, I captured her bouncing breast, squeezing them together. My tongue flicked over the right nipple then the left one before I sucked the small swollen nub into my mouth.

Peaches hands went to my chest, pushing me back down. She started riding my dick at a steady pace. Grabbing her hips, my legs bent at the knees and I thrust upward.

"Ah!" Peaches gasped out loud and her nails soon dug into my shoulders as her movement became faster to match mine. "Ooh, shit. Blaze, baby,"

I gripped her ass tight, bouncing her faster as my tongue played with her nipples.

"Aah, fuck, baby, oh, my fuckin'!" She moaned as her head fell on top of mine. "Ooh, fuck!" She cried out as I held her to my pelvis and thrust deep and hard into her pussy, once then twice.

Filling my nut build up, I turned us around on the lounge chair. I pushed Peaches legs up to her shoulder, leaning into her body, I pounded into her pussy frantically.

Peaches hands went to my thighs. "Oh, my fuck, Blaze! Oh my, ooooh!" Her pussy muscles tightened around my dick as her body tightened and shook.

"Gotdamn, Peaches, fuck!" My hips pushed into hers as I released my nut inside her love box. "Fuck!" I grunted as my hips jerked into her. "Shit!" Reclining the lounge chair fully back, I widened her legs and laid on top of her. I wasn't pulling out until I was certain one of my little niggas reached her eggs.

Peaches arms went around my neck and she brought her mouth to mine, kissing me. Her lips parted and my tongue slid into her mouth. She captured my tongue between her teeth and sucked on it.

Groaning, I pushed into her and she moaned rolling her hips as her pussy muscles began milking my dick. Peaches ass knew exactly how to work her damn pussy muscles. It only took a few minutes before my dick was twitching and growing hard.

Once again, I started thrusting inside her and didn't stop until we've both reached another mind-blowing orgasm.

***

"Oh, my God. That was…" Peaches panted as she laid between my legs, placing kisses on my chest.

"I got that out of this world dick, huh?" I hit her ass, then squeezed it.

Peaches started laughing. "Something like that." She breathed out, sounding breathless. She kissed my chest once again then looked up at the sky. The nights air blowing across our overheated body's felt good as hell. "It feels so good out here." Peaches grabbed my arm and pulled it into her body. I put the other one around her, holding her tight. "I wish we had some candles lit to make it more romantic. Making love under the stars with candles." She sighed dreamily while looking up into the sky.

I looked up into the sky seeing what she saw exactly. Licking my lips, my head shook. "Sweetheart, we ain't got no damn stars out here, those plane lights."

Peaches was quiet for a few seconds before she broke out laughing. "You are such a damn asshole. Yo ass forever ruining the moment. If I say those are damn stars let them be shit."

Kissing the side of her head, I laughed. "You got it baby, those some dope ass stars too. The red one and the white blinking one."

Peaches looked up at me and started laughing again. "You get on my damn nerves for real." She kissed my chest, then leaned up and pressed her lips to mine. "How's everything going with Joshua?" She asked, kissing my chin, then my jaw.

Grabbing the long beach decorative towel from the side table, I covered Peaches' naked body with it. "Shits cool…" My words were cut short as she licked my bottom lip, then sucked it into her mouth.

"So, things are going good between y'all?" She asked between pecks.

"Mmhm…" I pulled my head to stop her from kissing me. "How the fuck am I supposed to answer your questions when you're doing all this?" I popped her on the ass, and she laughed.

"I'm sorry. Tell me what's up with your brother?" She settled back against my chest, placing kisses on it.

I just chuckled at her ass and answered her question. "Dude is cool, though, I might've misjudged his ass off bat because I didn't want to fuck with him at all. I gave him a job just to really keep an eye on his ass. Honestly though, Peach, I don't think he have any other motives aside from him wanting to know me and Brittany. We're the only family he got basically aside from Joseph. So, I'mma fuck with him for the time being."

I felt Peaches smile against my chest before I heard it in her voice. "I was glad to see the two of you together. I was hoping you would reach out to him, after talking to Joseph about Joshua, I felt bad for him because he doesn't have anyone. I wanted y'all to link up, but I didn't want to push you to do it, because you would've only been reaching out to him for me and not yourself."

My eyes closed and I laughed at that because she was right. She was the reason I met with his ass the first time. "Don't act like you know me, Mrs. Carter." I felt Peaches gaze on me, and I peeked out of one eye to see her staring at me. "What?"

Her hand came up and she stroked my cheek with her thumb. "I really love you, Blaze." She sat up and kissed me slowly.

Chuckling, my hand tangled into her hair and I returned her kiss, then pulled her head back. "I really love you too, Peaches."

"No, I'm being serious, B. Like I've seen your growth throughout the years and yet, you still find ways to amaze me. And it's not just about you reaching out to your brother, but as a father and husband, you just… continue to make me fall even more in love with you as time passes." A small laugh left her mouth and she sat up fully, pulling the towel over her naked body.

"I heard you talking to BJ the other morning. I've never heard you speak to him in that tone or like that before in general. Don't get me wrong, I know you love all our kids equally, but… I thought you were always tougher on our boys because they're boys, who would one day become men, you know? Anyway, hearing your proud tone and the joy in his voice that your words brought him, really showed me that I couldn't have found a better partner to marry and have kids with. Blaze, a lot of men that has grown up like you had, doesn't really see a bigger future for their kids, they always want them to follow in their footsteps, not elevate them to pursue bigger dreams in life."

"Like my dad for instances. He brought King into his lifestyle and raised him to perfect that craft instead of something legit, even though he made that dumbass go to college. Still, these past million years with you, although rocky at the beginning, just watching you become this man that I've always known you could be and more has been the best parts of my life. You are an amazing father and husband that any wife or child could ask for. So, when I say, I'm really and truly in love with you, I wholeheartedly mean it to the depths of my core, for all the reason's I just said."

Peaches knew how to tug at a niggas heart, I felt everything she said and knew they were true. However, I couldn't form the right words that was needed to really reply to what she said. Not that I was incapable of doing so… then again, maybe I was because my ass was stuck on what to say back to her. I didn't know how to be that expressive with words like she was. Then again, she knew that shit because she married my ass. That woman knew every fuckin' thing about me, shid, she knew me better than I knew my gotdamn self at times.

"Peach, I love the fuck out yo ass man. I'm only the man I am today because I had a strong ass woman backing me through all my bullshit. I really want to impress her ass and became the man she needed me to be. So, you should thank yoself Mrs. Carter, this all you baby."

Peaches smile was wide as she kissed me. "I guess I did have a hand in all of this, huh?" She mumbled against my mouth.

My hand gripped her ass cheeks. "Mmhm."

She smiled against my lips. "I love you, Blaze DeShawn Carter."

I pulled her into my lap, so that she was straddling my hips. "I love you too... now come make love to me under these moving stars."

Peaches broke out laughing as she looked up at the planes moving overhead. "I can do that..." Her lips fell on mine as I slid her down on my dick.

Chapter 29

Blake

I think my momma and your daddy had something going on back in the day." Janae said while brushing her hair into a ponytail.

I strolled through Janae's newsfeed on Facebook, which she had logged into on my phone. I wasn't looking for shit, I was just seeing what the hell was going on while waiting for her to get ready.

"Babe, you hear me?" She came over to see what I was doing. "Wait…" She stopped at a picture of Shantell and loved the image. "You think they did?"

I shrugged. "Shid, he probably did fuck her before he got with my momma. It wasn't shit serious."

She popped her lips and hit me on the back of my head. "Don't say it like that."

I laughed at the attitude in her face. "How the fuck you gon' get mad because yo moms was just a fuck to my pops? Shid, it is what it is, she ain't fuck'd up about it. Plus, she learned something from him, she went and started a whole business. You should be happy he gave her a little game with the dick." She hit me again, and I pushed her on the bed.

"You a legit asshole in real life. You get on my nerves." She pushed at my shoulders as her eyes rolled.

"I'm just being honest." I told her as my phone went off with a text. Janae grabbed my phone before I could and glared at me. Laughing, I shrugged. "It ain't nobody but probably Ace. Why yo stupid ass jumping up like that."

"What the fuck?" A glare formed on her face as she looked at the screen. "So, Ace got a pussy now?" She snapped, hitting me in the chest with the phone.

"What the fuck is you talking about?" I looked at the phone and it was a coochie on the screen. "I don't know who the fuck that is or the number. It's a pretty pussy though—"

Janae punched the shit out of me in the chest. "That bullshit ain't fuckin' funny, Blake!"

"Man, you better lower yo fuckin' voice. I said I don't know who the fuck that is or that fuckin' number. I don't talk to no bitches, damn sho' ain't gave nobody my fuckin' number so yo ass need to chill for real."

"So why would somebody send you a random pussy pic, Blake?" She asked serious as hell.

Again, I shrugged. "How the fuck am I supposed to know that, Janae? Text that bitch or whoever the fuck it is and ask them." I tossed her ass the phone back and laid back on my bed.

"Some bitch sends you a pic of her pussy and you just cool as fuck about it?" She continued to snap at me.

"What? I'm supposed to be mad about the shit?" I didn't know how the fuck she wanted me to react. "I don't give a fuck about some random pussy I ain't fuckin'." My phone pinged again, and I grabbed it.

Unknown: *We miss you. When am I going to see you again Blake?*

Janae snatched the phone from me. As she read the message her face turned red as her grip tightened on the device. She glanced at me.

"I don't know who the fuck that is, Nae. If I had bitches sending me pics like that why the fuck would I even let yo ass hold my damn phone, man?" I wasn't stupid, I knew it had to be Mariah. I had deleted our messages and blocked her number so that she couldn't hit me up.

"Blake, then who the fuck is it? Why would some random bitch be texting you out of the blue? Is it Squeaky?" She snapped and I reached for my phone, but she pulled it back. "Is it that bitch Squeaky? You done fuck'd that hoe, so yo ass know what the fuck her pussy look like."

My hand rubbed over my head and I laughed to myself. "I don't know if that's her or not. I never got face to face with her pussy—"

She slapped the fuck out of me. "You always think shit a fuckin' joke, Blake—"

My hand went to her throat and I slammed her into the wall. "If yo ass hit me like that again, I'mma knock the fuck out yo ass, Janae. I ain't bullshittin', hit me again and I'mma slap the fuck out yo stupid ass. Like I said, I don't know who the fuck that is. Maybe it is Squeaky, I don't fuckin' know, I ain't never had no fuckin' face time with that bitch pussy. You pissed at me because I ain't mad and don't know who the fuck it is? Man, gon' with that dumb shit." I pushed her into the wall once more before letting her go. It took everything in me not to slap the fuck out of her.

"It's one of the bitches you were fuckin' with recently for them to be saying they miss you."

I sat on the bed and grabbed my shoes. I wasn't trying to listen to that bullshit. "Man, think what the fuck you want. I ain't fuck'd no other bitch since we got back together."

"So, who was that?" She asked.

I pulled on my shoes and tied them up. "Man, I ain't about to get into all that. It don't fuckin' matter who it was. I ain't fuckin' the bitch now. Man, shut the fuck up. Don't nobody wanna hear this bullshit. If you wanna know who the fuck it is, call the damn number, just leave me the fuck alone." My phone went off again. That's when I started to get pissed off. It was most definitely Mariah's stalking ass.

"When I knew it was real and forever." Janae read out loud. My phone pinged again. "Oh, my fuckin…" Her words trailed off before my phone grazed hard against the side of my face.

"What the fuck!" That crazy mothafucka had thrown the phone at my head.

"You lying sonofabitch!" She yelled before she jumped on me with her fist flying.

Grabbing her arms, I slapped the fuck out her ass. The hit shocked the shit out of her because she went still. "I told yo dumb ass to keep yo fuckin' hands off me. What the fuck is wrong with you?"

Janae broke into tears. "You are such a fuckin' liar. I fuckin' hate you. Get off me." She was bawling hard.

"Janae, I don't know who the fuck that is, yo—"

She grabbed my phone and threw it at me. I caught it that time. "Get off me! I'm so fuckin' done with you."

I unlocked my phone and looked at it. "What the fuck…" I mumbled.

Unknown: *When I knew it was real and forever.*

The message read and underneath it was a picture of the exact same tattoo Janae had with my name, the locket and key, everything. It was in the exact same place, right above her pelvis, but it wasn't Janae.

Unknown: I love you Blake. I can't wait to see you again.

That was the text underneath the image. That's why Janae had snapped. That bitch had lost her fuckin' mind. What the fuck was Mariah thinking?

I grabbed Janae before she could leave out my room. She pushed at my chest trying to get out of my hold. "Nae, I know what that look like—"

"Blake, let me go. Just let me go. It's not a fuckin' coincidence that some hoe got the exact same tattoo I have. What? Did you fuck that bitch good and sweet talk her ass into getting your fuckin' name on her like you did me? Huh, Blake? Don't even fuckin' answer that. I'm so fuckin' done with you."

"If that's the case, why the fuck is your name the only one on me and not some other bitch? Janae, I would never hurt yo ass like that man, real shit. Nae, that some jealous bitch that saw yo fuckin' tattoo and got the same one."

"Why would somebody do that, Blake? You sound so fuckin' stupid! So, some bitch just claims to be in love with yo ass, get you tatted on her and you don't know who the fuck it is? Blake, fuck you! Let me go, I wanna leave." She pushed at my chest and shoulders hard, trying to get out my hold.

I wasn't letting her ass go though, not while she was thinking that way. I wanted to tell her ass what was really up. But I knew that shit wasn't going to go well at all, especially by it being with Mariah's ass.

"Blake!" Her nails dug into my face before she bit my shoulder.

I slammed her on the bed. "Nae, calm the fuck down. On my life I ain't have nobody else get that shit. I be with yo ass every day of the fuckin' week. When do I have time for any other bitch, Janae, man think!" She was starting to piss me off. If we weren't at school or I wasn't at practice, we were together. I didn't have time to fuckin' cheat.

"I don't care! I don't want to hear that shit. Blake, get the fuck off me! I wanna leave! Let me go!" She screamed loud like I was trying to kill her ass. "I wanna leave! Let me go! Get off me!"

"What the hell is going on in here?" My mom yelled as my room door burst opened.

My momma and dad were standing in the threshold, but my mom was staring at me like I had lost my mind. "Rashad, what the hell? Get off her."

"Blake, what the fuck is going on?" My dad glared at me then to Janae.

"It ain't shit." I grabbed my phone and keys, pushing past them, leaving my room.

A Love Like Ours: *The Carter Family*

"Blake, where the hell are you going?" My momma called after me. Ignoring her, I kept going.

"Boy, you don't fuckin' hear yo momma talking to you?" My pops deep voice was loud behind me.

"I'll be back, man, damn." I was pissed off at Janae's stupid ass for screaming like I was hurting her. And at Mariah for that bullshit she had pulled. I stepped into the living room to see my aunties all sitting in there. I didn't say shit to either of them as I left out the house. Outside was no better, because my Unc, Mac, Joshua, Parker, Chris, Bell—fuckin' everybody was out there. I didn't want to talk to anybody, I was so damn pissed. I jumped in my car and once it was started, I took off.

***

"Blake? —" Mariah's confusion soon turned into one of shock as my hand went to her throat and I pushed her back into the apartment, slamming the door behind us.

"Yo, what the fuck is wrong with you? Why would yo stupid ass send that shit to my fuckin' phone and yo ass knew Janae was there." I wanted to snap Mariah's neck. I squeezed her neck as tight as possible before letting her go.

She fell to the floor gasping for breath. I had to turn away from her so that I wouldn't give into the urge to stomp on her fuckin' head. When her breathing was somewhat normal, she glared at me.

"I didn't know she was there, but I didn't care either. This is your fault, Blake!" She yelled while getting up off the floor. "You made me fall in love with you. Now you're trying to just walk away like I never meant anything because I'm not her?"

I was confused as fuck. How the fuck I make her ass fall in love? "How, Mariah? I fuck'd yo ass twice because you were there and wanted it. That's the only reason I fuck'd yo ass. Bitch, I don't even fuckin' like you—"

"Don't say that, Blake!" She suddenly screamed. "Please, don't say that." She repeated in a more even tone. Mariah walked over to me, her hand coming to my chest. "I love you, Blake, and you love me too. I know you do, I felt it. You just need to remember how it felt." She whispered against my chest before grabbing my dick.

I slapped the shit out of Mariah and pushed her hand away from my dick. That slap seemed to shock the hell out of her. Gripping her arms, I shook her ass hard. "Me fuckin' you ain't love. I don't fuckin' love you, I don't like yo ass. Get that shit through yo fuckin' head and leave me the fuck alone." I shook her ass again.

She gripped the front of my shirt hard. "You're just saying this because of her, Blake. Why don't you see that? Janae isn't right for you. She's a little ass girl who's in way over her head with you. I'm better for you than her and you know I'm right. You just have to remember. Let me help you remember what it was like making love to me…" She pushed my hand to her pussy, and I was surprised to realize she didn't have shit on under the dress she wore.

Feeling her pussy, the tattoo came to mind and I raised her shirt. Seeing my name tattooed on her lower abdomen, I jerk my hand from her and moved back. "Bitch, you fuckin' nuts for real. Yo ass got my name tatted on you." The shit looked exactly like Janae's, every damn detail. "Yo…" Seeing something through a phone screen was nothing compared to seeing the shit face to face. It made the shit more real.

"You need to go get some fuckin' mental help. Stay the fuck away from me, Mariah. Stop fuckin' calling and texting me. We don't have shit going on, I don't fuckin' love you, I don't even like yo ass man, get that through yo fuckin' head and leave me the fuck alone."

"It's because of Janae. Blake, what does she have that I don't? I can give you so much more than she can. I can love you better. Why do you want to keep pushing me away? Just give me a chance to show you—" As she spoke, she grabbed hold of my face and tried to kiss me. "Just tell me you love me."

I pushed her ass off me. Never in my life had I ever dealt with a crazy chick like her ass. To hear about crazy shit like that and to witness the bullshit was two different things. "Man, go get yo crazy ass some fuckin' help and leave me the fuck alone." I walked to the front door.

"I'm not going to let you go, Blake! I love you!" She yelled after me as I left her apartment.

Once I made it to my car, I grabbed my ringing phone. My momma name popped on the screen. I let the phone ring until the voicemail picked up. I had fifteen missed calls from her and five from my dad. I had just as many text messages from my momma. Not one from Janae.

That mothafucka was stupid as hell. After every fuckin' thing I done told her ass, she would really think I'll fuck her over like that and so fuckin' quick after promising I wouldn't do the shit.

My momma called again, and I groaned. I was definitely going to have to let her know what was up now that Mariah had lost her fuckin' mind. And by my momma working with her ass, I didn't know what to expect from her and I didn't want my mom caught off guard by some shit Mariah did, if she did something.

"Fuck!" I hit the steering wheel as I thought about telling her every fuckin' thing. That was something I didn't want to do but had too. "Fuck!"

-*Blaze*-

Between Peaches worrying my ass about Blake taking off and Brittany getting on my fuckin' nerves about Kordell leaving, I was about to lose my fuckin' mind. It would be the day I made plans for everything to go down for everybody to start acting fuckin' stupid.

I wasn't worried about Blake's ass because I knew he was going to be straight. His ass just needed to calm down from the blowout he had with his girl. Kordell on the other hand, shid, I respected what he had to do, so I wasn't going to go looking for that nigga like Brittany wanted me to.

"B, Blake hasn't called you back?" Peaches asked, grabbing my phone. I took my phone back from her. "No, Peaches, leave that man alone. Once his ass done calmed down, he'll be back. Is that damn girl still here?"

She sat down at the foot of the bed before getting back up and pacing. "Yeah, she's in his room laying down. She said she was calling one of her cousins to come pick her up. I just never seen him that mad before. I want to know what's going on with him."

I tucked my gun in the back of my jeans as I shook my head. She damn sure didn't want to know what the hell was going on with his ass. Especially not the part about him fuckin' her co-worker.

"Don't be in that niggas face, Peaches, when he's ready to tell you what's up, he'll do it. Don't try to force his ass to though. Whatever him and that babe going through that's their shit. It ain't got shit to do with us." I pulled on my black hoodie.

"I know that. I just want to know that he's okay. It's nothing wrong with me wanting to know that my son is okay. I want to know what the hell that fight was about." She flopped down on the bed. "We don't talk like we use to. I miss that. I can't remember the last time Blake came and laid next to me and we just watched tv together. Blaze, he's growing up way too fast for me." Peaches rolled on her side as she stared at me. A heavy sigh soon left her mouth.

I went over and kneeled beside the bed next to her. "Blake will always be your first baby,

Peach. But loosen up that rope you're trying to bind him to, he ain't going nowhere, sweetheart." I kissed her forehead then stood up. "I got to go. Peach, look out for Brittany. Don't let her ass leave this house. Knock that mothafucka out if you have too."

Peaches laughed and got up. "You be careful out there, B. Don't bring your ass back here beat up or shot. I'm not playing, Blaze." The look she gave me told that much.

"I got you."

Peaches arms went around my neck and she pulled my head down to hers. "I'm serious, Blaze. You better come back to us."

"I hear you, Peaches." Pulling her head back, I started kissing her.

Before the kiss could get to heavy, she moaned and pulled back. "Mmm, hold up." She ran into our bathroom. "Papa Bear, one of your seeds planted." She walked into the room and tossed me the pregnancy test. I didn't need nobody to tell me that I was grinning hard as fuck because I felt that shit. "You better come back to us, Blaze." She repeated.

Grabbing the back of her neck, I kissed her hard. "I am. I love you, Peaches."

She smiled against my mouth. "I love you too, baby."

***

"Josh, yo boy out here yet?" Once I left the crib, I met up with everybody at the apartment.

"Yeah, he's on his way to the bar now. I'm supposed to meet him there in about fifteen minutes." He informed me.

"I'ight, gon' take off and hit me if anything changes." I told him and he nodded then took off. I looked at everybody else. "Y'all know what to do, let's get this shit over with." We all grabbed our shit. I had to get Parker, Chris, Mane and James a few things, them coming down was unexpected but after catching them up on everything, those niggas were down to ride. I wasn't against them coming though, shid, the more hands on deck the quicker and smoother shit went.

The four of them seemed excited as hell about it too. Plus, Parker and Chris had cribs down there where we all were going to meet up at, once everything was over and done with.

Once we left the apartment, we all got into our cars and took off.

***

A Love Like Ours: *The Carter Family*

It took us an hour to reach our destination before we split up, going to our spots. While everybody else were posted up at Sean's crib and the club, Mac, King, Bellow, and I were at Saul's house. He was the one I wanted because his ass called for Brittany to be taken.

He was the biggest threat in my eyes. I motioned for Bellow to go ahead and deactivate the security cameras and the alarms. It took him a minute to do it all. Once everything was down, he motioned for us to go ahead. I sent out a text for the rest of them to burn Sean's crib down and that damn club.

After I sent out that message, the four of us made our way to the back door. King made quick work with picking the locks, we then moved inside. I motioned for them to get to work and they began dousing everything on the first floor of the house with gasoline. While I made my way upstairs, I did the same, leaving a trail of gasoline behind me.

The only thing that could be heard on the second floor was a tv. From the male moaning, I knew the nigga was watching porn. I had to laugh to myself at the irony of him dying while getting off his final nut, one his ass wasn't going to enjoy.

Sitting down the large gas can, I grabbed my gun and went to the master bedroom. The door was opened slightly, but it was big enough so that I saw the tv. What was on the screen fuck'd me up.

Saul and Sean were on the video, but what fuck'd me up and made my ass sick was the fact that, they were fuckin' their brothers, Tony and Turk.

As I kicked the door open the two bodies on the bed pulled apart. "Yo, what the fuck kinda sick shit, you two bitches got going on?" Saul and Sean pushed from each other. Never in my life had I seen no shit like that before.

I heard about sick shit like that, but never witness the shit before. Sean made a quick reach for the gun on the side table and I shot him dead in the head. His body immediately went lump over the side of the bed.

"Bitch nigga, don't be stupid." I turned my gun on Saul.

He glanced away from the gun on his bed side table and his gaze fell on his brother, the nigga looked devastated. "You killed my fuckin' brother." He grabbed Sean's lifeless body and pulled him into his chest. His head fell on top of his.

"Y'all some sick, nasty mothafuckas."

Saul looked up at me with teary red eyes. "Nigga you picked the wrong fuckin' house to rob. Do you know who the fuck I am?" He yelled.

I shrugged. "I didn't come to rob yo ass. I came to kill you. Guess I got two for two." I smiled at him and raised my gun at his head. "I didn't know you, but yo ass fuck'd up with me. You should've done yo homework before you sent yo niggas after a chick, you should've made sho' she ain't have a fuckin' brother like me." I pulled the trigger as Sean's body was pushed upward, blocking Saul. The nigga used his brother as a fuckin' shield. I shot again and he quickly rolled off the bed.

"B!" Mac yelled from the hallway.

I quickly backed out the room. "Get out of here, I ain't leaving until that bitch dead. Start that fire, I'm right behind you. Go!" I pushed him and he took off. I peeked around the door and bullets started flying. Once they stopped, I glanced back inside to see Saul running to a door. Aiming for his leg, I shot his ass.

"Ah fuck!" He fell into the room before closing the door behind him. I ran over to the door, tried the knob but it was locked. I kicked that bitch, but it didn't budge.

Pop, pop, pop!

Three shots came through the door. "Fuck!" I dropped to the floor. The flames flickering caught my eyes, the fire that they started downstairs had grown quick as fuck, reaching the second floor in no time. The hallway and entrance to the room was engulfed in flames. "Fuck!"

Chapter 30

Blake

After leaving Mariah's crib, I drove around for hours thinking of ways to approach my momma with everything. I soon realized there was no right or wrong way to tell her, I just had to get the shit out.

When I walked into the house my aunties all looked up at me. "What's up." I spoke to them with a wave.

"I didn't know if we were speaking or not." My auntie Angel said before giving me a hug. "Hey, baby."

"Yeah, I'm sorry about that. Got a lot of shit going on." I told them as I gave each one of them a hug.

"You get a pass for today don't let it happen again." My aunt Ebony said, smiling.

"I'm not trippin' I know who yo daddy is, so you're good. But if it's girl troubles, just let us know. We'll fuck them bitches up for you." I started laughing at the seriousness on my aunt Missy's face.

"I'mma remember that for next time." I said before walking out the living room. My momma wasn't in there, so I knew she had to be in her room. I knocked on the door.

"Come in." She called out and I walked into her room. She looked flushed, like she wasn't feeling good. However, when she saw me her whole demeanor changed. "Hey, baby, what's up, is everything okay?"

At that question, my head unintentionally shook. My hand rubbed the back of my neck. I couldn't even look at her. I didn't want to disappoint my momma and I knew what I was going to say would do just that, especially with the whole Mariah thing.

"Blake, what's going on." She sat at the edge of the bed staring at me. I couldn't hold her gaze for too long, that damn stare of hers was like she could read my every fuckin' thought. If only it was that easy. "Baby, come talk to me and tell me what's up." She patted the spot beside her and like a little ass boy I went and sat next to her. My momma's hand came to the back of my head and she started rubbing it. "Baby, you know you can tell me anything. Talk to me, Rashad."

My head fell back, and I let out a groan before I started telling her everything. The moment, I spoke about Janae and the abortion, the caressing of her hand stopped.

"Rashad, you made her get an abortion? Rather you was ready to be a father or not, an abortion shouldn't have been an option. Y'all actions created that child and you made her abort it knowing she didn't want to. What the hell, Blake? I guess, what's done is done. I really wished y'all would've came to me, we could've all figured something out."

"So, you're not pissed at me about that?"

My mom's hand came back to my head. "No, Blake, I'm not mad at you. I understand where your head was at, I still wish you would've come to me. Baby, you're young and you're entitled to make several mistakes, but learn from them and don't make a habit of repeating them."

I let out a heavy breath, that was the easy thing to tell her. Taking in my paused she groaned. "It's more?" She asked and I nodded. "What is it, Rashad?"

"It's about Mariah." When I mentioned Mariah's name, it looked like she had stopped breathing all together, but I didn't stop talking. I told her everything about Mariah, from when she first sucked my dick at the restaurant, to when I fuck'd her on my birthday.

To say my momma was furious would've been an understatement of the fuckin' century. She was an entirely different person. I moved the fuck away from her as she paced the floor with her arms swinging back and forth.

"Blake, that girl is fuckin' twenty something and you had sex with her?" She repeated for the hundredth time. "You were fuckin' sixteen and she seduced you! Oh, that bitch is dead. That whore couldn't get your father, so she came after you? She's sending yo ass fuckin' pictures of her nasty ass coochie! Oh, I'mma kill that stank hoe ass bitch!" She was going the fuck off. "I'mma go to fuckin' jail." She talked to herself as she put her hair into a ponytail.

"I'm about to stomp a hole into that bitch's slutty ass fuckin' face." She tore off her shirt and walked into the closet. She returned moments later in some sweatpants, a red tank top and some gym shoes. She then grabbed her phone and walked out the room. "Come on, Rashad!"

She yelled and I followed behind her, making sure to keep my distance.

"Oh shit, what done happened?" My aunt Kim asked looking at my momma's changed outfit.

"I'm about to beat the fuck out this bitch." She told them.

"I'm coming." The four of them chimed in at the same time.

"Well let's go. Sha'Keema, Tink and Peewee," she called to my cousins and they ran in the room. "Y'all are in charge while we're gone, don't fuck up my gotdamn house. Understand me?" I guess they could tell she was pissed off, because they didn't say anything, just nodded. "Let's go, Rashad." I knew she was irate because she kept calling me Rashad. She went to the front door and walked out. The four of my aunts were right on her damn heels.

I walked out last and locked the door. My aunties filed in the back seat of my dad's truck, while my momma hopped in the driver's seat. I opened the door to the passenger side and got in. My momma started the car and backed out the driveway quickly.

"So, where are we going?" Angel asked her.

My momma hit brakes. "I don't fuckin' know where I'm going. Rashad, come drive me to this bitch's house." She threw the truck in park and got out.

I did the same. "Momma, I'm not about to take you over there—"

Her short ass grabbed my shirt and hemmed me up against that truck so gotdamn fast and with so much damn strength, I shut the fuck up surprised as hell. My momma was roughly 5'3 and I was 6'2 but in that moment, her ass looked way taller than me as she jabbed her little finger in my face.

"Rashad, with the way I'm feeling, I will kick your ass. So yo best bet is to shut the hell up and do what I tell you. Now get in the damn truck and drive me to the bitch house." She pushed me in the chest before letting me go. She then went and got in the passenger seat.

Now I saw why my dad didn't want to be around when I told her. She was scary as fuck when she was enraged.

***

When we made it to Mariah's house, my momma banged on the damn door like she was the police.

"I'm coming!" Mariah yelled from the other side of the door. Hearing her voice, my mom banged harder on the door. "I'm coming, just hold on!" Mariah snapped then opened the door. "What the—" before she could finish her sentence my momma punched her square in the mouth, then the nose. It was at that moment I saw the brass knuckles on her hands.

Mariah was caught off guard and stumbled back into the apartment, tripping over a pair of shoes. Once she fell to the floor, my momma kicked her in the face, then the stomach.

"You nasty, triflin', bitch ass hoe! You gon' fuck my gotdamn son?" She kicked Mariah hard in her pussy. "Yo ass couldn't get my fuckin' husband so you went for my fuckin' son, bitch!" She screamed at Mariah. "Get yo bitch ass up!"

"What the hell is going on..." Janae and Shanny ran from the back room. "Mrs. Peaches? What?" Janae looked confused as she stared at my momma beating the fuck out of Mariah. Shanny on the other hand looked ready to jump in and help her cousin.

"Little girl, if yo ass don't want to be leaking like that bitch, I suggest yo ass think smart. Because if you touch my bitch, I'mma walk yo little ass all through this fuckin' apartment. Please fuckin' try me." Missy threatened her.

"What did she do? Blake?" Janae was looking at me for answers.

"You nasty ass bitch!" My momma voice suddenly rose as she continued to beat Mariah's face in. "You had the fuckin' balls to seduce my fuckin' son! He was only sixteen! You're a grown ass fuckin' woman, you pedophile ass hoe!" She was panting hard, but she wasn't letting up on Mariah as she got up and kicked her in her pussy once again, then her stomach and face. As the words left my momma's mouth, both Shantell and Janae looked at me.

"Wait, Mrs. Peaches, what she do?" Janae asked my momma.

My momma turned on me and pointed to Janae. "She doesn't know." She stated as a matter of fact. She put her hands on her hips and glared at me. "Tell her why I'm beating this bitch ass, Rashad."

That was not how I wanted Janae to find out. Hell, I didn't want her to find out at all. "I fuck'd Mariah—"

"She fuckin' seduced him!" My momma cut me off as she started kicking Mariah again. "She fuckin' seduced him, by sucking his fuckin' dick in a bathroom while he was only sixteen!" She kicked Mariah in the mouth. "Before she took advantage of him on his birthday and had sex with him. Your friend, Janae!" She told her. "That whole fight y'all had this morning is because of this nasty, grown ass bitch! This bitch lucky I'm whooping her ass and not sending her to fuckin' jail!"

I wanted to choke the hell out of my momma. I knew she was pissed but damn, she didn't have to put that shit out like that.

"The pictures were of Mariah? The tattoo too?" The devastation on her face said everything.

I nodded. "Yeah it was her."

Janae went to Mariah and pulled up her shirt, showing off the tattoo she had. "Oh, my God."

"I love him…" Mariah mumbled out.

Janae's hand went to her mouth and she quickly ran to the back. I followed her and found her hunched over the toilet getting sick. I went to her and her hand came out. "Don't touch me." She grabbed some tissue and wiped her mouth. "This whole time and you didn't say shit, Blake. I feel so fuckin' stupid and played. You're the fuckin' guy she was crying over. Oh, my God!" She hunched back over the toilet and once again started getting sick.

Once she was done, she wiped her mouth. Shanny came in the bathroom with a cup of water. "Are you okay, babe? Nae, I swear I didn't know any of this." Shantell tried to hand her the cup of water but she didn't take it, Janae just broke out crying.

"I'm so damn stupid. How did I not know? Everything she was saying should've been a dead giveaway. She talked me into really going through with my abortion, I wouldn't have done it if she hadn't told me it was the best thing to do for the both of us. I thought she was really trying to be there for me when this whole time it was for her, so could have him." She was bawling hard.

Hearing what she was saying and to see her crying so hard, hurt me. "I'm sorry, Janae—"

Her eyes snapped to mine. "You're sorry?" She threw the water in my face before throwing the cup at my head. I managed to duck back just in time for it to smash against the wall and shatter. "You're fuckin' sorry, Blake? You could've fuckin' told me everything, but you didn't! I'm out here looking stupid in this bitch's face, confiding in her about every fuckin' thing between us and you ain't said shit, when you knew this! Why didn't you just tell me, Blake?"

My hand rubbed over my head as I stood up. "I didn't want to hurt you, Nae, I've already done that with the abortion and everything. I didn't want to hurt you again."

"You didn't want to hurt me?" She got off the floor and pushed me. "Well guess what, Blake, I'm fuckin' hurt. Out of all the shit you've done to hurt me, this is the one thing you decided to keep to yourself. Someone I thought was my friend of all people. That fuckin' girl held me at night and cried with me for days after my abortion. Her, Blake? Why?" Her fist balled up and she punched me hard in the chest.

There wasn't a real reason aside from her just being there at the time and I wanted to. I couldn't tell her that. It would no doubt only make her feel worse. "I don't know."

She laughed. "You don't fuckin' know. Do you know what it's like to lay on a bed to get an abortion? To hear the vacuum going, knowing your baby is about to be torn, literally torn out of your body piece by fuckin' piece. That girl was there for me after I had to go through all of that! And she was sucking you off way before any of that happened and you didn't say shit!" Her hands brushed at her cheeks roughly as she chuckled humorlessly. "You've failed Blake, that whole promise you made, you've rip that to shreds. Not only did you manage to hurt me, Blake, you've fuckin' broken me. I hate you so gotdamn much. Stay the fuck away from me and out of my life for good. I'm done." She pushed passed me and ran out the bathroom.

Shanny shook her head at me, then chased after her. I didn't though. I saw the resolve in her eyes when she looked at me, I knew it was done and over.

I had really gotten in over my fuckin' head with everything.

Don't go losing yo fuckin' focus over these little ass girls. They ass gon' always be here, yo gotdamn career ain't. Once you fuck up that opportunity yo ass can't get it back.

My dad's voice was loud in my head. He was right, I had fallen off my game and was losing my focus. I needed to get that back and letting Janae go was the only way I would be able to do that. So, I didn't go after her, even though my entire body urged me to. I had to do what was best for the both of us and that was letting her go.

Chapter 31

Peaches

I paced around the living room stressed the fuck out given everything I had learned that was going on with Blake. Although my girls, my freaking best friends were there with me, I really wanted—no needed Blaze to talk too. I needed him to confide in. I was still so pissed off about the Mariah thing. I just couldn't believe she took advantage of him like that.

My thoughts were so damn contradicting. Deep down, I knew the sex thing wasn't solely her fault, Blake partaken in it as well. He was to strong of a man to be overpowered by someone like Mariah. He was in fact his father's son, so I knew he willingly had sex with her. But I was still more so pissed at her because she was a grown ass woman.

The other thing that weighed so heavy on me was that I overheard what Janae said to Blake. And the shattered look on his face when he came from that back room. Not only was Janae broken, so was Blake.

They were both so young and I felt for them, to have such emotions and love like they both shared for one another, only to be torn apart from heartbreak was tragic.

When we had gotten home, Blake had locked himself in his room. I wanted to go comfort him, but he had shut me out.

It was eleven at night and I was waiting to hear from Blaze. I tried calling Mac and King, but still nothing. I knew the job they had done earlier should've been over hours ago—unless something went wrong. I immediately stopped my thoughts from wondering to any dark places. I knew everything was fine, it had to be.

"Peach, come sit down before you walk a damn hole into the floor." Kim patted the spot beside her.

I waved her off. "I'm okay. Ang, Parker haven't called you?" I asked her as I sat on the arm of the couch.

She looked at her phone and shook her head. "No, he hasn't. I'm sure they're okay, though, Peach, so just calm down. Blaze is fine, that nigga is legit unkillable for real." She reassured me.

"I know he's fine... I guess I just want to hear from him, though." I was right back up resuming my pacing.

"How's Blake doing?" Ebony asked. "That poor dude, I felt his pain." She let out a heavy breath as the girls mumbled their agreement.

"He'll be alright in time." I looked down the hallway as if expecting Blake to show up there. "Y'all I can't believe that bitch had sex with my son. Like for a whole fuckin' year she was on Blaze, then Blake chokes the little bitch and she's on his shit. Did y'all hear that bitch talking about she loves him? I tried to stomp that hoe pussy out. I wanna go whoop her ass all over again." I couldn't believe that hoe. How could she possibly be in love with him after a few minutes of meaningless sex.

Never did I expect Mariah to turn out to be looney as hell. I felt like when she was flirting with Blaze so hard, she was only doing that to get on my damn nerves. I couldn't have guessed she was far more psychotic.

"Hell, my damn coochie started to hurt when yo ass was kicking her shit in." Missy groaned and her hand covered the front of her crotch, making us laugh.

"I think they're here." Angel said, as headlights flashed through the front window.

"I hope Kordell's with them." Brittany perked up.

I doubt he was, there was no way Blaze would bring that man to our home. The apartment, maybe but not to our home. Even though I thought that I kept it to myself.

I quickly went to the door and opened it. I watched as each man filed into the house. Mac was the last in and the look on his face was one of sorrow. On top of that, he didn't even look at me. Then again, he didn't seem to be seeing anything, like he was just on autopilot.

I grabbed his arm stopping him. "Mac, where's Blaze?" When his eyes met mine, my heart shattered. "No, no, Mac, where is he?"

"Peaches—" King grabbed my arm, but I snatched away from him.

"No, go fuckin' get him, now!" I screamed at them. How the hell were they all standing in his living room, but he wasn't with them? They all left together, and they should've returned together. "Go get Blaze. If he's not here none of you should fuckin' be here. Where the fuck is my husband!" Mac's arms went around me, and my body went limp as I began to sob. "Mac, go get him, go bring my Blaze home."

"King, what happened?" Ebony asked him.

"It was a fire and he got trapped in the house—"

"No!" A loud high-pitch scream rang out and it took me a minute to realize that I was the one screaming. "No, no, no. God, no, please no." I sobbed, hoping I was hearing him wrong. I had to be. "Please, go get him. Y'all just left him there? Go get him, he needs to be home, please go bring him home." My vision was blurred, the talking around me was gone, all I heard were my own cries. Our time couldn't have been over. It was too soon. I needed to see him, hold him, kiss him. I needed him. "Please, go get him. He's there by himself. Y'all left him there. King, Mac go get him, please."

"The police and fire department were all over the place, Peaches, we couldn't get back in. Beforehand, though, the fire was too wild, we couldn't get back in there to get him. I'm sorry, Peaches."

"No! King, no! Just go get him, please." I didn't care how I got him back, I just needed him.

***

I sat on the couch watching the news tell about a night club, belonging to Saul and Sean Washington going up in flames. However, there were no deaths involved with the night club because it was closed due to renovations.

The image on the screen changed showing a house that was up in flames. The fire was wild and seemed unattainable as the firemen fought to put the flames out. The house was Saul's. I watched emptily as the flames blazed through the roof top.

Blake's arms tightened around me and he kissed my head. I squeezed his arm, not being able to voice any words. I had cried and screamed so loud until I had nothing left. Although my head pounded and my eyes felt swollen, I wasn't leaving from in front of that tv until I knew for sure Blaze was gone. They hadn't said how many bodies were found in Saul's house.

The twins sat at my feet hugging my legs tightly. They didn't know what was going on, they only knew that I was sad and had been crying. I didn't have the heart to crush them without knowing for sure if he was really gone. Blake knew everything that was going on, though.

Apparently, Blaze had told him what was going on just in case something went wrong. That was typical Blaze, though, there was no doubt in my mind that he told Blake to look after us.

I just hoped and prayed that everything was one big ass dream. I was waiting for the moment when I would jump awake with Blaze holding me to his chest and telling me I was just dreaming. That moment hadn't come yet.

I just wanted the pain in my heart to stop.

***

"Ma…" Blake shook me awake. I didn't know I had fallen asleep. "They found two bodies in the house so far, with all the debris they're still looking." He informed me and I once again broke down crying.

"Peach, I am so sorry, baby." Kim came over and sat to my left, pulling me tight into her. "I am so, so, sorry."

I couldn't speak. What would I say if I could? It's okay? Thank you? I couldn't voice any of that, because it wasn't okay, I wasn't alright and would never be again. What would I be saying thank you for? That I lost my husband, my soulmate, my lifeline? My body shook violently as sobs racked through my entire being.

-*Blake*-

Seeing my momma break down the way she had, hurt the hell out of me. I wanted to take her pain away, but I didn't know how too. In that moment I could really see the love she truly had for my pops. She had completely come undone.

I was hurt about my pops being gone too, the pain in my chest was unbearable, I felt cheated out of time with him. Regardless of my agony, I couldn't break, especially not with my mom so broken.

But most importantly because of my dad's voice in my head, going back to the conversation we had a few days ago.

***

A Love Like Ours: *The Carter Family*

"Lil B, if something goes wrong and I don't make it back, I need you to do something for me."

My arms folded over my chest and I nodded. "You know I'll do anything for you, dad."

"Look after yo moms for me. Her little ass might seem tough, but she a big ass baby inside, this shit gonna break her, but I need you to bring her back from it. Don't let her stay in that state of mind frame. I already know you gon' do right with BJ and Brianna little badass. You gonna be the man of the house until you leave for school, and when you do go, Blake, don't forget about them. Do that for me and when the shit comes to light, don't break in front of nobody, if you gon' cry do that shit alone, never in front of anybody. Understand me?" His hand grasped the nape of my neck tight as his eyes stared into mine.

"I'll look after them, promise. I'll make sure momma good, swear." I reassured him.

I understood why my pops did the shit he did. In any case, he would always put his life on the line for family. He was so damn loyal to those he cared about, no matter what, if shit went down, he was always in the front of the line, ready to go.

"I'ight." He pulled me into him, hugging me tight, after kissing the side of my head he pushed

me back. "Check me." He threw the basketball at me and we started balling.

"So, I should probably help her find another man, huh?" I asked and my dad stopped bouncing the ball.

"Why the fuck would you say some shit like that? Lil B, I don't know if you realized it or not, but yo pops a selfish mothafucka. If I die, Peaches bet not find another nigga or I'mma haunt her ass from the fuckin' grave, that nigga and yo ass too for allowing that shit. Hell no, fuck that, she can't have no other nigga, Blake, I ain't bullshittin'." From the anger tension that grew in his voice, I knew he was serious.

"Then yo ass bet not die. Don't do shit stupid, don't talk to fuckin' much, get the job done and get the fuck out. And you won't have to worry about another man loving yo wife." I threw the ball at him. "Check me."

He looked at the ball, flipping it in his hands, he chuckled, then glanced at me. "I hear what you saying, Blake." He checked me and we once again started playing ball.

***

"Blake…" Brianna walked into the living room, pulling me from my thoughts.

618

"What's up, sweetheart?" I focused on her and she was looking at our momma.

"What's wrong with momma? Is she going to be okay?" Her eyes quickly filled with tears.

Picking her up, I left out the living room, going into her room. Sitting on the bed, I sat her on my lap. "Yeah, momma will be alright in time." My chest grew tight and my throat burned. Telling Brianna and BJ what was really going on wasn't something I wanted to do.

Brianna grabbed her phone and unlocked it. "I tried to call daddy and tell him momma was crying so bad, and he really need to come check on her, but he's not answering or texting me back. See." She put her phone in my face, showing me the text messages.

"That's because he's not coming back. He's dead." BJ stood in Brianna's doorway, tears rolling down his face, but he wasn't sobbing. "Ain't he, Blake? That's why the news on, ain't it?"

"No, he's not. Don't say that BJ!" Brianna screamed at him.

"He is, that's why he's not answering your calls—"

"BJ, shut the hell up, why the fuck would you tell her that shit?" I glared at him, wanting to knock his ass out.

BJ chest puffed out as anger filled him. "Fuck you, Blake! Tell me is my daddy dead." He yelled, walking up to me like he was ready to fight.

At times I had to remember BJ was only seven, he was still a child. I didn't want to crush either of them by telling the truth. Given how I was feeling from the loss, I could only imagine their pain.

"No, he's not BJ, he's at work. Tell him, Blake." Brianna urged me.

I couldn't and I couldn't tell them the truth either. "We don't know yet. Pops was seeing a friend and the house caught fire. We don't know if he was in there or not, we're trying to find that out."

"My daddy not dead! He's going to text me back. He always texts me back. I'm about to call him." Brianna pulled up our dad's number and called him. The voicemail picked right up. "Daddy, please call me back and tell me you not dead. I love you, daddy." She ended the voicemail and started texting him the same thing.

Brianna broke out crying at the same time BJ went to his knees and started crying. The twin's sobs were in sync, the pair bawling hard together. Seeing them like. That the shit broke me, even so, I didn't let a tear drop. Instead, I grabbed BJ and pulled him to me. The pair of them wrapped their arms around my neck and continued to cry their eyes out.

Kicking off my shoes, I laid back on Brianna's full-size bed, with the twin's tucked into my neck. I held the pair tight, letting them cry until they fell asleep.

-*Peaches*-

After peeking in on the kids, sleep in Brianna's room, I went into the kitchen, trying to busy myself.

"Hey, babe, how are you feeling?" Ebony walked into the kitchen and came to stand beside me at the counter. Seconds later, Kim, Missy and Angel came in. The four of them refused to leave my side given everything that was going on. I was thankful for them, but I just wanted to be alone.

"Terrible, Ebony, I'm not feeling good at all." It was seven-thirty the following night, and I was honestly waiting on the police to show up and tell me they found Blaze's body. However, I doubt I would get that courtesy visit because from the news the bodies were burnt beyond recognition. Grabbing the wine glass, I filled it up with Ciroc and took a big gup.

Kim snatched the glass from me. "What the hell are you doing, Peaches? You're at least six weeks pregnant, you can't be drinking."

I didn't care, I just wanted the pain to stop. "I just want him back home. Even if he's really gone, I want his body home. I need him home." I slid down the counter until I was sitting on the floor.

Missy came and sat next to me. "Peach, I wish there was something I could do for you. I can't even imagine your pain, baby. I can't tell you everything is going to be alright and shit will get better, because I don't know that. But I'm here for anything you need..." Missy voice cracked, and she threw her arms around me. "I am so fuckin' sorry, baby." She held me tight as she too cried.

I just wanted everything to just stop for a second, with everything I felt, I couldn't breathe. The sound of glass shattering caused me and Missy to jump.

"What the fuck?" Kim tone was freaked out.

"Oh, my God." The collective voices spoke at once.

"Peaches..."

I looked at Missy before I jumped up off the floor. I just broke down once again. Blaze stood at the sliding door, his clothes were dirty and cover with some type of white powder, his face was smudged with dirt and marks and something else. I didn't care though.

"Oh, my God!" I ran and threw myself at him. He caught me and groaned. Dust flew from his clothing, still I didn't care, my hands moved over his face, then chest. I needed to make sure he was real.

Blaze grabbed a hold of my face, lifting it to meet his gaze. "It's me, baby, I'm here."

My vision blurred as I sobbed, kissing him. I didn't care about the dirt on his face or the taste of it, I just kissed him. "You're really here."

"I'm here." He repeated, returning my kiss.

Chapter 32

Blaze

Josh held my ass tight, damn near squeezing the hell out of me. "Man, you scared the fuck out of me. I thought I had just lost my fuckin' brother when I just got yo ass. Don't do this shit no more man, fuck!"

I hugged my brother back, patting him on the back of his head. "I'm good, bruh, I ain't going nowhere."

"Yo ass bet not, we got twenty years to go before I can get that apology from you." Josh said before letting me go.

I chuckled at that and nodded before I went and sat down. Once I did everybody literally came and stood around me.

"So, what the fuck happened?" Mac asked, crowding around me like everybody else. They all stared at me like they were seeing a damn ghost.

"How the fuck did you get out that fuckin' house, B?" King chimed in.

Shid, I couldn't believe I wasn't dead either to be honest. I knew for sure once those damn flames entered Saul's room, I was fuckin' dead.

"Would y'all stop crowding him, damn. Let him breathe." Peaches snapped at them. I had to laugh at that because she had her ass right on my lap as if it was her chair.

"Shid, I'm surprised I got out too, for real." I finally spoke. "I knew for sho' I was done when that nigga started shooting through the bathroom door. It got the vest though. Anyway, after I shot the door down, I caught that mothafucka trying to go down a fuckin' laundry shoot. After I popped his ass, I went down that bitch and ended up in a fuckin' underground basement. I ain't know that crib had a fuckin' third floor." I told them.

Saul was a sick ass bitch nigga, but the nigga was kind of smart. Dude had hiding spots all through that fuckin' house. Places mothafuckas would never think to look. I would have never thought of using a laundry shoot as a fuckin' getaway. It wasn't an easy drop though and the clothes on that floor broke my fall.

"That nigga was smart as fuck to get that shit in there. But shid, once I landed in the basement, I couldn't get back upstairs because of the fire, and I wasn't opening that damn door to blow myself up. The fire didn't really do no damage to that third floor." Even though I found that strange, I wasn't going to dwell on the whys.

"Once I heard the police and shit, I started moving shit around in the basement to find somewhere to hide. I move the fuckin' dryer and it's a trap door behind that bitch." I motioned to my dirty clothes. "So, I got my ass in there and had to hideout in that bitch until the police and shit took off. Then I stole a car and drove my ass back out this way, ditched the car and footed it to the Lot. Got my little car from there, now I'm here." I ran down everything to them. "The shit sound insane as fuck but living through that shit is a whole other thing."

The room was quiet for a while before Missy let out a huff. "Yo ass is one lucky sonofabitch. Like you got fuckin' nine lives or some shit. Somebody in the heavens definitely favors your ass."

"Damn. That shit is nuts, yo. But I agree with Missy. If I wasn't looking at yo ass right now, I wouldn't even believe the shit." Mac stated still looking at me as if he couldn't believe I was sitting there.

I nodded in agreement. I couldn't believe I made it out that shit either. Hell, being trapped in that wall for hours, made you reevaluate everything in life. Shid, I already valued everything I had, but going through that shit only made me appreciate it more.

"I couldn't leave just yet." My hand went to Peaches stomach. "I still got a football team to build."

Peaches nodded, taking hold of my face. "You really do." She kissed me. "Don't ever scare me like that again."

Reaching in my pocket, I grabbed my phone. "I busted my shit when I fell through the laundry shoot." I showed her the busted up black screen.

"Next time steal a phone, please... matter fact." She looked at everybody in the room. "Ain't gon' be no fuckin' next time. Whenever any of y'all in some bullshit, leave us the fuck out of it. My gotdamn heart can't take no more of this shit. I love all y'all but he ain't getting involved in shit else. I don't care if we're all together and niggas get to shooting at y'all—"

she looked directly at Brittany when she said that.

It was funny because I got involved in the shit because of Brittany and her nigga. From what Brittany told me, Kordell was all good after he had taken care of the workers who betrayed him.

"He ain't getting involved, period, I don't fuckin' care. I'm not about to lose him behind y'all shit, man, I swear I'm not. And I really do love y'all, but I cannot be without him for real. We done had to many fuckin' close encounters, I'm not taking no more, and I'm not sorry for saying this either. He's done with this shooting and burning shit down mess. He's out."

"Shut the fuck up." King told her. "You ain't running shit but yo damn mouth. I knew that stubborn mothafucka wasn't gone nowhere."

Peaches glared at him. "No, King, I'm dead ass serious right now. Like you ain't just have to live these past few hours thinking the love of your life was dead. I don't want to feel that shit ever again. So, y'all, please keep y'all shit away from him."

I had to laugh at Peaches, she was smart to address them and not me. She no doubt knew my thought process. I was always down to ride for family no matter what. After surviving everything, though, it really did make me appreciate what I had, and I wasn't ready to lose that. I loved Peaches ass to death, she was my life, so were my kids.

"Y'all heard what she said. My guns are retired ain't no more of this shit for me." Peaches turned to look at me in surprise. I nodded at her unasked question. "I mean that shit, Peach. For you and my babies, I'm done." They meant way more to me than a temporary rush I got from shooting a nigga or setting some shit on fire.

Peaches eyes teared up and she hugged me. "I love you so much, Blaze."

Tangling a hand in her hair, I pulled her head back, kissing her. "I love you too, Peaches." After kissing her again, I got up. "Let me go check on my babies." I hadn't seen the kids since I got back. I didn't know if they knew what was going on or not, but I needed them to see me and I needed to hold them.

"They're in Brianna's room." Peaches said from behind me.

Nodding, I went to my baby girl's room. Sure enough, they were all in there. Blake was in the middle with the twins on each side of him. Brianna's face was tucked in his neck while BJ was on his chest, their arms were wrapped tight around him. That was most definitely a picture-perfect moment.

As if knowing what I was thinking, Peaches was beside me with her phone. "You look like you want to capture this moment."

I nodded at that. I really did. "Take it." Once she took the picture, I leaned over and kissed Brianna's head, then BJ. When I sat back up Blake's eyes shot open. He stared at me for the longest before he got out the bed and threw his arms around me.

"Dad." He squeezed me tight. "I thought you were dead." His voice shook as his arms tightened around me.

"Nah, y'all ain't gon' get rid of me that fast." I told him, hugging him back.

"Pops, I thought you were dead." He repeated.

Pulling his head back, I stared into the tearful eyes that mirrored mine. "Lil B, I'm here, I ain't going nowhere. You hear me?"

He nodded. "I hear you."

I pulled my oldest back to me, my hand grasping the back of his head. "I love you, son." I kissed the side of his head. I love the fuck out my kids, it wasn't a better feeling than being with them. So, I knew I made the right choice with putting all that bullshit behind me.

"I love you too, Pops."

The groaning coming from the bed had Blake releasing his hold on me. I glanced around his shoulder to see the twin's waking up. Once Brianna's focus was clear, her eyes went wide.

"Daddy!" Brianna jumped up and threw herself at me. "I knew you wasn't dead. I was so scared." She whispered as her little body shook in my hold.

That broke my fuckin' heart hearing her say that. I held onto my baby girl tight, kissing her head. "I'm alright, baby. I promise." My eyes locked with BJ's and a second later his arms and legs were wrapped around me too.

"I thought you were gone, Pops. Don't do that to me." There was so much aggression in BJ's voice as he damn near choked my ass out, that's how tight his arms were around my neck.

It was all from fear though. I felt his anger and fear in that tight ass grip of his. "It won't happen again. I'ight?" The pair nodded. I kissed both of their heads, then sat them on the bed. "How about y'all let me get cleaned up and then we all chill in the movie room and watch whatever y'all want?" I offered and they smiled wide while nodding. "I'ight, bet, give me a minute." I got up and left out their room.

"Hey, Peach, we're going to take off and give y'all some time together. If you need us, just call and we're here. I'm glad you're alright,

Blaze." Kimmy smiled at me and I nodded to her before going into my room.

Going into the bathroom, I pulled off my clothes then hopped into the shower. I had just finished washing myself for the second time when I felt Peaches watching me. I glanced back to see her naked but standing outside the shower.

"It took yo ass long enough to get in here." I told her while rinsing the soap off me. Once the soap was off, the water soon followed. She motioned for me to get out, when I did, Peaches had a dry towel and began drying me off. When she was sure she got all the water off, her arms hooked around my neck and I picked her up, walking us back into the room.

"B, I just want you to hold me. I just want to feel you." She mumbled in a sad tone. I gave her what she wanted. I laid down with her on top of me. My arms tightened at her waist and held her naked body to mine.

Leaving out the movie room, I went into mine. I was fuckin' exhausted from all the drama that had played out. To see my dad again, was something I never thought would happen. It messed me up to see him standing in Brianna's room. After that damn scare of losing him, I knew not to take the time I did have left with him for granted.

It also made me take everything he's ever told me to heart. It was like I had a second chance with him, so I wanted him to see me accomplish so much, just to make him proud.

I also thought on my mom's breakdown, I never in life wanted to feel no shit like that or be that deep in love, ever. I didn't want to bear that shit at all.

After taking a quick shower, I went and hopped in the bed. I laid there thinking about all my pops near misses when it came to his life. That nigga had an Angel or some shit riding him hard. He had overcome so much shit and survived harsher bullshit. No matter what was thrown at him he always found a way to survive that shit. It was hard not to idolize the hell out of that man and I really did.

Somewhere along my running thoughts, I felt myself doze off to sleep. I didn't know how long I was out for before my body suddenly jolted awake.

"What the fuck!" I jumped out my bed quick, from the body that laid next to mine, holding me tight. I flicked on the light and what I saw shock the fuck out of me. "Momma! Pops!" I yelled for them. "What the fuck did you do?" I ran back over to my bed.

Mariah laid in my bed bleeding badly from the writing in deep cuts on her arms. *I Love U* was cut into her right arm and Blake was written on the left one.

"Why the fuck would you do this?" Mariah wasn't moving and her breathing was faint. I shook her. "Mariah!"

Slowly her eyes fluttered opened. Focusing on me, she smiled. "I love you, Blake… You love me too…" She whispered as her eyes closed.

"Ma! Dad!" I called for them again.

"Why the hell you yelling—what the fuck happened? Peaches!" My pops yelled.

"I woke up to her in here like this." I told him.

"Oh, my God! Blake, call the police." She urged, while grabbing the clothes off the floor and wrapping them tightly around Mariah's arms. "Blake, what happened?"

After giving the information to the police, I ended the call and addressed my momma. "I don't know, when I woke up, she was in here like that. Why the fuck would she do that?"

634

My mommas head shook. "Baby, I don't know."

"She came in through the kitchen." My pops said coming back into the room. "It's a blood trail from the sliding door that leads to here."

"Is she gon' die?" As I spoke Mariah's eyes found mine.

"I don't know, baby." My momma mumbled.

I knew she had some screws loose in her head, but never did I think that her ass would try to kill herself all because she thought she was in love with me. After seeing her dying, I felt bad for her. I couldn't help but wonder about the fuck'd up shit she may have been through in life. It had to be something terrible if it made her think a night of sex would equal love.

I hoped like fuck she didn't die because I didn't need her death on my conscious.

Epilogue

Blake

I just wanna say, ma and pops, thanks for everything you've done and sacrificed for me. Just know without y'all I wouldn't be who I am today or striving to become a better man. I love y'all." I toasted to them. My mom and dad were all smiles as I held up my number 17 jersey for Purdue University college basketball team.

There were several other colleges that were offering me scholarships, but I decided to stay close to home. I didn't want my momma to think I was moving to far away from her and that she was losing me—*her baby*. Although she just had my baby brother, Blayson Dmitri Carter—*who would be keeping her busy, along with the twins*—I knew she still wanted me close. I wasn't complaining, though I loved the hell out that woman and would live anywhere she asked me too.

I glanced around the backyard looking at all my family and friends who came out to celebrate with me. Although I was excited as hell to see everybody, the one person I really wanted to celebrate with wasn't there.

"Who are you looking for?" My momma linked her arm through mine.

My head shook. "Nobody, just looking around."

She chuckled at that. "You're a terrible liar, Blake." She stopped walking and stood in front of me. "Baby, I am so damn proud of you and I'm honored to say that I'm your momma. Just know that wherever this journey takes you and no matter the decisions you make, you can never, and I mean that literally, you can never disappoint me, Rashad." Her hand cupped the side of my face as she smiled hard and proudful at me.

"Thanks ma. I'mma hold you to that. You know I tend to do some dumb ass shit." I warned her. "And college with a bunch of chicks—"

My momma punched me in the stomach. "As long as they don't hurt you and yo ass stay focus and keep that thang wrapped up, I'm fine with whatever you do."

"He bet not bring no damn babies' home, I know that much. 'Cause I ain't taking care of no more damn babies. Tell'em Blayson." My dad held my baby brother up.

I looked at Blayson who was only six months then down to my momma's three-month pregnancy belly. "Pops, yo ass about to be taking care of two babies and two kids, shid, I can add one more, y'all won't even notice."

"I will fuck you up, Blake. Blay-Blay tell'em pops will beat yo ass." My dad moved Blayson's mouth with his finger, making me laugh. My pops was happy as hell that he had another boy, and he was praying for another one. "I'm bullshittin' with you, Blake. Real shit though, I'm proud of you and like yo momma said, yo ass could never disappoint me. You haven't so far." My dad's hand came out and he pulled me into a hug.

"Thanks, dad." I returned his hug before I pulled back with my nose twisted up. "Blay, yo little ass stank man, damn." I gagged, rubbing my nose.

"Damn dude. Yo ass about to get off that damn milk. Peach—"

"As I was saying…" My mom's arm linked with mine once again and walked us away from them.

"That's fuck'd up, Peaches." My dad yelled from behind us laughing.

"Like I said, I'm fine with whatever you do." She repeated, ignoring my dad. My momma was dope as fuck.

Laughing, I wrapped my arms around her, then kissed her forehead. "I can promise to do all that." I glanced around the yard again and my momma hugged me tight.

"I'm sorry she didn't come. I called and invited her to come, but she was busy. Blake, she needs more time, that could be another year or two, maybe even more. She went through a lot, just continue to give Janae space and if it's meant to be, y'all will find a way back to one another. Trust me." She reassured me, giving that smile I loved.

"I do, thanks." I hadn't talked to Janae since the night at Mariah's apartment. It was hard seeing her every day at school and not being able to talk to her, but I did. I didn't bother her at all because I wanted to give her that space she needed.

I couldn't shake that hurt and broken look that was in her eyes. I didn't want to cause her ass no more pain, so I stayed my distance. I also wasn't ready for those type of emotions we both had for each other. I loved the shit out of Janae, but I wasn't really ready for that shit. I still had a lot of learning and growing to do on my end.

Although the decision was hard, it had to be done for the both of us. The shit was crazy how everything had played out though. Everything really felt like a dream as the events played in my head.

The shit with Mariah was crazy as hell. Luckily, she didn't die that night in my bedroom. My momma was able to stop the blood flowing from her wounds in time. Later, I did find out from her sister that she had her committed to get the psychiatric help she needed.

Mariah suffered from borderline personality disorder, and my aggressive ways toward her is what had her so drawn to me, and what caused her to think that she was in love with me.

I regretted ever meeting her ass and even interacting with her that first night at my game, that was when all the bullshit started for her. The shit was nuts, but I was glad she was locked up somewhere far away from me and getting the help she needed.

The shit with Mariah was definitely a life learning lesson.

I glanced at my momma and smiled. My pops had one arm around her, rubbing her slightly protruding stomach, while holding Blayson in his other arm. My momma was definitely a hell of a woman and I saw why my pops was so in love with her. She was right though, if me and Janae were meant to be, we'll find our way back to one another.

Everything that has happened the past year and a half was a learning lesson for me.

I glanced around the yard again and chuckled to myself realizing I was really looking for Janae to show up like she had on my birthday. She wasn't coming, my momma was right, Janae really needed time. She had her space for the time being, until we ran into each other again.

That I was sure of. I had to chuckle to myself at that thought as it made me think of what my momma told Janae, who repeated it to me.

He's not going to let you go. He might leave you alone for a minute, but if he's anything like his dad, he'll be back.

With my thoughts and that random memory, I had to believe she was right.

Until then, I had the tattoo of her name and lips still on my chest, reminding me of what we had and what the fuck I lost. I was cool with that because now it gave me room to really focus on my basketball career.

"Lil B, we about to get this game going, come on." My dad called before tossing the ball up and throwing it to me.

"I'ight." I jogged over to the basketball court. I tossed the ball in the air and caught it. A laugh left my mouth as I shot the ball, making the basket.

Yeah, she had her space for the time being.

A Love Like Ours

The End!

Made in the USA
Monee, IL
01 September 2021

76930577R00356